Sols & Shades Book One

THIS SAFE DARKNESS

ALEXIS MARAGOLD

ISBN 979-8-9933623-4-2 (hardcover)

Dust jacket, reversible dust jacket, cover, and title page art by Kasia Jasmina (@kasia.jasmina on Instagram)

Map design, interior graphics, formatting, and author headshot by Alexis Maragold

Published through Foreword Books LLC

TRIGGER WARNINGS

This Safe Darkness is intended for adults, and contains subject matter that may be difficult or disturbing for some readers.

Sensitive material includes, but is not limited to: ableism, misogyny, socio-economic power imbalances, emotional abuse, harassment, explorations of implied mental illness (anxiety and trauma), implied disabilities (chronic migraines, hypopituitarism, infertility, and neurodivergency), profanity, sexual content, divorce, grief, violence, gore, murder, and death.

Although *This Safe Darkness* does not contain explicit, open-door sexual intercourse, there are explicit conversations surrounding sexual encounters and sexual themes that will escalate over the course of the series.

Reader discretion is advised.

PRONUNCIATION GUIDE

Orelle: *oh-RELL*
Kalden: *KALL-din*
Taurance: *TORR-uhns*
Meridna: *muh-RID-nuh*
Twilynn: *TWY-lin*
Aruna: *uh-ROO-nuh*
Yvonne: *yuh-VON*
Faron: *FAIR-uhn*
Niles: *nilez*
Aurick: *OR-ik*
Caligo: *kuh-LEE-go*
Deor: *DEE-or*
Scuros: *skur-OHS*
Lucis: *LOO-sis*
Sols: *sohlz*
Pyres: *PIE-irs*

PROFANITY GLOSSARY

sun's pits = *fuck*
shadows swallow me = *well, shit*
burning pits of the sun = *hell*
go piss yourself above = *fuck you, fuck off*
by the shadows = *goddamn, holy shit*
shadows' mercy = *shit*
a shadow's fuck = *fuck (but with style)*
sun-damned = *goddamned*
holy shadows = *holy shit*

SCUROS
LUCIS
CALIGO

AUTHOR'S NOTE

Dear reader,

Thank you so very much for being willing to read my debut, *This Safe Darkness*. When I first wrote the original version of this story in October 2022, I set out with a fairly clear goal: to write an epic fantasy centered around a disabled woman who learns that she is whole exactly as she is. It's a lesson that I've had to relearn over and over throughout the many years of living with an invisible disability.

So much of this book has changed since that first draft—the plot, the cast, the world—yet that goal has remained. If you're someone who's well acquainted with pain, I hope Orelle's story leaves you feeling celebrated for your resilience, and that it serves as a reminder that life doesn't have to be painless to be full.

Once you finish reading, it would mean the world to me if you would consider sharing an honest, public review on your platform of choice. As a debut indie author, reviews can make all the difference in helping this little story of mine reach more readers and maybe encourage them to take a chance on an author they've never heard of.

With gratitude & solidarity,
Alexis Maragold

To all those who battle to leave their own safe darkness,
and the ones who ensure we don't have to do it alone

CHAPTER ONE

I can't take my eyes off the full moon, even as lips press against the base of my throat. The celestial body basks in the glow of the unseen sun, forever taunting me, as if it knows this is the closest I've ever gotten to beholding its counterpart and revels in having my full attention. Shameless tease.

The moon and I have that in common, I suppose.

Hot breath skirts along my collarbone, and I reluctantly tear my gaze from the star-flecked sky to the man lapping at my skin like I'm something to be devoured. His chin brushes against the plunging neckline of my shift. I grab it, digging my fingertips into the wiry black-and-gray beard along his jaw with enough force to pry his tongue from my skin, though not so rough as to bruise his ego.

He flinches anyway, eyes burgeoning like a wounded animal's. "Whatcha do that for?"

As much as I want to tell him his saliva feels like sticky wax, my teeth gnaw along the inside of my bottom lip, keeping the words restrained. I need this man, or rather, I need his crazed infatuation to lead to a proposal. So, I nod towards the eastern horizon and speak a different truth. "Dawn is coming."

Moonlight highlights the lingering drool on his downturned mouth, and my muscles tense to refrain from recoiling. I force a pout as if I, too, resent the imminent sunrise for interrupting us. Fortunately, he can't hear the silent gratitude I send to the sliver of pale navy streaking along the space where sand and sky collide. Blue hour is nearly upon us. Soon, sunlight will illuminate the black nightstone gate at my back and the surrounding dunes, bathing the world in its lethal golden rays . . . and magic.

A heady shiver races along my spine. Though it has nothing to do with the man beside me, his gaze misses nothing. He is a Guard of the Gate, after all—one of Caligo's most prestigious positions, selected for his lethal perception and agility. It's a shame that perception skews towards what he wants to see, not what's truly there. Mistaking my movement for an invitation, his hands snatch my waist, pushing me flat against the closed gate.

"I can be quick," he whispers, fists traveling lower to bunch up the loose chambray fabric of my dress.

A second, more violent shiver chills down my back as it presses into the stone.

I take his hands into my own and laugh. "I may not be a maiden, but I have taken the vow of celibacy until I remarry."

It's nonsense, of course, but I'm trusting that his reputation as "one of the good ones" will prove true. In case it doesn't, I shift my weight, readying to knee his manhood.

"Understood." He takes a sizable step backward. "Forgive me. I shouldn't have assumed you wanted—"

My shoulders sag.

"I do." The lie rushes past my lips as the glimmer of interest singes out in his gray-blue irises, undoing months of careful glances, shy smiles, and whispered invitations. There isn't enough time to find and coerce another mark—not when the selection ceremony for the Hunt is less than twenty-four hours away. Fingertips dancing along his leather-clad arm, I trace the pair of silver bands denoting his two decades of service and wrap my hand around the back of his neck. "But don't you think it'll be worth the wait?"

My words are a caress against his ear, and he swallows hard before his untended brows pinch together. "Hold on. You aren't talking about marriage, are ya?"

I bat my lashes and fiddle with my tawny curls, ignoring the feverish warmth flooding to my cheeks. "Haven't you considered it?"

He frowns, retreating another step from the imposing stone archway. "I couldn't do that to my wife."

Your *dead* wife, I mentally correct him before giving my mind a good slap. Reminding this man that, as of ten months ago, his wife of twenty-two years is no longer present on this earth is hardly the best way to win him over.

Turning, I tear a blade of marram grass from the brush grazing the edge of the pure black gate. It's the only plant plucky enough to survive in the shifting sands, high winds, and nutrient-poor conditions of Caligo's dunes. Its existence is a marvel. A rebellion, even. I twirl the green blade between my fingers, channeling its audacity.

"Wouldn't she want you to find joy again?" I glance over my shoulder, allowing him to view the full weight of my longing. "Or maybe even love?"

The deep lines in his forehead soften as he shakes his head. "That's what she wanted for me. To move on. Remarry. Get myself a good woman who'd dote on our boys, though they're nearly grown men themselves now." He chuckles, and the sound is heavy with bittersweet pride. "But replacing her? Don't think I ever could."

Great. This is what I get for choosing a widower as my mark, but what other choices do I have? Despite his eagerness to get under my dress, the man's clearly still in love with his wife, and no lack of a pulse will change that. A woman in his bed is one thing; a woman in his heart is another.

"It's nearing curfew." He assesses the brightening sky with a growing heaviness, then picks up his black sword and helmet from the ground. Sand spills out as he resettles it atop his head. "We should go. Do ya mind?"

I respond by once again turning my back towards the gate recessed within the rocky surface of the gorge, giving him privacy as he pulls the two dangling keys from his belt and inserts them into the secret locks. After the second click, he taps against the frame. The knock is methodical and changes nightly—there's no use memorizing the shifting rhythm, even if there were some way to survive the day up here. The arched nightstone doors groan open, and I swivel back around as another Guard of the Gate ushers us inside. Back to the glorified cage we call home.

"Cuttin' it close." The guardsman snorts through his helmet, and I could swear the two men share a wink.

The shifting sky draws my glance one more time as handles turn and hinges creak. In less than an hour, the blackness above will give way to hues I've only ever seen in faded texts and on the common area screens during the annual broadcast of the Hunt. My leg spasms with the urge to run back outside before the guards finish closing the gate. It's an absurd thought that I dismiss, frowning at my legs as if they have a mind of their own, one that's entirely void of logic. Sure, it would be nice to witness an aerial landscape that isn't an inky canvas interrupted by specks of white. But given that it would likely be my first and last time witnessing the sun, that's a theory better suited for dreams.

I continue fidgeting with the blade of grass while the doors grate back into place, sending echoes throughout the shallow cavern dimly lit by an oversized pendant made in the moon's likeness and aglow with a violet bioluminescence. My sandals clap against the polished granite steps as I descend into the landing chamber, giving the two guards space as they share a hushed exchange.

Damp, nipping air chases off the final gust of warmth. A familiar weight settles over my lungs, and I tense, re-triggering the ache I'd been trying to ignore along my neck and above my right brow. If I'm lucky, I'll convince this hopelessly devoted widower to change his mind and make it back to my cabin all before the nausea flares up.

Easy. It's only my life on the line.

I pocket the grass and rub circles along my throbbing temple.

My companion claps the other guardsman on the back before angling towards me.

I lower my hand, but not fast enough. He strides over, boots resounding against the cavern floor, and my face heats. It's *my* duty to be the caregiver, not his. I'm already competing with the ghost of this man's wife, so the last thing I need is to give the memory of her an edge in my moment of weakness.

He offers up an arm. I accept it with a too-wide smile.

"Something wrong?" he asks, voice muffled by the helmet, while guiding us towards the darkened archways that stretch along the landing chamber's gray walls like scattered black teeth. Though his eyes are now covered, the side of my face tingles under the weight of his attention.

"I'm fine," I say, but my voice comes out higher than intended. I swallow, easing the strain. "Why do you ask?"

"I know about your condition."

The blunt confession weighs down my leading leg. Luckily, the smooth floor accepts the stutter of my footstep, allowing it to go unnoticed.

Even now, ten years after my very public divorce from Chancellor Bren's son, people speculate that I'm barren and broken. But few are bold enough to acknowledge those rumors to my face. I stare pointedly at my sandaled feet, ignoring the urge to glance at the mangled skin on the back of my left hand where I once proudly wore the branding of my marriage.

"I don't mean to pry," he rushes to add. "I only mention it in case you'd like to go slower."

"I'll manage," I reply with what I hope is a reassuring smile. I have no other choice if I hope to earn my keep.

He nods, and we stride past the pair of silent guards manning the transport tunnel's steel-clad entrance that leads to Deor, one of Caligo's two brother cities. Though the westbound train rumbles through the ceiling of my cabin with its nightly departures, it's been years since I last made the eight-mile trek to visit my parents. Longer still since they've deigned to visit their only child—and greatest disappointment.

My jaw clenches as we pass beneath the centermost archway into the main stairwell and descend its aged spiral steps. Despite my prior assurance, I tug on my companion's arm, trusting he'll interpret it as a wordless request to slacken the pace instead of a discreet maneuver to buy more time.

"About earlier, I'm sorry for pressuring you. I have no intention of replacing your wife."

He clears his throat. "I'm sorry, too. I didn't realize you had interest in remarrying, especially since . . . well, ya know."

"I get it," I say, rubbing at an invisible tear that becomes real as I consider what's at stake if tonight doesn't go to plan. "It's just . . .

I don't want to die."

It's a risk. Discovering that I have ulterior motives for courting him—that his convenient circumstance of being a widower with an established family drew me in more than his spirited impressions and clever puns—may wound his pride. But if soliciting his carnal nature is no longer an option, perhaps I can appeal to his empathy.

The purple glow of the sconces mounted to the rough limestone walls shines through his helmet, and I think I see his blank eyes blinking as he attempts to deduce how my urgent desire for marriage links to my fear of death.

I continue, "The selections for the Hunt will be chosen at midnight tomorrow."

He halts mid-step. My stomach plummets as he shifts his arm away from my grip, fists clenching at his sides. "You want to marry me to get out of being drafted for the Hunt? Why would you want to desert your duty?"

My hands clamp onto the rusted rail along the inner ledge of the spiral staircase that continues for miles, stretching to the depths of this underground haven—a haven that will always protect those like him from the sun and from those mutated by its corrupting light. He'll never stand before a Sol. He'll never know the consuming fear that rises with every image of the charred shells of humanity displayed on the ceremonial screen. Not a single Guard of the Gate will ever have to face eviction into the merciless world of light, never have to lose sleep from the looming probability that they will be killed by the golden-veined monstrosities or, worse, become one.

Protection comes at a cost.

Only one of us will have to pay it, and it isn't the man across from me.

"My *duty*?" I practically spit, tone darker and sharper than it should be. Though the lapse in the facade is cathartic, I can't make a habit of wielding my words like a knife, not if I want to be heard. I take two measured breaths before my voice returns to false levity, its own kind of subversive weapon. "The Hunt is a death sentence."

"The Hunt is an honor," he corrects, reciting word for word from Chancellor Bren's speeches. "It allows those who contribute least to Caligo's welfare to make the ultimate contribution of eliminating the threat above."

He speaks matter-of-factly, as if hunting and killing Sols is a simple enough task. As if thousands of women haven't lost their lives in futile attempts to accomplish that objective. As if I should be eager to follow in their footsteps in the name of honor and duty.

"You really think the only significant contribution a woman can offer is to marry and multiply? Is it not enough to be a hard worker and a considerate neighbor?"

Unwed, childless women are those who "contribute least" to society, according to Caligo's warped constitution. Strange how everyone seems to forget it was drafted at a time when men were the significant minority after the massacres from the Last War. Although I loathe the notion that single women who hadn't procreated were seen as more dispensable, I somewhat understand the logic from the repopulation angle. But now that the male-to-female ratio has long since recovered to a near even split, the mandate holds more so out of tradition than necessity. If those of us with uteruses fail to serve as wives or wombs, we risk becoming sacrifices.

He bristles. "Not as much as serving your family. Without a husband or child, you have no direct stakes in Caligo's future; no one you love who'll outlive you, who'll feel the lasting impact of every choice you make."

I hate that it stings, hate how his regurgitation of the tired narrative stirs up a tightness in my throat. But most of all, I hate my body for putting me in this position—pleading to a man who believes I can't possibly care for anyone who'll live long after my death until I've pushed a wailing newborn out of my womb.

"What about those of us who want to be a wife? Who'd give anything to have a child? There are no exceptions for women who are eligible for the Hunt by no fault of our own." Though my voice breaks, I force myself to hold his gaze. He needs to hear this, needs to believe that it's not as simple as we're all taught.

His fists unfurl, spurring me to continue.

"I'd give anything to have all of those things. I want someone to wake up beside me every night. Someone who'll appreciate my secret sourdough recipe and boast about my shoulder massages to his friends. He'll swear he has the best wife out of all of 'em."

My lips curl as I welcome the familiar daydream of a husband wrapping me in his arms as soon as he comes home. He'd pull me away from the sink and lift me onto the bed. I'd scold him for messing up the pile of laundry I just folded, and he'd promise to help refold after we're finished. That's the future I once envisioned for myself. Being needed. Treasured. A woman of infinite value to a man who'll keep his vow of "till death do us part."

I'd thought I had it, once. I should've known dreams weren't meant to last.

A warm palm braces my shoulder, squeezing once before dropping it. "Maybe someday you'll get that."

But he won't be the one to give it to me.

I shake my head at the unspoken implication.

"I won't if my name gets called tomorrow. No matter how many times I've tried, what I have to offer has never been enough." Before he can interrupt, I plead, "Please. I'm begging you. I can be whatever you want me to be, do whatever you want me to do. I'll be the perfect spouse. You'll see."

His knuckles turn white. "I won't betray my wife to help you avoid your duty."

A hot tear streaks down my nose. I turn my head away and offer a curt nod as a final goodbye, knowing it's the last we'll see of each other. There's nothing else I can say to this man that would break through decades of purist brainwashing. As quickly as my laden legs will carry me, I trudge down the worn stone stairs.

No footsteps follow.

No objections to my exit.

Not that I expected either.

With a sigh, I take the remaining steps two at a time while avoiding the foundational cracks from the ever-shifting fault lines that Chancellor Bren has sworn to fix since he was first elected three terms ago. I wipe the tear from my face, and glide down the last few steps.

An arched doorway etched with *R1* marks the first residential level. I slink beneath it, in tow with a line of tiny brown beetles that greet me with their musty spritz. The breathy moans that drift beneath more than one poorly sealed threshold remind me that the reeking insects aren't the worst of my neighbors. At least the six-legged creatures don't advertise their romantic activities well into the late morning hours, making it a near daily gamble on whose orgasms will haunt my dreams.

Yet another punishment of failing to find a husband: being sentenced to live among the other "low contributors" in compact cabins that are within spitting distance of one another. Could be worse, I guess. At least the housing is free, albeit positioned in an echo chamber with a proximity to the surface that's a bit too close for comfort. If Caligo is ever breached, we'll be the first to go.

I quicken to a jog and cover the side of my face as I pass by a particularly vocal bunch that makes a habit of leaving their door wide open.

Most of the sconces on this level have been dimmed as folks settle in for the day, ready to sleep off the sun's waking hours, yet the one beside a dented steel door painted with three constellations remains fully lit.

Of course they're waiting up for me.

I brace myself, then shove my key into the knob. Before I finish twisting it to the right, the door swings open, revealing two identical pairs of disapproving green eyes.

"Where in the burning pits of the sun have you been, Orelle?"

CHAPTER TWO

Before I can get a word out, Taurance yanks me into her chest. "We thought you'd left!"

"Without us," Gem adds with a grunt.

"Never." I wrap my limp arms around Taurance to pat her back before she gently shoves me away. "I wouldn't go back on our promise. If we leave, we leave together."

Taurance's lips thin as she turns to stand side by side with her sister. Rarely are the twins' similarities on display. Taurance's waist-length locks, husky voice, and less-is-more approach to clothing stand in contrast with her soft-spoken twin, who keeps her raven hair close-cropped and her body hidden beneath several layers. But seeing them stand before me now—their arms folded and jade irises hooded in scrutiny—the resemblance is unmistakable.

Together, they block off the narrow path between our off-kilter dining table and the partition curtains concealing our washroom. Taurance tugs on a chair, gesturing for me to sit. I'm eager to comply, if only to have the chance to lean back and rub at my closed lids.

"What took you so long?" Taurance presses while Gem disappears behind the curtains. "You've never gotten back past curfew."

I pause the massage long enough to peek at the sand clock we keep on the center of the table. It's been flipped upside down, reset to track the daylight hours. Few particles dust the bottom of the glass. It couldn't have been flipped for long—maybe a minute or two.

I point out, "I got back right *at* curfew. Not past it."

Gem tosses a damp washcloth at my face. "The last grain of evening hours fell nearly a full minute before your hand touched the door."

I wrap the cloth around my neck, and the warmth of it eases the stiff knot of tension. A satisfied groan escapes me. "I was with the guard, and it's not like he'd arrest me."

My fingertips halt on my brow bone. That might not be true anymore. Whatever we had is over. If he were to catch me out past curfew now, would a purist like him really think twice about detaining me?

A second chair scrapes against stone. I don't have to open my eyes to know it's Taurance. Her vanilla-almond body oil cloys at my senses, triggering a fresh wave of throbbing behind my right eye.

"What happened?"

Squinting through my heavy lids, I admit, "I picked another bad mark."

"Lousy kisser?" Taurance asks, leaning over to brush the stray curls from my forehead.

"No. I mean, his kisses felt more like mucus exchanges, but nothing I couldn't acclimate to over time."

Gem makes a sound like she's holding back bile as she perches along the table's edge.

Taurance waves off her sister's dramatics. "Was he not interested in taking it further, then?"

I pinch the bridge of my nose. "Oh, he was *very* interested, but only if he could get a release without attachments."

"What?" Gem jumps to her feet. "Did he hurt you?"

Taurance's black brows lift, wrinkling the smooth, pale skin of her forehead.

"No. He stopped as soon as I made it clear that I'm looking for an engagement, not a casual entanglement. He said he couldn't do that to his wife."

A huff escapes Taurance's scowling pink lips. "So, he has no problem burying himself inside you as long as you don't try replacing his buried wife?"

Gem swats Taurance's shoulder. "Sun's pits, T! That's bleak. He's a widower."

"A horny widower," Taurance corrects, then pats my leg. "You really are awful at picking 'em."

"In my defense, there aren't many options for a thirty-year-old disabled divorcee. I was hoping his neglected libido would override his grief. How was I supposed to know he'd have that much willpower still in him?"

Taurance leans in to ask, "What happened after you dashed his dreams of getting under your skirt?"

Gem groans, turning away to raid our cupboards.

"I told him the truth."

A cabinet door slams. "You did *what*?"

I shift in my chair, stuffing my hands into the pockets of my dress. "On the way back, he admitted he knew about my condition and offered to go slower. That's more empathy than I normally get. I thought if I told him why I wanted to get engaged, maybe he'd get it."

"You told a Guard of the Gate you wanted out of the Hunt?" Gem asks from across the room, pale cheeks flushing.

Taurance's palm presses against my forehead. "Are you sick?"

I swat her away. "Not any more than usual."

"Dehydrated, then. Did you drink enough water today?"

Taking her sister's cue, Gem rushes back to the washroom, sending the partition curtains billowing.

Ignoring the sudden, acute awareness of my tongue's dryness, I argue, "I drank plenty."

"Drink up." Gem reappears with a mug in hand. The cracked ceramic thumps onto the table.

"Yes, Mother," I jibe without thinking.

Gem's face falls, and mine follows suit.

"By the shadows, Gem, I'm so sorry."

Her frown breaks into a lopsided grin. "Gotcha!"

I flick the damp washcloth at Gem, and she ducks behind Taurance, who's watching us with a halfhearted smile.

"Your sister is cruel," I tease, but my smile falters as I take a better look at Taurance. Her green eyes glisten brighter than usual, which only happens when she's on the brink of tears. The levity falls from my lips as the moment passes. "What's wrong, Taur?"

She stands up from her chair, gliding over to her cot at the back of the cabin.

My gaze darts to Gem, lifting a brow in a silent question.

She shakes her head, then moves to follow her sister. "It was a joke, T."

"It's not that," Taurance says, fetching a folded parchment from beneath her cot. Gem and I step in closer to get a better look while she unfolds the paper with shaky hands. "I found out earlier tonight, but I wanted to wait until we were all together."

"Wait for what?" Gem asks, eying the parchment. "Is it from Ma?"

"No." Taurance cradles the paper close to her chest.

I lower myself onto the cot beside her, rubbing circles on the small of her back. "Your mystery suitor, then?"

"No. It's, um . . ." She blinks, sending two beads of tears rushing down her flushed cheeks.

Gem nudges her sandaled foot into her sister's. "Come on, T. You're scaring me."

"I'm—" Taurance sniffles, then tries again. "I'm pregnant."

Gem goes completely still at the barely audible confession.

My hand pauses on Taurance's back. "What?"

"I'm pregnant," she repeats, turning the paper around to reveal the official declaration of pregnancy signed off on by the Department of Midwifery. "I heard their heartbeat. A hundred sixty beats per minute."

"Taur!" I wrap both arms around her shoulders. "This is good news, right?"

I may be childless by force—thanks to my defective body—and Gem by choice, but Taur's longing to be a mother has only grown in the years since we first decided to room together.

A weighted smile stretches across Taurance's face as she nods, glancing up at her twin who's yet to budge an inch. "It is, but this means I won't be able to go with you."

I wrap my fingers around Taur's, attention drifting to the satchels leaning against the kitchen cupboard. Over the past few nights, we've packed a few bags of hazelnuts, a loaf of sourdough, an old wine bottle refilled with water, and a few other essentials in case my plan of wooing the widower fell through.

"What if we stay? Take our chances. We've made it this far without our names being called. You're ineligible now, Taur. And Gem, this is only your sixth year of eligibility. Maybe they won't—"

"Ten," Gem says, tone thick. "This is your *tenth* year of eligibility, Orelle. If you don't leave today, you will be drafted."

Few who make it into the double digits escape the Hunt. Our entries double with every year of eligibility, and the system heavily skews towards candidates who've aged past their twenties. It's a bitter truth we usually refrain from acknowledging aloud.

My voice breaks as I counter, "You don't know that."

A muscle flexes in Gem's jaw. "We have to leave."

"No, we don't." I rise to my feet, folding my arms across my chest. "I'm not going without meeting Taurance's child. That baby will need their aunties. Taur will need us."

Delicate fingers wrap around my wrist. "I need you alive. If not for my sake, then for Gem's. Once the baby is here, we won't be allowed in the same cabin anymore. You're going, even if Gem has to drag you all the way to Deor."

The twins share a loaded look, and Gem swallows hard before dipping her chin.

"I'll join you." Taurance glances at her stomach. "As soon as she or he is born and we're both recovered from birth."

I droop back onto the cot, shoulders hunching forward. "What about the father? Won't he want you to stay here?"

Taurance fidgets with the shorn hem of her sleeping gown. "I'm not entirely sure who the father is."

The space between Gem's brows creases. "How many contenders are there?"

"Two," Taurance says, head down as she picks at a loose thread.

"Shit, T. You really want to follow in Ma's footsteps?"

I stiffen. The twins rarely speak of their mother, though I've gleaned enough to know she'd gotten pregnant out of wedlock after sleeping her way into the beds of several male suitors and placed the blame of her disheveled life on her daughters, as if they'd chosen to be born into the lower rungs of society.

Taurance meets her sister's scolding gaze. "I will never be like Ma. You think you're so superior because you're a virgin, but at least I won't die alone."

"Woah there, Taur." I rest a palm on her leg, but she brushes it off. "I doubt she meant it like that."

Gem shakes her head. "That's *exactly* how I meant it."

"Go piss yourself above," Taurance spits back.

I insert myself between the galling green gazes of the twins. "Enough! You know Taur is nothing like your Ma. She's gonna spoil that baby every single day of its life. Smother it in far too much love, the way she smothers us." I shift my glower from Gem to Taurance. "And just because Gem has no interest in sleeping with anyone does not mean she'll die alone. We're her family: me, you, and a niece or nephew who honestly might prefer their Auntie Gem over their own mother sometimes. So, let's not waste our last couple hours together exchanging low blows, hm? You're making my brain hurt."

I kick off my sandals and scoot further onto the cot, releasing a heavy exhale.

Taurance is the first to surrender. She scoots closer to me, patting at the space on her other side. "Truce?"

It's a few tense seconds before Gem breaks. "Truce."

The cot's thin mattress deflates as she joins us, but I don't mind. This might be the last time the three of us are together, at least for a while.

Or for good.

I shoo away the thought.

Soon, Gem and I will sneak up to the transport tunnels while the city's sleeping. We'll slip past the guards by taking the utility stairwell instead of the main path. And we'll make it to Deor right before sunset.

Our plan *will* work.

Because if it doesn't, my name will be chosen for the Hunt.

There's no way of knowing that with absolute certainty, yet the knot that's been festering in my chest doesn't doubt it's true. It's that same intuition that haunted me in the days prior to the divorce—a deep knowing that something's about to change.

I pull out the blade of marram grass from my pocket, desperately praying that change will be for the better this time, not the worse.

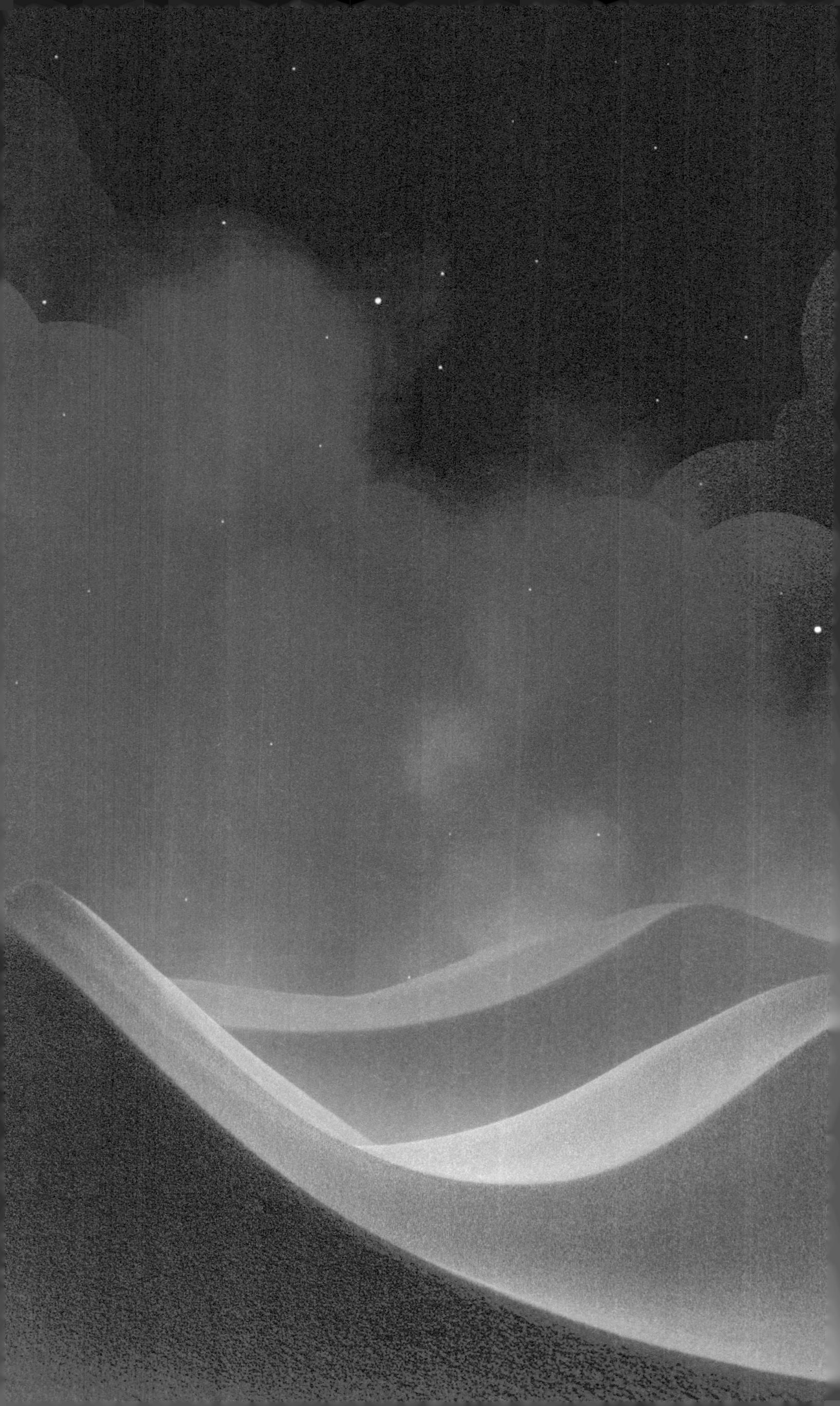

CHAPTER THREE

A bead of sweat streams down my temple as I reach for the next rung and question all the recent choices that led me here. Maybe sticking around for the Hunt wouldn't be so bad; preferable, even, to climbing the utility staircase that's more of a slanted steel ladder than true stairs.

I rub the back of my hand against my forehead and frown at the dark gray smudge staining my ashen skin. Gem spent her past few kitchen shifts scrounging up a pail of soot from the oven, so we could dye my hair. We'd hoped the ashes would darken my conspicuous tawny curls to a shade closer to the twins' raven locks. The actual result is more of a lifeless gray, but it should suffice as a temporary disguise long enough to get us into Deor.

If I can make it there.

Gem halts a whole flight above my head. Neither of us dares to speak a word aloud—not while our every move is reverberating through the unforgiving stone and steel surfaces—but I could swear I can hear her questioning in the silence whether I can keep going.

I respond by hoisting myself up, rung after rung.

This is fine.

I'm fine.

It's not like the moist, moldy air from the adjacent water pipes is goading my stomach into joining the protest of my muscles. And my brain certainly isn't threatening to implode if I don't rest soon.

The ladder sways beneath my touch as a dizzy spell calls bullshit on my lies. By the grace of the shadows, I glance up to see the top of the stairwell. Just fifteen more steps. Gritting my teeth, my fingers grip more tightly on the rusted steel rungs. Black orbs creep along the edges of my vision. I hasten my ascent, climbing the remaining steps with as much vigor as I can muster. When my hand latches onto the top ledge of the round platform, I heave myself up and sprawl stomach-side-down across the chilled metal floor.

Gem pushes off the rough limestone wall to kneel at my side. I hold up a single finger, and she nods, understanding that I need a minute.

The kiss of cool steel against my cheek and temple chases off my unsettled vision, but the acid along my tongue is slower to recede. Once the pasta salad I downed an hour ago is no longer threatening to make its way back up, I roll into a sitting position.

Gem pulls the wine bottle of water from her satchel. I snatch it and pluck the loosened cork, taking a swig.

"Ready?" Gem silently mouths.

I want to shake my head and tell her no. I'd rather go back to our cabin, pass out on my cot, and not wake until the selection ceremony is over. But if my name gets called and I'm not present, the cabin would be the first place Chancellor Bren's men would look.

Although escaping to Deor isn't a plan without flaws, it buys us time. Once the henchmen come knocking, Taurance will be ready and waiting with my alibi: my new fiancé whisked me away to the north. All we need is to divert their attention for twenty-four hours.

That's how long it's taken in past Hunts for new names to be chosen once the women who'd deserted weren't found. Of course, we'll never be able to fully lower our guard, even after hours turn into days, weeks, and months. Desertion is treason. If we're ever found out, it'll be a lifetime of imprisonment without parole.

So, my options are to return to our cabin and accept the likelihood that I'll soon be sent above like a sacrificial lamb prime for the slaughter, or keep going and pray to the merciful shadows we don't get caught.

One leads to an imminent death. The other, an inhibited life.

My shoulders roll back as I stuff the wine bottle into my own satchel and finally offer Gem a nod. She helps me to my feet, then cracks open the sliding steel door. Having a few extra inches over Gem's five-foot frame, I peek over her shoulder at the compacted clay walls and rusted rail lines bathed in dim purple light by interspersed sconces. Thanks to a brief fling with a maintenance technician around last year's Hunt, I've gleaned that stationed guards keep tabs on all the primary entrances to the transport tunnels around the clock, but none should be present during daylight hours to monitor the seldom-used utility doors.

As expected, nothing stirs within the violet darkness.

We slip through the doorway, keeping to the raised pathway along the tunnel's edge to avoid the central trench and its five-foot drop-off. The cool metal beneath my tattered sandals shifts into something more pleasant. Not warm, but almost.

I tilt my neck as my amber eyes drift to the clay ceiling. The tunnel runs just below the surface, leaving only a few feet to separate us from the world above. A world opposite our own. A world of light and heat—a contrast to these suffocating walls and bitter air. Perhaps a world that could chase away the ice in my soul, or the pulse in my heart.

Gem, who's ten steps ahead, checks on the miniature sand clock

I stashed in her bag.

I hasten my pace, focus returning to the path. We fall into a rhythm, the sconces creating an ebb and flow between light and shadow.

As we pass the first mile marker, a low rumble carries through the tunnel.

Gem glances over her shoulder. "Earthquake?"

Given the last one was three nights ago, we're past due.

We bend into a crouch to wait out the tremors for the usual thirty seconds, but the groaning grows louder as the seconds pass. Loosened rocks cascade over the platform's edge into the trench. The low groan sharpens into the whining shriek of metal against metal.

"The train!" I say, pulse accelerating in tandem with the growing screech.

Gem curses under her breath. "But it's hours past curfew! Who'd be traveling this late?"

"Maybe Chancellor Bren called in more guards for the selection ceremony."

My head whips side to side, searching for an alcove to conceal us from any eyes peering through the train's windows, but the nearest recessed corner I can recall is by the utility stairwell's entrance a mile back.

I tug on the brown sleeve of Gem's oversized jacket, pulling us into the cloaking darkness between the scattered light of the sconces. Then, after pulling a black wool shawl from my satchel, I stretch the fabric over our hunched forms and pray to the merciful shadows it'll be enough.

Seconds later, the eastbound train comes around the bend ahead. Though the thick wool is nearly impossible to see through, there's a tear in the fabric. I squint through it, holding my breath as the locomotive approaches. Its brakes scream their protest while they try to slow the rapidly rotating wheels. Unlike the usual train that transports residents between the two brother cities, this cart is shorter, yet wider. Its side windows have been painted over, and platforms protrude from its ends where four armed guards stand patrol: a pair in front, the other in back. But instead of directing their attention outward, the guards angle themselves towards the cart, as if the real threat lurks within.

A prisoner transfer.

They must be sending someone from Deor into the Abyss—prison cells at the lowest level of Caligo. But why arrange the transfer during daylight hours?

A reverberating crack emanates from the rear window as the cart passes in front of us. A shadowy profile refracts through splinters in the glass.

Gem winces, letting out a small squeal.

All four guards stand straighter as they swivel around.

My whole body tenses, preparing to bolt.

"That one of you boys?" asks a gravelly-toned guard stationed at the front of the cart. He scoffs. "Sounded like a scared little girl."

The shorter of the two guards in back replies with a grunt, while the other folds his arms against his chest, flexing his muscles. "Wasn't me. You sure you can hack it, old man?"

"I've been doing this since you were in diapers, son. It's gonna take a whole lot more than that to rattle me. Probably just a nail or something on the track."

Despite their talk, all four shift further from the cart as the hazy black outline of a fist slams against the glass, then pulls away before striking again—and again.

The shorter guard thumps the hilt of his sword against the window before calling to someone inside. "Give 'em another shock."

Any responses are lost to the grinding retreat of the train as it winds around the other side of the bend.

Our lungs deflate a minute later.

"Sorry about that. Almost got us caught," Gem says, bunching up her side of the shawl and passing it to me.

"Nothing to be sorry for." I stand, folding the wool over my arm. Adrenaline rushes through my aching noodle legs, making them halfway useful as we continue down the path at a brisk pace. When we've put another two mile markers between us and the Caligo end of the tunnel, I ask, "Don't you think it's weird that they're transferring a prisoner this late?"

"Maybe they didn't want to distract from the festivities of the Hunt?"

"Maybe." I chew on the inside of my bottom lip. Normally, the chancellor has prisoners paraded like warning signs to dissuade people from falling out of line. My brows pinch together as I consider why he'd switch tactics.

The thought distracts me from minding the path until my heel catches on a crack in the clay. I stumble sideways, arms flailing. Gem lunges back, but she's too far ahead to grab me as I topple over the ledge into the trench of the central rail lines.

My satchel takes the brunt of the fall.

Something shatters inside and splinters through the canvas material directly into my right ass cheek. The sting distracts me from the rest of the aches while I hiss out a breath and roll forward onto my hands and knees.

Gem rushes to the edge of the platform. "Orelle! Are you okay?"

A strained laugh bursts through my lips as I push myself back to standing. "Never been better."

Her furrowed brows relax. "Guess it's not too bad if you think this is funny."

"C'mon, it's a little funny. Survived a near spotting from a prisoner transfer train, only to get taken down by my lack of coordination."

"Are you hurt?"

"Fairly sure our wine bottle cut into my ass, but nothing feels broken." I give my arms and hips a wiggle, proving my bones are indeed intact, then use the wool shawl to swipe at the wet stains along the backside of my chambray dress.

"Thank the shadows for that. Come over here so I can pull—"

A groaning rumble shakes through the ground beneath my feet, sharper than the previous tremors.

Violet light illuminates the whites of Gem's eyes. "Another train?"

A growing roar nearly drowns out her words, and I shake my head. This isn't the metallic grating of the train. This is deeper, more violent. Clumps of clay and rock rain down around us.

"Take cover!" I shout, kneeling to do the same.

The meager purple light pouring into the trench forsakes me while falling debris clouds my vision. A sandy avalanche descends as a fissure rips through the ceiling. I bend further into a crouch, wrapping my arms behind my head to protect myself from the cascading rubble.

A plume of grainy dust fills the air. I shelter here, waiting for the series of thundering snaps and violent tremors to subside. Seconds feel like minutes as the earth finally settles. I fight the urge to inhale, but my resilience has already been pushed too far today. I succumb to the breath my body so desperately desires, accepting the consequences. Coughing violently, I cradle my nose into my shoulder and try to blink my eyes open to assess the damage, but an unforgiving light makes it a near-impossible feat. Blinding streaks of gold pour into the tunnel from a split in the earth above, diffused by the haze enveloping the trench.

Finally, my lungs begin to clear, but my voice chokes through the debris in my throat.

"Did my clumsy ass somehow cause a real earthquake this time?" I ask rhetorically—but Gem doesn't respond. "Gem! You okay?"

Still nothing.

My stinging eyes refuse to stay open. Relying on touch alone, I swing my arms around until I find the edge of the trench and lean into it, rising on unsteady feet. Something hot spreads across the back of my right hand, and I pull back.

"Gem!" I call again, straining to peel my lids open long enough to adjust to the onslaught of light. In all my three decades of life, not once have I seen something so painfully bright. It takes several watery blinks before I'm able to peer through squinted lids.

When I do, I immediately wish I could unsee what's in front of me.

My hand is . . . glowing.

A golden, tingling energy pulses through the veins in my fingers, traveling down my palm and stopping just past my wrist. The heady warmth of it stands in contrast to the permanent chill residing within me.

I gawk at the appendage like it's betrayed me.

No.

It can't be.

Head whipping upward, my gaze fixes on the dusty shaft of light beaming through the parted ceiling. Though narrow, the vertical spotlight stretches dozens of feet across, from the surface above to the packed earth along the edge of the trench. Particles of clay dance in its illumination.

Sunlight.

In the exact spot where I placed my hand a mere moment ago.

My *exposed* hand.

"Are Sols human?" I'd once asked my mother. She was in the middle of a history lesson, and I'd just learned that the monsters that lurked above began as humans. Prior to that, I'd thought the Sols

were evil creatures from birth.

"Not anymore," my mother replied. *"As soon as they allow the sun to mark their veins, they lose their humanity."*

I'd gulped, knowing from that day forward that I'd have nightmares about getting trapped outside with no shadows to shelter me from that fate. *"Forever?"*

"Forever," she'd confirmed.

My chest heaves, the weight of that memory condemning me.

How long do I have before the mutation begins? Will I still remember who I am? Who my friends are?

Gem.

"By the darkness," I whisper as I look past my tainted flesh at the pile of rubble cutting an angled line across the raised pathway—exactly where I'd last seen Gem.

"Gem!" I shout, dismissing my concern of being discovered. There's no way an earthquake of that magnitude went unnoticed. A horde of day-shift guards will likely arrive in a few minutes to inspect the damage.

Stumbling closer to the edge of the trench, I skirt around the edge of the beam of sunlight and attempt to pull myself up onto an unmarred portion of the path. My wrists buckle, unable to bear my weight, and a few rebellious coughs escape my lungs expelling the last of the debris.

"Sun's pits." I groan, wiping my palms along my dress as if clamminess is the issue and not my lack of upper body strength.

After the fourth failed attempt, my shoulders hunch, and I scan the surrounding debris for a rock large enough to use as a stepping stone.

"Here," a masculine voice says from behind.

With a yelp, I clasp my glowing fingers behind my back and spin to find a broad-shouldered man cradling a small boulder in one excessively toned arm. He's notably shirtless, and I'm taken aback by the vibrancy of his deep olive skin—how it lacks the usual ashen undertone found on those of us who reside in the safe darkness. But unlike mine, his veins show no sign of the sun's corrupting light.

"What are— Where did you— Who?" I stop and start, not knowing which question to lead with. As he nears, I settle on a warning. "Look out for the sunlight!"

Without a glance in my direction, the stranger kneels beside me, his dark curls inches from brushing against my exposed calves. Raised scars stretch across his muscled back as he shoves the boulder against the wall of the trench.

I should put some distance between myself and this bare-chested man who came out of nowhere and potentially saw the damning evidence of my compromised hand.

Unwilling to heed logic, my legs stay firmly planted while I breathe in the stranger's distinct scent that reminds me of smoky bergamot. A nightstone pendant thumps against his chest as he rises. Eyes like molten gold flick down to mine, gleaming with predatory intent.

I finally step back.

Those narrow golden irises leer at me through dark lashes. As if *I'm* the one who snuck up on him. As if *I* forced him to fetch the boulder for me.

And, shadows help me, I glower back. "Who are you?"

There's a reckless bite in my tone—one I should temper if I want to avoid this man dragging me to the guards, though I'm banking on the fact that he, too, is out past curfew.

Between his loose linen pants and the absence of armor, he's obviously not a guard himself. Or perhaps if he is, he's off duty. He does have the build of one. I suspect there are more muscles in his back than there are in my entire body. Yet there's something untamed about his overgrown black curls and incandescent irises that makes me doubt this man would ever agree to the subservient life of a guardsman.

So, what exactly is he doing here in the transport tunnels in the middle of daylight hours, if he isn't one of the chancellor's men? What's he trying to hide?

Our gazes lock in a silent battle of will. I raise a single brow. Both of his lift, like my reaction doesn't align with his hastily constructed impression of a damsel in distress. He doesn't strike me as a man who's accustomed to his expectations being subverted or proven wrong.

I'd like to do it again.

The impulsive thought is enough to make me fold. I lower my head, breaking our prolonged eye contact.

"That should be enough." The man clears his throat and nods to the boulder before turning on his heel, leaving my questions unanswered.

I stare at his retreating form for several seconds, then return my focus to the more important matter: Gem.

The boulder is just over knee-height—tall enough for me to climb atop and hoist myself over the ledge. My ass cheek stings in protest as I do so.I stand, then twist to survey the cut. Sure enough, there's a blot of crimson leaking through the thin chambray material of my shift. I tug the black wool shawl from where I draped it on my satchel, ready to tie it around my waist, but pause as the dense fabric extinguishes my glowing fingers. I glance over my shoulder to verify that the stranger is truly gone and wrap the shawl around my hand. Although the resulting makeshift cast is bulky, it's less conspicuous than waving around my sunlit veins like a beacon of my transgression.

With the wrap in place, I rush over to where Gem last stood and clamber up the pile of rubble. Several rocks dislodge and tumble during my ascent, but I scale the stockpile without further injury.

I spot Gem's prone form instantly, sprawled out on the packed clay path, a scarlet puddle encircling her head.

"Gem!"

Falling to my knees, I lower my ear to her chest. Fresh tears rush down my cheeks as her steady pulse beats against the side of my face.

Alive. She's alive, thank the shadows.

"Gem, can you hear me?" I intertwine my left hand with hers. A new wave of panic chases away the brief relief when she remains unresponsive, and my grip tightens.

"Gem, I need you to squeeze my hand if you can hear me."

Nothing.

We can't stay here. She needs help, and I can't carry her, nor do I think the guards will be particularly inclined to do so when they realize we're deserters—or would-be deserters, if it weren't for the earth itself halting our path to freedom.

I curse, then release Gem's fingers. "Be right back."

Once I'm on the other side of the rubble, I jog along the path, following the same direction as the gruff stranger. Flashing orbs dance along my vision as it readjusts to the shadows, and I call out, "Sir? If you can hear me, I really need your help."

I wince at the raucous echoes.

There's no way that man *didn't* hear me.

Still, no one responds, so I press forward. "Please? I wouldn't ask if—"

A callused palm wraps around my mouth.

The basic training offered twice annually to eligible women of marital age comes rushing back, and I slam my elbow backward, aiming for my attacker's solar plexus.

Although a whoosh of air escapes his lips, the hand around my mouth doesn't relent.

Before he can catch his breath, I raise my heel, preparing to stomp on his sandaled foot, but the stiff muscles in my leg slow me down.

A second arm wraps around my waist, lifting me off the ground entirely. Warm breath scalds my ear in warning.

"Do you have a death wish?"

CHAPTER FOUR

Though he'd spoken no more than six words, I immediately recognize the gravelly voice and subtle scent of smoky bergamot. And against my better judgement, I relax a little.

"No," I try to mumble against his palm.

The man huffs a bemused breath, like he's unconvinced, then asks, "If I put you down, do you promise to stop screaming?"

His grip on my mouth loosens enough for me to answer. "Sure, but only if you promise to help me."

"Help you how?" He lowers his hand from my face, but instead of setting me down, readjusts his free arm to brace across my shoulders.

"My friend, Gem. She was hit by the falling rubble. Her pulse is steady, but she's bleeding and non-responsive. I need to get her to someone that can help, and I'm not strong enough to carry her on my own." The admission has me biting the inside of my lip.

"I can't—" he starts.

"*Please.* I'll owe you a favor." Desperation heightens my pitch. "Anything you need."

Offering an open-ended favor is a gamble, but there are two things

I've gleaned about this man: he's clearly up to something, yet he was good-natured enough to give me an unprompted hand with that boulder. Plus, little does he know I have an impending expiration on my time as a human. He won't have long to cash in that favor.

The scruff along his jaw brushes against the side of my head as he asks, "Anything? No conditions? No questions?"

"Anything," I agree, praying to the shadows that I've gambled correctly.

He releases me instantly.

I stumble a little, unprepared to bear weight again on my limp legs. Once I stabilize, I return to Gem with the stranger in tow. He frowns when he sees her lying in the puddle of blood, then delicately slips a hand beneath her neck.

I lower into a shaky squat. "You get her head. I'll get her legs."

Lifting a single angular brow, he blinks pointedly at me before bracing his other hand beneath Gem's knee and raising her off the ground. I catch her torn satchel as it slips off, frowning at the unexpected heaviness of it.

The man readjusts his grip on Gem, cradling her in one arm while lifting the other in offering. "I'll take it."

"You sure?"

He responds by grabbing the strap and tugging it onto his shoulder with a scowl.

"Is it too heavy?"

"Not for me," he says.

I wince at the implication. How can someone be so simultaneously rude and so generous? I mean, he isn't wrong; the satchel would significantly slow me down if he hadn't offered to carry it. But wouldn't most people keep that deduction to themselves? I glance at the stranger, whose arms are full with Gem's prone body and her bag, then shake my head. Most people wouldn't have bothered to help.

"Where to?" he asks.

My head twists to the side. There's a metal mile marker a few feet down the wall with two lines of text. The first denotes a distance of three and a half miles between this check point and Caligo. The second shows four and a half miles to reach Deor. Blood rushes to my cheeks at the realization that we hadn't even made it halfway.

Wishing I didn't have to make this decision alone, I point to the east, towards Caligo.

Gem's going to be pissed when she wakes and discovers we backtracked, but I won't prolong her receiving medical care for the sake of escaping the Hunt. She has so much more potential, more value, than I'll ever have. If it's her life or mine, I'll choose hers. Every time.

We carry on in silence, and I try to keep up. Even with the added weight of a grown woman, the stranger's stride doesn't falter. If only I could say the same for myself. By the time the first mile marker returns to view, I've long since given up on matching pace. Instead, I busy myself with staring at the gruesome scars cutting along the left side of his back and disappearing around his rib cage. Perhaps I was wrong to assume he's not a guard, though I've seen the unclothed backs of several guardsmen and not once have I seen wounds so grim. Despite their role as primary protectors of Caligo, the Guards of the Gate rarely see battle. Thanks to their dependence on direct sunlight and wariness of the underground, Sols seem to reserve their attacks for the Hunt, when their prey is more easily available. So, where did this stranger earn such a fierce wound, and how did he survive?

Distant voices break our wordless progression. We rush to push our backs into the wall. The guards must finally be coming to inspect the commotion. It's a miracle it took them this long, but it seems our good fortune is running out. I lean further into the wall, my arm pressing into the chilled, metal sign denoting we're a mile from the transport tunnel's main entrance, which means . . .

"There's a utility stairwell a quarter mile down from here on our right." My words are barely louder than a breath. "If we hurry, maybe we can get to it before the guards."

Problem is, hurrying means no more being quiet on our feet.

We'll need to run.

"Don't wait for me," I urge, knowing there's a chance I won't be fast enough. "Even if they catch me, go down the stairwell. Look for the doorway marked R1. Hook a right and follow the bend. There's a cabin with three constellations painted on the front door. Knock six times."

There's more I want to tell him, but the voices grow louder, so I shove the stranger's arm with the unspoken plea to *move*.

He bolts.

I follow, clutching my stomach and begging in vain for my useless legs to go faster. But I've already pushed my body well past its usual limit. The adrenaline from the earthquake abates, allowing my prior fatigue to come barreling back, more prominent than before.

The guards shout something, no doubt alerted by our rapid footfalls. But I keep moving, eyes fixed on the fading figure ahead. The stranger soon disappears into the alcove of the utility stairwell entrance, and a hopeful smile tugs at my lips.

Gem's going to make it. He's going to get her to Taur, and she'll make sure Gem gets the medical attention she needs. Maybe I will, too. A few more seconds and I'll be ducking into the doorway before the guards get close enough to spot me.

I nearly convince myself it's true when three guards round the corner, jogging in my direction. They're on the opposite path, across the rail lines. They'll have to cross the trench to catch me. A small mercy—one I can't let go to waste.

I dive forward, swinging my arms back and forth more aggressively, as if that'll increase my speed.

"Is that a lady?!" one guard calls as they jump into the trench.

"Ma'am!" They break into a sprint, and another yells, "Stop right where you are!"

The first is already at the ledge when he warns, "In the name of the chancellor, stop or we will arrest—"

The door to the utility stairwell clicks into place behind my back, and I've never been so happy to be greeted by the scent of mold.

Without pausing to savor it, I dash down a flight of steps and barge through the doorway marked *P1* for the first level of the water purification system. I won't make it to the secondary utility stairwell on the opposite side of the five-hundred-acre reservoir. Instead, I aim directly for the bridge that divides the two basins, eyes wildly scanning the steel ledge until I find it—the ladder I once followed a boy down what feels like a lifetime ago.

I tighten the straps on my satchel before grabbing onto the ladder's slick rail. Cool water chases off some of the escalating fatigue as I partially submerge into the reservoir. Using the ladder to keep from plummeting the twenty-foot depth, I tuck myself behind the bridge's support beams. A purple sheen from the suspended tube lights glistens off the water's lapping surface while I fix my attention on the door and wait.

One . . .

Two . . .

Three hurried breaths later, the door slams open.

I squint through the perforated platform and hold as still as possible to avoid disturbing the reservoir's natural current.

It's a small relief to see that the guard is by himself. They must've taken the divide-and-conquer approach. But a second look at his brawny frame tamps that relief.

He won't need the helping hands of his fellow guardsmen if I'm caught.

The guard stomps forward, twisting his head right to left. He checks behind the row of groundwater pumps lining the reservoir's edge first before moving onto two mixing tanks at the nearest corner of the chamber, and I'm grateful I didn't go for the more obvious hiding spots.

His boots clang against the steel bridge, and my pulse grows so loud it's practically shouting.

Clamping my lips together, I hold my breath until the guard is several feet past the ladder. Once there are nearly two dozen feet between us, I relax into the support beam.

Something yanks on the shawl. The tear in the fabric has snagged on a protruding screw jutting from the ladder's steel rung, unraveling most of my makeshift cast. Though my glowing fingers are still covered, one good nudge from the reservoir's current might be enough to change that.

Slowly, I tug on the damp wool, hoping to unhook it from the screw. It doesn't budge. I try again, giving it a better yank. The stitch relents, releasing the shawl—but the motion casts a ripple along the surface. I tense, attention flicking back to the guard, who's halfway across the bridge. Unless he turns around, he won't notice a couple tiny ripples.

The door swings wide a second time.

"No sign of her in the archive," the newcomer calls across the chamber. "And the dayshift janitor swears she hasn't seen anyone come through. Boss is heading to R1 to do a head count on the feeders, see if anyone's missing from their cabin."

My teeth grind at the mention of feeders.

Feeders. Rats. Bait. Nicknames given to those of us unfortunate enough to call the first residential level home.

"Maybe she's in the greenhou . . ." The first guard trails off, his gaze homing in on the space to my left, where the dwindling ripples ebb across the water.

I squeeze my eyes shut.

Not for any good reason, really; it's not like my inability to see the guard will prevent him from seeing me. But I'd rather not lock eyes with the man who's about to drag me off to a cell in the Abyss, which is rumored to be kept in total blackness. Not even the dim bioluminescent sconces are allowed. Perhaps it'll feel like floating. Or like a thick blanket. Or maybe, like the feeder rat that I am, I'll develop enhanced night vision.

A rumble vibrates across the chamber, stirring up countless more ripples across the reservoir's expanse and interrupting my feeble attempts at persuading myself that a life of imprisonment might not be as bad as it sounds. I brace for a repeat earthquake.

Though the aquifer above the reservoir groans, it holds steady against the tremors.

"Aftershock?" the second guard questions as the trembling subsides.

"Must be," the first mumbles, then lifts his gaze from the water.

A minute later, I'm alone again. It's another five before I dare to move. I lean my head back into the water and release my hold on the support beam. My legs rise to the surface as I sprawl out, eager to release the burden of my aching body and weighty worries.

Twelve years have passed since I last felt the chilled embrace of the reservoir cushioning my back. We were newlyweds, drunk on declarations of love and the endless possibilities of our future. I'd wanted to stay in our cabin that night, but he'd insisted on sneaking up here.

"How perfect would it be if we conceived our firstborn son in the same spot I proposed?"

"*Or daughter.*" I'd smacked my palms against his chest. "*And you're not playing fair.*"

He'd given me a dimpled smirk. "*Life's not fair, Elle. But you certainly are.*"

Water trickles down my throat as my fingertips follow the phantom trail of kisses he'd once traced down my neck. Kisses that had crumbled my shaky resolve on more than one occasion. Kisses from a man I'd given everything to—my heart, my body, even my last name—only to be cast out like a shredded rag for the one thing I couldn't give him: an heir.

I spin onto my stomach and sink beneath the reservoir's surface, letting the current carry away the chafing memories of his haunting touch.

When I come back up, my ex-husband's name is long gone from my mind. And when I ascend back onto the steel bridge, I don't recall the time he gripped my waist and yanked me back into the water with a hungry gleam in his midnight-blue eyes.

The last of the soot stain drips from my drenched locks onto the steel bridge as I aim for the secondary utility stairwell. I shouldn't go home, not when I have no way of knowing how fast the mutation will spread through my veins. My very presence could put Taurance and Gem in danger. But I have to check on Gem. And I'm so damn tired. So, I resign myself to getting some rest in our cabin before saying goodbye.

By the time I arrive at our dented steel door, it's all I can do to lift my arm and knock.

Taurance grabs me by my sopping chambray shift, and I vaguely register her mentioning something about a half-naked man carrying her half-dead sister before I collapse in her arms.

CHAPTER FIVE

"He said nothing else before he left?"

After I woke, Taurance recounted what happened after the stranger made it to our cabin with Gem, who was as white as a corpse. He laid her out on the cot while Taur fetched some supplies from the retired midwife two doors down the hall.

"You mean *after* he raided my drawers and stole my clothes," Gem huffs as she maneuvers into a sitting position on the cot beside mine.

Taur tuts her tongue against the back of her teeth, then rises to fetch the tea tree oil from the kitchen table. "It's the least we could offer him for saving both your asses."

Not only did this man give me a hand with the boulder and with Gem, he also acted as a stand-in body on my cot when a guard came knocking on our cabin door for the head count.

I meet Gem's gaze and give a *"she has a point"* tilt of my chin.

Her green irises roll. "But why did he need my clothes? What was he doing sneaking around the tunnels half-naked in the middle of the day? For all we know, he could've been the prisoner they were transferring in that train."

In other words, what have I gotten us into?

No one speaks. Even if we allow ourselves to consider the questions we'd rather avoid, we don't have the answers, and I'm not so sure I want them.

There's a strong chance the man we welcomed into our home is a criminal. What other reason would someone have to traverse the tunnels—with few clothes and zero belongings—during daylight hours, if not to avoid notice? Perhaps he was caught having an affair. It's not unimaginable that a man of his physique might attract the forbidden attention of a married woman, or a man, for that matter. A ridiculous image comes to mind of the stern-faced stranger scrambling to tug his linen pants back on after getting caught in an indecent entanglement.

That must be it. Or maybe I'm indulging myself because it's more palatable to think we harbored a red-handed lover instead of someone truly nefarious.

The sound of running water from the other side of the partition curtains fills the notable silence as Taur drenches a fresh cloth using the midwife's recommended mixture of tea tree oil, magnesium sulfate, and chilled water. She's back a moment later, tossing her braid behind her shoulder and peeling away the soiled cloth wrapped around the crown of Gem's head.

"Sutures are holding up okay," Taur comments before dabbing at the few blots of crimson surrounding the wound before covering the sutures with a dry compression cloth.

Gem winces. "It's only been a few hours, T. Fairly sure stitches are meant to last at least a week or two."

Taur swats Gem's leg with the dirty cloth. "I've assisted the midwives with postpartum tears, but this is my first time using sutures on a scalp. It's a bit different from a perineum or vagi—"

"Okay, okay, we get it," Gem says, splotches of pink bringing color back to her wan cheeks. "Can you stop hovering now? Go bother Orelle. She got hurt, too."

"My ass is as good as new," I quip, hoping the twins will leave it at that.

But of course, they don't.

Taurance arches her brows. "And your hand?"

My pulse trips on itself.

"Fine," I practically chirp as I swing my legs off the cot, thankful that the nap was enough of a reprieve to ease the pounding in my brain and stomach, if not the aching in my calves.

Ignoring the prickle of eyes on my wrapped arm, I amble over to the table, where our belongings from the satchels are neatly organized in rows. The bags themselves are hanging from the curtain rod. Taur must've cleared everything out to give them a good scrubbing. Gone are the bloodstains and dirt, and I can easily patch the tears with my . . .

The sight of my black makeshift cast dashes any ideas I have about sewing up our battered bags. I haven't felt the warm tingle of energy since waking from my nap, but the thought of unraveling the wool fabric to check on how far the mutation has spread makes my skin crawl. So, I return my focus to the table, ready to assess the damage to our belongings. My mother's recipe journal lies warped at the table's center. I pick it up and try to peel apart the first two pages. The paper rips, its fibers brittle thanks to my dunk in the reservoir.

At least the sand clock should be safe. I set the leather journal down and search for the other heirloom. My brows pinch together when I don't spot it among the orderly piles. I'm about to ask Taurance if she tucked it away, when I spot the leftover sourdough. It's mashed on one side, but by some highest of miracles, the bread isn't soggy. My stomach groans, reminding me I've skipped at least two meals.

"Are you seriously ignoring me right now?" Taurance snatches the loaf out of my grip. "Let me take a look at it."

"The bread?" I ask, intentionally obtuse. I know she means my hand, but I'm not ready to have that conversation yet. Can't we have just one more hour of them treating me like a chosen sister instead of a monster in the making?

Taurance's face twists into *that* look—the one I've seen my mother wear dozens of times. The one making it clear we both know that's a lie.

"It barely hurts." I fold my arms tight across my chest, tucking my cast beneath my good arm. "And it's not like there's anything you can do."

"If it barely hurts, why do you need to keep that on?" Eyes narrowing, she nudges her chin at the shawl.

Shadows swallow me. Looks like I'm not getting that extra hour.

Metal scrapes against stone as I tug a chair out from the table and spin it around. Taurance clutches the sourdough for emotional support as she too takes a seat.

Gem scoots to the edge of her cot. "You're not about to tell us you're pregnant, too. Are you?"

"*Gem,*" Taurance chides, tossing the loaf of bread at her twin. But her aim is off, and the sourdough lands on the floor instead, joining the dust bunnies beneath Gem's bed. "You can't make jokes about that."

"Sorry for trying to lighten the mood," Gem says while using her feet to slide the loaf back out and punt it at Taur, who huffs.

"Since when is mocking infertility a mood lightener?"

Gem's jade eyes meet mine, and she shrinks into herself.

I offer her a smile before hunching over to scoop up the misshapen loaf covered in a layer of grime. "Don't worry about it. What you two should both be sorry about is ruining my sourdough."

I've had a decade to come to terms with my infertility. Sure, the echoes of my loss of choice sting every once in a while, especially when I catch glimpses of the tiny humans who share the midnight blue eyes of the man whose surname I still bear. But I've made peace with knowing there are other ways to indulge my nurturing instincts—instincts I may no longer have once the mutation spreads.

"My bad." Gem brushes a hand through her close-cropped hair, flinching when her fingers ruffle the edge of the compression cloth.

Taurance's crossed knees twitch, and I know she's fighting the urge to check on Gem's bandage again. Sensing my attention, Taurance turns back to me, her furrowed brows relaxing as her bouncing legs go still.

"Sorry. You were saying?"

I fidget with the black wool wrapped around my right arm, slowly loosening it.

"You know how that man showed up to help me out of the trench?" They both nod, and I continue, "A few minutes before that, right after the ground stopped shaking, I tried to lift myself up to get to Gem. But there was this bright light. I couldn't keep my eyes open. So I felt around the ledge, but something . . . hot touched my hand."

Chest heaving, I begin to unravel the wrap.

"What do you mean, something hot?" Gem rises from her cot to stand at my side, her knuckles turning white like she's itching to bury them into the stranger's face. "Was it that guy? Did he try to hurt you?"

I shake my head, but the single tear trailing down my face does nothing to ease their concerns, so I reiterate, "No. He did nothing but help."

Taur leans forward to rest a palm on my shoulder. "Was there someone else there, then?"

"No," I repeat. "Part of the ceiling split open during the quake."

Taurance's grip on my shoulder tightens, and I know she's catching on.

My voice falters. "And my hand—"

"Orelle." Gem's spine straightens. "You didn't. Tell me you didn't."

I can't. The words are too big to make it through my constricted throat. So, I give a final tug on the wool, letting the evidence speak for me.

The whites of Gem's eyes briefly widen before constricting to a grimace. She grabs at my wrist before I can warn her to not touch me. Logically, I know the sun mutation isn't contagious, but I can't bear to see the condemning glow of my veins against her skin, or the hurt on her face once she realizes I'm endangering them both by being here. So I flinch, twisting my head away like a coward.

Gem grunts as she tosses my hand aside. "And T thinks *my* jokes are bad. Why would you mess with us like that? You genuinely had me convinced you'd been exposed."

"I—I *was*," I say, twisting back around and splaying open my fingers.

But my olive skin is as dull and lifeless as usual, revealing nothing abnormal lurking beneath it. Gone is the unnatural golden light that illuminated my veins.

As soon as they allow the sun to mark their veins, they lose their humanity. Forever.

My mother made it clear there's no going back for a human who's been marked by the sun. Their loss of humanity is inevitable.

So why does my hand look and feel normal again?

"I swear my hand was glowing a few hours ago." I rotate my wrist and blink forcefully, sure I'm not seeing correctly. Either the mutation has gone dormant, or there are more nuances to sun exposure than we've been led to believe.

Taurance grabs my cheeks, rotating my neck from side to side.

"What are you doing?" I breathe, getting a good whiff of her vanilla-almond scent.

"Checking to see if you hit your head, too." Taurance releases my cheeks only to run her delicate fingers through my hair, mussing my tangled curls. "No lumps or swelling. Tell me if I touch a sore spot."

I duck away from her meddling grip. "My head is fine, Taur."

The twins wear mirrored arched brows, and I can't help but note the deep circles beneath their matching eyes. These last few hours have been a lot. Between the earthquake upending our escape plans, a stranger showing up on our doorstep with Taur's unconscious sister, and my delayed return, I can't really blame either of them for being unwilling to accept this latest turn of events as truth.

"That five-foot drop into the trench looked like it hurt. Maybe it sloshed your brain around a bit." Gem eases back onto her cot and shrugs, like that's more believable than the absurdity of me being exposed to sunlight.

"What you went through was traumatic," Taurance says over her shoulder as she rises from her chair to roam the cupboard. Snatching a tin of crackers, she adds, "It's not unheard of for trauma to cause hallucinations. I've seen it a few times in the postpartum ward. Mothers complaining about someone wailing when all the newborns in the nursery are fast asleep. Just last week, there was a mother who drifted off with her son still latched, though she swore she remembered tucking him back in the crib."

She pops a cracker into her mouth, then reaches on her tiptoes towards the slightly crooked wall shelf for the peach jam I mashed and jarred last night.

I wave at my empty womb. "I'm not a postpartum mother."

"All I'm saying is you wouldn't be the first to misremember something after experiencing mental and physical shock," Taurance says, still struggling to reach the jam.

Grabbing the jar for her and unscrewing the lid, I relent, though intuition tells me otherwise. "Maybe you're right."

The last thing I want to do is add to their worries. Though none of us dare to point out the repercussions of this morning's failures, our hunched shoulders say enough about the weight of the impending selection ceremony. Gem's earlier words are more prudent than ever.

"This is your tenth year of eligibility, Orelle. If you don't leave, they will draft you."

Our fears may be proven wrong. Perhaps there's a future reality where the three of us stroll out of that shadow-forsaken ceremony with none of our names called. I cling to that image, pleading to the merciful darkness for it to manifest, as I reach around Taurance's shoulder to grab a few crackers from the tin, only to find it empty.

A young boy pulls at his oversized navy shirt, using it to hold as many of the glossy red apples from the top of the produce stand as he can fit in the stretched cotton. I kneel at his right, hunching over to grab the two bruised fruits sitting abandoned on the bottom shelf, placing them in my basket alongside the wilted broccoli florets, sprouting white potatoes, and a can of kidney beans with an expiration date of last week.

An apple slips from the kid's little fingers. I fetch it before the perfectly ripe fruit can touch the scuffed granite floor of the food bank. "Here you go."

The boy's green eyes crinkle at the sides. "Thank you, ma—"

"*There* you are," a woman with the same chestnut locks as the boy says as she rushes around a barrel of watermelons at the end of the aisle. She reaches to grab her son's shoulders while cradling a sleeping baby wrapped snugly against her chest. "What did I tell you about running off?"

The kid lifts his bounty and beams. "Look, Mama!"

The mother smiles, though it doesn't reach her hooded eyes. "I see. You plan on eating all of those?"

He bobs his head up and down, but his grin falters as he spots me rising from my squat to place the fallen apple back on the top shelf. "Mine!"

I pause, turning to the boy's mother, whose lips pull back down when she spots me. I lift the shiny red fruit like an offering. "He accidentally dropped this, but it should be good. I grabbed it before it could touch the floor."

The woman grimaces, but the boy doesn't wait long for his mother's approval. Raising up on his tiptoes, his little fingers clench around the apple, forehead puckering as he catches sight of the marred skin on the back of my left hand.

I hold back a wince while tucking my arm inside the shawl.

"What's that?" he asks, pointing at the concealed scar.

His mother ushers him into the next aisle over, yet doesn't lower her voice to explain, "She got her marriage brand taken away."

"Why?"

"Well, she didn't do what she was supposed to . . ."

My cheeks prickle as I walk towards the attendant's stand on the opposite side of the food bank, even though I haven't checked off everything on my list. It's slim pickings today, anyway. Stock is always low around the Hunt, especially for the items available to those in my tier.

No resident has to pay for food or housing, courtesy of Caligo's generosity. But it's a skewed generosity based on our level of societal contribution. At the bottom are the women like me—unwed and childless. Tier Three is our legal classification, though most call us feeders, rats, bottom-shelfers, or eligibles, if they're feeling benevolent. Our unused uteruses and unbranded hands mean we haven't earned the privileges given to those in the upper two tiers.

I take my place at the back of the line, shuffling the basket to my opposite arm while I wait.

An expectant mother with an ill-fitting brown dress and unmarked left hand arranges her groceries on the metal counter. The attendant—an older woman with permanent frown lines—inspects each item thoroughly before placing them back into the woven basket, halting when she plucks a banana by the stem.

"Is something wrong?" the expectant mother asks, rubbing a hand along the top of her swollen stomach.

The attendant eyes her. "Which shelf did you take this from?"

"The middle one."

The older woman shakes her head. "There's only a few brown spots, see? This is a Tier One banana. You gotta look for the ones with more browning."

Since mothers who've procreated out of wedlock have only fulfilled half of their expected contributions, they're given Tier Two handouts. The midgrade groceries are more reliably unexpired than the bottom-shelf stock, but never quite as fresh as what the Tier Ones get.

"I swear I grabbed it from the second shelf."

"Then someone must've shelved it incorrectly. Sorry, ma'am, but I can't let you take this."

The man between me and the expectant mother leans to grab the banana from the attendant's hands, taking it for himself. As an owner of testicles, he's allowed to do so. All men are automatically Tier One, thanks to their status as Caligo's highest contributors. Their wives get to share in the benefits of that status, relishing the best our great city has to offer.

The expectant mother hangs her head and shuffles out of the food bank with the rest of her approved groceries.

My knuckles whiten as they clench around the handle of my basket.

"Happy Selection Day," the banana thief says brightly to the attendant.

The older woman nods politely. "Is there something I can help you with?"

"Yeah, all the tomatoes are bruised." He plucks one from his basket. "See these marks? Belongs with that bottom-shelf junk."

There are few reasons a Tier One would wait in line, given bypassing the attendant's stand is one of their many perks. Reporting a complaint is at the top of the list.

The attendant's mouth thins. "That's a striped cavern tomato. Its skin naturally has orange stripes."

"What happened to the regular tomatoes?"

"We ran out of the globe variety last night. Should be getting a fresh batch from the greenhouse next week."

He scoffs. "Next *week*? You expect me to eat this feeder crap for a week?"

"I can assure you that our striped cavern tomatoes are up to par with Tier One standards. They're an excellent heirloom variety suitable for stuffing, grilling, slicing, and they pair great with a salad."

The man shakes his head, muttering under his breath something about how this is why he usually sends his wife to fetch groceries. Then, he tosses the tomato over his shoulder and stalks off.

The propelled produce hits me square in the chest before splatting onto the gray granite floor. I glare at the back of the man's balding head, fantasizing about how satisfying it would feel to pour my can of expired beans over his haughty face. Even the attendant's lips pinch together as she appraises my half-empty basket.

"Orelle?"

Throat tightening, I spin towards the woman exiting the food bank with three stuffed baskets. Her silver locks are a near match for the tailored silk dress that drapes effortlessly down her petite frame. And though there are at least fifteen feet between us, I swear her signature floral fragrance tickles at my nose. Familiar amber eyes widen as they assess my patchwork dress, worn sandals, and meager findings.

I collect my basket from the metal counter and take a deep inhale before striding towards my mother.

CHAPTER SIX

I pat her back in a stiff hug, then gently nudge her away from the food bank's narrow doorway as two teen boys come barging through. "What are you doing here?"

Although my mother's arms are full with her three baskets, she manages to free a hand enough to tidy up my errant curls. "Your father and I decided to come visit for the Hunt. We swung by your cozy little cabin, but no one answered, so I thought I'd stock up on the usual fixings to hold us over during our stay."

I ignore the look she casts at my paltry provisions and nod like that makes perfect sense, although my parents haven't attended a single Hunt since I've been eligible. "Oh. Uh, well, you're welcome to swing by again before the selection."

"Nonsense! Come back with me. I know your father would love to see you, and I could use a hand, anyway."

We don't have long until the ceremony begins—maybe two hours, three, tops. Not to mention Gem, Taurance, and I agreed to meet back at the cabin beforehand for what could be our final meal together.

I reach for the sand clock in my dress pocket, only to remember

I've misplaced it. "I can swing by, but only for a few minutes. I still need to prepare for tonight."

My mother's smile strains as she transfers a basket onto my free arm. "Wonderful!"

We walk in tandem across the open bridge that connects the commerce district with the residential quarters. Violet lights twinkle across the city's expanse, making up for the lack of stars in the massive cavern ceiling suspended above. A bluish-white beacon sweeps across the shadowy expanse from the top of the watchtower—the tallest of Caligo's buildings and one of the few powered with electricity. The spotlight glides across the stone bridge, illuminating the deep-set hollows beneath my mother's eyes before moving past.

"How have things been in Deor?" I ask as we turn left at the split, aiming towards the main stairwell.

Her shoulders perk up. "Deor's been as wonderful as always. Your father's taken up pottery. If you're running low on mugs or bowls, we've got plenty."

"We're fine, thanks." I tuck a few curls behind my ears, though it's a useless gesture since the strands don't stay put. "What about you? Are you still taking dance lessons?"

She blinks. "Oh, I stopped those ages ago."

"Why? I thought you said moving your body like that was the most alive you've felt since I was little."

Her pupils go distant as she shrugs. "The newness wore off, I guess. I spend most of my free time in the racket rooms these days. Have you played?"

I sigh. "Not since . . ."

She winces. "Right. Sorry, sweetie. I forgot that silly rule about Tier Threes needing chaperones for certain recreational activities. You could play a couple rounds with me while I'm here. Your father's got an extra racket you could borrow."

"I'm not sure if I'll have the time."

"Just one hour. Who knows when we'll get to visit next? I miss spending time with you."

Whose fault is that?

I refrain from asking the question aloud. We're walking on a tight rope enough as it is. The last thing we need is to address how my parents can't bring themselves to face the discomfort of having a Tier Three daughter. So, I nod and say, "I've missed you, too."

The descent to the lower residential levels takes longer than I remember, or perhaps it's the tense silence making every second stretch. No insects or moaning neighbors greet us when we pass through the R5 archway. The only similarity to our R1 home is the faint stench of mildew, but that's inescapable no matter where we go in Caligo. At least R5 has spiced fragrance added to their bioluminescent sconces to somewhat conceal the bitter odor.

"This is us," my mother says, transferring her load to knock on the first cabin on our right.

Seconds pass with no response.

She clears her throat and leans closer into the polished steel door. "Honey, it's me. You'll never guess who I ran into."

Nothing.

My mother rolls her eyes before setting both baskets on the sparkling granite floor. She digs through them until she finds an ornate black key, then inserts it into the knob. The bolt unlocks, and she scoops up her groceries before ushering me into the entryway of their temporary lodging, which is spacious enough to fit the entirety of my cabin.

"Would you mind taking your shoes off? For some absurd reason, they gave us all-white rugs. Can you believe that? How am I supposed to keep these clean for two whole weeks?"

I slip off my sandals beneath a circular marble table with a metal floral arrangement, eyes catching on the six tiny pearls that sit on the ends of the stamens within the center of the lifeless black lilies. A matte black tag engraved with a cursive B in silver-foiled letters sits beside the mirrored vase.

"Is that how long you plan on staying? Two weeks?" I ask, swallowing past the tightness in my throat while joining my mother, who waits by parted glass doors, dainty silver flats still on her feet.

She nods. "Your father thought that should be plenty of time for the Hunt to conclude."

The knot in my throat thickens.

Fourteen days. Plenty of time for ten women to be selected and slaughtered, their life's essence sucked dry by the Sols.

"I hear you talking about me in there," a deep voice calls from one of the rooms further within the cabin. Despite the years and distance, that rasp still feels like coming home to a soothing hug.

My mother places her baskets on the brown marble counter of their generous kitchen. "Oh, so you can hear when you're mentioned, but not when your wife is banging on the door with her hands full?"

"How'd you knock if your hands were full?" My father strolls into the kitchen, his smirk turning into a full grin when he sees me. Wrinkled hands leave the pockets of his tailored gray trousers as he lifts his arms. "Come here, kiddo."

I set down my own groceries before falling into my father's warm arms.

"What happened to your hair? I don't remember it being this frizzy." He pulls back while patting my mussed curls away from his mouth.

I rub the top of his fully bald head. "What happened to yours?"

He leans in to whisper, "Your mother shaved it off in my sleep."

"I did not." My mother crosses her arms against her chest. "You asked me to shave it, remember?"

He tugs her close to his side. "You're right. Thank you for putting up with my jokes."

"Forever and always." Her amber irises glitter as he rubs at the marriage brand on the back of her left hand—two overlapping crescent moons.

I glance down at my bare feet as I ask, "So, why'd you two decide to visit?"

"I told you, sweetie. We came to watch—"

"The Hunt. Yes, I know." I lift my head, our matching eyes locking. "But why now? Is it because it's my tenth year of eligibility? Are you here to say goodbye?"

A whimper escapes my mother's taut lips, so my father answers for her.

"We missed you and thought you could use some company." He clamps a palm on my shoulder. "But this isn't goodbye. You're not gonna be selected. Bren wouldn't do that to us."

Bren.

As kids, my father and Chancellor Bren were inseparable. That friendship carried into their adult years. So, when my mother gave birth to her first and only baby girl months after Bren's first wife birthed a son, it was only natural that they'd come to an agreement about their children's future nuptials.

I wasn't the only one blindsided by the divorce, hence my parents' abrupt move to Deor. As far as I'm aware, their friendship hasn't been the same since, though it must be on the mend if the gifted floral arrangement is any indicator.

I shake my head. "Why would he make an exception for me? I'm not his daughter-in-law anymore. He owes me nothing."

My father's permanent smile lines pull downward, as does his hand on my shoulder. "He wouldn't have those six grandsons if you hadn't graciously agreed to the divorce. The least he could do is spare you from getting drafted."

"*'Agreed'* is a generous description, considering I didn't have a choice." I exhale, running my fingers through my curls. "Look, I'm glad you came, but you have to know that we can't count on an old, fractured friendship to save me from my fate. I've accepted that. You should, too."

His nostrils flare. "You're talking like it's set in stone."

"Something I learned quickly as a Tier Three is that it's better to expect the worst and be pleasantly surprised than have your hopes ripped from you." I shrug, then turn to pick up my groceries from the marble counter.

"You're leaving?" my mother asks, stepping towards me.

"I promised Gem and Taur I'd be back by now. We've gotta eat and change."

With a nod, she haphazardly dumps one of her baskets into mine.

"I can't take these," I say, reaching to remove the head of fresh lettuce from the top of the pile.

She swats my hand away. "Yes, you can. It's a gift from your mother. I can't send you home to starve."

"I'm not starving. We have enough to get us by."

"Well, now you'll have more than enough," she says, lifting her chin in a way that makes it clear she won't accept any arguments.

I sigh, rearranging the items so my broccoli florets and apples sit above the gifted groceries—to avoid any accusations of taking Tier One goods from the food bank—before wrapping an arm around her. "Thank you."

She squeezes me back. "I understand you've accepted a grim

reality for yourself, but you can't talk me out of clinging to hope on your behalf."

My father rests a palm along my mother's spine in solidarity. "Let's plan on having an early dinner together after the ceremony. You can come back to our cabin once you're released."

"I'd like that," I say while ignoring the voice inside my head telling me it's pointless to make plans I can't keep. But my parents still see things through the delusional lens of their Tier One perspective. Why shouldn't they? They've gotten everything they've ever wished for, with the one exception being grandchildren. I don't see the harm in enabling their ignorant optimism a while longer.

I take a deep inhale, savoring the potent blend of floral perfume and musky patchouli cologne, despite the way it provokes my throbbing temples. Then, with a forced smile, I say, "Time for me to go."

Both my parents walk with me as I fetch my sandals and tug open the front door.

My mother's polished nails dig into my father's arms as they send me off. "We'll see you in a few hours."

I nod, not letting the smile fall until my back is to them.

A family of five passes me by at the end of the hall, heading in the opposite direction. The husband eyes my tattered clothes and brimming basket, but doesn't comment.

When I turn into the main stairwell, I drape the edge of my shawl atop the groceries to conceal them from further scrutiny.

"Are you hiding something?"

The question comes from a young woman approaching from behind. Given the plump youthfulness of her face and heightened tone, she can't be more than twenty. Yet two babies rest soundlessly in her wrap—a fresh newborn on her front, and an almost-toddler on her back. She points at my basket with her left hand, proudly brandishing her marriage mark.

"No," I say. "Just trying to keep my produce from falling out."

The woman ascends the steps between us, then swipes the shawl off my basket. "Where did you get this much food?"

I tilt my chin up, mustering the scraps of my dignity. "My mother."

She shakes her head, waving over a patrolman who's descending the stairwell. "Sir, I think she stole from one of the Tier One cabins."

I grind my teeth. "My mother gifted me some of her groceries. If you want to check with her, she's on R5 in the first cabin on the right."

The man's bushy brows tug together as he aims a flashlight at my basket, then at my eyes. "Is that so? Why doncha take me there yourself?"

My shoulders roll forward, and I prepare to do precisely that.

"That won't be necessary," calls a voice from above, a voice that sounds too close to the one I've spent ten years trying to forget. An impeccably dressed man with perfectly coiffed silver hair, four personal guardsmen, and a plethora of badges pinned to a navy suit materializes around the stairwell's bend. The violet glow of the sconces reflects off eyes so light, they're practically void of color. Those icy irises lock on mine. "I vouch for the lady myself."

The young whistleblower and patrolman both bow. "Yes, Chancellor Bren."

I follow suit, dipping as far forward as I can without toppling over.

"Come, Orelle," the chancellor says, inviting me forward with an outstretched hand. "Allow me to escort you back to your cabin."

I nod, though it's not like I have a choice in the matter. If the chancellor asks you to follow, you follow. If he asks you to kiss his pristine leather boots, you drop to the floor. Not even his son is exempt from the precedent of obedience.

I place my fingers in his open palm, fighting back a wince at the chilled touch of his skin. Thankfully, he relocates my hand to his arm, relieving me from the hair-raising contact.

Musings about his mercy and generosity bounce off the limestone walls of the stairwell from the young mother who trails behind.

The chancellor pauses to give a whispered order to the nearest guardsman. He retreats back several steps, then pulls the woman aside. Her cheeks redden as she nods and turns around.

"I thought you might enjoy some privacy."

Since when does this man care about what I might enjoy? Hazy memories tell me there must've been a time. Flashes of a younger version of him, before he'd been sworn in as Chancellor of Caligo and his auburn hair had yet to turn silver, appear in my mind. Back then, my mother kept my curls tamed in tightly braided buns. And every so often, Mr. Bren showed up at our door with a gleaming smile and a small gift bag filled with hair ribbons to weave through the braid. By my eighteenth birthday, I had a whole chest's worth in every color and fabric. After his son and I married, the visits gradually diminished, as did his gifts, until one day he'd shown up with divorce papers in place of a shiny new ribbon, any prior warmth long gone from that crystal gaze. But he did save me from the humiliating fate of returning to my parents' door with a presumptuous patrolman, so perhaps I was wrong to dismiss my father's hope that a certain fondness may linger.

Regardless of his motive, I dip my head in thanks, willing to play along. "Thank you, sir."

We continue our ascent towards R1.

Minutes pass before Chancellor Bren speaks again. "As you know, there are certain rules in place that keep our great city at peace. Although no laws were broken, it creates the potential for dissent if enough witnesses were to see you carrying items above your tier.

Your peers may question what other loopholes may exist. They may stoop to bribing or even threatening superiors for gifts, depriving our precious youth of resources and stoking friction between tiers."

I refrain from pointing out that friction already exists as he continues. "Despite our history, I trust you can discern why I cannot make a habit of showing you special treatment."

"I understand, sir. Caligo first, above all," I say, using one of his favorite mottos.

He pats the hand that's still tucked around his arm. "Precisely. Our duty to Caligo must come first. Always. Which is why my mercy ends here, Orelle. The next time you fall out of step, I will not stand between you and the consequences."

Raised hairs race along the back of my neck. The warning seems a bit extreme, considering all I did was accept some gifted groceries. Unless . . . unless he knows about my attempted escape.

There's no way. None of the guards got close enough to see my face. If they had, surely the chancellor's men would've come knocking earlier.

"I understand," I repeat, hoping he doesn't notice the sweat building on my palms.

"Good."

When we arrive at the R1 archway, he releases my arm. Fighting the urge to run, I bow once more.

"Do try to get some rest before the ceremony, Orelle. I suspect you didn't get enough this morning."

I swallow to keep my voice neutral. "Why do you think that?"

Chancellor Bren gestures beneath his eyes. "The dark circles, dear."

The pressure in my lungs deflates. With a strained chuckle, I wave a dismissive hand. "I appreciate your concern, but I'm afraid those never go away these days."

I dip my head and turn to stride down the hall.

Though he makes no move to follow, my neck doesn't stop prickling, even once I lock myself back inside the cabin.

CHAPTER SEVEN

I am no one in a sea of bowed, cloaked heads as the pulsing wail echoes through the cramped corridor. Sconces flash in sequence with the alarm, creating a bizarre sense of warped time. It's no different from years past, yet this time the flashing feels personal—like the ticking of a timer about to expire.

"Mama," a child whispers at my back. "Does the Hunt start tonight?"

"No, my lovey. Tonight, they'll select this year's Huntresses," the woman trills, like the title is some glamorous honor, "but they won't be sent above until the dawn after tomorrow."

"Awww," the little one groans. "The selection is boring. Why can't they send them up tonight?"

The mother chuckles, amused by her child's impatience to witness televised deaths. "The Huntresses need time to prepare for their task."

A scoff escapes me. I lift my billowing black sleeve to my face, rushing to disguise it with a cough.

Thirty hours. That's how long these women will have to prepare for their mission of eliminating Sols, who are superior to us in nearly every way, with one exception: their intrinsic dependence on the sun.

A shoulder presses firmly into mine, and I know it's Taurance's way of offering both reassurance and a warning.

My lips press together as I return to picturesque obedience, sandals shuffling dutifully forward on the polished granite floor.

When we near the fork in the corridor, a guard ahead drones in a nasally monotone voice, "Two single-file lines. All Tier Threes who are eligible for selection, to the right. Exempts, the left. Exemptions include females who are legally wed or have filed an official intent of marriage co-signed by their male partner, females who have at least one living child or have been declared an expectant mother by the Department of Midwifery, females not yet of marital age, and all males of any marital status, parental status, or age. Have your proof of exemption at the ready."

A bit of animation livens the guard's tone as he clasps his arms behind his back and strolls up to the fourth female in the line forming on the left, whose trembling increases the closer he gets. "We will be verifying all those who claim exemption, so if you're eligible and thinking about sneaking into the opposite line, don't."

He says that last word directly into the woman's ear, and she whimpers.

The guard's thin, chapped lips pull back, revealing a set of too few buttery-yellow teeth.

The child behind me speaks up again. "I wanna be like him when I grow up."

Bile coats my tongue, but I keep silent and brush my arm against Taurance's one last time before making my way to the right side of the corridor.

Gem does the same, then slides into place behind me. My fingers itch to reach for her hand, if only to calm her practiced breathing and remind her it'll all be fine. At least, for her, it will be.

In two hours' time, she and Taur will be back to bickering about whose turn it is to take our sand clock to the horologist to be adjusted for the shifting seasons. And now that Taurance is pregnant, maybe Gem will stop pulling out pitiful excuses—like the time she'd feigned a sprained ankle, though we all knew damn well she'd been walking fine enough three minutes prior. And yet, we'd both caved. Taurance had fetched her sister a cool rag from the washroom and lent Gem a pillow to elevate her foot while I set off with the sand clock in hand.

A snap of fingers an inch in front of my nose jars me out of the memory.

"Oy, full name and date of birth," grunts the guard who'd turned nearly gleeful at the prospect of catching would-be deserters. I can't help but marvel that *this* is who that child aspires to be—this man whose breath reeks of sour ale, whose life is so devoid of true pleasure that he's left to find it in the discomfort of others.

"You deaf or something?" He spits on my face, and my teeth grind with the effort of not scowling in disgust. "Full name. Date of birth."

"Orelle Bren. The twentieth of June in the two-hundred-forty-ninth year of shadows."

The guard's face distorts into a mockery of a smile as he beams and grabs my left hand, rubbing a grimy thumb across the scarred remnants of my marriage brand. I stiffen, knowing there's nothing I can say or do as he nudges his companion.

"See this? Found myself Bren's throwaway runnin' with the rats." He steps further into my space until his chest presses into my own, then leans down to whisper, "You know, if you aren't selected tonight, I might be willing to get down on one knee, but only if you get on yours first."

He reaches a hand beneath the hood of my cloak and tugs on my bottom lip.

I'm yanked backward as Gem feigns a stumble. The guard's cheeks redden.

"Ope! I'm so sorry." Gem dips into a bow, then staggers back to standing, cloak falling to reveal the bandaged wrap. "Feeling a bit woozy."

I'm pulled forward by his accomplice as the crude guard demands of Gem, "Name and date of birth."

I proceed around the bend, slowing my steps as soon as the stiff hand releases my forearm. It's not until I've reached the part of the path that slopes into a sharp decline that Gem emerges from the corner.

I wrap her in a hug, but release her before she can protest about the mushy affection. "Why'd you do that?"

Gem shrugs and stalks past me. "He was being gross."

"That's nothing new, though," I say, matching her stride down the ramp. "And a guard is one of the last people you want to piss off right now."

She winces. It's only for a second, but I catch it.

"What did he say to you?" She says nothing, so I press, "Gem, what did he say? You were gone too long for the usual check-in."

Gem wraps her arms tightly across her chest and exhales a shaky breath. "He wanted to know what happened to my head, and what my whereabouts were from sunrise to sundown."

"What?"

This is worse than I feared. If the guard suspects that Gem was in the transport tunnel during the earthquake, then getting through selections is just the beginning of her concerns.

Sandals clack on the granite behind us, and we pick up the pace.

It's not until the footfalls are nearly inaudible that I ask, "What did you say?"

"That I tripped over a crack in the main stairwell on my way home from my shift."

I've got to hand it to her, it's one of Gem's finer excuses. Some of those cracks are almost as wide as my foot. If there's a prime spot for a concussion waiting to happen, it's that stairwell.

"Did he believe you?"

"He asked if anyone was there to verify my alibi. I told him we were walking home together, and you saw the whole thing." Gem's whisper grows quieter. "So, if anyone asks—"

"I've got you," I promise.

More eligibles trickle in behind us as the sloped passageway spills out into a room large enough to hold at least two hundred women, as long as we stand shoulder to shoulder, like we're no better than herded cattle. I scoff internally while someone's elbow nudges into my spine.

It's one of six identical receiving chambers interspersed around the arena's perimeter. The muffled rumble of thousands of restless spectators slips through the cracks in the steel double doors ahead, dividing us from them—the eligible versus the exempt. None of us speak, yet the volume of our silence is greater than the booming chatter of those searching for a good seat among the countless rows throughout the stadium.

"Keep it moving!" a man calls from the back of the cramped chamber. "There's more of yous coming. Make way."

My gaze fixates on the sliver of bright light between the two doors as another nameless guard tugs me closer to the entrance.

The last time I was this close to the front of the line was my very first year of eligibility. A week had passed since Chancellor Bren had signed an amendment to the constricting marriage laws, making it possible for a man to divorce his wife if she bears no heirs within the first twenty-four months of their union. Before the ink on the amendment had dried, his son finalized our divorce. Since we'd married the day I turned marital age, the Hunt was something I hadn't needed to worry about. And why would it be? We were childhood sweethearts. Even after the divorce, I thought surely he'd petition his father for my exemption. My naivety shattered the night one of Chancellor Bren's henchmen burst into my cabin and escorted me to this very spot. I'd insisted they were mistaken, pleaded to be released, until my words gave way to incoherent sobs the moment those double doors split open.

That was the first time I'd had to face the cruelty of the position that sun-damned constitution forces too many of us into—the first time I had to face the callousness of what happens in this room. Where's the honor in drafting unwed, childless women into battle with no chance of survival?

Unlike then, no tears race down my cheeks when the doors swing wide. A fresh wave of cheers carries down the stands.

We wait at the threshold. Though the doors to all six receiving chambers are now open, it is not yet our cue to enter. How long we stand here, on display for all of Caligo's superior tiers to gawk at, depends entirely on the whim of the chancellor.

Two men in the row above our entrance lean over the concrete ledge. They point at us, taking bets on which of us are more likely to be selected. Most of their words are stifled beneath the ruckus, but I hear mentions of withered hands and jowls.

The speakers crackle to life, halting the chatter. A silver spotlight illuminates the circular stage in the heart of the arena floor that rotates as it rises. The double-sided screen dangling directly above comes to life with Caligo's official crescent moon emblem. Our city has limited resources and strict rations for energy usage, hence the reliance on bioluminescent sconces, yet no resource is spared for the chancellor and his theatrics.

Chancellor Bren's crystal eyes glimmer like a proud father's as he strides into the beam of light and stretches his arms wide. Spectators rise to roar their admiration, hoisting babies onto their shoulders and throwing fists into the air. The chancellor mouths his thanks while clutching a palm over his chest—a humble public servant basking in the praise. A minute or so into the ovation, he flips over his palms, signaling for voices to lower, heads to bow. As one, thousands of chins dip in reverence.

"Welcome, sons and daughters of Caligo. Before we begin, let us first pray. Merciful shadows, we thank you for shrouding our great city from the abominations above. We invite your blessed darkness to guide us tonight as we choose the next round of Huntresses to further our noble cause of eliminating the Sols, so that we may one day know true peace above and below. If the shadows will it, let it be."

The whole of the arena concurs, *"Let it be!"*

Chancellor Bren beams, lapping up the attention of this call-and-response. "Two hundred seventy-nine years ago, the Sols drove us to the brink of extinction after the Last War massacres. The shadows welcomed us, gave us shelter, time to multiply. Our enemies' fatal dependence on the sun deterred them from following us, but our founders—may they rest in the peace of eternal darkness—knew we'd never attain full freedom until every last Sol was eradicated. Thus began the Hunt."

On cue, the spotlight dims and the crescent moon emblem fades from the screen as the highlight reel begins. Almost three centuries' worth of footage edited down to showcase the most thrilling moments of past Hunts.

A collective gasp echoes through the stands when a Sol appears in frame. Charred flesh stretches across its vaguely humanoid face as it cocks its head and blinks its iridescent eyes—eyes that are only capable of a single feeling: guttural thirst. Cursed to crave the humanity burned away by the golden sunlight pulsating through its veins.

The video jumps to a full-body shot, filmed at an angle close to the ground, likely from the camera of a fallen Huntress. A black-and-gold figure lunges across the screen, grabbing a woman by the throat and lifting her. She attempts to lift her nightstone sword, arcing it toward the Sol's neck. But the creature moves faster. It dodges the attack and pummels the Huntress into the ground so hard that the weapon slips from her grip.

Another angle switch, filmed from the point of view of the Sol's current victim, shows the scorched skin around its mouth peeling back. Its tongue extends, splitting into six needle-like pincers that burrow past the woman's fighting leathers straight into her chest.

Then, it drinks.

The woman's flailing arms twitch violently before going limp as the last of her life essence is drained from her.

I lower my gaze to the empty arena floor.

Perhaps I shouldn't. Perhaps I should study more of the Sols' movements, so I can have a semblance of a strategy when my name gets called.

But the barbarity of it all is no longer a novelty. Not to me. There's nothing new to see in these clips that I haven't seen before. The Huntresses who attack get killed. The Huntresses who run get killed. No matter the strategy, the result is the same.

Three women, since the formation of Caligo, have defied the odds. Not by landing a blow or outrunning the Sols. No, each of these women used their comrades as bait, waiting until the creatures were thoroughly engrossed in ripping apart their prey. Covered in the blood of their peers, they laid motionless among the viscera, waiting until sunset. As soon as the Sols retreated for the night, they ran home.

Only one of those exceptions happened during my lifetime: Jacqueline Winters.

I was a young teenager with little interest in the Hunt, since I'd been under the impression even then that I'd never have to worry about eligibility. But from what I remember, Jacqueline wasn't exactly given a hero's welcome when she found her way back.

We're told that being selected for the Hunt is a chance to fulfill your duty by fighting for our collective freedom. Yet Jacqueline didn't fight for her city or her comrades. She fought for herself.

And I don't blame her one bit.

Colors and shadows flicker across the arena as the screen cycles through dozens of gruesome deaths, glamorizing them with slow-motion sequences and a dramatic build-up in the soundtrack.

My eyes rove around, eager to look at literally anything but the screens, when my neck prickles with the sensation of being watched.

I shift my cloak back the tiniest bit and scan the visible faces of those in the first row directly across from my entrance. They're all dutifully glued to the video, pupils dilated and mouths parted.

My attention returns to the stage. Though the spotlight is off, I could swear the man standing there is angled directly towards me.

Why would Chancellor Bren take an interest in me? I've done my part. Stayed away from his son and his thriving new family. An exemplary ex-daughter-in-law and citizen, minus my audacious action of accepting gifted groceries and my failed attempt at running away. But there's no way he'd know about the latter. We weren't caught. The gruff, half-naked stranger got Gem to the cabin before the headcount. I made it back unseen. If the chancellor had any reason to suspect us, I'd know by now.

Stop being so paranoid.

I release my hood and pretend my pulse isn't racing while the video builds to the grand finale—an illustrated future where the final Sol falls, leaving humans to roam the surface of the Earth in peace. Only under the protection of night, of course, lest we expose ourselves to the sun's mutation and rebirth the problem.

The narrator closes off the presentation with Chancellor Bren's favorite chant: "If the shadows will it, let it be."

With a shout, the crowd pumps their fists and claps like victory has already been won.

The spotlight returns to the stage, where the chancellor sits in a lavish, black velvet chair—a throne for a quasi-king. To his left sits his third wife in picturesque stoicism. And to his right, Gabe Bren.

My ex-husband.

He's as painfully handsome as I remember. From the perfectly coiffed swoop of his auburn hair to the thick lashes framing midnight irises, his is a beauty that demands your full attention. So, I oblige, studying his pink lips and the way they tilt up in a smile.

It's false, of course. The absence of his dimples gives him away. Then again, I haven't seen him share a true, dimpled grin in over a decade. Perhaps they've disappeared with age along with his decency and desire to do better than his father.

The thought is enough to break the allure.

My gaze wanders a few feet to the right, to Coraline Lunam. The newly promoted hostess of the Hunt boasts a too-wide grin as she steps up to the podium. "Wow, wow, wow! I'll tell you what, I'll never get tired of seeing our brave Huntresses in action, fighting for our freedom. Will you?"

More like dying for the unattainable concept of our freedom.

Cries of "No!" and "Never!" and "Woo!" blend in a jumbled roar.

"Tonight, ten lucky women will be selected to carry on that legacy. I know you're all anxious to skip to the selections." Coraline rubs at her swollen stomach and giggles. "Oh! Looks like he's ready, too. But first, let's welcome our eligible candidates!"

The drummers flanking each entrance begin beating their mallets to a building rhythm.

Here's our cue.

Tens of thousands of rabid faces swivel in our direction. Their feral eyes gleam, and I'm not sure if they're more keen to see which of us will finally seize the unattainable victory over the Sols, or to watch us break. Likely a mix of both.

This is just a game to them. Our lives. Our deaths.

Last night, we were neighbors, if not friends. But tonight, we're nothing more than glorified pawns that exist for their benefit and entertainment. And what's more morbidly fascinating than watching someone suffer?

A manic laugh catches in my throat as I recognize that that's one of the few things I'm good at: suffering. Perhaps this is exactly what I deserve, the purpose I'm meant to fulfill.

I stride forward, shoulders shrinking inward, until I'm three feet in front of the stage, six feet from my ex-husband, and a minute from finding out if the knot that's been tightening in my chest for weeks now was right to worry.

CHAPTER EIGHT

"So, please lower your hood and step to the base of the stage when your name is called, understood?" Those of us on the arena floor nod as Coraline finishes explaining. Her gaudy rings thump against the microphone as she claps and bounces. "Wonderful! Shall we get to the best part, then?"

The cluster of women to my right parts, forming a path for the two marching guards carrying a cloaked barrel-shaped object: the drafting drum. A black cloth embroidered with the crescent moon emblem covers it, but the steel-plated drum is a sight etched into my nightmares. The machine itself is simple enough, consisting of a rotatable perforated barrel the size of a small child, with a tarnished copper lever on one end. Over a thousand names sit inside its belly.

The bulk of eligible candidates are young—eighteen-year-olds who haven't been snatched up yet by a bachelor looking to marry. But thanks to the system of doubling entries with every year of eligibility, their names will only appear once or twice, whereas the few of us lucky geriatrics in our tenth year of eligibility are in there 512 times each. Gamblers call us the safe bets.

While I wonder how much of a jackpot my name has collected, the guards ascend onto the round platform and position the drafting drum on a black marble pedestal beside the podium. The two men then take up a position behind the chancellor, and one leans in to relay a whispered message. The flash of yellow teeth confirms the man as the guard who gave Gem and me trouble during check-ins.

For a moment, it seems as though his head tilts in my direction, but I dismiss the paranoia. There are hundreds of women on either side of me; he could be gesturing to any of them. Or perhaps it was an unintentional tilt of the head.

Then Chancellor Bren's silver brows lift, and his icy gaze flicks to mine before dismissing the guard with a nod.

Out of everything I've seen tonight, that glance is the most chilling. As much as I detest the glamorized death montage and barbaric chants, at least they're expected—normalized, if not normal. This reaction from the chancellor—sensing his attention on me during the video and now, in response to his henchman's debrief—is an unwelcome deviation.

Even if he suspects that I was the woman in the transport tunnel, he has no eyewitnesses. No proof. Not that it'll matter in a few moments.

I chew on the inside edge of my bottom lip as Coraline unveils the drafting drum with a flourish, inciting a crescendo of "ooohs," as if it isn't the same aged contraption Caligo's been using since the dawn of the Hunt. Coraline rotates the lever, jostling the scraps of paper. On squeaky hinges, the steel barrel spins five times before coming to a halt. Coraline unlatches the front flap, flipping it open and pulling out a single slip. Her berry-painted lips stretch wide as her charcoal-lined hazel eyes scan the paper.

"Our very first Huntress in our two-hundred-seventy-ninth annual Hunt is . . ." Coraline pauses, and the exempts lean in while us eligibles lean away. "Meridna Nox!"

The crowd erupts, jumping to their feet and clambering to get a good look at the first sacrificial offering.

I know Meridna. She's one of the few eligible women older than I, but this is only her third year of eligibility. As a single mother, she met the requirements for exemption until her preteen son died three years ago.

Perhaps that's why her gaunt face and gray eyes are devoid of emotion as she lowers her hood and walks over to the stage.

The second victim of the drafting drum is Twilynn Rayth.

There's a break in the applause when no one steps forward. A woman a few rows to my left trembles in place.

Move, I want to tell her. Better to obey instructions willingly than be forced into submission.

The foul-breathed guard follows the trail of eyes in the crowd and spots her at the same moment I do. He leaps off the raised platform and yanks her hood down, revealing high porcelain cheeks with twin streams of glossy tears. He grabs her by the back of her cloak, spinning her around so the others can get a good look at her. "This Twilynn?"

At first, the surrounding women shake their heads, and I dare to hope that maybe we've grown a united backbone against the powers that be. There are other ways of verifying her identity, of course, but the idea that we as a collective would force Chancellor Bren's men to pursue those alternative methods . . . Who knows what that one simple act of defiance could lead to?

"Yes." A woman to Twilynn's right breaks, and my chest deflates.

It's the only confirmation the guard needs. Fist still buried in her cloak, he drags Twilynn forward and tosses her beside Meridna.

Five more are selected. Each time Coraline slips her perfectly trimmed nails into the barrel, I hold my breath, waiting for my name to be called. Only three spots remain, yet I'm no less convinced

I'll be one of them.

But the eighth name that echoes through the speaker is one more terrifying than my own.

"Gem Samard."

My stomach twists in on itself as my widened gaze swivels to the woman directly to my right.

"No!"

Thundering cheers drown out my denial. But the celebrations falter as Gem uncloaks, revealing her bandaged head. A splotch of red has bled through the back of the compression cloth, roiling my already tempest stomach. Shouts turn to murmurs as spectators spot it, too. Even the exempts have qualms about sending an injured woman into the Hunt, though it's unclear if their reaction is born from a flickering ember of empathy, or concerns about selecting a wounded soldier to defeat our greatest threat.

I shuffle my weight on my feet, aching to grab Gem and run, then shake away the reckless thought. The guards would catch us almost immediately and make a larger spectacle than they did with Twilynn.

But how am I supposed to stand here and accept this?

I can't.

My hand lifts, and Gem subtly shakes her head. There's a hint of an apology in the upward tilt of her black brows before she pulls away from my reach and strides forward to take her place among the selected.

That should be me. *I'm* the statistical probability. Not Gem.

Her thirty-two entries are nothing compared to all of mine.

She wouldn't even be here if it weren't for me slowing us down this morning. She would've made it further down the tunnel by the time the earthquake hit, away from the collapsing debris. Instead, she's here, being forced into the fate that should've been mine.

I glare at the drafting drum as if the weight of all my fear and fury could set fire to every name ensnared within, but the steel barrel remains unaffected. Even if the mechanism could be destroyed, the selections would go on. Chancellor Bren would make sure of it. So, I shift my focus onto the true source of the problem and find that he's already staring back at me, mock sympathy pulling at his lips. My skin crawls with the revelation that the chancellor must've found out about our failed escape. But why risk the unflattering perception of sending a wounded young woman into the Hunt? No one would bat an eye if it was me up there. Then again, what better way to punish me than by taking it out on someone I love?

And that smug tilt of his chin tells me he knows he can get away with it.

Once the thrill of the Hunt begins, most exempts will get over whatever discomfort they currently feel about the condition of a Tier Three rat.

I barely register the final two selections until Coraline repeats the tenth name into the microphone . . . Ten names were called, yet none of them were mine. I don't understand. Why haven't I been released from this annual cycle of misery? I can't handle another year of desperately awaiting a random man's approval only to face rejection, especially not without Gem. If only all of us packed onto this arena floor could force the chancellor's hand. In unison, we could say, *"If the shadows will it, let* us *be!"*

The chant pushes its way to the edge of my tongue. I dig my teeth into my bottom lip, keeping the words restrained knowing they'd send me on a one-way trip to the Abyss.

Before I can revisit the notion of us eligibles banding together, another guard rushes to the stage to mumble something in Coraline's ear.

She clears her throat. "Um, it seems Novah is no longer a

viable candidate."

Confusion sweeps through the arena. Since the Hunt's origin, not once has an ineligible name been called.

Why now?

I tense as Chancellor Bren rises from his seat and reclaims the microphone.

"Apologies for the disruption. We have been informed that Novah was found deceased in her cabin." The chancellor raises his hands to silence the outcry spreading through the rows of flustered spectators. "I'm told Novah was an upstanding citizen of Caligo. A young woman who longed to start a family of her own and believed in our vision of freedom. As such, I wholeheartedly believe the best way to honor her memory is to carry on with the selection, don't you agree?"

No.

My internal rebuttal is nothing compared to the shouts of concurrence carrying down to the arena floor.

Coraline shifts closer to the drafting drum, ready to follow orders, but the chancellor halts her while asking the crowd, "Is it all right with you if I select our tenth and final Huntress myself?"

Men and women alike clap their approval.

Chancellor Bren waves his palms in a *"you're too kind"* gesture before grabbing onto the barrel's lever. He rotates it ten times—drawing out the suspense, no doubt. Because this truly is a show to him. And despite myself, I played right into his hand.

I close my eyes and await my fate.

On cue, the chancellor declares, "Orelle Bren."

CHAPTER NINE

My face is a neutral mask as I lower my hood and break from the line of eligibles to claim my place among the selected. The earthy musk from the packed clay floor of the arena combines with the pungent scent of perspiration emanating from my fellow Huntresses.

My eyes lock onto Gem's.

At least I won't be facing death alone. Her presence is both an unwelcome tragedy and a balm to my battered heart.

I'm so focused on Gem that it takes a few seconds to note the stifled reaction to my selection. In place of applause, hushed whispers travel across the stadium. Thousands of faces shift between my direction and the stage.

My brows pinch together.

I've done everything right. Lowered my hood. Joined the selected at the base of the circular platform. Kept my mouth shut. Has the evidence of my sun exposure returned? My heart threatens to punch through my rib cage. I clasp my hands in front of my abdomen in what I hope is a casual waiting stance. The billowing sleeve of my black cloak inches down my forearm. The damning glow is nowhere to be seen, thank the shadows.

Coraline's nervous chuckle brings me out of myself. I turn, angling to look up at the stage—and my thundering heart stops altogether.

Gabe stands halfway between his vacated chair and the platform's ledge. His jaw hangs open, and the whites of his eyes frame deep blue irises fixed directly on me.

I gape back.

What in the night's mercy is he doing? Why is my ex-husband looking at me like that? Like he cares?

The spotlight reflects off Coraline's wrinkled forehead as she asks what we're all wondering. "Surely, you aren't attempting to volunteer . . . are you, Mr. Bren?"

Though the chancellor holds the microphone, Coraline is close enough for her words to echo through the cavernous walls of the arena.

Chancellor Bren turns away from the podium to cut a glare at Gabe before retraining his expression to one of sympathy. "Don't be absurd, Mrs. Lunam. You must understand that the sight of my son's ex-wife is still upsetting for him. One doesn't forget that pain so easily, even if it's been ten years."

There's a barely concealed bite in his undertone that implies that the chancellor disagrees with his own words.

He's not the only one.

Gabe unfreezes, shaking his head as he releases me from his perplexing stare. "What have you done?"

"Excuse us for a moment." Chancellor Bren pulls his son further from the microphone and out of the spotlight entirely.

They're no longer within earshot, yet Gabe's vigorous arm movements speak enough about his anger. I turn away when he points at me, not waiting to see the chancellor's reaction.

Gem leans around the woman between us and arches her brows.

I shake my head.

Gabe's strained relationship with his father is no longer my business, and he'd do well to remember I'm no longer his. What he *should* concern himself with is what his wife and children think about his public outburst.

My neck prickles with awareness, but I ignore the unwelcome attention, keeping my back to the stage even as Coraline returns to the podium.

"Sorry for that, folks. I got so swept up in all this excitement that I completely forgot that immediate family members of elected officials are disqualified from participating in the Hunt."

Her voice is raised, as if the increase in volume will make the words any truer. Anyone who's bothered to read the rules of eligibility outlined in our constitution will know that it makes no mention of exemptions for elected officials or their family members. Fortunately for the chancellor, most haven't bothered learning that, because they haven't had to face the fear of eligibility.

With no one calling bullshit on her capitulation, Coraline goes on. "Please accept my sincerest apologies for implying that the future leader of our great city would entertain breaking such a rule. Now, let us wrap up—"

"I'd like to volunteer."

The declaration comes from my left, where a man is hoisting himself above the concrete barrier separating the exempts in the front row from the arena floor. He's missing his ceremonial cloak, and the hem of his too-tight trousers hits an inch or two below the kneecap—details that are easily overlooked, considering the way the silver spotlight illuminates smoldering gold irises, full lips tugging into a stern line, and a familiar brown shirt that clings to the many contours of his upper body.

Why is the stranger who saved us, then stole Gem's clothes as repayment, jogging through the parted crowd of unselected eligibles towards the stage with the intent to join the Hunt? Surely, he can't be volunteering on my behalf.

On the off chance that he recognizes me as the haggard woman from the tunnels, it's not like I left a flattering impression. He'd met me with dirt on my cheeks, soot in my hair, and blood on my ass. Not to mention, I can't write off the possibility that he saw my glowing veins.

Don't be so self-absorbed.

The few times he'd interacted with me during our illicit excursion, he was curt, louring like I was a nuisance purposefully sent to distract him. His gaze held no fondness, no attraction.

Whatever his reasoning for volunteering, it doesn't involve me.

Two guards descend from the stage to grab the man by each arm and force him to his knees.

"I'd like to participate in the Hunt," the stranger insists. "Or has the chancellor ratified an amendment to disqualify all men from volunteering?"

"Watch your mouth," warns the older of the two henchmen, veins protruding from his forehead like the question was a personal insult.

The stranger's molten gold irises almost seem to glow with the challenge. Considering he's nearly as tall as the two men while on his knees, those eyes alone hold more of a threat than any spewed words from the guard.

Chancellor Bren squints down over the ledge and gestures for the brazen stranger to be released. "What is your name, son?"

"Kalden Tonalli," he answers, voice carrying even without the microphone's aid.

"Tonalli," the chancellor repeats. "I'm unfamiliar with that surname."

Kalden just blinks at him, as if to say that isn't his problem.

The chancellor's lips thin. "Why do you wish to volunteer, Kalden?"

"I question whether this current group is fit for the Hunt." His eerily bright gaze travels from the still-trembling Twilynn to Gem to me. The implication might offend me if it weren't so painfully true. "If I'm there, we'll stand a better chance against the enemy."

I scoff under my breath. Leave it to this overgrown man to think a few extra inches of height and a pair of toned arms are all it takes to defeat the Sols.

The chancellor sucks his teeth, mulling it over. "Our constitution is clear. Only ten are allowed in the Hunt."

"So, let me take the place of another," Kalden suggests, like it's an obvious solution.

Gabe, who's been inching closer to the commotion, grabs his father's wrist. "Let him."

Others may mistake the two words for a plea, but Gabe's clenched jaw helps me hear it for what it really is: a demand.

Chancellor Bren goes as still as stone.

Gabe releases his grip, but raises his voice so it echoes through the microphone. "The volunteer clause does not require your permission for his participation."

The chancellor smiles, but it's a contrast to the ice in his narrowed eyes.

"Indeed. It does not. What an adept pupil you are, my son." He claps a firm hand on Gabe's shoulder before nodding to Coraline. "The young gentleman may proceed. Now, if you'll excuse us. This ceremony has incurred too many delays, and our great city won't run itself."

"Of course, sir!" Coraline bows while the chancellor ushers his wife and son down from the stage. Once they reach the steps, Coraline smooths the wrinkles in her cloak and addresses the crowd. "It seems we have a volunteer. Kalden here believes so strongly in our noble vision for Caligo that he's willing to trade places with one of our selected in hopes the Hunt will prove more fruitful with his presence. Isn't that wonderful? Which young lady would you like to exchange places with?"

We eligibles are not permitted to speak during the ceremony. It's not so much a rule as it is an expectation. But now that the chancellor is leaving, what's worse—getting reprimanded for petitioning on Gem's behalf, or staying silent while Kalden swaps places with another?

The first would be unfortunate. The second would be unforgivable.

So, while everyone's eyes lock on Kalden, mine find Gem's.

My intention must be obvious, because she shakes her head, but it doesn't stop me from saying, "Pick her."

Kalden steps toward us, his golden gaze scrutinizing Gem's bandage while she scowls at the borrowed pants. He notes her displeasure, and I could swear the corner of his mouth twitches, like a smile is trying to break through his stony facade.

Fidgeting beneath his assessment, Gem folds her arms tightly across herself. "Don't bother. If you try swapping places with me, I'll volunteer to take *her* place."

"You can't go up there like this," I argue.

"Neither can you. What are you going to do once you get hit with a debilitating migraine? Do you think the Sols will take it easy on you because you don't feel well?"

"Gem." My voice breaks, but I know she's only lashing out this way in an attempt to save me, so I try to ignore the sting. "Please. Taur needs you here. And that baby is going to need its Auntie Gem."

"What about Aunt Orelle? You're needed here, too."

"You can take my place," offers the woman standing between Gem and me, glancing at us both with lifted brows. I can't remember her name, only that she was the ninth to be selected.

Kalden frowns at the three of us before nodding.

Without sticking around for a verbal agreement, the woman bunches up her too-long cloak and jogs towards an unselected eligible, who's waiting for her with open arms. Her partner mouths *"thank you"* to Kalden before planting a kiss on the woman's forehead.

Hot tears blur my vision. I angle my chin up towards the wide expanse of the arched cavernous ceiling and swipe at my eyes. I don't begrudge the woman for seizing this second chance at freedom. It isn't her fault Gem chose misguided loyalty over self-preservation.

"Is now a good time to collect that favor?" Kalden asks while assuming the newly vacant position.

So, he *does* recognize me.

I turn, giving him a glare that communicates that now is the absolute worst time.

But he keeps his head forward, not bothering to face me as he orders, "Stop crying."

"Excuse me?"

How is this callous asshole standing beside me now the same man who saved our lives hours ago?

"What's done is done. Crying won't change anything." Kalden finally deigns to look me in the eye as he says, "Whether you like it or not, you're a soldier now. Soldiers can't afford to feel. We are one distraction away from death."

I'm loath to admit he has a point. There will be time later to process, *if* I focus on making sure there is a later. If not for myself, then for Gem.

I nod, and Kalden returns to standing at attention, awaiting Coraline's next orders.

"Huntresses—and, er, Hunter—please make your way onto the stage, so our great city can give you a proper sendoff."

One by one, we shuffle up the steps onto the circular platform.

Meridna is the first to receive the blessing of the shadows.

"Meridna Nox." Coraline dips her thumb into a jar of black ink and swipes it beneath both eyes. "May darkness guide your sight and spirit. May it strengthen and protect you from the corrupting sunlight. Your victory is our victory. If the shadows will it . . ." She pauses, glancing towards the audience to signal their cue.

"Let it be," they proudly respond.

By the time it's my turn to receive the blessing, Coraline's words are rushed, my bones ache with the need to be horizontal, and the audience's echo lacks its earlier vigor. Trickles of the black ink run down my cheek from Coraline's hastily dipped thumb. Now that the fun part is over, nearly a third of the seats sit empty as spectators trickle out of the stadium. And the glazed glances that remain reaffirm what I knew to be true: these people are here to be entertained. Coraline rushes through the closing script without so much as pausing for a breath, and the silver spotlight flickers off.

While our eyes are still adjusting, I allow myself one last indulgent shudder before clenching my jaw and following the line of soldiers marching dutifully towards our inescapable fate.

CHAPTER TEN

A camera operator walks backward in front of Coraline, who escorts us across the inclined bridge that connects the ceremonial arena along the city's edge back to the hub of Caligo. Onlookers press against either side of the bridge's iron railing as they point and cheer at our ragtag group of soon-to-be martyrs. Fighting against the instinct to lower my head, I scan their faces, spotting a few familiar ones, yet failing to find Taurance or my parents. Gem cranes her neck, jade eyes lingering on a woman who could be a distant cousin, but not her twin.

With both of our heads turned, we don't notice that those in front of us have slowed until Gem walks into the backside of a redheaded woman. If my memory is correct, I believe she was the third to be selected, right after Twilynn.

"Oh! Sorry about that, Faron," Gem says while flinching back.

She waves off the apology. "Don't be! I was distracted, too. Checking to see if my sister's here."

Gem runs her fingers through her close-cropped hair, avoiding the bandage. "Same."

"They're probably keeping our loved ones away for now to build tension before filming our final goodbyes," whispers a willowy brunette on Faron's left.

My nose scrunches. "You know, I'm not sure why I expected anything else."

Once we reach the end of the bridge, Coraline guides us away from the swarming crowd into a private stairwell, not stopping until we reach an unmarked door six levels down. She pulls on the longest of her three silver necklaces, producing a key from the neckline of her cloak.

"Welcome to your training facility," Coraline singsongs while flourishing an arm into the now open doorway. "Uniforms have been provided in the changing stalls on the left. I'll be back in two hours to escort you to your temporary living quarters before curfew, but don't fret. You'll be in good hands. I'm so pleased to announce that your training instructor is one of our highly esteemed Guards of the Gate!"

Boots thud against granite as the instructor in question marches up the steps. We fall back against the limestone wall, giving him space to lead the way into the facility. My shoulders raise as I lock eyes with the man who was lapping at my throat less than twenty-four hours ago—the widower who thought me better to bed than to wed. At least he has the decency to flush when he averts his gaze and waves at our group to file in.

Coraline prances off before the door clicks back into place, and our instructor clears his throat. "Help yourself to the equipment. Towels are on your left here if you spill any blood."

Piles of raggedy towels lie haphazardly in a basket to the left of the door. Floor-to-ceiling mirrors line the right side of the room, and the reflection from the bioluminescent tube lights casts a dim glow throughout the surprisingly large space.

"If you gotta puke, aim for the buckets. I won't be cleaning that filth up for you. If you miss, you know where the towels are." The guard points at the tin pails scattered along the room's perimeter before putting a sand clock atop a shelf lined with circular weights. "Like Mrs. Lunam said, you got two hours till curfew, and she'll bring you back here first thing tomorrow evening for another two."

He turns to claim the metal stool beside the exit.

Kalden strides up to him. "Aren't you here to oversee their training?"

Their training. Not *our* training. He doesn't see himself as one of us, and why should he? With his six-foot-plus frame and disciplined muscles, Kalden is years ahead of us in terms of physical proficiency. My stomach flutters as I acknowledge that a handful of hours isn't enough time to change that, let alone adequately prepare us for what awaits above.

"Training is self-led," grunts our instructor.

"Self-led? You expect these women to instinctually know how to prepare for battle?"

The guard stiffens at Kalden's escalating tone. "They've all been given basic training. Twice a year, we host an entire week of mandatory combat exercises for Tier Threes. And the chaperone requirement doesn't apply to the communal fitness facility, so they've had plenty of opportunities to practice those skills all year round."

Kalden folds his arms, and the borrowed brown shirt squeezes against his muscles, stirring a warm flutter within me. "And how has this training worked out so far for past Huntresses?"

Veins protruding from his forehead, our instructor rises from his stool, but Kalden cuts him off.

"A couple weeks here and there of basic combat lessons isn't enough to turn these women into soldiers. And if you really believe it is, I'm not sure whether that makes you a mindless moron, or simply unconcerned because it doesn't affect you whether they live or die."

Someone gasps behind me.

Kalden isn't just challenging our so-called instructor with his words. To question how things are done for the Hunt is to question Chancellor Bren. And, if you ask a purist, questioning the chancellor may as well be an act of rebellion.

Face nearly as red as blood, the guard's right arm uncoils in an uppercut, but Kalden shifts, dipping low into his hips and evading the blow.

The guard's nostrils flare as he swings his elbow downward, aiming for Kalden's face. I wince, expecting to hear his nose crunching beneath the impact.

It doesn't. Kalden crouches and rolls, pivoting back to his feet on the guard's side.

Golden eyes flick to mine, as if to check whether I'm watching, and comprehension lifts my brows. This isn't a spontaneous brawl. This fight was purposefully instigated. And what better way to begin our training session than with a demonstration?

The guard rushes forward. A second before he lunges, Kalden jumps over his hunched back.

Panting, the man braces his hands on his knees. As he's catching his breath, Kalden fetches a towel from the basket and wipes away non-existent sweat from his temples.

"None of you are warriors, so evasion is your best bet at survival. Offensive attacks are useless in a one-on-one combat scenario with a more powerful opponent," Kalden says to the group while tossing the rag at the panting guard, whose frown lines deepen as he realizes he played right into Kalden's reckless training lesson. "Tonight, we'll go over some basic dodging and blocking techniques. Tomorrow, I'll check your running form. Sprinting for speed will help you get away, but once there's enough distance between you and your opponent, you'll need to adjust your technique for longevity."

Our instructor mutters under his breath and stomps out of the room, locking the sliding door into place behind him.

Kalden strips off the too-small shirt, which had bunched halfway up his abdomen during his skirmish. He smooths a palm over his collarbone, brow furrowing, then searches through the discarded shirt until he pulls out his nightstone pendant and secures it around his neck.

Something coils low in my stomach. I tell myself it's fear stirred by Kalden's warnings.

Gem nudges her elbow into my rib cage. "You're drooling."

"*Gem,*" I chastise with a whisper, head whipping around to make sure no one heard her.

Thankfully, our comrades are busy swarming around Kalden, who's rolling out gray mats halfway across the room. He reaches up to grab another folded mat from the top shelf, stretching a pink jagged line that spans across his right shoulder blade.

Whatever gave him those brutal scars, is that what made him so . . . rigid? Not in *that* way, but in the sternness of his clenched jaw, taut brows, and near-permanent scowl.

"You're doing it again," Gem teases. "It's not too late, you know. Maybe you can convince him to marry you before they give us the boot tomorrow."

I roll my eyes. "Sure, let me push him down and seduce him into proposing right on the mats."

I ignore the warmth flooding through my veins at the prospect, reminding myself that it's a ridiculous notion. There's a reason I stick to marks who are considerably older and less coveted. It takes a certain level of desperation for a man to desire the attention of a broken throwaway. Even if I were to throw myself at Kalden, I'm more likely to believe he'd implement one of those ducking maneuvers than welcome my advances.

"I've already been selected, Gem," I say while ambling towards the changing stalls. "There's no way the chancellor would pardon me now. Him, maybe. But not me."

Once we're in our uniforms, we slip into the back and join the others in a series of stretches.

Reaching her fingertips to the mat, Gem asks, "So, you won't even try?"

"There's no point," I whisper as we shift, rotating one arm to reach up as high as it can go while keeping the other hand on the floor. My boobs threaten to spill out of the provided top, which is a generous word to describe the sleeveless sliver of fabric that is both too tight to be comfortable and too loose to be supportive. "If you're going, I'm going."

Switching arms, Gem grunts. "You know, you used to be so amenable. Now you're almost as stubborn as me."

"You're a bad influence," I concur, and we both chuckle.

By the shadows, it feels good to laugh. After the stress of our failed getaway and the selection ceremony, we need this. Our giggles swiftly escalate into a full-blown laughing fit, like we're no better than rambunctious children.

Through my tear-blurred vision, I spot booted feet approaching. Kalden, who's now in the provided dark gray uniform that's barely larger than the previous borrowed clothing, frowns while stalking towards us.

I double over.

The gold in Kalden's irises flares. "What's so amusing about your certain death?"

"It's not—" I try to collect myself enough to say. "It's not that."

He stands there, waiting for further clarification, but neither of us can explain the manic outburst.

"We have less than four hours total to give you a marginal chance of survival. If you don't care enough about your own lives to pay attention, consider the lives of your fellow soldiers."

His prior warning resurfaces. *"Soldiers can't afford to feel. We are one distraction away from death."*

I won't be the distraction that costs Gem her life. The reminder is enough to sober me as I wipe the tears from my face. "Okay."

"Let's start with the first technique." Kalden tilts his head toward Gem. "Punch her face."

"What?" My brows pinch together as I give him a look that questions his sanity.

"I'm not asking you to hurt her," he says, drawing out the words as if to aid my comprehension. "Throw your fist slowly, so she can practice dodging."

"Oh," I say, cheeks burning. "Right."

Once Gem and I adjust our stances, I lazily swing my arm, knuckles aiming towards her nose. Gem squats straight down, away from my attack, but Kalden shakes his head.

"Bending down without sliding back or to the side keeps you vulnerable for the next attack. Remember, it's all about adding distance between you and your opponent. Like this." Kalden does a two-step shuffle backward while bending at the waist and lifting his arms to block his face. He repeats the move, explaining, "Keep one leg behind the other and your arms in tight. Again."

After our seventh run-through, he relents, "Better. Now switch places."

Sweat beads down my neck as I mimic the technique. The quick bending motion sloshes my brain, and by my fourth try, I swear the mat beneath my feet begins to ripple like a wave.

"Woah." Gem rushes to grab my wrist, stabilizing me. It takes a few measured breaths before I can focus on her downturned face. "Do we need to take it slower?"

"Your opponents will not make accommodations," Kalden says matter-of-factly.

Gem shifts defensively in front of me, but I step around her to admit, "I know."

The admission weighs on my hunched shoulders. I'm well aware that no Sol will take it easier on me simply because I require it. We're already practicing at a pace that's far more leisurely than what we're likely to encounter. And if I can't hack this, I'll be done for within seconds of a true attack.

I don't want to die, but perhaps it's time I come to terms with the inevitability of it. Hands shaking, I massage my scalp as the tension in my throat threatens to suffocate me.

Kalden assesses my trembling fingers, then my face. I imagine what he sees there: taut lines along my forehead and deep under-eye hollows beneath hooded lids.

I've had many years to shape a façade. A polite smile will trick the eyes of many into ignoring the subtler signs of my weakness. Only those who care to do an attentive examination will catch the evidence of my pain. Lucky for me, few care.

Kalden, however, takes his time. A single black brow raises as he studies me thoroughly.

"If a simple practice round has this much of an impact on your stamina, relying on the standard evasion techniques against your enemies will lead to your death," he says, confirming what I already suspected.

"No," Gem says, reaching out to grab my hand in hers. "I won't let that happen."

Her rare initiation of physical contact is a gesture of solidarity meant to bring reassurance. Instead, it tightens the knot in my throat.

"I won't let you go down with me." I squeeze her hand back. "If anything, I can provide a distraction while you hide. It's worked for others before."

She shakes her head, refusing to accept what I'm proposing. "There's got to be another way."

"Your opponents won't make accommodations—" Kalden starts, but Gem cuts in, jade eyes sharpening like daggers.

"You already said that."

Kalden ignores the interruption. "But you can make your own. The usual techniques will fail you, but there are . . . other methods that may prove useful in prolonging your time above ground."

He briefly meets Gem's scalding gaze and nudges his head towards the others. "Keep practicing your dodges. Those of you taking the offensive position, stop holding back. Strike as quickly as you can. No more waiting for your partner to catch their breath or slowing your punches. Your opponent won't stop, so neither should you."

Gem hesitates at my side. "I'm not letting Orelle train alone."

Kalden's eyelids twitch, and I get the feeling he's trying not to roll his eyes. "She won't. I'll train her separately."

"Why not teach all of us these other methods?"

"Because what you're learning is more effective for those without physical limitations."

Gem still doesn't budge. "What about my head? Doesn't that count as a physical limitation?"

Kalden sighs, like he's dealing with a petulant child. "It does, but you seem to be handling yourself well enough with the basic maneuvers. As long as you drink plenty of water during our last few meals and avoid strenuous activity outside of training, your youth should lend itself to an adequate recovery."

"Fine," Gem relents, then shoots one last warning glance before partnering up with Twilynn.

Kalden stalks off towards the farthest corner of the room.

Assuming he intends for me to follow, I trail behind, lowering my tone to ask, "Why do we need to be this far from the others?"

Those eerie eyes trail down to my hand. My *right* hand—the one I'd exposed to the sun. In the tunnel, I'd feared he glimpsed the glow of my treacherous veins, but he'd given no indication of it.

Until now.

My breath catches as I plead to the shadows that I'm wrong.

"You felt the sun's kiss, didn't you?" Kalden asks. "I saw the light flaring through your fingers."

Though his voice is low, I glance over my shoulder while wracking my brain for any excuse. "I . . . I spilled some bioluminescent liquid. Last night. Our lantern . . . I was refilling it and got some on my hand."

It's not even a good lie. The glow emanating from within me had been a brilliant, near-white gold. Not violet.

A muscle ticks in Kalden's jaw. "You and I both know that isn't true."

"Of course it is." A hurried tone threads through my whisper. "If I'd been exposed, I wouldn't be talking to you now, would I?"

The beginnings of a smirk lifts one side of his lips before he leans in to say, "Once again, we both know you're lying."

"Then why are you asking if you already know?" I snap as quietly as possible, stepping into his personal space.

His pupils constrict.

Sweat buds in my palms, and I try to step back.

Kalden grabs my wrist, lifting it between us. His touch is warm, almost uncomfortably so, as he studies my fingers like he can still see the evidence of my treason.

"What did you feel?" He taps the center of my palm. "In here?"

I squirm, but his grip remains firm. "I didn't—"

"I haven't told anyone, nor do I plan on it. I'm trying to help you, but I need you to be honest with me."

Prickled nerves raise hairs up and down my arms as I recall the tingle of energy that I'd been so sure would spread throughout the rest of my body, mutating it into something unrecognizable.

"I felt power. Almost like an itch that could only be scratched by releasing it."

"Did you?" His voice is rougher than before—heady, almost.

"Did I what?" I breathe, intoxicated by the recollection, like I can still sense it.

Another gleam shines between Kalden's thick lashes before he blinks, letting go of my wrist. "Did you release the power?"

Nose crinkling, I try to shake off the lingering warmth of his fingers. "Absolutely not. I don't want to become a monster."

"You don't look like a monster to me." Kalden dips his chin towards my hand. "Despite holding the power of the sun within your palm, you look very human."

"I *am* human," I insist, stuffing a balled fist into my dress pocket, only to remember there are no pockets in the skintight pants of the provided uniform. "I don't know how or why, but the mutation didn't spread. When I woke earlier tonight, the light was completely gone."

Kalden peers over my shoulder at the others, who continue to spar while none the wiser to our treasonous conversation, then drops his voice lower. "What if I told you there's a way to harness the sun's power without sacrificing your humanity?"

I scoff. "I'd say you're a worse liar than I am."

"It isn't a lie," Kalden says firmly. "You can either choose to arm yourself or continue playing dumb for the sake of upholding misguided disarmament, even if it means getting yourself killed."

I shake my head. "It's not possible. Sun exposure mutates us into Sols."

"Then explain what happened to you earlier," he challenges.

"I don't know." I shrug. "Maybe it's gone dormant?"

Kalden squints as if searching beneath my skin. "You'd sense it if that kind of power remained within you."

"Okay, well, maybe I wasn't exposed for long enough." Though it's only a hunch, it would go against everything I've been taught, but what other explanation is there for why I'm still me?

A single brow lifts as Kalden considers my words. "So, you admit there's a threshold of exposure that would, theoretically, make it possible for someone to channel the power for limited bursts of time without experiencing permanent mutating effects?"

I chew on the inside of my bottom lip while searching for any hint of deceit.

He doesn't cower or shift uncomfortably under the weight of my scrutiny. Instead, his shoulders pull back, proud and tall. The set of his jaw and upward tilt of his chin project a confidence that he believes what he says is true. But how can he be so sure of this theory?

Unless it *isn't* a theory.

Unless he's already tested it and has firsthand proof.

"You've done this before, haven't you?" I ask, voice nearly inaudible over the pounding in my ears.

His head dips, but just barely.

My eyes unfocus as I consider how this could change everything. If he isn't lying, and we can truly wield the sun without becoming what we fear, maybe the Sols will finally be the ones on the losing side of the Hunt's death sentence.

And if he's wrong . . .

I can't let myself go down that path—not when this is my only feasible chance of getting myself, and hopefully Gem, through this alive.

I swallow, fighting to get the next words out, because if I speak them aloud, it means I'm really considering this. "And you're sure I won't become a Sol if I do this?"

Kalden nods, but it isn't enough.

"Promise me I won't turn into one of them." I raise my hand between us once more, this time as a request.

A pulse promise is not to be taken lightly. Touching the pulse point on the thumb side of your wrist to another's is a profound act reserved for vows not intended to be broken. I've only ever engaged in one once. With Gabe. On the night of our wedding, we both vowed that it would be forever. Little did I know that forever would end in twenty-four months.

Brows pressing downward, Kalden raises his wrist and crosses it against mine.

My mouth falls open as his heat singes away any lingering thoughts of my ex-husband.

Is his touch always like this?

Agonizingly warm? Invasive? Consuming?

Kalden rolls his tongue across the fullness of his bottom lip. The movement is swift—done in a blink—yet my breath hitches, eliciting the hint of a smile so brief, I'm almost convinced I imagined it.

If only I could write off my pounding heart as foolish imagination. Surely, he feels its rapid thrum pulsing against his skin, just as I can feel the steady beat of his.

"I vow to you, Orelle Bren, that you will not become a monster."

He remembers my name—my full name. And the sound of it on

his lips is so unlike the usual taunts I receive from other men that it takes me a moment to realize he's saying more.

"—between us?" Kalden waits, expectant gaze on mine.

"Sorry," I say as the fever from our joined wrists licks across my entire body, culminating in my cheeks. "Would you mind repeating that?"

His lucent irises glimmer. No matter how much of a stony façade he wears like a mask, the miniscule expressions in those molten eyes are his tells.

"Do you promise to keep what I reveal to you in our training between us?"

Only now do I pause to consider how much trust he's putting in me. We're little more than strangers, and yet he's confessed to experimenting with wielding the sun's power—an unpardonable offense that could very well land him in the Abyss. Granted, he could drag me down with him, now that I've confirmed my own exposure to the golden rays.

Withholding this from Gem won't be easy. I can already feel her curiosity prickling the back of my neck. An interrogation awaits the second she gets me alone. I can't guarantee she'll accept my lies at face value.

"I vow to you, Kalden Tonalli, to keep your secret between us."

Your secret. I can't promise to keep Gem from discovering my secrets. But maybe I can give her a portion of the truth—one that doesn't compromise Kalden.

Satisfied with my response, Kalden dips his chin, yet makes no effort to lower his wrist from mine for several more seconds.

The pulse beating against my skin accelerates.

Is it his, or mine? Both?

My arm presses more firmly against his, as if to discover the answer, but Kalden pulls away. A chill spreads across my skin in the absence of his heated touch.

I fold my arms tight against my chest, trying to disguise the shiver rocking through me as I ask, "Where do we start?"

CHAPTER ELEVEN

"A simple slice in the palm of your gloves will allow you to absorb a portion of the sun's energy without overexposing yourself to its corrupting effects. You'll want to angle the blade like this, though, so you don't nick your skin," Kalden explains, brandishing his finger like a blade that slices along his palm. "As long as you keep the cut small enough, the modicum of light emitting from your hand should be easy enough to hide from your comrades."

The slight tension in my shoulders abates, knowing I'll be able to disguise my treachery from Gem and the others. "How will I be able to tell if the exposure is too much? Will I feel it if I start losing my humanity?"

"It's more about how much you draw from the sun's power than exposure alone. You should feel a pleasant warmth wherever the sunlight kisses your skin. And as you harness that energy, you may feel a subtle increase in your internal temperature, but nothing that passes the point of minor discomfort. If that heat becomes scorching to the point of being agonizing, you'll want to stop channeling and seek shade immediately." Seeing me swallow, Kalden adds, "It's highly unlikely you'll get anywhere near that point, especially if you stick to short bursts of solar flares."

"How do I do that?"

He maneuvers himself behind me, hovering an arm around my neck without making contact. "You won't have the speed or agility to escape your opponent, but you will have the element of surprise. They won't expect you to wield the sun. So, the moment you're in their grasp, do whatever you can to get your hands on them."

"Does it matter where?" I ask.

"No. All you need is for the sliver of exposed skin on your palm to come into direct contact with them. Once you do, you'll release the energy."

"What does that mean?" I grab onto the sleeve of his borrowed tunic. His arm twitches at my touch, despite the layer of cotton separating my fingers from his skin.

Kalden's voice is a breath in my ear. "That buzz you felt before was radiation bonding with your body's natural magnetic field. If you channel that energy out of your palms, you'll create a solar flare that will incapacitate your opponents."

My fingers slacken on his arm. "Will it kill them?"

The thought doesn't sit well, which is ridiculous. These are the monsters that left my ancestors on the brink of extinction—the monsters that have slaughtered generations of Huntresses, and which threaten to be my own undoing. And yet the thought of ending a life, even a life void of humanity, brings bile to my tongue.

Kalden pulls back. "It depends on the strength of the flare and how strong their own magnetic barrier is, but death is unlikely. I'd say it's better to assume it will leave your opponent immobilized for at least a few minutes, but perhaps a few hours at most."

We run through several more maneuvers, mixing in a few standard combat sequences to dissuade wandering eyes from getting curious.

"What if the Sol prevents me from using my hands?" I ask while sprawled on the floor, Kalden hovering above me on his forearms. "So far, the positions we've practiced have made it easy enough to place my palms against my opponent. But what happens if I can't?"

Shifting his weight onto his left arm, Kalden wraps his right hand around both of my wrists, locking them into place above my head.

Again, I'm struck by his scalding touch. Though he limits his contact to my wrists as he keeps the rest of his body supported several inches above mine with his opposite arm, I can feel the burn of it everywhere.

"You mean like this?" he asks in a tone so low my back arches, straining to hear him.

I'm certainly not arching my back for any *other* reason.

His pupils narrow in on my parted lips, stealing the air that escapes between them the longer his gaze lingers. The arm supporting the weight of his body begins to bend as he lowers himself closer, fingers tightening their hold on my wrists.

My spine lifts higher off the floor as I wait for the space between us to be eliminated by a single inhale. And when the breath comes a moment later and our bodies finally touch, a tremor rocks through me, breaking the spell.

Kalden rolls onto his side and rises to his feet, but not before grimacing down at me, effectively dousing my building warmth in a bucket of chilled water. "If they get your hands in a lock, you're dead."

I stay there, pressing my eyes shut and wishing the floor would devour me whole.

When I finally blink, Gem's standing over me with her black brows lifted so high, they nearly disappear beneath her bandage. "I thought you'd written off your plans of seduction."

I push myself into a sitting position, gaze darting over to Kalden, who's rejoined the others to run through a forward roll maneuver. His hands briefly wrap around Meridna's back leg, guiding it into a position better suited to push her forward into the roll. A rosy hue blossoms across her waxen cheeks, mirroring my own flushed face.

My focus returns to Gem. "If anyone's the seducer, it's him."

"Is he making you uncomfortable?" she asks, all humor disappearing from her darkening tone.

"Not like that. I mean, he's an ass and has little faith in my survival abilities, but at least he's trying to help. And he barely touched me, even when we were sparring. But when he did, it felt . . ." I search for an adequate word to describe his engrossing touch, yet come up short.

"Clammy?" Gem's nose pinches.

I chuckle. "No. He *is* warm, but not in a sticky or sweaty way."

Her scowl doesn't soften. "I think if T were here, she'd say something about ovulation raising your basal body temperature."

"Maybe," I say, though I suspect there's more to it than hormones.

As we rejoin the group, Kalden tells Gem to sit this one out to avoid splitting a stitch. So, we study the women's forms, critiquing the angle of Faron's bent knee and admiring how well the willowy brunette beside her—whose name I've learned is Demi—lands on the balls of her feet. Despite what we've all gone through tonight and the weight of what lies ahead, they run through the drills repeatedly without complaint.

A shared fervor has been set alight in all ten pairs of eyes, a refusal to accept our fate without a fight.

Each of us has been taught it's better to stay in the shadows than be burned by the sun. But now that the shadows are rejecting us, what if we become the ones that burn?

The Hunt was intended to make us an example, not a threat. Maybe this is the year that changes.

A pot of steaming black beans with diced red onions and a garnish of cilantro is placed next to a silver platter of baked potatoes. If it weren't for the two servers and three camera operators stationed around the dining chamber of our temporary living quarters, keen on capturing one of our last meals before our impending departure, I'd jump from my chair to secure a slice of the fluffy cornbread before it's gone. My knee bounces as I restrain myself to avoid playing into the feeder rat stereotype. Judging by the sideways glances the other women cast over their shoulders, I'm not alone in that hesitation.

Gem and Kalden, however, don't seem to share that qualm. The metal legs of Gem's chair squeak against the granite floor as she snatches two slices of the sweet yellow bread and drops one onto my plate, not having to ask whether I'd like a piece. Kalden goes straight for a potato, ladling the black beans into the steaming split.

A melody of metal against ceramic fills the silence as the rest of us take that as our cue to help ourselves. I ladle the black bean soup into my split potato and scoop a generous portion onto my spoon. My eyelids flutter shut the moment the flavor melts onto my tongue. The creamy inside of the potato blends quite well with the soup, but the cornbread is the true masterpiece of the meal, with its perfect balance of savory and sweet. Crumbly, but not too dry.

Though Taurance often praises my skill at turning our scraps into pleasant meals, there isn't enough seasoning in this city to fully mask the bitterness of food on the cusp of expiring. Nothing in our cabin has ever compared to fresh ingredients reserved for Tier One cuisine.

When I reach for second helpings, I spot Kalden making an intense face of displeasure at his plate. The deep frown is at odds with his usual stoic nature, so I can't help but pry. "Something wrong with your food?"

His features neutralize as he glances up. "It's edible."

I laugh. "Edible? Are we eating the same thing?"

Kalden squirms. Legitimately *squirms*.

"Is there a spider in your soup or something?" I ask, because I'm not sure what else would have this stone-faced man so unsettled.

Twilynn, who's on Kalden's left, flinches away on instinct. And Yvonne, the woman with waist-length braids on his right, scoots to the opposite side of her chair.

Kalden shakes his head. "There's no spider. I guess I prefer the food from back home."

"Where are you from?" The question comes from the other end of the brown marble banquet table, where the youngest of the selected is seated. Irina, maybe? No, I'm fairly sure it started with an A. Anira or Arima, perhaps?

"The north," he answers before taking a measured bite of the food he clearly doesn't enjoy.

"Scuros?!" Maybe-Arianna squeals. "That's where my fiancé is!"

"Your what?" Gem asks, nearly gagging on a mouthful of cornbread.

The girl blushes, and the color is a near match for the red-berry liquid in her glass. "Well, my *future* fiancé. We haven't met yet, but he's left hints in his letters that he's planning our engagement."

"Why didn't he propose before the Hunt?" It's nosy of me to ask, but I can't help but think that if a man is already committed enough to discuss engagement details, why would he leave his future bride susceptible to the draft?

Arianna—or is it Anara—thumps her mug of water down onto

the marble surface. She winces, doe eyes darting to the nearest camera before she drops her voice. "Just because your tragic love life is public doesn't mean I want mine to be."

I bite my tongue to prevent myself from pointing out that *she* was the one who brought it up. I get why she's lashing out. She shouldn't be here. None of us should, really, but especially not a twenty-one-year-old with a pen-pal lover who's reluctant to make an official proposal. She's pissed. At me, currently, because I'm the easiest scapegoat. But also at the situation. Likely at her partner, too.

So, instead of getting even for her petty retort about my public divorce, I say, "You're right. I'm sorry, Adrina."

"Aruna," she corrects with a grunt.

Beneath the table, Gem nudges her knee into mine, and I bite back a snicker.

"Aruna," I repeat. "Sorry."

Aruna lifts her chin, which I choose to interpret as an acceptance of my apology.

The clatter of silverware bites through the renewed silence as the meal comes to a close. By the time I swallow the last of my potato, over half the group has disappeared into their respective bedchambers, leaving only Kalden, Meridna, Gem, and myself to clean the mess. Funny how the attendants and serving staff are nowhere to be seen now that the cameras have stopped recording.

I scrape and stack the beige ceramic plates from the marble tabletop while Gem grabs the mugs and forks. We carry them over to Kalden, who's stationed himself at the oversized copper sink.

"Have any of you seen where they keep the broom and dustpan?" Meridna asks, pulling open each of the cupboards.

Kalden wipes off the suds from his left hand to grab the small broom from atop the wall cabinet, all the while rinsing off a fork with his right. The sight of a man helping with the dishes is both strange and welcome. Perhaps Scuros's recipes aren't the only things that differ from Caligo's customs. Maybe the men there are taught by their parents to divide the domestic duties. The thought is so ludicrous, I scoff while collecting the remaining platters.

"What a bizarre man."

I startle, not expecting to see Meridna—a woman of few words—leaning against the metal chair behind me.

"He's certainly different," I say once the surprise settles, the sound of the running water concealing our whispered exchange.

"I can't believe he volunteered. Makes me wonder what's wrong with him." Her pointer finger taps against her temple.

My grip tightens on the stack of silver platters. "He seems sane enough."

"Honey, those of us who seem the sanest are usually the ones with the most to hide." Pity fills Meridna's gray irises as she strides out of the kitchen behind Gem, leaving me alone with Kalden while I process her words.

Perhaps I should heed the warning. After all, I still don't know what he was doing half-naked in that tunnel, or why he was so insistent on participating in the Hunt. I'd be a fool to let my guard down around him just because he's offering an alternative path to survival.

As if that's the *only* reason he's growing on me . . . My palms grow clammy as I'm brought back to the engrossing anticipation I felt with Kalden's wrist on mine.

Shadows help me, this libido is getting out of control.

I swiftly discard the platters into the sink, holding my breath as if one good inhale of Kalden's masculine smoky bergamot scent is enough to undo my renewed resolve.

"Are you okay?" Kalden asks, glancing down at me with

pinched brows.

"Fine."

"Your face is turning purple."

"Must be the lights." I turn away, lungs greedily inflating as I finally allow myself to inhale. "Would you like a hand?"

He shakes his head. "I've got it."

"You sure? It'll be good to feel useful."

Kalden pauses his scrubbing, then relents. "I'll wash. You'll dry."

"Perfect," I say, pulling on a drawer only to find it empty. "Where'd you find the towel?"

"In the middle drawer. That one there, to the left."

I tug it open and grab a fresh white hand towel from the top of the neatly stacked pile.

The occasional scrape, thunk, and squeak of my cloth against the clean plates interrupts our companionable silence until I work up the nerve to ask, "Who taught you to wash dishes?"

Kalden leans the last silver platter against the marble backsplash and unplugs the drain. "My parents have always split up chores evenly. If one of us cooks, the others will clean."

"Wow. I bet your mother loves that."

He shrugs. "It's just good manners."

"So, you *are* aware of what manners are?"

I freeze, mouth agape as I realize I voiced the jibe aloud.

Kalden lets out a low chuckle, igniting a fresh warmth in my stomach as he rinses his hands and turns off the faucet. "Was that ever in question?"

"Well, you can be a bit blunt," I say, wiping off the beads of liquid from the tilted platter before folding the dampened towel along the sink's edge to dry.

"Does honesty equate to a lack of manners?"

I tilt my head. "I guess it depends on how you deliver it. There's a tactful way to tell the truth without sounding like an inconsiderate ass."

The corner of Kalden's lips lift the smallest amount. "Is that your tactful way of telling me *I* sound like an ass?"

I stiffen against the counter's ledge.

Did I just unintentionally call a man an ass to his face?

My hand flies up towards my mouth, as if I could pluck my previous words from the air and stuff them back into my too-tight lungs. "I didn't—"

"You're allowed to be honest with me, you know." The line between his brows deepens. "I'm aware I can be . . . gruff, and I won't fault you for calling that out. In fact, I'd prefer it."

No words can pass through my swollen throat, so I offer a nod instead.

His smirk fully disappears, and I excuse myself a moment later, chest heaving as I slip into my temporary bedchamber.

"I hope you didn't think you'd get away with not filling me in on your private training session," a voice calls from somewhere within the chamber's inky shadows.

I jump and reach blindly for the nearest wall sconce, twisting its dial until the dark-gray walls and sparse black-metal furniture are illuminated in a familiar violet hue.

Gem is perched on my cot, her knuckles bracing her chin and jade eyes glittering.

"Sun's pits, Gem! Are you trying to kill me a day early?" I scoop up my cloak, which I'd aimlessly tossed on the floor after our training session, and throw it at her face. I miss, of course, and the heavy garment falls to a heap at the edge of the bed as I lean over to peel off my sandals. "When did you sneak in here?"

"A couple minutes ago," Gem replies, plucking at the fraying seam of my navy cotton pillowcase. "I walked right past you, but I guess you were too busy salivating again."

"Don't make me throw more things at you." I wave my sandal towards her as a threat, then offer, "Truce?"

She lifts my pillow like it's a shield and shakes her head. "Not until you tell me everything that happened between you two."

My shoe drops to the floor with a thud. "Just now?"

"Don't be daft."

"I already told you. We sparred," I say while searching through the trunk at the cot's base. A shapeless gray dress has been provided by the chancellor's staff as a customary change of clothes. The linen material unfolds as I hold the dress to my body. I can't help but think it looks more like the attire of an inmate than that of a supposedly esteemed Huntress.

"You're too slow to outrun a Sol, but strong enough to fight them?" Her flat intonation suggests she's not buying it.

"I won't have a choice, Gem. Evasion is obviously the better option, but you know how much all that up and down makes me dizzy." I tug off the too-tight black pants of my training uniform, and the skin along my legs practically sings in freedom. "Kalden agreed to teach me a few offensive techniques as a last resort."

I slip into the gray dress before peeling away the provided top that's basically a bra, and it's a tense moment before Gem asks, "You believe that'll work?"

Despite my sagging shoulders, I understand her doubt. If Kalden had told me I'd have to rely on my physical strength alone as an offensive tactic, I'd share Gem's concerns. Little does she know there's a loophole—a way to turn the Sols' power against them without becoming one, assuming Kalden's techniques prove true.

But I can't tell her that. Not only would it endanger Kalden, it might jeopardize Gem, too, if the chancellor deemed her guilty by association.

So, I twist my features into feigned hurt. "Just say it. You think I'm too weak for this, don't you? That I can't possibly survive up there?" Her eyes widen, and my voice breaks. "Please, by all means, tell me how you fully expect me to be the first to die tomorrow."

Gem shakes her head, unable to speak the words we both know are true.

I hate that I have to do this—that I have to guilt trip Gem into thinking I resent her lack of faith in my abilities. But even more, I hate the true throb in my chest telling me I *do* resent her doubt. Yes, it's justified. Yes, I'd rather my closest friend be honest rather than spare my feelings. And yet, it stings to hear the person who knows me best admit I'm too weak, too broken to survive.

Instead of answering my question, Gem asks her own. "You think I'd turn down Kalden's offer to swap places if I was confident we're doomed to be goners?"

A wet heat builds in my eyes. "Yes, I do."

Her mouth falls open. "Seriously?"

I lean against the footboard for support while explaining, "You're a realist, Gem. Not an optimist. I think you chose to stick with me, despite the obvious risks, for the same reason you wanted to escape to Deor: to avoid being cast aside while Taur adjusts to life in a superior tier."

A tear silhouetted by the room's purple glow trails down Gem's cheek.

"Soldiers can't afford to feel."

With Kalden's earlier words echoing in my mind, I take two measured breaths before saying, "Let's get some sleep. We're both tired, and we've got a big day ahead of us."

Nodding, Gem rises from my cot and shuffles to the door. Her fingers pause on the knob. "You're wrong, you know. Not just about me. You're the most resilient person I know, Orelle. If anyone can defy the odds, it's you."

Before I can respond, Gem slides out into the hall.

The door clicks shut, and I collapse onto the cot. Why should I bother to slink beneath the soft cotton sheets when I'm already covered in a compressing blanket of shame?

CHAPTER TWELVE

I didn't expect to spend the last few hours of my life in a private bathing chamber far too large for me and my assigned beautician, getting plucked like a caged bird primed for slaughter.

"How exactly does my lack of body hair prepare me for defeating Sols?" I ask as she scrapes a blade down my armpits.

Her red lips pinch together. "You'll thank me once you're in your suit. Less hair, less friction and odor."

Half an hour later, I'm sewn into the suit in question by another personal attendant. From the neck down, black leather covers every inch of my body like a second skin. And once I put on my helmet, not one part of me will be exposed.

My chest rises and falls rapidly as soon as the last attendant leaves the oversized space. I take a measured inhale, reminding myself it's for my protection. Although my previous encounter with the sun didn't have the disastrous outcome I'd expected, the last thing I want to do is expose too much of myself to its mutating light. Like Kalden said, all I need is a slit in the palms of my gloves.

I lift the headgear from the wrought iron vanity's glass top, intent on securing the final piece of protection. But I hesitate when I catch sight of my reflection. My tawny curls have been subdued into an orderly braided bun near the nape of my neck. The purple lamplight reveals a tint of color enhancing my small but full lips, and there's a dewy glow to my normally ashen cheeks. If it weren't for my mother's almond-shaped amber eyes staring back at me, I'd sooner believe the woman in the mirror is a stranger than a true reflection of myself. She looks too . . . vibrant. Healthy. Ironic, that I'd appear more alive than ever on the brink of death.

I wipe at my mouth with the back of my hand, but the rosy stain doesn't budge. So, I tug a few strands loose from my bun, disheveling the too-perfect updo. Now that the reflection's more of an acquaintance than a stranger, I ease my head onto the vanity. Cool glass kisses my forehead as I tilt side to side, letting the solid surface massage away the building tension behind my brow bones.

Metal screeches against the limestone floor as the door to the chamber cracks open. I flinch, nearly tumbling off the stool before catching myself and jumping to my feet.

"Shadows' mercy," Gabe whispers as he shoves the door shut. Pressing his back to the wall, he waits, presumably to see if anyone is coming to investigate the disturbance.

Several seconds pass. No one comes knocking, and he peels himself from the stone wall.

He's swapped his ceremonial cloak for a familiar navy suit that's impeccably tailored. The silver threads of the crescent moon crest sewn above his heart reflect the lamp's violet glimmer.

"So much for sneaking in." He smiles sheepishly, and a shadow of a dimple flashes on one side of his tilted lips for a split second before his face sobers. "I'm so sorry, Elle. This wasn't supposed to hap—"

I hold up a palm. "You need to leave."

His apology, his presence, and that sun-damned nickname are not welcome here. His guilty conscience can go piss itself above.

"I know," he says, ruffling a hand through his auburn hair. "I won't stay long. I just needed to see you before . . ."

He trails off, so I finish the sentence for him, folding my arms against my chest.

"Before your biggest mistake is gone for good? I thought you'd be happy. You won't have to alter your commute to avoid running into me anymore. Won't have to explain to your children why that strange woman has the same surname as them."

His pinched expression sharpens. "They have nothing to do with why I'm here."

"Oh, I'm sorry. Did I cross a line? Am I supposed to pretend like they don't exist? Or would you rather I'm the one who disappears?" I laugh, though there's no mirth in my voice. "Good news: looks like you're getting your wish."

"Do you truly believe I want that?" Gabe takes a step forward, and I shift backward. At my silence, he presses softly, "The last thing I want is for you to disappear, Elle."

I close my eyes. There was a time I would've devoured those words, greedy for any breadcrumb of affirmation he deigned to toss my way. Now, I reject them, no longer willing to accept breadcrumbs as sustenance.

I square my jaw and force my eyes back open. "Even if that's true, it doesn't matter what you want or what I want. What's done is done."

Distant footsteps carry through the crack of the metal doorframe.

Instead of backing away, Gabe draws closer—close enough for the familiar fresh scent of clean linen to scratch at once-blissful memories now buried.

His breath ignites every nerve in my ear as he whispers, "What if it isn't?"

There's a gleam in those deep blue irises that's almost as terrifying as it is baffling.

"What do you mean?"

Gabe's lips part, ready to explain, when the thud of boots grows closer. He pulls back, searching for a place to hide. Though this bathing chamber is generously sized, its furnishings are sparse. There are only two good options for hiding: behind the partition curtains concealing the iron soaking tub, or beneath the vanity, though the latter is barely large enough to accommodate *my* frame. Gabe isn't much taller, but his broad shoulders give him an added width that may prove too difficult to squeeze beneath the vanity.

He climbs into the tub as the door groans open.

I adjust myself on the stool, spinning around with a sigh as I prepare to face the snooping guards.

But it isn't a guardsman standing before me with eyes that could freeze the sun itself.

Spine straightening, I lock gazes with my ex-father-in-law.

His suit is much like his son's, yet with far more embellishments. Being the elected leader of Caligo, his crest has a star above the crescent moon emblem. Two silver peace pins with engraved depictions of a handshake—pins he awarded himself at the end of his prior two terms for lowering the number of violent crimes while doubling the birth rate—are fastened beneath his breast pocket. A black ribbon encircling his right bicep denotes his oath to serve the shadows first, the people second.

And those are just the badges I recognize.

Chancellor Bren is a well-decorated man. It's why many continue re-electing him, although the elections themselves are hardly representative of what the city as a whole truly wants, since Tier Threes aren't permitted to vote. It doesn't matter that he over-promises and under-delivers on most of his campaign objectives. As long as he continues delivering on his primary focus of lowering crime, increasing birth rates, and upholding tradition, his loyal purists will keep voting him in while overlooking the rest.

"It's good to see you again, Chancellor." I rise from the stool to dip into a bow, hoping to distract from my too-high voice.

The chancellor smiles softly, heeled boots clacking against the floor as he stalks forward to sit halfway on the ledge of the vanity, gesturing for me to retake my seat. "Come now, Orelle. I was hoping we could be honest with each other. Would it be all right with you if I went first?"

Lowering back on the stool, I nod, though the question's rhetorical. Chancellor Bren doesn't require my permission, or anyone else's. "Of course, sir."

"Seeing your hair like this takes me back." His eyes crinkle at the sides. "They even wove in a black ribbon."

I raise a hand to touch the braided bun, eyelids fluttering as my fingertips brush against a sliver of silken fabric I hadn't noticed before. "They did."

"You look years younger."

"Thank you," I say, dipping my chin as if the backhanded compliment has made me bashful. "Is this what you wanted to have an honest conversation about? My hair?"

"Oh, sweet shadows, no." The chancellor chuckles before his smile sobers. "No, dear. I came to ask what you know about the woman who was spotted in the western transport tunnel during the daylight hours prior to the selection ceremony."

My legs spasm with the ache to run, like cornered prey.

I stave it off. Not only would I not make it far, I need to stay and glean how much he knows. The chancellor mentioned that *a* woman was spotted, not two. It's possible he doesn't know Gem was with me. If there's a way I can protect her from being implicated as an accomplice, I'll find it.

Contrary to my escalating pulse, my brows arch in vague interest. "A deserter?"

He leans further back on the vanity's top. "Perhaps. My shadows described her as well endowed, with graying untamed hair and a limping gait. One of our elderly, they presumed."

The assumption almost makes me laugh. Though the limp was unintentional, I can admit in hindsight that it paired nicely with my soot-drenched curls, casting the illusion of a much older woman.

Chancellor Bren continues, "It would be odd, though, for a woman of advanced age to travel alone while the city slumbers. Odder still for a senior female to fear the Hunt enough to desert, since the oldest eligible this year was in her mid-thirties. I couldn't make sense of it . . . until my men found this among the rubble."

The chancellor's hand disappears behind the navy lapel of his suit, procuring a small object from a hidden pocket. His palm unfolds, revealing a miniature sand clock.

Recognition hits me in the chest. My heart beats like a frantic bird pining to escape its cage, escalating the pressure behind my right eye.

"One more truth, my dear. Do you recognize this?"

Pocket-sized sand clocks aren't uncommon. In fact, almost every working adult carries one to track the time for their shifts. Most are a simple design—frameless curved glass with black sand and a small plug in the bottom. This hourglass, however, has an aged bronze frame and grains the deep color of plum. And if the chancellor flips it over, I suspect we'll see the compass my father etched into the bronze base along with the words, *In case you lose your Way*. A cheeky wedding present for his bride, Mrs. Way, turned heirloom on their daughter's wedding day—*my* wedding day.

Chancellor Bren places the hourglass upside down on the vanity, confirming my suspicion. "Tell me, why does this bear your maiden surname?"

I remember noting the sand clock's absence from our belongings organized on the table, but hunger had distracted me from looking further into it. Gem must've dropped it in the tunnel when she was pummeled by the falling debris.

The chancellor rotates the hourglass and points at a smudge of crimson streaking down the side. "Is this your blood? Curious that I see no injuries marking your flesh. Your friend, however—"

"Yes," I rush to say, "it's mine. I tried to leave for Deor before the Hunt. When the earthquake hit, I fell onto some glass and sliced my backside. I must've dripped blood on my sand clock after dropping my satchel."

The chancellor lifts a single gray brow. "That was almost believable, dear."

"It's the truth."

His lips tug downward. "Unfortunately, you have no evidence to support your claims."

Blood rushes to my face as I realize what I must do. If it'll absolve his implied suspicion of Gem, I'll show him proof.

"I do have evidence," I say, standing to undo the buttoned flap between my legs that allows for necessary bodily functions.

Chancellor Bren's silvery blue eyes widen, but he makes no effort to move or stop me.

The last button snaps apart, and I turn, preparing to show him the jagged cut across my right ass cheek.

"Father, enough!"

CHAPTER THIRTEEN

Gabe rips aside the partition curtain and bounds forward until his body is between mine and the chancellor's.

"Ah, I was wondering how long you were planning on hiding," Chancellor Bren says while rising from the vanity and smoothing out the invisible creases in his suit.

"How'd you—"

"My shadows saw you sneaking in here a few minutes ago." The chancellor shrugs. "I'll admit, I'd expected to see you buried between her legs, not cowering in the tub."

Pink rushes to Gabe's cheeks, and his father *tsks* his disappointment.

My nose snarls as I retreat towards the wall and hastily refasten the buttons of the flap. "He's married."

The chancellor waves a dismissing hand. "He's a Bren. We cannot be expected to refrain from indulgences, no matter who we indulge within, and your infertility is rather convenient. There'd be no need to worry about concealing the potential fruit of the transgression from the public. Although your history would complicate things, if you two were to be seen together."

Bile burns in my throat. "I can assure you that won't happen."

"Unfortunately, dear, it already has."

He's right. Between Gabe's reaction at the ceremony and conspicuously sneaking into my private room, people will talk.

"Well, it won't happen again," I say, lifting my chin.

"Finally, a truth." Humor returns to the chancellor's cold eyes as he collects the sand clock from the vanity, re-pocketing it. "You don't mind if I hold onto this, do you? You won't be needing it during the Hunt."

Finding his voice again, Gabe asks, "You're not actually making her go up there, are you?"

"It's her duty."

"We had a deal." Gabe jabs a finger at his father's chest. "The only reason I agreed to the divorce was because you promised—"

"Our deal was annulled the moment she stooped to desertion." Chancellor Bren flicks his son's finger away like it's nothing more than a minor nuisance. "Would you rather she be imprisoned in the Abyss for treason?"

Gabe's shoulders deflate.

The chancellor claps a palm on his back. "If I didn't hold my friendship with the Way family in such high regard, that's exactly where I'd send her. Be grateful for this mercy. Now, fuck her, if you must, and say goodbye. You have five minutes until my shadows return."

He offers me one last smile before spinning on his heel and stomping into the hall.

Silence descends after the door clicks into place.

Gabe's soft auburn brows furrow low as our gazes lock. But while his pupils dilate in and out, searching for what to say, mine remain unmoving.

What does he expect from me? Gratitude? His intervention saved me from baring my backside for his father, but perhaps the chancellor wouldn't have bothered paying me a visit if his henchmen hadn't seen Gabe sneaking in here.

My head pounds with the all-too-familiar effort of trying to make sense of why these Bren men insist on bringing chaos into my life. I tilt my neck back, fighting to keep my hooded lids from closing.

Gabe is the first to break. "I'm sorry, Elle."

"For what?" I whisper, relying on the steady presence of the wall at my back, holding me upward as a decade's worth of walls are crumbling within me. "Sorry for divorcing me? For showing up now, pretending like you care whether I live or die, after ten fucking years of nothing? Right when I was *this* close to erasing your name from my mind. Or are you sorry you still haven't found the balls to stand up to your father, even while he speaks about me like I'm no better than a whore for the taking?"

My voice rises as the words continue spilling out. "What exactly are you sorry for, Gabe? I'd love to know before deciding whether to accept your apology."

"For all of it!" Gabe throws his hands in the air before bunching them in his mussed hair. "None of this was supposed to happen. My father . . . I made him promise you'd have permanent exemption from the Hunt, as long as I agreed to the divorce."

"You *what*?" I sink down the stone wall, legs unable to bear the weight of this revelation.

He steps forward, then halts when I flinch.

The man standing before me now is capable of causing infinitely more pain than the one who threatened imprisonment. The chancellor can harm me physically, but only his son can harm the one thing more fragile than this impaired outer shell: my heart.

He didn't just break it. He tore it into a thousand pieces and tossed them out, along with a trunk of my belongings and a mangled remnant of our marriage brand. It's taken ten years to find those pieces and stitch them back together into a mockery of what it was. A patchwork heart, one wrong move from tearing apart the seams.

"Why didn't you tell me?" I finally ask.

Gabe lowers himself to the floor, meeting me at eye level—reminding me of how gentle he used to be with me.

"It was part of the agreement. My father didn't want word to spread of your exemption. If others knew, they might question why you'd be excused from doing your duty. They could accuse him of abusing his power."

I can't help the breathy scoff that escapes through my nose. The chancellor's been abusing his power since well before his first term. The notion that my exemption from the Hunt would be the catalyst to stir up dissent after eighteen years of his actions going unchecked isn't even a good lie.

"And you believed him?"

The lines along his forehead deepen. "I had no choice. You know I have a different vision for Caligo's future, but none of it will happen if he doesn't back me as his successor. And I need our people's trust as much as I need his."

And there it is.

Gabe's love for this city runs deep. Deeper than whatever love he felt for me—a bitter truth learned too late.

The lamp on the vanity illuminates Gabe's silhouette in a violet aura while he stares at me expectantly, begging me to understand. And I do. I understand why he replaced me with a woman who could bear his heirs. It isn't a mystery to me why he bends the knee to his father time and time again.

"Okay," is all I say, knowing it isn't what he wants to hear, but it's all I'm willing to give.

"Okay? Does that mean you forgive me?" Gabe presses.

"It means I understand. You are your father's son." I shrug, like it's as simple as that. Because it is. Despite their differences, both Brens crave power. More than anyone or anything.

Before Gabe can push any further, I shove myself back to standing and tug open the door. "You can go now."

And then my ex-husband does what he does best. He walks away, leaving only the ghost of his clean linen scent behind.

CHAPTER FOURTEEN

A ticking mechanical sound alerts me to the hidden cameras pivoting for a better view as the ten of us are shepherded into the war room.

You'd think the production staff that's in charge of condensing the daily footage into a half-hour episode got enough material with our makeover reveals that they wouldn't need a clip of us silently walking into a room. But now that it's two hours till our impending eviction, I suppose they're ready and willing to catch any potential meltdowns that would make for an intriguing first episode.

The war room is bigger in name than in reality. A large circular table fills most of the space, leaving just over three feet of walking room between the table's edge and where the ten of us stand shoulder to shoulder against the concrete wall. Several unrolled maps, weighed down by flickering lanterns and miniature figurines, overlap each other like a puzzle across the corkboard surface.

Every publicly accessible map is of the underground city systems, so this is my first time seeing the world from this vantage point. A push pin with our black-and-silver crescent moon flag denotes the location of our capital city of Caligo within the sliver of sand cushioned between lush western forests and an expansive eastern ocean.

The few times I've ventured outside the Gate, all I saw was a long stretch of dunes. If it weren't for the moments in past video montages showing the rare instances of women who'd made it to the western tree line, I would've presumed a boundless desert stretched above our haven. But our "great city" is little more than a dot in a world far more vast than I'd thought to imagine.

A camera operator stationed in the room's corner holds up a thumb, and the theatrics commence as the Commander of the Guard approaches the head of the table.

"As you're aware, the primary objective of the Hunt is to eliminate any Sol you come into contact with, but your ancillary goal is to act as a second pair of eyes for our team of cartographers. Each of you has a visual recording device built into your helmet."

I lift my helmet from where it rests on my hip and frown when I spot the telltale pinprick of red light in the space that will rest above my brow bone. The camera is already recording. How long has it been watching us?

Is this how Chancellor Bren knew his son had snuck in to see me?

At least it's a mercy we were given the headgear *after* our training sessions. Otherwise, my private lessons with Kalden wouldn't be so private anymore.

Commander Guffian continues, "These devices will not only provide footage for the nightly updates of your progress, but also an opportunity to fill in potential gaps in our understanding of the terrain above and the enemy numbers. We have strong confidence in the accuracy of the inner zone here." He gestures with his finger in an oblong circle around Caligo's dunes. "But the confidence decreases the further we get into these outer zones due to distance and the Sols' frequent mutilation of the land."

There's movement in my peripheral vision where Kalden stands at my right, but my attention is on the hundreds of tiny black pushpins scattered along the map.

Noting the direction of my gaze, the commander explains, "Each of these represents a fallen Huntress from the past three decades. The locations of these deaths provide data that help us track our enemy's movement. As you can see, though a few outlying nests were encountered further inland, Sols tend to congregate closer to the coast. Any guesses why?"

He peers over the frameless rim of his glasses at the group, fixing his beady eyes back on me.

I point out the obvious answer. "To avoid shadows."

It makes sense that creatures dependent on sunlight would gravitate away from densely packed forests or any terrain that would get in the way of a direct view of their source.

"But why just the past three decades?" I ask. "Were the locations of prior deaths not recorded?"

Commander Guffian's lips thin. "After thirty years, the data is considered obsolete. The more recent the death, the more useful it is for adapting our intel on the Sols."

A metallic taste fills my mouth as I bite the inside of my gums hard enough to draw blood. Hundreds of women gave up their lives in futile service to this city, only to be reduced from useful intel to obsolete data.

The commander carries on with his orders. "Once you're released, you'll be split into pairs to cover more ground. There are five hotbeds of Sol activity noted over the past several Hunts, one target for each pair."

His finger traces around several large patches of black pins only a few miles from Caligo's entrance, though what sends my skin crawling is the heavier density of pins surrounding the Gate, producing a teardrop shape. The forest. The majority of our predecessors tried to make it to the tree line. Most didn't succeed, but the pins all but disappear inside the splotchy cluster of green and brown ink.

"We understand that Sols are coming from areas primarily to the north and northwest. Note the locations where past Huntresses have already searched. Each pair will be provided with directions to their target location. Follow them exactly, and you'll fulfill your purpose. Find their dens. Neutralize all Sols in the vicinity. And finally free Caligo from the soulless scourge above!" Commander Guffian leans back and pauses triumphantly for a raucous cheer that never comes.

Aruna's hand shoots up. "What if we run into a group of Sols that outnumbers us?"

"Do you know how many of them are up there?" asks Demi, who's standing beside Yvonne.

The line between Commander Guffian's gray brows furrows deeper. "Sols are inherently selfish creatures that often travel alone, though there have been exceptions. The largest horde we've seen is a group of five. It's fair to suspect there are more, perhaps dozens of others, that lurk farther from our borders, but those posing a more immediate threat should be no more than ten. Fifteen, at most."

Whispered dismay echoes through the cramped room, and the commander reengages. "You'll have about half an hour before the sun rises. The more distance you cover in that initial window, the more likely you are to find the Sols at their weakest."

On my left, Gem mutters to me under her breath, "Like thirty minutes will be enough time."

Our eyes meet. It's a relief to see no evidence of bleed-through on the fresh compress cloth, but the way she hugs her arms tightly around herself deepens the creases in my forehead.

From the neck up, Gem looks more like herself than I do. Her attendants used a light hand with her cosmetics. A dab of dewy blush on the apples of her cheeks and a thin smear of liner along her lashes enhance her naturally striking features. The effect reminds me just how young she is, though there's an acute heaviness in her jade eyes—multiplying with every passing hour—that ages her compared to her twenty-four-year-old peers. But the rest of her is unrecognizable. As long as I've known Gem, she's kept her body hidden beneath layers of oversized clothing. Seeing her forced into having herself on display like this makes my teeth grind together.

It's all my fault. The accusation festers from my lungs into my throat. Gem had the opportunity to walk away from the Hunt, and the only reason she turned it down was so I wouldn't be alone. And how did I repay that sacrifice? By picking a fight with her on the final night before our deployment.

I need Gem. I've always needed her, but especially right now.

Her twin and I were instant friends. With Taurance's infectious optimism and magnetic passion, it's impossible not to love her. But when I'd first invited the twins to share a cabin with me, Gem had her misgivings about welcoming a stranger into her heart and home. The roots of their mother's abandonment ran deep. Still do. So, day by day, I proved to her I had no intention of walking away. And once she decided to let me in, I knew it was a forever type of friendship—the kind with a foundation not easily fissured. Her steadiness will be the only thing grounding me as we traverse into the unknown.

The center of my brows raises: an apology and silent plea.

With a nod, the corner of Gem's lips lift, and she reaches her right hand toward mine. A peace offering. I accept it eagerly, my chilled fingers wrapping around hers before she can change her mind about the physical contact.

"—weapon of choice," the commander says, bringing my attention back to the room at large while gesturing at the array of nightstone blades and weaponry mounted on the concrete wall.

The others stride towards it. Gem releases her grip, yet stays at my side while I shuffle behind.

I stare at the swords, daggers, and spears. Unlike the other natural stones mined from Caligo's underground quarries, nightstone has no polish or sheen. Instead of reflecting the room's dim light, its flat black surface seems to eradicate it, absorbing only the shadows. It's those same properties that make nightstone our only resource capable of causing true damage to the Sols. With every cut, the golden energy flowing through their veins depletes. I should be grateful that such a resource exists. Yet there's something disconcerting about being this near to the inky black weapons, like they're void of more than just light.

"How are we supposed to know which blade to pick?" Gem asks as she too eyes the weapons warily, reluctantly stepping towards the row of swords on the far left.

Yvonne leans in. "My Pops has been working in the nightstone mines since before I was born. He says any nightstone with a brown patina has been diluted with iron. The pure stuff should be matte black."

"A blade is a blade," Kalden says.

Yvonne continues, "But untempered iron jeopardizes more than the purity. It might make the weapon more brittle."

I wave an arm at a section of untarnished swords. "So, any of these, then?"

Kalden releases a grunt. "Longer blades will enable you to defend yourself while keeping some distance between you and your attacker, but they're heavy and will slow your movement."

Gem moves to shove her hands into her pockets before remembering that our bodysuits have none. "What weapon do you recommend, then?"

"For you . . ." He leans to the right, scooping up a thinner, more tapered blade. "A poniard should suffice. It's slender, so it won't weigh you down. And the nine-inch blade is more than enough to impair your opponent, should it come to that."

Kalden shifts the poniard's hilt into Gem's open palm, and she tests its weight, twirling the weapon before slowly thrusting it towards my stomach.

"Got ya!"

Though the narrow tip is gentle as it presses into my leathers, my spine curls inward as I groan dramatically, "How could you?"

Kalden's brow pulls more taut, but he voices no critique while arming himself with two throwing knives.

"Really? You're not gonna give us a warning about how 'if that's really your form, you'll both be goners'?" I lower my voice to mock his deep timbre.

He ignores me, and Gem snorts before securing the accompanying leather scabbard around her waist.

I lift onto my tiptoes, reaching up to grab an identical blade from the wall.

Kalden steps in front of me. "You're too slow to use this effectively. The blade cuffs would be better suited."

"The what?"

He twists, grabbing two of the smaller weapons from the wall.

"These straps wrap around your wrist and forearm," he explains while tugging my left hand through the cuff, and I'm grateful for the layer of leather gloves separating my skin from his sweltering touch. He tightens the bands so the steel-plated mechanism rests firmly against the top of my arm. "And see this wired ring? If you put that around your finger and flick your wrist, it'll release the folded blades."

He demonstrates the motion, and I mimic it, jumping when

the two nightstone blades spring outward on each side of my wrist. I repeat the motion, and the blades tuck themselves back into place.

"Piercing something vital might be trickier with these, but you could easily sever an artery just by doing what comes naturally, like flailing." Kalden heaves a breath that sounds suspiciously like a snicker before securing the second blade cuff to my right arm. "Erratic movements might even dissuade your opponent from trying to disarm you."

I can admit that his logic is sound. A weapon that requires little to no strategy on my part is likely the best fit for me. Plus, the tight formation of the blades near my palm could make for a good excuse, should I need to explain why a Sol would flinch from my touch if I succeed in releasing a solar flare.

But does he have to be such an ass about what I can and can't do?

Once both blade cuffs are in place, I rotate my arms in front of me, acclimating to the sight and feel of the weapons.

Gem arches a brow. "Are you sure that will be enough? Those blades look tiny."

"Like yours is much bigger," I say, tilting my chin.

"Bigger than yours," she retorts.

Kalden interjects. "They won't cause as much damage to an attacker as a poniard or a sword, but they won't rely on a tight grip or stamina, which is why they're the best option for Orelle. The only drawback is that she won't be able to wield a second weapon, since most wrist movements will trigger the release. But considering that she lacks the proficiency required to wield a longer blade, it's not much of a concession."

I flick my right hand, taunting him by lifting the unfolded blade inches from his face. "You should watch what you say to an armed lady."

Kalden's pupils dilate as they narrow in first on the nightstone, then on me, and the corner of his mouth twitches up ever so slightly.

"Sun's pits, Orelle!" Gem tugs downward on my arm, warily eying the blade cuffs while whispering, "You can't threaten him like that."

"Relax. I was joking," I say, retracting the blades.

"I'm not sure he finds you waving a sharp weapon in his face funny."

Kalden's hint of a smirk deepens. "It's a little funny."

Gem looks between us before rolling her eyes.

"W-When will we get to come home?" Twilynn asks, blanching at the dagger in her quivering hand.

The commander peers through his glasses. "After you eliminate the threat."

"But what does that mean?" Gem presses. "What if we reach our target, and there's nothing there? Can we just come back?"

He flips through a pocket-sized version of our constitution, as if he hadn't thought to memorize the Hunt's conditions of return, because no one truly expects us to return.

"I, um—"

As someone who *has* studied it yearly on the eve of selection, I interrupt his blustering. "The drafted soldiers may return under the following condition: for each Huntress remaining alive at the time of repatriation, the irrefutable proof of one Sol destroyed by each requestor's hand must be presented at the Gate, thus furthering suitable circumstances for the city of Caligo to emerge and establish a secure fortress impenetrable from future attacks."

I glance at Gem, hoping she pays close attention to these next words. "Requestors may also be repatriated if they are found to survive for more than seven days outside of the Gate; however, the requestor will be dishonorably received. A trial may be held to determine whether the circumstances of their return are defensible or an act of dereliction of duty, but they cannot be denied access to the city, emergency medical care, or the right to legal representation."

"So, if one of us kills ten Sols, we can all come back?" Twilynn asks, perking up a little as she glances at Kalden.

The commander shakes his head rapidly. "No, no, that's not how the rules are interpreted. If there are ten of you alive, all ten need to be at the Gate with proof that each of you killed a Sol. The cameras in your helmets will allow us to see who has accomplished their mission. It's everyone or no one."

Pinpricks trace down the back of my neck and along my spine as the eyes of the other Huntresses slide to me. Each of us holds the fate of nine others in our hands, and mine are too slow, too weak. Even if by some miracle the others could kill enough Sols, the only way they'd be welcomed back into the city without the threat of a trial is if I kill one too . . . or if I die.

The grim set of their jaws tells me they've come to similar conclusions.

"We're expected to kill almost every single Sol in the area? It might not even be possible to make sure everybody is able to kill one without going past the northern edge of the dunes." Gem's green irises flare. "It could take weeks. We won't be able to fit enough food in these knapsacks to hold us over that long."

The Commander of the Guard straightens, rolling his shoulders back. "You will face hardship, but duty is not without sacrifice."

What sacrifices have you *made?* I clamp my mouth shut, keeping the question contained in my mind, not without effort.

Unlike us, most guards will never know the misfortune of direct encounters with our greatest enemy. They limit their outside patrols to the evening hours and cower behind the nightstone barrier during the day. To my understanding, the commander never even leaves the lower city. What does he know of sacrifice beyond a sore ass and boredom?

The commander's voice resounds once more through the war room. "All of your questions have been answered, Huntresses . . . and Hunter. You are soldiers of Caligo now. Your city expects you to act like it. Show bravery and courage in battle. And when your time comes, die with dignity."

That's all we are—a sacrifice meant to appease, not to live. My fingers clench, finding minimal comfort in the whirring release of the curved blades.

To my right, Kalden's irises are bright with unspoken judgement.

Lifting his chin, the commander takes note of the piercing intensity. He grabs onto the handcuffs dangling from his belt as he prowls forward through those surrounding the table. "Tonalli, is it? Do you have something to add?"

Before Kalden spits out one of his reckless critiques, I nudge my elbow into his side. This isn't the right place or person. The guard who "oversaw" our training might've dismissed Kalden's accusatory tone, but as the head of Caligo's armed forces, Commander Guffian may not be so forgiving.

Molten gold eyes lock onto mine before flicking back up. "No."

With a satisfied nod, the commander releases the handcuffs and clasps a hand on Kalden's shoulder. "Mind your face, boy. Your attitude is unbecoming for a man of Caligo."

"I agree, sir," Kalden grits through his teeth.

A hunched-forward Coraline Lunam perks up when she spots us rounding the bend of the main spiral stairwell.

The massive moon pendant illuminates a small crowd gathered around the perimeter of the landing chamber. Only Caligo's most influential are invited to witness the official departure of the Hunt in person.

Still, I scrutinize the faces, searching for my parents or Taur.

Standing proudly at the top of the stairs to the left of the towering gate is Chancellor Bren, with his dutiful wife at his side, followed by his personally selected daughter-in-law—my replacement. We share a similar stature and hair color, but that's where the resemblance ends. There's not a single tangle or stray frizz in sight in her slicked-back ponytail. No wrinkles in her figure-hugging dress or pristine complexion. Dense lashes frame her blue-green irises, which stare unblinkingly forward while her six sons fidget and snicker beside her. *Gabe's* sons, I remind myself.

Yet Gabe himself is nowhere to be seen. The coward couldn't be bothered to look me in the eye as I'm evicted from our haven.

Coraline's heels clap against the polished granite floor as she strides forward to greet us and gestures for a camera operator to follow.

"Look at you all! What a transformation! Let's give a hand to our team of beauticians and attendants responsible for getting our soldiers battle-ready," she gushes, taking special notice of Kalden, who's assumed leadership at the front of our group.

The gathered crowd claps politely while I try not to roll my eyes at the notion of a makeover being deemed necessary for battle preparation.

"Do you all hear that?" Coraline waits for the general muffled noises to settle before squealing, "The sound of freedom! I know my mother used to say this at the start of every Hunt, but I really do believe *this* will be the year Caligo claims victory!"

Applause echoes throughout the arched landing chamber.

Coraline beams more widely, her teeth like tiny sponges soaking up the attention. "Now, before we get to our final interview, each of our esteemed Huntresses has loved ones who'd like to bid them farewell."

Yvonne leans forward and whispers to Demi. "You were right. We can't even say our goodbyes in private."

One by one, the family members of my peers are escorted through the leftmost darkened archway. The production crew swivels their wheeled camera equipment around the landing chamber, hunting for the best angles to capture the new arrivals rushing forward to embrace a daughter, sister, cousin, or friend.

Throat swelling, I drop my helmet to the stone floor as Taurance and my parents are among the last to enter. All three wear wan, sunken faces, like they've aged years instead of hours since I last saw them. Noting my attention, my mother tries her best to pull her unpainted lips into a reassuring smile. Taurance reaches Gem at the same time that my parents draw me into their arms, enveloping me in floral perfume and bitter tears. I savor it—savor them and this moment that makes me feel like a child whose heaviest burden is passing a timed history exam. My eyes squeeze shut as I linger in the nostalgia, though unlike then, I'm in no hurry to leave the safety of their embrace no matter how compressed my lungs are.

My mother is the first to pull back, dabbing at the glossy streaks staining her cheeks with the back of her hand before fussing over a few face-framing curls that broke loose from my bun. "Coraline's right, you know. This will be the year that you claim victory. I can feel it."

"You can?" Brows arching, I lift my eyes to my father, who's too busy glaring at Chancellor Bren to give more than a half-hearted nod. "I wish I could agree with you."

Manicured fingernails clamp onto my shoulders.

"Now you listen to me. You are still a Way," my mother says with no small amount of pride. "Do you remember what that means?"

I dip my chin, repeating the trite yet sentimental family motto drilled into me through the various challenges of years past.

"Ways always find a way."

She mouths the words with me, then leans in. "Promise me that you won't give up on yourself. That you'll do whatever it takes to survive, just like you always have."

"Promise." I glance at Kalden, who stands alone, wishing I could assure her that I've been working on a contingency plan.

She follows the direction of my attention. "Be careful with him."

"With Kalden? He's actually been helping us with our training. He's taught me more in our past two sessions than I've learned in ten years of the mandatory combat lessons." Nevermind the fact that he's also a blunt asshole with zero tact in that perfectly honed body—a body that is currently shifting uncomfortably as those around him exchange emotional goodbyes.

My mother sighs. "That's wonderful, sweetie. Truly. Thank the shadows he decided to volunteer. He seems like a great asset."

"But?" I prompt.

"But I worry that he's a bit reckless. Just don't let yourself get caught up in anything dangerous, okay?"

I chuckle, though there's little mirth in it. "You mean beyond hunting our greatest enemy across foreign territory? I'll try not to, but I promise he should be the least of your worries."

She squeezes my shoulders once more before releasing her grip.

My teeth bear into my bottom lip as I watch Kalden angle away from the older man standing defensively beside the blonde Huntress whose name is Blair, if I remember correctly. It seems my mother isn't alone in her distrust of Caligo's first ever volunteer. The man's eyes narrow into slits on the one person who's willingly participating in the Hunt. For darkness's sake, Kalden is about to risk his life for this city, and this is how we repay him: with glares and seclusion?

I shake my head before calling out, "Kalden!"

His golden gaze finds me instantly, and I wave him over.

My mother pinches her lips together, but I ignore her to nudge my arm into my father's. "What about you? Any words of wisdom or warnings?"

My father reluctantly turns his reddened face away from the chancellor back towards mine. "If anything happens to you, I'll kill him myself."

Face blanching, my mother whips her head around to make sure no one heard. "You can't say things like that, especially not in public!"

"It's not like anyone can hear me over all that blubbering," he says, gesturing towards a middle-aged woman sobbing over Aruna. "And even if they could, who cares? It's nothing I wouldn't say to his face."

"Whose face?" Kalden asks, weaving through the small crowd surrounding Faron to stand between me and my father.

"No one," my mother and I reply in unison.

Kalden arches a single black brow, yet leaves it alone as Taurance spins me around into a tight hug.

I kiss the side of her head, then pull back. "You're not wearing your vanilla-almond body oil."

She huffs a breathy laugh, cheeks turning pink. "That's what you're worried about right now? Do I smell that bad?"

"Not at all, but you always wear that oil," I say. "Even when you're sick."

"I guess I forgot to put it on. I haven't really slept much since . . ." Her jade irises look between Gem and me, brightening with tears as her words trail off.

Gem nudges her boot against her twin's sandal. "You've gotta take care of yourself, T. No matter what happens."

Lip quivering, Taur shakes her head. "Don't talk like that. Don't even think it. You're coming back home. Both of you are. I can't raise this baby alone."

"You're pregnant?" my mother asks, her strained voice lifting a bit.

Taurance nods. "Seven weeks along."

Kalden is the first to respond, offering a stiff hand. "Congratulations."

Taur accepts it while my mother echoes the sentiment before asking, "Do you have any names picked out yet?"

Looking down at her stomach, Taur says, "I'm thinking Gemelle, after both her aunties."

"Oh, how lovely!" My mother clasps a hand to her heart. "You already know it's a girl?"

"Not officially. Only a hunch."

I intertwine my fingers with Taur's. "I love it."

Gem turns to swipe at a few rebel tears. "What if it's a boy?"

Frowning, Taur asks, "Gemelle is gender neutral, right?"

Gem and I exchange wide-eyed glances, neither of us certain if she's joking.

"Maybe you could tinker with it a bit," my mother suggests tactfully. "Something like Gemol, perhaps? Or you could go shorter with something like Gor?"

My father leans forward to chime in. "Darling, let the girl name her child whatever she wants to name it."

"You're right. I'm sorry, Taurance. Gemelle truly is a beautiful name. And if you need anything at all, especially while our girls are gone, our door is open."

Taur gives her a soft smile. "Thanks, Mr. and Mrs. Way."

The oversized moon pendant flickers twice, signaling for the room to quiet down. Coraline announces we have one more minute to finish our goodbyes, though I swear we're only given half that before the guards begin ushering our family and friends back through the doorway.

My father is the last to go, planting a kiss on my forehead and whispering, "You send those creatures straight to the fiery furnace of the sun, okay? Whatever it takes. Don't stop fighting."

A nameless guard puts a hand on my father's arm. "Sir, it's time for you to leave."

He shoves the hand away. "I'll take as long as I like saying goodbye to my daughter."

"Sir, you cannot obstruct—"

"You should go," I say, fighting to keep my voice from wavering. "I love you."

"Love you too, kiddo." My father pats my shoulder, then spins to leave, but not before shooting a final scowl at the chancellor.

Once the double doors close behind him, I fetch my helmet from the stone floor while Coraline breaks the silence with her too-cheery falsetto. "I know you're all eager to hear from our soldiers one last time before they depart. Shall we begin the last interview with our brave volunteer?"

The sconces flicker as Coraline scoots closer to Kalden.

"Do you have a special lady you'd like to send a message to?"

Standing stiller than a statue, Kalden replies with a simple, "No."

"Really?" Coraline places a palm on her chest, like this is the most shocking thing he could've said. "No wife or partner? Someone who'll be counting down the days until your return?"

"No," he repeats.

"Well." Coraline leans toward the camera with a conspiratorial smirk. "I'm sure some of our eligible ladies would be glad to give you a true hero's welcome once you come back."

I expect Kalden's neutral expression to hold firm, but a scowl breaks through.

Coraline chuckles tensely before moving on to Gem. "Speaking of heroes, we were all moved by your insistence on serving in the Hunt, despite your injury. Were you compelled by your sense of duty?"

Gem glances at me while answering, "You could say that."

"Can you believe that, folks? Wow! Now *this* is a woman whose heart is fully devoted to our merciful shadows. We love to see it!" Coraline directs her next question at me. "What's it like being friends with someone so dedicated?"

"Gem is . . ." I start and stop. Despite our unspoken amends, this is my chance to verbally affirm what she means to me, so I want to get it right.

"Not many can say they have a friend loyal enough, or stubborn enough, to walk with them into battle. Someone who's willing to leave behind their comforts, or maybe even their lives, so the person lucky enough to be loved by them won't have to face their deepest fears alone." Coraline's forced smile falls, and a shaky exhale passes through my lips as I admit, "I can't say I'm glad she's here. I'm terrified, actually. But I also couldn't be more grateful that we're facing this together."

Gem's cheeks are rosier than usual as she squirms at my sappiness and having everyone's focus on her, but the soft smile she dips her head to hide tells me all I need to know.

Coraline tugs her silver neckerchief loose to dab the inner corners of her black-lined eyes, which she closes while shaking her head, like she's trying to shake away the distressing sensation of empathy.

By the time her eyes reopen, the glossy detachment is firmly back in place.

"Let's have production cut that last part," Coraline whispers to the camera operator before switching her sights over to Aruna. "Miss Aruna here is the youngest of this year's selected. Tell me, Aruna, do you think your youthful energy will give you an edge out there?"

Aruna, who perked up a bit at being called, deflates. "I had a better chance at getting engaged in the next month than I do at making it through one week against the Sols."

Coraline sighs and shares another look with her camera operator. "Cut that, too."

Meridna's the next victim. When Coraline asks why she chose a short sword as her weapon, Meridna simply shrugs.

A few minutes later, Coraline gives up entirely on getting good content out of us. To her crew, she instructs, "Let's get a good wide view of the group and a few up-close shots of them putting their helmets on. Oh, and their weapons! Folks go crazy for that kind of footage."

My fists clench at the pageantry of it all, and I mistakenly trigger the mechanism on my cuffs. The metallic whir causes Gem and Twilynn to flinch back. Before I think to move my arms away from my sides, one of the blades slides through the leather fabric on my thigh, releasing with it a small stream of blood. An icy pinprick dances across the cut, though the pain is secondary to the crushing weight of the crowd's eyes.

"Sorry," I rush to say, retracting the blades and making a mental note that even the slightest hand movement can release the trigger.

"Hold places, everyone," Coraline declares before waving over an attendant. "Please take care of the tear and wipe away the blood. We can't have people saying we don't care for our Huntresses properly."

A girl who can't be more than eighteen hurries toward me with a towel, needle, and fine thread. I watch as she wipes the beads of crimson from the leather and meticulously begins to sow the suit back together while blood continues to seep from the wound.

"Could I get a bandage before she finishes sewing?"

"No time," Coraline responds gruffly.

Chatter rises from the spectators.

Cheeks heating, I resume watching the attendant sow loop after loop after loop. Too many minutes pass before the girl wipes the last traces of blood from the leather. When she finally leaves my side, the crowd cheers.

Shadows, swallow me now.

The Commander of the Guard inadvertently grants my wish a moment later when he signals it's time to don our helmets.It's as heavy and uncomfortable as I expected. My fingers itch with the urge to rip the bulky headgear off, but I hold still, not wanting to repeat my embarrassment. A polarized lens stretches across the front of the mask, offering a shaded view of my surroundings. And there's a line of perforations along the base for moderate airflow, yet I find my breaths stilted as the commander waves to four Guards of the Gate, who obediently fall into line at our flank, seeming much more at ease in their own masks and uniforms.

They order us into pairs, placing me next to Twilynn and sending Gem with Meridna behind me. With our heads covered, I lose track of who's standing where, except for Kalden. With his added height and distinct build, he's unmistakable from the rest.

Once the guards move past us, Gem grabs Twilynn's arm to swap places, pairing her with Meridna instead.

"Together," she whispers, voice muffled by the helmet and the creaking of the Gate's locking mechanisms releasing.

This is happening.

The Hunt is about to begin.

As my chest rises and falls, the edges of my vision threaten to blur. Not from a migraine, thank the darkness, but from the intoxicating surge of dread and anticipation. I'm about to see the sun. Not through a video screen, or a sliver of sunlight beaming past the tunnel's fissure, but in the limitless expanse of the open sky.

Metallic groans reverberate across the chamber as a guard cranks a lever. The two massive slabs of nightstone begin to part, and I sway into Gem. She places a steadying palm on my back.

Commander Guffian beckons us forward to the Gate's threshold, where Chancellor Bren waits with a grin. "May the shadows lead our esteemed soldiers forward in honor. Let the two-hundred-seventy-ninth annual Hunt commence!"

He extends a sweeping arm, and the gathered sycophants cheer as we're ushered forward to our doom.

CHAPTER FIFTEEN

Thunder booms across a densely packed cloud-ridden predawn sky, mocking any expectation of witnessing my first sunrise as we're transported a mile north of Caligo's entrance. Though daybreak will be imminent within the hour, the roiling storm blots out the aerial light from the moon and constellations, leaving only the silver beam of headlights on the front of the motorized cart to enhance visibility.

"Do you think it'll rain?" The question comes from a woman sitting two rows ahead of me in the motorized cart. Judging by the huskiness of the tone and the rapier on her hip, I think it's Faron, though it's hard to tell with her red hair covered by the helmet.

"Looks like it might," I say.

"I wonder what it's gonna feel like," another remarks.

"Wet," Kalden states simply, and I almost crack a smile as the cart comes to a halt at the top of a large dune, overlooking the expansive sandscape.

We file out one by one onto the ground.

A more nasally voice whispers to the few women within earshot,

"Why did they bring us all the way out here? Why not let us walk from the entrance?"

I shrug. "Maybe they don't want to lead Sols to the entrance of Caligo."

A commotion on the other side of our group drowns my words out. Three of our escorts have climbed back into the cart they used to transport us across the dunes, but the fourth guard makes no effort to join his comrades.

"C'mon, we gotta get back," calls the man sitting behind the cart's steering wheel.

The dissenting guard shakes his head and tugs off his helmet, revealing tousled auburn hair and an all-too-familiar smirk.

My stomach twists in on itself as my ex-husband commands, "Head back without me. I'm right where I need to be."

The Guards of the Gate freeze, and I almost pity them for having to decide between obeying the orders of the next-chancellor-to-be or earning the current chancellor's ire.

I stomp forward through the group. "What are you doing?!"

Gabe's lopsided smile falls as he faces me. "The right thing."

"How is leaving your family behind the right thing?"

"I have to, Elle. You wouldn't be here if it weren't for me."

"No." I shake my head, though the bulky headgear makes the movement more clunky than intended. "You can't just make your wife a widow because you don't want the death of your ex-wife weighing on your conscience."

"That's the thing, though. None of us have to die. Not if we use this," he says cryptically, thumping a hand against the large pouch looped around his waist.

"You can't know that."

There's no telling what weapon he's got in there, but how can it guarantee that all eleven of us will make it out of this Hunt unscathed?

Gabe moves closer, voice lowering. "Trust me, Elle. This will work."

"What if it doesn't?" I step forward, contemplating whether I'd be fast enough to snatch that helmet out of his hands, plop it back on his head, and send him on his merry way back to safety.

"It will," he insists.

"But what if it doesn't?" I repeat, voice thick with a plea for him to understand what's truly at stake if his secret plan doesn't pan out as expected.

Gabe's throat bobs as he lessens more of the distance between us. "*If* it doesn't, then my boys will know their father died with honor." His deep blue eyes dip to my own, and I know he's now speaking to me instead of the camera. "And I could only hope they'd be willing to do the same for the women they love."

For the first time since I've put it on, I'm grateful for the helmet, if only for its ability to disguise the emotions on my face. Like how his confession widens my eyes and tugs at the corners of my lips, only for the near smile to crumble a second later. He chose to throw what we had away, to ignore me for ten years, despite his so-called "love" for me.

I need him to believe my next words. Need *myself* to believe them.

"I don't want you here, Gabe. There's nothing you could ever do that would atone for what you did. Your honor died a long time ago, along with any love between us. Out here," I say, swinging my arms out at the surrounding dunes and overcast sky, "there's no room for cowards or distractions. So, leave your secret little weapon with us, if you must, and go back home while you still can."

Gabe smiles.

Smiles.

My arms shake as I stave off the urge to clench my fists.

His eyes move lower, catching the movement. "You gave yourself away earlier, you know. In your interview with Coraline. What you said about Gem . . . If you really didn't care about me, it wouldn't matter to you if I stayed. The fact that you're trying this hard to get me to leave—"

"Stop," I say, but he talks over me.

"—tells me you do care. You care a lot."

Gabe lifts a hand towards my helmet.

What's he going to do? Rip it off? Forsake his vows to his current wife for the sake of resuscitating ours? It would be a lie to say I haven't dreamt of this—or something like this, minus the hostile environment and shit timing. But those dreams faded years ago.

"Don't," I breathe, stepping back.

But Gabe's not ready to let me get away. He shifts forward.

"Stop it, Gabe."

A hand comes between us, but it isn't Gabe's or mine. I know from the charged energy alone that it's Kalden.

"She said stop," he warns, spreading his palm against Gabe's chest.

Gabe's deep blue eyes narrow as he peers down at the hand, then between Kalden and me.

"Your chivalry is admirable, but unnecessary," Gabe says while brushing aside Kalden's hand and taking a few steps back. "I would never hurt Elle."

"Sounds like you already have," Kalden counters.

Gabe holds up his palms. "Fair enough, but I'm here to prove it won't happen again."

Kalden stands silent for several seconds, and I get the sense those molten irises of his are assessing my ex-husband. Finally, he says, "Get your helmet on, then. Let's head out."

Gabe hesitates, unaccustomed to following orders, then does as he's told. But not before he calls back to the guards, who are still waiting on the motorized cart. "I'm not going back. You can't force me to return without restraining me, and legally, you can't. So go."

The three Guards of the Gate need no other permission. The cart's wheels kick up grains of sand as it takes off across the dunes, its rhythmic whir disappearing a minute later.

I angle back towards the Huntresses. They look like statues, each one fixated in a different direction, slowly surveying the cloud-covered landscape that dips and crests for miles. A gentle wind flows through the helmet as I, too, fall under the spell.

There are no walls. No doorways or stairwells. Nothing to hold on to. Nowhere to hide. Even the ground gives way, like an endless void that won't stop spinning while I fall through a vortex of sand and sky.

My knees collapse against the surface. I lean forward, bracing my palms on the cool earth while I attempt to convince my brain that the tunnels of Caligo aren't trying to swallow me back inside.

"Being out here makes me feel like I'm stuck inside a sand clock." Gem's words ease their way through the tempest. She scoots up next to me and presses her knee into my own, providing the anchor point for the world to stabilize.

We stay in the quiet expanse for a few moments more.

When my vision settles, I notice Kalden returning from the large dune toward my right. He leaps gracefully down the steep decline while my feet sink and stick as I trudge my way back to standing. As he arrives, our group seems to come to attention, turning toward him without prompting.

"I know the commander ordered us to split up, but we'll have better odds of making it through an attack if we stick together. Groundcover isn't the priority here. Survival is." Kalden's neck tilts back as he takes in the clouds, which have brightened from a near-black gray to a slightly brighter shade of charcoal. "We've got a little less than half an hour till sunrise. If we head west for the tree line, we may make it before dawn."

Before our enemies awake.

"Remember what we practiced. Adjust your form for long-distance running. Stamina over speed, until a threat arises."

Kalden spins on his heel, leading our group towards the darker side of the horizon.

Gem falls into step on my right, Gabe on my left. Their pandering makes me want to push myself faster, but I refrain from doing so. The last thing I want to do is burn myself out in the first half hour. So, I focus on what Kalden taught me during our second training session: lean forward, higher cadence, shorter strides. The movement is gentler on my ankles and knees, redirecting the stress to the balls of my feet and my glutes.

Minutes pass, and I fall into a rhythm. Because of the angle, I'm able to avoid too much vertical oscillation, and my brain is grateful not to be jostled around. Like usual, there's a pressure behind my eyes that pulses with every heartbeat, but it hasn't reached a stabbing level of pain.

Yet, whispers an intrusive thought.

I ignore it. Worrying about when my next debilitating episode will strike will do me no good. If it happens—or *when* it happens—I'll have to lean on the borrowed power from the sun instead of my own and pray to the shadows that it'll be enough.

CHAPTER SIXTEEN

Silvery light illuminates the gnarled branches of the tree line ahead. Even with the dense cloud cover, the sun's brilliance is already more than the dull violet lights my sensitive eyes are accustomed to. If this is dim, how much brighter will it be when the sky clears?

I inhale, catching a sweet floral scent mingling with the earthy marram grass, the forest ahead greeting us through the wind. It's a nice change from the musty aroma that lingers throughout most of Caligo, despite the spiced fragrances they mix into the bioluminescent liquid to cover the stench.

I've spent most of the past thirty hours preparing myself for the horrors awaiting us above. Scorching heat. Formidable terrain. The scent of death closing in. I hadn't once considered it might be . . . pleasant. Since dawn broke a handful of minutes ago, a comfortable warmth has permeated the steady breeze. Not too hot, but enough to chase off the chill beneath my leathers. If it weren't for the weight of the steel resting atop my forearms or the sheathed weapon bouncing against Gem's thigh or my ex-husband's panted breaths, maybe we could forget that we're running for our lives. Maybe we'd find enjoyment, even, in the shifting landscape and how the golden hues of the sand spill into lush greenery.

A low rumble cuts through our silence.

Gem glances over her shoulder. "Guess the storm's back."

Though the thunder had relented a minute after the guards parted ways with us, the reprieve seems to be ending. Yet when a second, third, and fourth *thump* reverberate through the charged air, unaccompanied by the telltale flash of lightning, alarm bells ring in my mind.

A screech pierces through the gentle wind, shattering the last remnant of the blissful illusion.

"Shift!" Kalden shouts from the front of our group—our signal to shift into speed sprints.

I elongate my strides, but my cadence suffers as the added impact makes my booted feet burrow further into the sand.

The ground rumbles in time with the thudding impacts, growing closer by the second.

Kalden is the first to disappear beneath the forest's canopy, and the others soon follow. The dense woods won't stop our assailant, but it might slow them down—or better yet, weaken their magic from the stifled sunlight. I want to scream at my legs to move faster, but my legs aren't the issue. A familiar aura smears the edges of my vision, and my stride turns sloppy.

Gem and Gabe slow.

"Don't you dare!" I yell at both idiots while clenching my fists, releasing the folded blades from my cuffs, readying to slice the palm of my gloves as soon as their backs are to me.

But neither listens.

The hairs on the back of my neck raise, and I know the beast of my nightmares is closing in.

Gabe grabs a teardrop-shaped object coated in a black shell from his pouch, along with an igniter. He stokes it and tilts the fire onto a wire jutting from the bottom of the shell.

Kalden reappears from the forest, sprinting back towards us.

Towards danger.

Has everyone lost their sun-damned minds?

Kalden unsheathes one of his throwing knives, discreetly running its sharp edge against his glove, all without halting his stride.

I look away, hoping the movement blurs any footage the camera in my helmet might've captured of his subtle treason. My head whips to the right, anxious to see if Gem took notice, but her helmet is angled toward the man at my left.

Gabe stops running altogether, and I choke on a scream.

He spins on his heel, aims the weapon, and launches the shell into the air. The missile arcs across the dune, aimed perfectly toward the charcoal-skinned blur leaping down the hill some sixty feet behind us.

"Gabe! Run, dammit!" The words finally rush out of me as I wonder why he's standing there with the Sol closing in faster than any human could.

Gabe finally unfreezes, darting forward several steps before crouching onto the ground.

Once the creature is three leaps away from Gabe, the missile explodes.

Black powder and smoke erupt in a dense cloud that billows skyward impossibly fast, enveloping the entirety of the Sol. The already overcast sky darkens considerably as smoke laps onto the low-hanging clouds. Gem tugs me into the sand beside her as the wave of thick black air disperses over us.

Seconds feel like minutes as visibility slowly returns. There's movement in the fog ahead. I roll onto my hands and knees, bracing myself for the end.

But the figure ambling through the dissipating smoke isn't a Sol.

"It worked," Gabe chokes out with a manic laugh.

I rise to my feet, dusting the sand from my pants. "What worked?"

"Is it dead?" Gem and I ask our questions simultaneously.

Gabe doesn't respond to either of us, so Gem shuffles forward to see for herself, knuckles tightly wrapped around the hilt of her poniard.

"It's not moving," she calls from ahead. "Unconscious, at the least, if not dead."

Kalden, who's caught up to us, tips his head at the still-expanding blackness shrouding our surroundings in a false night.

"What is that?" When Gabe doesn't immediately answer, Kalden grabs him by the front of his guardsman vest. "What did you do?!"

"I-It's something I've been developing for a while now. I thought if we could find a way to make nightstone airborne, we'd be able to disarm the Sols and protect ourselves from exposure without having to wear all of this." Gabe gestures at his helmet and full-body leathers.

His words pull at a long-buried memory.

"Do you ever wonder what it would be like?" I'd asked Gabe a lifetime ago during what used to be our typical evening cuddles. I'd woken from a dream where he and I had decided to explore the world above. In the dream, I dared to envision what it might feel like—the sun's warmth and the sheer openness of not living in a cramped underground city.

"Of course I do," Gabe had admitted while rolling me further on top of him and rubbing circles on my back. His eyes had gotten that glazed look—the one he'd always get when dreaming up all the ways he could bring about a better future—as he continued, *"I love this city, but I love our people more. And they deserve to have the option of seeing the world beyond the confines of tunnels and caves. You know, I've explored the concept of building polarized dome structures*

above the entrances. We could use them recreationally, maybe. Or even as residences, if there's enough interest. But father is skeptical of the cost and longevity, not to mention the impossible logistics of sending enough guards to defend the construction from attacks. As long as the Sols are still lurking above us, we're stuck here."

I'd shifted myself atop him, longing to erase the building sense of hopelessness tugging at his perfect lips. *"If only it could be night all the time."*

I said it casually, hoping he'd catch the implication of desire in my tone as I kissed his neck. In no way had I meant it to be a true solution.

Yet Gabe had perked up. He'd grabbed both sides of my cheeks and stared at me like I'd solved some great mystery. *"That's it! What if we can make an airborne version of nightstone that bonds with the atmosphere? Even if the sun rises, it won't touch the earth. We could explore and expand above without worrying about the Sols using their power, or becoming a monster ourselves."*

I blink back to the present.

Eleven years. That's how long Gabe's been working on making nightstone airborne.

And he's finally done it.

The vapor now stretches above us like a foreboding black cloud.

"How long will it last?" Kalden demands, fists still clenching onto Gabe.

Hearing this much emotion break through his controlled, stony facade sends a fresh wave of pinpricks down my arms.

Gabe, though, seems unfazed as he basks in his accomplishment. "We carbonized the nightstone so it could easily form a strong covalent bond with the oxygen in our atmosphere."

Gem crosses her arms tightly around herself. "Are you saying you turned nightstone into a greenhouse gas?"

Gabe nods. "The carbon nightoxide molecules are dense, so their rate of dispersion is low. Which is why we struggled to find a sufficient method for infusing it into the atmosphere. The missile has to be a specific weight and ignited with a temperature of at least twelve hundred degrees." He shakes off the dazed expression and blinks down, as if just noticing Kalden's grip on his vest. "To answer your question, it could take a day or two for the carbon nightoxide to decay, though some of the finer nightstone particles may linger in the air for longer."

Kalden finally releases him with a shove and stalks towards the fallen Sol a few yards away.

"What's his problem?" Gabe asks, coming down from the high of his experiment proving successful.

Gem shrugs. "Maybe he's pissed that you stole the hero moment from him."

"A hero, huh? I guess I did. What about you?" Gabe angles towards me, and I can hear the smug grin in his voice. "Aren't you glad I'm here now?"

I respond with a knee-jerk, "No."

"Seriously? That thing was seconds away from sinking its talons into you."

I tilt my chin up. "That's one less Sol for those of us who need to prove a kill. We could've handled it without you."

More like *Kalden* could've handled it. Me? Unlikely.

I retrace my steps back up the dune, sparing myself from Gabe's gloating.

Inky smoke rises from the bare, charred corpse. The area around its heart took the brunt of the explosion, judging by the gaping wound splaying out its chest cavity. Any trace of the golden light flooding its veins has been extinguished, along with the unyielding thirst in its now colorless eyes.

It almost appears . . . human.

Well, a human with skin blackened to a crisp. But those parted lips? They might've been soft and rosy once. And the dainty, upturned nose reminds me so much of Taurance that a pang stabs my chest.

Who was this person, before they became this thing? Do they have a family? Is there someone out there right now missing them as fiercely as I miss Taur?

Stop empathizing with it.

Regardless of what it might've been once, there's no humanity in the Sol sprawled before me. If our positions were reversed, it certainly wouldn't mourn me.

Kalden, who's knelt beside the creature, presses his gloved fingers against the pulse point on the side of its neck, right above what looks to be a collar. Seconds pass, and he lowers his head.

The gesture is so close to tender mourning that I freeze in place.

"Dead." Kalden confirms what we both already knew, voice returning to neutral as he rolls back on his feet.

"That's great, right?" I ask, taking a cautious step forward.

He shakes his head as he walks past me. "A life lost is never something to celebrate."

I double my pace to match his. "Even if it's our enemy?"

Kalden halts. "How are those who revel in the death of someone who was once human any better than the monsters they're taught to fear?"

I place my palm against the forehead of my helmet, covering the camera inside, and whisper, "You can't let them hear you say that."

"Why?" Kalden challenges. "What can they do to me out here?"

My mouth falls open, then shuts.

He has a point. We're already living in one of the worst-case scenarios. The only alternative that could be worse is imprisonment in the Abyss, but would Chancellor Bren risk the valuable lives of his men by sending them out to detain us? Doubtful.

I suppose he could have us arrested, *if* we return home at the end of this. But that's a big if. Assuming Gabe has enough nightstone missiles for each of us to kill ten Sols, what happens when we miss or encounter more creatures? My teeth bite into my inner cheek as I imagine what would happen if we face another ambush, but without the intervention of the explosive.

As if he senses the direction of my thoughts, Kalden sighs. "Focus on right now, not tomorrow or next week or a future that isn't guaranteed. If you don't stay in the present and stay alert, that could be you." He tilts his head at the smoking corpse.

I roll my eyes, though he can't see it. "You're awful at motivational speeches, you know that? Why do you always end these pep talks with some vague threat about my imminent death?"

Kalden leans in so close I can see my reflection in the polarized lens of his helmet. "Because your will to live is what drives you. Not because you fear dying, but because you fear losing. You believe your death would confirm you are too broken, too weak for this world. So, you push forward out of spite, to prove yourself wrong—that you are worthy of existing."

Heat floods my cheeks, and I think I hate him a little bit. I hate how much he sees through me. Hate how his words pry at unhealed wounds. Because he's right. I'm not convinced I'm worthy of existing.

"But you're wrong." Kalden's low voice thickens. "If you die, it won't be a confirmation that you don't deserve to live. It'll just be a tragedy."

My knuckles clench, and my blade cuffs retract.

Part of me hopes he believes I intentionally sheathed the blades.

But if this conversation has taught me anything, it's that the man across from me is too observant for my own good.

A raindrop spills onto his helmet, saving me from whatever humiliating comment he was sure to make. Two more droplets fall on mine.

Kalden leans back, glancing at the blackened sky, then at the tree line at the base of the hill. "We should keep moving. Get further beneath the canopy before the storm picks up."

CHAPTER SEVENTEEN

I lose myself in the relentless patter of raindrops and crunching foliage as we traverse through the forest, dodging the occasional fallen limb and thorny shrubs. Shivers chase the water streaming down my spine. With every step, splashes of mud assault the fringes of my leathery suit before being washed away by the torrent.

The aimless trudging stirs the bubbling cynicism among the group to the surface. Though the beating rain across my helmet drowns out most of the conversations, I recognize Gabe shouting toward Kalden. "Where are you taking us? I can't tell which way is northeast, but I don't think this is the right way!"

Kalden yells back over his shoulder. "We should be going in any direction *but* northeast right now, and we shouldn't be drawing attention to ourselves! Let's keep well within the tree line and head back towards the dunes once visibility returns and everyone has had a chance to dry off!"

His voice resembles the thunder cracking through the wind, carrying with it a charged command. The chaotic whispers cease as we all hear the order and obey.

For a while, the false night moves with us, concealing the true sky from view and making it difficult to know how much time has passed since we left the Sol's steaming carcass. Eventually, the black-tinted raindrops taper to a clear mist as we reach the edge of the nightstone cloud.

Now that we're free of the unnatural darkness, I stand a little straighter.

Stay present. Stay alert. I repeat Kalden's advice like an anthem. His delivery was tactless, per usual, but the advice itself is sound.

Everywhere I look, there are trees, animals, and insects I've yet to learn the names of. Birds with bright red feathers dive for cover beneath the green canopy. A furry four-legged rodent, whose gray-and-copper tail is longer than its body, scuttles past our group with its foraged fruit in hand. The movement stirs a fresh waft of bittersweet fragrance.

There's so much life here. So much sound. I'd thought Caligo's melody of echoing footsteps and muffled conversations was noisy, but this . . . It's entirely overstimulating. Still, I press on, refusing to be the first to request a break.

Mercifully, Gem folds a few minutes later. "Sun's pits, I'm starving. Can we pause to eat? There's enough cover beneath the canopy here that we should be safe from direct exposure."

Gabe, who's hovered persistently at my side since our trek began, pulls out a yellow-orange fruit from his pocket before tossing it over to me. "I plucked this from that tree we passed a bit ago."

"Do you even know what it is?"

"Not sure." Gabe shrugs. "But it looks like a cross between an orange and a pepper, so I'm guessing it's good."

"Those are two completely different flavor profiles," I scoff, but consider the fruit anyway. It seems edible. No discoloration or strange sap. My mouth waters, ready to risk it.

Without warning, Kalden plucks it from my hand.

"Excuse me?" I toss up my arms. "Why'd you steal my snack? Is it poisonous or something?"

Kalden shakes his head, tossing the fruit back and forth between his palms. "It isn't ripe yet. The skin should be softer and a deeper orange. If you eat it now, it'll fill your mouth with a fuzzy bitterness."

The description dries my salivating tongue. "How do you know?"

He pauses his juggling. "We had a few persimmon trees back home."

"You know, I've heard that Scuros is stingy with their greenhouse," I say, stealing back the fruit from Kalden's palm. "They keep the good stuff for themselves and send us Southerners the scraps."

One of the Huntresses snorts. "Fairly sure us Tier Threes get the scraps no matter which city we're in."

"You're from Scuros, then?" Gabe pivots the conversation back to Kalden, and I swear he's actively flexing his crossed arms beneath the slightly too-tight guardsman uniform. "I suppose that's why my father is unfamiliar with your surname."

I lean against a low-hanging branch. "Let's not act like Chancellor Bren devotes his time to memorizing all the surnames of Caligans."

Gabe falls quiet.

Kalden takes a moment to scan our surroundings. "We shouldn't stop for long. Let's limit it to a quick snack. If you need to relieve yourself, now's the time. No more breaks until sunset."

"I brought crackers," the woman to my right says before digging through her knapsack. Meridna, probably, judging by the rich timbre of her tone.

I toss the persimmon into a thorned bush before pulling out a small bag of hazelnuts. "I'm happy to share."

After bartering for a handful of Meridna's salty crackers and Faron's raisins, I grip onto my helmet, eager to yank it off.

It doesn't give.

"Gem, could you give me a hand? I think my helmet's caught on something."

"Sure." She trails a finger around the base that's suctioned to the skin around my neck, then mutters through her own mask, "There's no wiggle room here. It's like this thing is glued on."

"What do you mean? Can you try pulling harder?" The questions come out high-pitched and rushed. I kneel so Gem can get a better grip. She wraps an arm around the helmet and tugs, lifting me off my knees. The material cuts into my throat. "Ow, ow, ow!"

Gem releases me instantly. "Sorry!"

"It's fine," I hiss. "It really won't budge."

"Mine's stuck, too," someone groans.

"Same," says the woman beside Gem. Demi, maybe? Or Blair. It's tricky to tell on voice and stature alone.

Even Kalden fails to remove his.

"Mine's fine," Gabe remarks, helmet resting at his side.

Gem's shoulders deflate. "Looks like yours is the only one."

Through quickened breaths, I point out to Gabe, "Your gear is different from ours."

Unlike the neck-to-feet bodysuits that cling to our bodies like a thick second skin, Gabe isn't sewn into his borrowed uniform. The Guards of the Gate get to wear standard-issue black clothing—long sleeves, high-necked vest, and cargo pants tucked into combat boots. The shape of his helmet is more spacious, too.

"I wonder," Gabe mumbles to himself, his light auburn brows pulling together as he studies my helmet. Seconds into the inspection, he taps on the crown of my head. "There's a solar sensor here. I think . . . I think the wardrobe team might've upgraded the helmet design to automatically keep the helmet sealed if it senses enough sunlight.

Likely as a preventative measure to avoid exposure."

My hands twitch as I refrain from fidgeting. "Can you cover the sensor with your hand? Trick it into thinking it's night?"

Gabe gives it a try, palm splaying out on the top of my helmet. He waits several seconds before pulling at the suctioned base, but it doesn't relent.

"Sorry, Elle," Gabe says, removing his hand. "The sensor must detect more than just light. Perhaps it reads the solar radiation levels, too."

The woman standing on Gabe's opposite side curses under her breath. "We can't take it off until the sun sets?"

"How are we supposed to eat?" Gem asks.

Gabe frowns. "I don't think you can. At least, not until later this evening."

I throw my hands up. "So, we're expected to fight the Sols while we're dehydrated, starved, and sleep-deprived?"

It makes me wonder if they truly want us to succeed, to survive, or if this is all a punishment for our nonconformity. I've always suspected that Chancellor Bren and his chosen cabinet members, like Commander Guffian, valued the Hunt first and foremost as a source of entertainment and tradition more than a viable path to victory. The lack of sufficient training suggests as much. Yet I'd interpreted their carelessness as a lack of faith in our abilities, not as malicious intent.

What if I presumed wrong?

We don't stop again until the sky's overcast silver light bleeds to a natural black. The cursed sun couldn't be bothered to make an appearance today, though perhaps that was the only thing that kept us alive.

Tall grass grazes my shoulders, smearing leftover droplets of rain against my leather suit as we set up camp in a meadow. Though it offers minimal cover, the break in the tree canopy should allow us to waken tomorrow morning at the first sight of the brightening sky.

Gem and Gabe continue hovering at my sides near the back of the pack. Between Gem's frequent side glances and Gabe's insistence on holding out his arm anytime I trip, their actions do nothing to staunch the fear that I'm too weak to hack it on my own, that I'll bring them down with me. But I refuse to be the reason Gem or Gabe don't make it through this.

I square my jaw, tamping down the growing urge to collapse into the dampened earth while setting my mind on doing exactly what my parents instructed.

Whatever it takes.

Even if it means ignoring every slicing ache as I push my body further than it's ever had to go.

"Thank the shadows." Gem sighs as she tugs off the helmet.

Gabe, who'd immediately put his own headgear back on as a sign of solidarity after discovering the solar sensor, removes his, too.

The night's steady breeze is quick to caress my cheeks as I follow suit, then take a deep inhale. My ill-fed lungs welcome the abundance of fresh air. When my eyes blink open, I glare at the round lump of anodized aluminum and tempered glass.

"You look like you're debating whether to toss that in the creek," Gem remarks.

I blink away the tunnel vision, realizing my feet must've subconsciously carried me to the lapping stream running along the meadow's edge. Would that be so bad? Limited sun exposure won't turn me into the soul-thirsty monsters we're meant to hunt. I know that, thanks to my firsthand experience in the transport tunnel and

Kalden's confirmation. What I don't know is whether exposing the entirety of my head for a prolonged period would be enough to tip my body past the point of no return.How long would it take for the sun's corrupting light to mutate my body and burn away my humanity? A few hours? A day? Longer?

My fingertips itch with the urge to test it. Maybe I could pretend to lose my balance and "accidentally" drop the helmet into the fast-flowing current.

Gem nudges my arm, careful to avoid the folded blades. "You okay, Orelle?"

I turn on my heel, preparing to shrug it off.

"Don't you dare say you're fine. I'm not fine. None of us are." Gem lowers herself to the ground, shucking off her boots and dipping her reddened toes into the water. "I've got blisters in places I didn't know were possible. My stomach is so starved it's queasy. And this suit is giving me one hell of a wedgie that keeps coming back no matter how many times I tug on it."

I snicker and collapse gracelessly at her side. "You could leave the flap unbuttoned tonight. Let it all air out down there while you sleep."

Her jade eyes widen. "And let all my bits be on full display? No chance."

"We can choose a spot away from the others," I suggest before adding, "though I doubt any of them would—"

"No, I know." Her shoulders deflate. "I wish we could have stayed in our little cabin forever: you, me, and T. For all the drawbacks we put up with as Tier Threes, at least we had the choice of sticking together. That was all I ever wanted."

"That was always going to change, though. Whether Taur got pregnant or we got selected, forever was never a real option for us in Caligo." We both fall quiet for a time while Gem stares at the ripples of the creek bouncing between blades of grass, until I press on, "Do you regret not pursuing marriage?"

"No." Her reply is quick and firm.

"Even if it meant saving yourself from this fate? I mean, you have to realize you'd make the perfect wife. You're young, healthy, radiant. Unlike me, you wouldn't have to beg for anyone's affection."

"I couldn't be with them in that way, romantically—not without forcing myself. But even then, how could I guarantee they'd never leave me? I've seen what you and T have gone through, how fragile relationships can be." Gem shakes her head. "So, no, I don't regret spending the limited time I've had with people who wouldn't leave. Well, until T got pregnant."

My brows pull together as I quietly ask, "Is that why you decided to stay in the Hunt?"

Muted moonlight reflects off the glistening streaks running down Gem's cheeks. She dips her hands in the water and splashes her face before nodding. "There would've been no one left for me to come home to. We'd all be alone right now. Me in our dingy cabin. T in her upgraded space. You out here. And I guess . . . I guess I preferred to be the one leaving rather than the one who got left behind. Does that make me an awful sister?"

I scoot closer to Gem's side. "No. I won't allow you to blame yourself for choosing to stick by me, and Taur doesn't blame you, either. Sure, she's probably not eating or sleeping very well right now, but I can't imagine she feels anything beyond pride for your bravery, and fear for your well-being."

She chews on her bottom lip. "I just hope she doesn't feel abandoned."

"We can't control that, though." Gem's frown deepens, so I add, "But I have a feeling my parents have unofficially adopted her by now. After a few days of my mother's hovering, she might get sick of their constant company."

The creases along her forehead soften, and I smile gently as I fold up the bottom hem of my suit to a few inches below both knees, then dunk my feet into the stream beside Gem's. The rushing water is an instant balm that sends shivers up my entire body. A moan escapes my lips, and I force a fake cough in a belated attempt to disguise it, for Gem's sake. She rolls her eyes and tosses a couple of raisins into her mouth.

We snack in companionable silence while continuing to soak our aching feet. Neither of us eats much. Like Gem, I've reached the stage of nauseous hunger, but I know I'll need sustenance to fuel me through tomorrow's nonconsensual fast, so I force myself to push past my lack of appetite.

Yvonne joins us a few minutes later with Demi and Aruna at her sides as she pulls back her braids and leans over the creek to cup some of its water within her palms.

"Shadows' mercy, that's good," she says, scooping up a second helping.

Aruna wipes her mouth with the back of her hand. "It's okay."

Yvonne arches her brows. "Better than that over-processed water they give us back home."

Aruna shrugs. "At least the drinking water there is safe. Who knows what's in this? What if it gives us sun poisoning?"

"That only happens with direct exposure to sunlight," Demi chides as she kneels beside the creek's edge. "You'll be fine."

"How do you know?" Aruna lifts her chin while backing away from the water. "It's not like you've done this before. None of us have."

Moonlight breaks through the parting clouds, illuminating the flush of pink on Demi's cheeks. "No, but I know someone who has. My Aunt Jackie was the last to survive the Hunt sixteen years ago."

"Jacqueline Winters is your aunt?" Yvonne gapes at her friend, then gestures to Demi's chestnut ringlets. "Holy shit, you have her hair! How did I not know this?"

Demi rubs her hands on her thighs, drying them off before picking at a half-buried pebble, loosening it from the dirt. "My grandmother had the whole family disown Aunt Jackie as soon as she came back. Told my mom she had to break off all contact with her sister. Said it would look bad on us, after what she did. We didn't reconnect until four years ago—my first year of eligibility. She wanted to share some survival tips, just in case, even though I'd ignored her for twelve years."

She tosses the pebble into the stream, and the current swallows it with a splash.

Yvonne rubs a palm along Demi's hunched back. "You couldn't have been older than—what, like, six or seven when she returned? Of course your aunt wouldn't blame you for following orders."

Demi gives her friend a half-hearted smile, leaning her head onto Yvonne's shoulder. "Thanks, Von."

"So, she told you the water's safe to drink?" Gem asks, bringing the conversation back around.

"She said I could drink any water I find, unless it's from the ocean. When I asked her why, she said it's too salty." Demi's nose scrunches up in what I imagine to be an echo of her aunt's expression.

My forehead bunches together. "How long was Jacqueline out here?"

From what I recall of that year's Hunt montage, the footage hadn't shown any of the women making it past the stretch of Caligo's dunes. But according to Demi, Jacqueline had at least made it far enough to drink from the ocean and a freshwater source.

"Don't you remember?" Yvonne asks. "The guards found her unconscious in front of the main gate seven days after the hostess declared that all the Huntresses were dead."

"Huh," I say, vaguely recalling the confusion I'd felt when our neighbors grumbled their displeasure at seeing that the woman was alive after all. It wasn't until I'd asked my parents that I understood it was because she'd forsaken her duty. "What about her body camera? Couldn't they have checked on her?"

Demi scoops up a second pebble and launches it into the creek. "It got damaged in the last attack that aired—the one where they assumed she'd died. The footage from another camera showed Aunt Jackie sprawled beneath one of her . . ." She stops, rolling a third pebble around in her hand as she searches for the right word. ". . . beneath a fellow Huntress who bled out. The stench of the blood and death masked Aunt Jackie's scent from the two Sols. Once they left and dusk fell, she ran. Chose the wrong direction, at first. Said she found her way to a forest, probably this one, before circling back towards Caligo."

"Wow." Gem whistles, then asks, "The Sols left her alone after the last group attack?"

Demi bristles, staring at the polished brown pebble in her hand, avoiding our gazes. "Before she ran, Aunt Jackie covered herself in as much blood as she could and never washed it off. She thinks that's what kept the Sols from sniffing out her humanity. Told me to do the same if . . ."

Her eyes close, fingers clenching the rock in her fist.

"Holy shadows," I breathe, both appalled and impressed by Jacqueline's unsavory survival tactic. My shoulders convulse as I imagine the sickly sensation of being covered in gore for seven days.

Yvonne places her palm atop Demi's. "Your aunt is a badass."

"More like disgusting," Aruna says with a pinched nose. "I can't believe she disrespected the fallen like that. If any of you get any ideas about doing that to me, I swear I'll haunt you."

Yvonne snaps, "Like you wouldn't do the same thing if the roles were reversed."

"Decorum doesn't exist out here," I say, in case Aruna hasn't yet concluded as much herself. "We do what we can to survive, even if it's disrespectful or foul or taboo. If I fall in battle tomorrow or the next day, I won't begrudge any of you for doing what Jacqueline did."

I look at Gem as I speak that last part, hoping she listens.

She shakes her head, yet whispers, "Same."

The others echo a chorus of agreement, except for Aruna, who stands by her earlier declaration.

We chat a bit longer about Jacqueline, greedy to hear more of her tips. Demi becomes more animated as she tells us about a golden bird that appeared on Jacqueline's third day of meandering without direction, when she was on the brink of dehydration. A glowing sparrow guided her to freshwater steam. The next morning, a luminous robin pecked her awake and led her to a cluster of grapevines. Every day, a new bird appeared, steering her towards sustenance, and eventually, home.

In hindsight, Jacqueline had suspected that these golden birds were a figment of her imagination, born from desperation, dehydration, and instinct.

But as we settle in half an hour later, using our knapsacks as pillows, I can't help but wonder if the unlikely guardians are real. And if they are, maybe they'll help guide us, too.

CHAPTER EIGHTEEN

"Elle."

I'm on the brink of unconsciousness when someone whispers my name. Well, my nickname. And there's only one person who uses it.

My heavy eyes blink open to scan through the surrounding meadow. Faint moonlight illuminates Gem's silhouette as she lies on my right, lightly snoring into her knapsack through parted lips. Beside her are our helmets, rotated so the cameras are facing away from us—we weren't keen on being watched while we slept.

Though I don't immediately spot my ex-husband, there's movement in the tall grass to my left. Before I can write it off as rustling from the wind or an animal, a hand rises above the foliage to wave me over.

Ankles popping and brain throbbing in protest, I hoist myself to standing. I wait several seconds for the nausea to settle, then tread through the thicket. When I reach Gabe, he holds a single finger to his lips and gestures for me to follow. It isn't until we're past the tree line encircling the clearing that he finally speaks.

"Look over there." He points to the black void deeper within the forest, but all I see are vague outlines and shadows.

"Wow," I say with no small amount of sarcasm. "I'm so glad you woke me up so I could see this."

"Just wait," he says, then adds, "I didn't wake you. You were still on your back. You roll over onto your left once you're asleep."

I squirm, unnerved by the casual implication that he remembers my sleeping patterns.

While I scramble for a denial or retort, a tiny orb of yellow-green light flashes a few yards away, disappearing a second later. But then a second light flashes. And a third. Dozens of orbs flicker in and out of existence, as if the stars themselves refuse to hide behind the thin haze of clouds blanketing the sky above, preferring to dance across the earth instead.

My feet carry me closer. "What are they?"

"Some type of winged insect," Gabe replies quietly, likely to avoid scaring them off. "One landed on my arm when I was trying to settle in beneath that tree back there."

He tilts his chin, then reaches towards the flashing orbs. When one ambles inches from his face, he jerks his hands up in an attempt to capture it. But the insect darts away. Three tries later, he ensnares one between his cupped palms. He lifts his hands to offer me a peek. A tiny black-brown insect flaps its wings, searching for an escape from the cage of Gabe's fingers. Seconds pass, and a yellow-green glow illuminates its bottom tip before going dark.

"I think they're creating their own biochemical reaction." Gabe's midnight irises glimmer as he studies the strange bug. "Similar to the bioluminescence we use back home."

Home. He says it with such adoration.

To Gabe, Caligo has always been home. There's no corner, cabin, or tunnel where he isn't greeted with a warm welcome. Why wouldn't he be? Not only is he the prized eldest son of the beloved Chancellor Bren, and the presumed chancellor-to-be, but he's also spent his entire adult life in service to the city, delivering on many of his father's unfulfilled promises. He genuinely desires to better his constituents' living conditions and quality of life. He's the one who ordered the installation of bioluminescent sconces for every cabin in the upper residential levels, which had previously been limited to one sconce per hall. He also investigated growing complaints about the orange tint in the tap water that the Director of Health had turned a blind eye to. Within a week, he discovered a section of corroding pipes and had them replaced.

When Gabe succeeds his father and holds the title of chancellor, he'll have earned it through more than just nepotism alone. He loves the city, and it loves him back.

Me? Not so much. If Gabe is the solution, I am the problem. As an unwed, childless woman, anything I do is seen as a personal offense. How dare I mooch off the rationed grocery scraps or seek employment? You'd think I make a habit of stealing ripe bananas from the hands of babies and comfortable jobs from the hands of more qualified men. In reality, the produce I'm given is usually on the cusp of molding, and the few jobs I've worked only offered mundane domestic tasks better suited for a "woman's touch," according to my previous employers.

No matter how much we "noncontributors" speak up for ourselves, we'll never be heard. Not when their minds are made up. In Caligo, opinions are truth, and facts are irrelevant. And the truth is made abundantly clear with every side-eye and muttered cursed: I am not welcome there. Haven't been since my demotion to Tier Three, thanks to Gabe tossing me aside like garbage. So, how can I call that place my home when it's more like a glorified cage that resents my very existence?

Claustrophobia presses on my chest as I stare at the flashing light between the cracks of Gabe's fingers.

"Let her go."

Gabe's soft smile flattens. "But I—"

I unclasp his hands, breathing a little easier as the insect flies off.

He wipes his palm against his pants. "I wasn't going to hurt it."

"I know. I just . . ." I close my eyes, and a shiver races down my spine. "She deserves to be free."

Gabe nods, then quirks his lips. "'She'? Did you give her a name, in addition to a gender?"

"Go piss yourself," I mutter, turning away from his dimpled smirk and stepping deeper into the glowing insects' den.

"Not my first pick of names, but it could grow on me." Gabe chuckles at his own joke as he rounds my side. His auburn brows pinch together at whatever he sees in my face. "What's wrong?"

I can't bring myself to meet his gaze as I answer with a question of my own. "Why do you keep doing this?"

"Doing what?"

I fold my arms against my chest, rubbing a palm along my upper arm. "Talking to me. Trying to get me alone. Pretending like . . ."

I struggle to name exactly what he's pretending, so I let my words trail off as I lower myself to the ground. I lean against a sturdy tree trunk, rolling the knotted bark against a stiff spot between my neck and shoulders—my body's warning that a flare-up is coming, especially if I don't get some sleep soon. But I can't leave just yet. Not before Gabe explains his sudden interest in barging back into my life.

Gabe settles in on my left. He's silent for a while, and I'm unsure if it's because he fears his answer or he doesn't have one.

"I miss you," he confesses, voice little more than a breath as he picks up a twig from the dirt and twirls it between his fingertips. Predicting my response, he adds, "I know it's been a decade, and I know I'm the one who agreed to the divorce my father was pushing. But I fucked up, Elle. I knew it the moment I signed that paper. I never should've let you go. I put my ambitions over our vows. Chose myself over you. And the worst part is, I told myself it was a noble sacrifice, putting my duty to our city above my selfish desires to be with you."

I scoff. "I'm not sure if 'noble' is the right word to describe getting your dick wet in another woman's vagina. That doesn't make you a martyr, Gabe. It makes you a—"

"Liar? Coward? Prick?" he cuts in with some suggestions, pushing the twig harder into his finger.

I nod and add a few more. "Hypocrite. Asshole. Scum."

"All of those are true." His hooded eyes darken, barely reflecting the yellow-green light of the flashing insects. "If it helps to know, my wife hates me, too. She moved out after the first month into the conjoining cabin to free herself from the grating sound of my voice. She'll tolerate me publicly, but more so to appease my father than out of respect for me."

It *does* help to hear that, yet it doesn't. As poetic as it is that Gabe's karma for turning his back on real love is a marriage void of it, I don't find joy in his unhappiness.

"It can't be all bad. You've made six babies together."

He's quiet for a beat, tracing circles in the dirt with the twig. "I love my boys. I swear they teach me more than I teach them. Like how to slow down and put the needs of another before yourself. Two things you're already good at, by the way. But their conceptions were purely transactional. There's no pa—"

"No." I hold up a hand. "I do not want to hear about how you fuck your wife."

"That's the thing, though. It's not even fucking. I mean, we tried that, at first. But neither of us were into it. She'd just lay there. Unmoving. Expressionless. The one time she showed some semblance of enjoyment, she moaned my father's name." We both snarl our disgust, and Gabe continues, "So we switched to a system where the midwives implant her with my pre-prepared ejaculate."

All these years, I've believed their projection of the perfectly happy couple. Convinced myself that she satisfied him in all the ways I couldn't. And I loathed him for that. So, although I believe Gabe's revelations about his marriage, I struggle to undo my presumptions and rebuild it with this new information.

"Damn," I finally say after several weighted seconds. "Never thought my married ex-husband's sex life would be more pathetic than my own."

Gabe chuckles without humor, snapping the twig in half. "Do you . . . ?"

He leaves the question unfinished.

"Do I what?" I prod, curious to see what has his cheeks turning so pink.

"Nothing. It's inappropriate for me to ask."

"Gabe, you just made me sit here while you complained about how your wife chooses to be impregnated through a *procedure* to avoid being touched by you. I think we passed the line of appropriate conversation topics several minutes ago."

His blush deepens. "Do you have a sex life?"

"Oh," I breathe, brows lifting and falling. "If you'd asked me this a day ago, I'd tell you what I do or don't do with my body isn't your business."

Which is still true, but since he was willing to be vulnerable with me, I can try to do the same. I exhale before continuing, "I spent the first year after our divorce abstinent. But I was a single woman in her early twenties, and I missed feeling wanted. At first, I think a part of me hoped that being intimate would convince them to propose. Maybe that would've been enough for some men, but clearly not for the ones I've picked. Hasn't stopped me from finding pleasure, though. Especially when I'm having a bad flare-up and I'm desperate for some relief."

Gabe nods, likely recalling the times during our marriage when I'd beg for an orgasm to help ease the migraine pressure. Not that I had to beg too much. He'd been all too willing to oblige, much like the handful of others I've been with since him.

I shift my knees closer, wrapping my arms around them. "I'd say it's a fairly even trade. I use them for the temporary reprieve. They use me to avoid long-term commitment."

He frowns. "You're not something to be used. Don't you want more than that?"

"Of course I do. But no one wants Bren's broken throwaway—not when there are plenty of girls who are younger. More malleable." My tone drops to a whisper. "More fertile."

One of the glowing insects lands on my kneecap. It shifts around for a few seconds, pivoting in a circle before realizing I have no sweet nectar to offer it, and flies off. Gone as quickly as it came. Just like all the men who've landed atop me.

I spot Gabe's pitying look and nudge my leg into his. "Hey, at least I'm getting laid. That's more than *you* can say."

"Fair enough." He nudges me back, but his leg lingers against mine.

Once, a giddy warmth might've traced up my thigh at the small touch. The nerves beneath my leathers might've prickled in heightened awareness. Now, all I feel is the cool sting of broken promises.

I feel his gaze drift to my lips, yet I tell myself to ignore it. Ignore him. Put some distance between us. But my traitorous body does no such thing as my eyes find his.

He swallows roughly.

"Elle." His tone is like a deep caress, stroking old memories back to life as he lifts his hand and hovers it above my leg.

I freeze, waiting for the contact of his fingers and gasping when they press into my leather-clad thigh. I wrap my hand around his, unsure if I want to stop this from going any further, or guide us both over that edge.

Eyes closing, I whisper his name. "Gabe."

He groans, but his fingers still, waiting for me to make the call.

I squeeze his hand, savoring this once-familiar touch for one last second.

"I can't." My head and voice lower, though I know I've made the right call.

Gabe isn't like the others. Being with him in *that* way will never be a balanced, casual exchange. If I let myself go down this path, I'd want more, and he can't give it to me. Not while he's still married. Maybe not even if he became single again. Because we can't erase what's been done. If we gave it another try, I don't know if I could trust it. Trust *him*. Or if I'd always be waiting to be abandoned again for his warped sense of duty.

Shadows flicker in Gabe's midnight irises, but he hides it quickly with a soft, non-dimpled smile as he pulls back. "I understand."

A shiver rocks through me, and he shrugs off his vest.

"Here." He drapes it around my shoulders before putting some extra space between our bodies.

Smiling shyly, I scoot closer.

"You're allowed to touch me. Not like *that*," I rush to add, "but in a more platonic way. We were friends longer than we were more.

Maybe we could go back to that?"

Long before our first kiss, we'd spent most of our childhood together, thanks to the close friendship between our parents. After the divorce, I'd grieved our emotional connection just as much as our physical one.

Gabe groans again, though there's much less gravel in it this time. "Are you putting me back in the friend zone, Elle?"

I jab a finger into his bicep. "You should consider yourself lucky to even be there at all."

He winces, feigning hurt before grinning with both dimples. "You're right. After all this time, I guess I'll take what I can get. Oh! That reminds me." He pulls open his vest, retrieving something from the satin inner pocket. "I believe this belongs to you."

In his palm lies a miniature bronze sand clock with deep plum grains.

"You got it back!" I say, fetching the heirloom from his hand and rubbing my thumb along the inscription.

Gabe nods. "My father left it on the shelf in his office. I wanted to give it to you sooner, but figured it was best to wait until we were away from the cameras."

"Thank you."

"Any time," he replies, then cocks his head. "I am curious to hear the story of how you dropped it, though. You tried to run away?"

CHAPTER NINETEEN

Falling asleep was easier than I'd thought.

Nocturnal sleep cycles are a byproduct of living in Caligo. It began as a superstition that too much movement during daylight hours would lead the Sols right to us. Over time, it morphed into an ideological rebellion against the sun itself and what it represents.

Despite my near-constant fatigue, I often spend far too many daylight hours awake, and I'd feared trying to swap my sleeping cycle would trigger another insomnia episode. Instead, I was out within minutes of my cheek pressing against Gabe's shoulder.

Staying asleep, however, is a different issue.

Gabe is fully out, not even stirring as I startle upright and wriggle away from his side, unsure if minutes or hours have passed. The star-riddled sky above does little to help. It could be midnight or four in the morning. Not a trace of yesterday's storm remains as I blink up at the inky aerial landscape. Constellations blur into shapes and faces the longer I stare, my mind running rampant with how yesterday's highlight reel must've been received back in Caligo.

Chancellor Bren is likely in an uproar over his son's deception.

I imagine he's ordered the production team to delete as much of the footage as possible, but surely they can't erase him entirely from all ten of our cameras.

And Gabe's wife . . . How is she handling the news of her husband's abrupt departure? If Gabe's to be believed—and I think he is—perhaps she's relieved to not keep up the act of being Caligo's favorite couple. Or maybe she's annoyed by the uproar his actions have caused.

I can hear the gossip now . . .

"Did you hear that the chancellor's son is risking his life and his marriage to participate in the Hunt with his throwaway?"

"I know! His poor wife."

"His poor children!"

"I can't fathom why Gabe Bren would give up everything for a Tier Three rat, of all people! Do you think they've been having an affair?"

It's exactly what his father had wanted to avoid—hearing dozens of folks uttering both our names in the same breath. Even if Gabe survives the Hunt, his public persona might not.

The man I thought I knew wouldn't have risked it. Maybe the shock of me being drafted would've upset him, but he'd ultimately choose his duty to his constituents over any echoes of feelings he has for me. The Gabe I knew lived by the motto: Caligo first, above all. Has that truly changed? Or will a delayed sharp regret hit him as soon as he wakes? Now that I've dismissed his advances, will he remember I'm not worth the risk?

The pads of my thumbs rub at my closed lids like I can erase all the painful questions, accusing whispers, and disappointed faces from my mind if I press hard enough. When that doesn't work, I stand, surrendering any lingering hope of blissful unconsciousness reclaiming me.

There's no other movement in the meadow to suggest any of

the others have woken yet as I leave Gabe and carefully pad over to the opposite tree line ahead, scanning the moonlit ground to avoid snapping loose twigs. I round the thick trunk of what I think is some sort of pine tree, using its privacy to relieve myself.

With only the chirping insects as company, I slowly trot towards the creek, intent on washing off and rehydrating before the day ahead. The stream's current sweeps gently across the rocks as if it, too, is groggily waking from slumber. After a few drinks, I succumb to its lure, easing the entire lower half of my body beneath its surface. It's deeper than I thought, forcing me to stand on tiptoes to keep my chin above water. Latching onto a boulder protruding from the shore as an anchor, I dip my head into the stream. There's a warmth near the surface that contrasts with the chill at my toes. The sensory juxtaposition relieves some of the mounting pressure on the right side of my skull. Not entirely, but enough to ease the stiff tension from my neck and shoulders.

A shadow glides past overhead when I resurface. A small bird, from the looks of it. Thoughts returning to Demi's tale of her aunt's survival, I wonder whether this could be one of the creatures that offered Jacqueline guidance when she needed it most.

I wipe away the droplets coating my lashes and haul myself back onto the creek's shore. Once the laces of my boots are double knotted, I set out in the direction of the sweeping shadow, not stopping until the dense thicket becomes sparser and something round catches me underfoot, rolling my ankle.

"Burning pits," I curse, trance broken as I balance on my good foot.

I bend over to inspect the culprit and find a misshapen peach, along with dozens more scattered along the grass. A peach tree looms overhead, its branches weighed down by the fuzzy reddish-yellow fruit. Did the bird lead me here, as if it sensed the growing hunger I'd yet to acknowledge, or is my happening upon this tree a lucky coincidence?

If luck exists, I'm certain I'd be its primary allergen, so I doubt that's it. But the bird I'd spotted—if it was, in fact, a bird at all—wasn't lit by golden light like those from Demi's story.

My stomach groans as if to say, "*Who cares?*" It doesn't matter what brought me here. Food is food. I'd be a fool to not to get my fill while I still can.

I pluck a peach for myself, pleased to feel its skin slightly soft to the touch. I lift it to my lips, yearning to see if its flavor matches its indulgently sweet fragrance. My teeth sink into the fruit's supple skin. Its juices swim along my tongue and down my throat, awakening my taste buds with pure euphoria. It's criminal that I'd ever considered any of the peaches from Caligo edible before now. I devour it faster than I should, making a sticky mess of my face and hands. I tug on the branch, grabbing as many peaches as my hands can hold, which turns out to be four. If only I'd thought to bring my knapsack along.

I pivot, intending to head back towards our temporary camp, then pause as a streak of near-white yellow along the distant horizon catches my eye.

Blue hour is upon us. Not only that, but it's nearly dawn. I'd been so enraptured by my pursuit of the bird's shadow and my subsequent hunger that I hadn't noticed the incremental brightening of the sky.

I really should head back.

But my feet have other plans.

They carry me past the peach tree and up a grassy incline with impressive speed. And when I trip halfway up the hill, I drop the peaches before scrambling back to standing, jogging faster in obedience with the irrational urgency. It isn't like the dreamlike trance from minutes prior. Every part of me is fully alert and aching to fill this acute, intrusive hunger—one that cannot be satisfied by the consumption of food, any more than a stomach is satisfied by sight alone.

Whatever it takes.

My parents asked me to find a way to survive, and this is it: my chance to no longer be a burden.

I continue to climb. The tree line gives way to a grassy ridge, sparsely populated with boulders and a few bushes bathed in a violet hue not unlike in the halls of Caligo. There's little else between me and the calamitous horizon.

"Orelle?" A masculine voice calls my name in harmony with the wind as I crest the hilltop.

Pinpricks of heat spread across my neck, down my spine. I slow to a halt, yet make no move to turn around to confirm what I already know.

Kalden has found me.

But I don't want to be found. Not now, when I'm minutes away from experiencing the one thing I should fear more than the Sols—the one thing that's plagued countless nightmares, and maybe a few dreams.

"Orelle," Kalden says again, striding up the hill to stand at my side, his smoky bergamot scent washing over me.

"What?" I snap, eyes refusing to move from the view in front of me. I don't want to miss a single detail or second.

In my peripheral vision, I sense his searing gaze switching between me and the skyline. I catch the curt nod of his chin, like he's decided on an unspoken question.

I expect his fingers to take hold of my arms and drag me to the shady cover of the forest at our backs. Or all the way back to camp, to where I left my helmet. Surely, he won't stand idly by and let me expose far more of myself to the impending daylight than what we discussed during training.

And yet, he says nothing. Does nothing.

I hold still, in case any movement will break whatever it is that's convincing him to not interfere in what's about to become my greatest act of treason. His treason, too, since his helmet is notably absent.

Deep indigo brightens to a more vibrant hue as a beacon of golden light ascends over the inky landscape. Rich oranges and yellows bleed from a near-white orb in the center, spotlighting the sky and stealing my breath.

"Is that . . . ?"

"It is," Kalden confirms.

The orb grows brighter and brighter. Inviting me forward. Painting the sky in colors far richer than those found in the murky underground of Caligo.

I take a few shaky steps, reaching out a gloved hand like I can scoop up this view—this devastatingly beautiful and unquestionably egregious view—and pocket it alongside my most cherished memories.

The light becomes overwhelming, violating my senses. My eyes shut of their own accord, unable to handle its purity. Golden orbs dance behind closed lids, and there's an audible shift in nature's ballad—birdsongs and gargled calls from unnamed creatures. A rush of heat licks my exposed skin like a sinful kiss trailing across my forehead, cheeks, and lips. My treacherous pores devour it.

Bit by bit, I open my eyes.

Head bent, I catch sight of a lock of my hair. The dull tawny shade is now a bright bronze. Tiny beads of moisture, leftover from bathing in the creek, glisten throughout my curls. I wrap a strand around my pointer finger, marveling at the glossy reflections.

When I draw my gaze up, my knees tremble. Gone is the expansive dull landscape. Along the horizon, fiery sand dunes and the glittering teal depths of the ocean in the distance embrace a brilliant blue sky. The narrow leaves on the scattered trees I'd once known to be a near-black shade of green are now a vivid olive.

Nothing is untouched by the sun's generosity, by its magic. It bathes the earth in life.

My refusal to blink brings tears cascading down my face. A deep ache takes root in my chest, realizing I've been robbed of this. All this time, I'd thought the world to be a hazy palette of muted tones. In reality, the saturated vibrancy had simply been dormant, waiting to be awoken.

I set my sights directly on the source of it all—and flinch.

Warm, gloved fingers wipe away the wetness on my cheeks before gripping beneath my chin, twisting it to the side.

"First lesson about the sun: don't look directly at it."

Floating white spots glimmer across my vision, along with flashes of a green-tinted inverse image of the landscape. I blink, and the optical illusions fade enough for me to really see Kalden.

Streaks of gold shimmer along the veins of his face, framing his cheeks, trailing into his lustrous curls and down his neck. My hand lifts, fingertips longing to trace the sparkling patterns. But I halt when my eyes meet his.

Molten irises shine like twin suns. The effect amplifies his already intimidating, mesmerizing presence into something entirely otherworldly. My pulse trips over itself as I openly ogle his face, yet I can't bring myself to turn away from this beaming, unrestrained version of him. His gaze is a scalding, tangible touch, burning through me directly to the core of my being, and I have never felt so laid bare while fully clothed.

His smile grows crooked. "You're staring."

There's no use in denying it, so I shrug and share a sheepish smirk in return. "You . . . Your face is . . ."

The foundation of our beliefs rests on the irrefutable fact that the sun is the source of all our problems, that Sols are a result of direct exposure to its vile, corrupting light. Caligo wouldn't exist—wouldn't be needed—if humans hadn't been driven to seek shelter from the sun and its murderous abominations. Yet in this moment, I struggle to align those beliefs with what's in front of me. There's nothing vile about the radiant landscape. No corruption to be found in Kalden's disarming eyes.

"Yours, too," he says simply, brushing a thumb up across my jawline before releasing his grip.

My hands fly to my cheeks, as if I can feel the warm markings of my exposure. And I can, but not through my gloved fingers. Energy floods my veins, chasing away the lingering chill on my neck from my damp hair. A part of me acknowledges that the heady tingle racing beneath my skin should be a cause for concern, but it feels so damn good. *I* feel good. Powerful, even. Perhaps a little reckless, too, because I make no move to retreat to the shade, unwilling to part with the intoxicating sunrise.

"You've truly never seen it before, have you?" Kalden asks, what could be seconds or minutes later.

"Never." I shake my head. "And you have?"

He nods, lips quirking up the smallest fraction.

"Is it always this bright?" I squint, immediately forgetting his advice to not look directly at it.

Kalden chuckles, and the sound of it is so unexpected, it draws my attention back to him.

For the first time since we met in the tunnel, he looks . . . lighter. The near-permanent crease between his stern brows has softened. His shoulders are rolled back. Even the shadows beneath his eyes seem to disappear.

He takes a long and slow inhale, like he's savoring the charged morning air. "The sun shines brighter for those who've seen the night."

"Huh," I say, considering the poetic words that don't align with what I know of this stoic, pedantic man. "I'm not sure whether to take that literally or metaphorically."

"I'd say it's more of an allegory," Kalden corrects with a teasing smile, transforming his usually hard features into something dangerously alluring and quickening my already restless pulse. "The sun has a way of revealing things that the shadows would prefer to hide. Like you."

He takes a step closer.

"What about me?" I ask, voice a mere whisper.

"You've seen more darkness than most. Its shadows clung to you, convinced you the only safety you'd find was within their grasp," he observes, and I think of how certain I was that leaving the shelter of Caligo would lead to my imminent death. If I were relying on the shadows alone to get me through this, perhaps that would prove true. The only reason I stand a chance is thanks to the very thing I've been taught to fear, to hate.

I turn my face towards the gold-drenched landscape below, feeling neither of those emotions within me as Kalden continues, "Right now, the sunlight illuminates more than just your skin and vision. It exposes your character. Your adaptability. Your willingness to keep an open mind and be proven wrong."

Trying not to squirm beneath the fervor of his attention, I lift my chin, stealing some of the sunlight's brazenness.

"You know, I'm not the only one exposed here." Kalden's smile falls, but he allows me to go on. "I hear the way you talk about the sun. See the way you look at it. Like it's your anchor. Like you'd sooner worship its light than stand in reverence to the shadows."

He lifts a brow. "Does that frighten you?"

"It should. If I didn't know any better, I'd say you sound like a Sol, if Sols could actually talk."

"But?"

"But you don't look like a monster," I say, echoing words he once said to me. "You don't look fully human right now, but I'm not frightened by you. Should I be?"

Yes, answers a distant voice in my brain.

If I were thinking rationally, I should walk away from this strange man's too-keen eyes and his measured words with hidden meanings. If I were thinking rationally, I shouldn't have run up this hill to begin with.

Unfortunately, rationality left me the moment I spotted the streak of dawn on the horizon, which is why I hold my ground while he leans in closer to ask, "The better question is: should I fear *you*?"

I blink. "Why would you fear me?"

"Because you're . . ." He pauses, pupils dilating as they search my own for the right words. " . . . an unexpected distraction."

The way he grimaces as he says distraction makes it seem like it's one of the worst possible things I could be. To him, maybe it is. What was it he said to me at the selection ceremony?

"Soldiers can't afford to feel. We are one distraction away from death."

Something flutters in my stomach as I process the implication. "If I'm a distraction, does that mean you feel things for me?"

I regret the words as soon as they're out. They're too bold, too vulnerable.

And yet, Kalden answers anyway. "Unfortunately, yes."

Before I can ask for clarification on why that's unfortunate, he lifts a hand to brush a few rogue curls from my face, tucking them behind my ear. Silencing my mind. Stilling my breaths and body.

"You make me feel . . . too many things." His fingertips trail a line from my ear to my chin

"Like what?" I dare to ask.

"Frustration," he breathes while tugging on my bottom lip, and I gasp at the hungry flames erupting beneath his touch.

"Curiosity." His thumb travels back and forth across my lip, the twin suns of his irises flashing brighter as he toys with me.

His thumb presses harder. "Desire."

Lifting onto my tiptoes, I lower my gaze to his full, crooked mouth in a silent plea.

He pulls his hand away, and I fear the moment is over before it's truly begun.

But then he wraps his fingers into my hair, gently tugging my head back while lowering his face to mine. His lips are tender as they press tentatively into my own, testing me.

Stoking the flames, I pull him closer, my hands roving along the bare skin of his neck. Like mine, it's pebbled. The knowledge that my kiss elicits the same response in him as his does in me emboldens me to press further into him.

A guttural vibration emanates from his throat, nearly stopping my heart from beating. Yet Kalden still restrains himself, and I've had enough. I nip at his lower lip, pulling his mouth further open, commanding him without having to say a word. And he obeys.

There's nothing tender about the way he claims my mouth, then the sensitive area at the base of my neck. Nothing cautious about the way I groan into his ear, or the way his fingers dig into my hips as I hook my legs around his waist. The energy beneath my skin rises and rises until it erupts, enveloping us both in an invisible inferno. I pull away, making sure I'm not actually causing him harm, but he tugs me back to reclaim my mouth. The contact of his lips against mine ignites another hot, pulsing wave that consumes my senses. And it's like I can feel his innermost essence exploring my own.

Kissing Kalden is like being devoured by the sun itself, and delighting in every second of it, while needing more. More heat.

More skin. More everything.

I pull back to glare at his leather bodysuit, wishing there was a better way to rip it off him without ruining his only attire. I suppose we could make do with loosening the buttons securing the thin removable strip of leather between our legs, but that's hardly ideal.

"You really are a distraction," Kalden says, noting where my focus has drifted. He chuckles into my lips before sliding me back down to my feet. "As much as I'm intrigued by the direction of your thoughts, we should retrieve our helmets before the others wake, if they haven't already."

It takes several seconds for the lust-induced ringing in my ears to settle down enough for me to comprehend Kalden's words.

"Oh," I say, inwardly flinching at the disappointment in my tone. I release my clenched fingers from around his neck and clear my throat. "Good point. Gem will probably freak if I'm not there when she wakes up."

Gabe, too, though I don't mention his name aloud.

Come to think of it, this is the first I've thought of my ex-husband since . . . Well, since I left him behind an hour or so ago. But now that I have, the last embers of lust extinguish as I consider how Gabe might feel if he discovers I threw myself at another man less than twelve hours after denying him and spending the night sleeping beneath his arm.

I remind myself that I don't owe Gabe anything. I made that boundary abundantly clear. Friends only—that's all I can give him.

But maybe there's a chance I could be more with Kalden. The physical tension is certainly there. And he has this way of stripping my façade bare, seeing straight into the core of my flaws and hopes. If only he'd allow me to do the same.

Kalden peers over my shoulder, getting one last look at the unobstructed sunrise.

"You know, I forgot to ask earlier about when you'd gotten a chance to see the sun before." I comb my fingers through my mussed hair, attempting to tame it. "Was it when you were a guard back in Scuros?"

The hint of a smile fades from Kalden's lips, and a haunted coldness flickers behind his blazing irises.

Shoulders slumping forward, I wish I could take back the question. I should've known this is a sensitive topic for him, especially if I'm right in my assumption that those scars along his torso and back are from his time in service.

"I'm sorry." I dip my flushed face. "I shouldn't have brought it up."

Kalden shakes his head, then sighs. "I wasn't—"

Screams interrupt whatever he's about to say.

CHAPTER TWENTY

"Shadows' mercy," I breathe, following Kalden, who's already a blur at the base of the hill.

I place the wired rings attached to my cuffs around both middle fingers and clench, releasing the folded nightstone blades. Before I dart beneath the forest's canopy, I slice through my leather gloves at an angle to avoid nicking my skin, just as Kalden instructed. Leaning forward, I sprint into the trees as the buzz of energy awakens in my palms.

Unlike Gem and Gabe, Kalden doesn't bother with reducing his speed to match mine. I'm unsure whether it's because my safety isn't a priority for him, or because he trusts I'm capable of defending myself, thanks to his lessons. I tell myself it's the latter as he disappears from view.

I find I don't need to see Kalden to know which path to take. There's a magnetic pull on my senses, guiding me forward. I suppose I should question it, but I don't. There's no time for doubts.

More shouts come from up ahead, louder now that I'm getting closer. It isn't until I pass my earlier bathing spot that I remember I left my helmet at our campsite.

Maybe they won't notice.

The logical side of my brain scoffs at my naïveté. I'm basically a human lantern. They're going to notice. And the cameras will, too. Which means I'll never get to return home, even if I survive the Hunt.

When I breach the meadow's edge, something round and black launches towards me. I flinch, deflecting it with my arms. The object whacks against my forearms before falling to the ground. I jump away from it.

Kalden, who's running towards me, shouts, "Put it on!"

On second look, I realize it's my helmet. As I dart out of the camera's range, Kalden fastens his own headgear, the tiny suns of his irises fully concealed by the deep tint of the polarized lens.

"The cameras are off," he explains, tapping above his brow bone. "I disabled them with a targeted solar flare, along with the sensor."

I hadn't considered that was possible.

"Thanks," I say a few seconds too late as Kalden abandons me once again, sprinting back through the trees.

"Orelle?" Gem calls from nearby. "Orelle!"

The swelling within my chest strains when Gem appears on the opposite side of the clearing, her nightstone poniard at the ready. I finish tugging on my helmet as quickly as I can, praying to the shadows that she was too far away to see the evidence of my treason.

Gem's sprint falters for a split second, and the knot above my heart grows, but I don't let it stop me from running towards her and wrapping her in a hug. I keep it short, giving her shoulders a squeeze and pulling back almost immediately.

"Thank the darkness you're okay!"

"Where were you?!" Gem speaks over me. Her helmet blocks her features, but I imagine concern pinches between her brows.

The tangy odor of blood and gore assaults my senses. Forgetting

Gem's question, my attention drops to the rumpled grass, where three bodies lay, unmoving.

The first is sprawled on her side, hand stretching for the rapier just out of reach. Coppery red hair juts out from the bottom of her helmet, identifying the fallen soldier as Faron.

A second woman lies beside her, face down in her knapsack, like she hadn't yet woken when the Sols attacked. Blair, judging by the mid-length blonde strands coated in crimson.

I startle when the third woman's fingers twitch. Her helmet isn't fully secured to her suit, revealing a sliver of ashen skin that pulses with the faintest golden light. Lowering to my knees, I cradle her head while pulling off the headgear to reveal glossy gray eyes.

"Meridna?" My voice cracks as I wrap her hand in my own and use the other to tuck her loose silver-and-brown locks behind her ear. Blood spills far too quickly from the six gaping wounds in her chest, and I wish I could do more than offer comfort.

Though her forehead contorts in pain, Meridna's pale lips pull into a smile.

"My Georgie," she whispers hoarsely.

"Meridna, it's me. O—"

"I've missed you so much, Georgie." Meridna blinks slowly, smile spreading, and I know it isn't me she's seeing, but her son—the one who died a little over three years ago.

"I've missed you too," I say as a tear slips through the ventilation slit of my helmet, spilling onto her cheek.

"Don't cry, my love." She gives my fingers the gentlest squeeze. "I'll never leave you ever again. Our forever . . . starts . . ."

The last of the golden glow drains from Meridna's pallid skin.

Gem begins to mutter the prayer of departure. "Shadows guide your spirit. May you find peace in the eternal night in the name of our holy darkness." She cups a hand in front of her helmet, symbolically shrouding her vision, and lowers it to Meridna's unseeing eyes in a final farewell.

Once Gem finishes, we linger for another silent minute.

I stare at the pool of crimson surrounding Meridna's body and leathers, recalling Jacqueline's method of survival. But how can I desecrate the last of her lifeblood? Take advantage of her death to prevent my own? I can't.

A fresh wave of cries cut through the morning breeze, and I leap to my feet.

"What are you doing?" Gem calls from behind as I take off towards the commotion.

"I need to make sure it isn't Gabe," I say over my shoulder, trusting that she'll catch up.

Seconds later, she does. "He's got those nightstone missiles, remember? I'm sure he'll be fine."

"Why hasn't he used one yet?" I ask while dodging spindly branches, chancing a glance at the cloudless blue sky above. Selfishly, I'm glad to see it hasn't been marred by the false night of Gabe's carbon nightoxide, but I can't help but wonder why he didn't use it against the Sols. "Were there too many to attack at once?"

"I don't know," Gem admits. "He woke me up maybe a half hour ago, all freaked out, saying you were missing. Kalden was gone, too. I figured you were together, but didn't know for sure, so we split up to search for you."

"Oh," is all I say as we continue weaving through the thicket, still following that inexplicable magnetic tug, as if the sun's energy coursing through my veins senses its likeness nearby.

Gem huffs a dry laugh. "That's it? No 'I'm sorry for scaring you shitless, and I promise not to do it again'? What were you thinking, Orelle?

Wandering off right before dawn without telling anyone? Without telling *me*?"

"I'm sorry for not saying anything. It was still pitch black when I woke, and I wanted to let you sleep."

"I don't give a shadow's fuck about sleep," Gem snaps. "You left your helmet behind, and I had no clue if I'd find you in time. I could've lost you."

"The Sols weren't near—"

"That's not what I meant." She lowers her voice, as if that'll prevent her built-in camera from picking up her next words. "You and I both know there are worse fates than death."

Like becoming the very creature we're meant to hunt. A creature who wouldn't hesitate to feed on people it might've once cared for, too ravenous to discriminate friend from foe.

An unwelcome image of Gem in Meridna's place materializes—except instead of me grasping her hand as she takes her final breaths, I drink from her bleeding heart until I've drained every drop of her life essence.

I stumble over a thick root, bile coating my tongue as I blink, evicting the image from my mind. Gem slows her pace, waiting for me, despite her frustration.

"That won't happen," I vow.

She folds her arms tightly across her chest. Though I can't see it, I feel her narrowed gaze slicing through her helmet, like she can sense the golden light flooding my irises and veins beneath mine. The polarized lens completely extinguished Kalden's illuminated features from view, but what if the tint on my headgear isn't dark enough?

Maybe I could tell her the truth . . .

I imagine how that conversation might go.

"I was exposed for a few minutes, but don't freak out. Minimal

exposure won't turn me into a Sol."

"*What?!*" Her eyes would go wide. "*How do you know that?*"

"*Because Kalden told me it wouldn't.*"

Except telling her that would break my pulse promise with Kalden.

"*Because I've been exposed before and turned out fine.*"

Except she and Taurance didn't believe my recounting of what happened in the transport tunnel after the earthquake.

I heave a sigh. No matter how I approach it, Gem is unlikely to respond well to the truth. Though she deserves to know, and there might come a time where there's no avoiding it, now isn't the right time. Not with her camera still recording and the magnetic energy in my chest tightening.

So, for now, I leave it at, "I promise I'll be fine."

Gem tenses like she wants to press further, but an ear-scraping screech stirs us back into motion.

We find the Sol less than a minute later.

Sols, my mind corrects. Unlike yesterday's stray, this one isn't alone.

Three of the unclothed charred-skin creatures close in on two of our fellow Huntresses, herding them towards the open dunes, away from the shaded shelter of the trees. The pair sprints along the forest's edge hand in hand, toeing the line between the foliage and sand. A streak of black zips atop a distant sandy crest, and I could swear I spot something that looks a lot like the motorized cart that transported us yesterday morning, but it disappears before I can confirm the hunch.

Another figure comes at the Sols from the side. It moves so fast that on first glance, I assume it's a fourth Sol. Then I see the two nightstone throwing knives clenched in his fists.

Kalden.

Though he's several yards ahead, I recognize his chosen weapons, and the tug in my chest strengthens. I quicken my cadence to keep up, Gem matching my stride with ease.

Kalden lifts his left arm, hurling a knife into the air. The nearest Sol dodges the blade while it zips past inches from its skull.

A strong gust blasts through the scattered trees, ripping dozens of leaves from their branches while redirecting the knife in what should be an impossible curve back toward the Sol. The blade strikes true this time, burrowing into the creature's singed neck.

Golden blood spurts from the wound. The Sol falls.

Kalden lunges atop it and restrains its flailing arms before removing the knife, only to drag the blade in a deep line across the entire front half of its throat. Then, with a grunt, he plunges the weapon into the Sol's chest, down to the hilt.

"Holy shadows!" Gem curses between panted breaths as we chase the other two Sols, who continue their pursuit of our comrades without faltering, either not noticing or not caring that their kin has fallen.

Kalden's brutal killing cost him distance. And although he outpaces Gem and me, he isn't fast enough to block the furthest Sol from catching up to the first Huntress.

"Dodge!" I scream as the creature's taloned fingertips lash out toward her shoulder. It's the same command Kalden shouted during the countless drills he made the group run through.

Thankfully, the muscle memory pays off. She bends at the waist and shuffles to the side, exactly as practiced. The Sol trips, not expecting her swift evasion, but recovers quickly. In a blur, it twists, preparing to strike again.

The woman rolls forward, and its clawed nails sink into the dirt instead. Before it can finish pivoting, her friend swipes her dagger into its side. The creature hisses and shoots out a hand, clenching the second Huntress's wrist. It twists its grip, snapping bone like it's little more than a pliable twig.

She bellows deep—a sound that will haunt me forever.

If he weren't distracted by his own face-off with the other Sol, maybe Kalden could prevent what happens next.

The creature pins the woman to the ground.

"Orelle, don't!" Gem cries as I run faster, only a handful of feet away now.

But I'm no Kalden. My vision falters, tunnels. I stumble.

Beneath the Sol, my fallen comrade's roar turns gargled as I throw my hands forward, harnessing the vibrating energy in my palms. I wrap my fingers around the creature's sinewy leg. The tips of my nightstone blades cut into its flesh. It howls, flinching away, but I refuse to loosen my grip. I clench harder and finally release the burgeoning energy.

Invisible flames erupt beneath my skin, licking through my veins and into my palms, burning me from the inside out, forging my body into something new: a weapon. Someone screams Yvonne's name, yet my focus is on the excruciating ecstasy that's more pleasure than pain. And when I release all the scorching heat into the monstrous creature, I nearly whimper in relief.

A tremor ravages through the Sol's charred body. Its arms and knees buckle, and it collapses face first into its pinned prey.

"Yvonne!" someone shouts again.

The Sol's body falls still for only a moment before it sluggishly lifts its head and peers deeply into the lens of Yvonne's unmoving helmet.

With blood streaming down the blades of my cuff, which is still embedded in the charred leg, I gather the energy into my palm again. I need more power than before. I flip my left hand over and expose the slit in my glove to the sky, absorbing every bit of buzzing heat I can muster into my right hand. I feel the tingling warmth draining from the tips of the fingers on my left hand, then my toes, pulsing with every heartbeat down through my right arm until an unfamiliar pressure builds at my fingertips. The heat culminates in my palm, bringing with it subtle vibrations like bolts of lightning racing down my wrist.

This has to be enough.

"Don't!" Kalden shouts, though his words soften as they bounce across the sand.

Before I can release the focused energy, the Sol rears its impaled leg back, dragging me several inches closer to itself before snapping its gnarled foot back into my poised jaw.

My blades unlatch from the Sol's leg as I slide against the sandy dirt until the back of my helmet collides against an unforgiving boulder, splattering starry flecks across my vision. The solar flare must've dazed the creature—otherwise, that kick likely wouldn't have ended with me conscious. Or breathing. I concentrate on realigning the hazy image of the Sol while I scramble to regain my footing, reform the energy, and reach Yvonne before it's too late.

As I attempt to climb onto my knees, a pointed blade embeds into the Sol's neck. The creature collapses again on top of Yvonne, this time with finality. Its furled fingers twitch for a few more seconds before going still.

It takes several seconds to reel the surging power back in.

Gem slides her poniard out of the creature. Shimmering gold droplets spill off the blade onto the trampled ground as she rushes over to extend a hand towards me. "Are you okay?"

I ignore it, not wanting to accidentally torch her with the heat still vibrating within my palms, and slowly push myself to my feet. "I'm fi—"

"Mentally, not physically," she clarifies, whacking my shoulder. "What in the sun's fiery furnace was that? Why would you throw yourself at a Sol?"

"I had to do something," I say with a shrug.

"Demi?"

The strained whisper comes from beneath the Sol's corpse, sparing me from Gem's interrogation—for now, at least. My neck prickles from what I suspect is her bewildered glare that tells me she'll have plenty of questions for me later.

Gem and I step towards the Sol once more, both of us more timidly than when the creature was alive. As Kalden and Demi reach us, we make room for them to roll the lifeless shell off Yvonne.

A small spark rhythmically jumps from the band encompassing the Sol's neck. Another collar? A buzz ruminates from the spot where Gem's blade pierced the edge of the bloodstained metallic strap.

"Demi?" Yvonne calls again, voice fainter and crackling now.

My attention returns to the death rattle of the next victim of the Hunt. Crimson flows steadily from the six punctures encircling her heart.

Demi crumples forward, choking on a sob. "Von?"

Yvonne huffs a weak, breathy laugh. "That bad, huh?"

Kalden kneels on Yvonne's opposite side, tugging a square cloth from his knapsack. Tone softening with a rare tenderness, he asks, "May I?"

Yvonne's helmet tilts down a fraction of an inch. Taking that as a nod, Kalden leans forward to cover Yvonne's gushing wounds, then pushes his palm into her chest.

Yvonne winces, and Demi snaps, "What are you doing?"

"Applying pressure to compress the surrounding blood vessels and staunch the bleeding," Kalden states matter-of-factly, like he's done this before. He probably has, if his scars are any indication.

The magnetic tug on my senses heightens. A hazy golden aura pulses above Kalden's gloved fingers, then disappears as soon as I blink.

What was *that*?

I step forward, waiting for Yvonne to flinch away from the flash of hot magic, but the sigh that escapes her is more akin to relief than agony. My eyes dart over to Demi and Gem, yet neither reacts. Was I the only one who saw that?

A minute passes. Then two.

Yvonne's lungs rise and fall more steadily now, and her voice is clearer as she asks, "So, are we just gonna wait around for another attack, or . . . ?"

Kalden releases the pressure, allowing Yvonne to scoot herself onto her elbows.

"Don't!" Demi tries to shove her back to the ground, but Yvonne shoos her off.

"Stop fussing." She crunches forward into a sitting position and groans in disgust while glancing down at herself. Leftover gore from the Sol's severed artery mixes with her own sticky blood coating most of her chest and midsection. Using the soiled cloth, Yvonne takes care to swipe gently across the torn leather and flesh.

Demi goes still. We all do.

Well, except Kalden, whose back is to us as he rubs his knife against the patchy grass.

"Stop staring at me like that," Yvonne grumbles, poking Demi's shoulder to snap her out of the shock-induced haze.

"How do you know I'm staring?"

Yvonne scoffs. "Because you're standing there like you've seen a reanimated corpse or somethin'. Still got a pulse, if you wanna check, and I don't think anything's broken."

She taps a hand against her heart. Now that most of the blood's been cleared, the six wounds surrounding the vital organ are more visible. Unlike the gaping holes in her leather, the puncture marks themselves are barely larger than pinpricks.

Demi grabs her friend's wrist for a gentle inspection. "But I heard the snap."

Yvonne rotates her hand in a circle and wiggles her gloved fingers. "It's fine. See?"

"How are you . . ." Gem starts to ask, then stops.

"Not dead?" Yvonne supplies, then lifts her shoulders. "Dunno."

"Perhaps the wounds were more surface-level than feared," Kalden suggests while rejoining our group.

My gaze narrows. The others might've missed his little display of magic, but I didn't. He did something. Healed her, somehow.

I get why he'd be dodgy about it with them, writing off their concerns like overreactions. But why keep it from me? If I'd known I could use this borrowed energy to heal, maybe Meridna would still be alive. Sure, our private lessons were abysmally short, but Kalden could've at least mentioned that we could harness the sun's power for more than just offensive attacks. A simple heads-up would've been better than nothing.

But he couldn't even be bothered to do that.

What else is he withholding?

Kalden's head swivels towards me, like he senses my growing suspicion.

I'm not alone in my skepticism.

"All that blood," Gem points out.

Yvonne rolls onto her feet, backing farther into the forest's shadows. "Look, all I know is I'm alive, and I'd like to keep it that way. So, we should probably keep it moving before death changes its mind, yeah?"

She tugs several large bandage strips from her knapsack, placing them across her ripped leathers before weaving her arm through Demi's, who nods.

"Should we head towards the meadow?" I suggest. "To check for the others?"

"They weren't there a few minutes ago," Gem reasons, "and I doubt they'd come back to the spot they were attacked. I wouldn't."

It makes sense, but I shake my head anyway. "We can't leave without them."

"They're already gone," Yvonne says, then rushes to add, "On the run, I mean. Not *gone* gone. Hopefully."

Sensing my discomfort, Gem softens her tone. "Gabe's fine. You saw him yesterday. He can handle himself—probably better than we can, since he's got those nightstone missiles."

"What about Twilynn though? And Aruna?" Though I agree with Gem's assessment of Gabe, I'm less confident about the odds for our two youngest comrades.

"Maybe they're all together?" she supplies, fidgeting with the hilt of her sheathed poniard. "But we can't wait around here, hoping they'll find their way back to us."

My pitch heightens. "So, we're just going to abandon them, then?"

"That's not what—"

"What if it was me you were leaving behind?"

It's an unfair question. If I were in Gabe's shoes right now, and he was here, I'd want them to continue without me. But I know Gem wouldn't do that. She knows it, too, judging from her silence.

Yvonne waves an arm out in front of herself. "Even if we wanted to find them, how would we do that? Unless Bren shoots off one of those big black beacons, how are we supposed to know where to go?"

"They could've gone deeper into the forest," Demi supplies. "That's what Aunt Jackie did, before the glowing birds guided her home."

"Glowing birds?" Kalden asks, deigning to rejoin the conversation.

"Long story," Yvonne replies, then adds, "If Aruna was doing more than judging your aunt and actually listening to her story, I bet that's exactly where she is. Probably the others, too."

"No."

We all angle towards Kalden, whose back is now turned to us as he peers out at the white-gold dunes.

Arms crossed, I position myself in front of him. "Care to elaborate?"

It takes him a few seconds before he gestures to the open landscape to our right. "Easier to launch a missile out there than in the thick of all those trees. If the chancellor's son is smart and has any hope of accomplishing his mission, he'll hang around closer to the forest's edge."

Without waiting for our agreement, Kalden strides forward.

"We'll be too exposed if we stick around the edge," Gem counters, picking at the leather strap on her scabbard. "Remember the map? The dunes were scattered with black pins."

Of course I remember. The barren sandy hills are both the perfect stomping grounds for the Sols, who thrive in direct sunlight, and a graveyard for the Huntresses who've come before us. And a day ago, I'd likely have agreed that the better strategy would be to tread towards the forest's depths. A day ago, I thought the chances of defeating a single Sol were slim to nil.

Things have changed. Four Sols have fallen in the past twenty-four hours, thanks to Gabe's airborne nightstone, Kalden's experience, and the power dancing beneath my fingertips.

What if the Hunt's original purpose is no longer a pipe dream?

I voice as much to Gem. "I think Kalden's right. Gabe believes in the Hunt, what it stands for, and he came prepared."

"But the map—"

"Things are different this year."

"How?" Her tone grows thick. "Three people died today. Tell me how that's any different from years past."

"I know," I admit with a shaky breath, rubbing a hand along my upper arm as I replay the screams and visions of three lifeless bodies in the strewn grass. "But we also killed three Sols today, Gem. And one yesterday. For the first time, we stand an actual chance of eliminating them."

She claps twice without enthusiasm. "Spoken like a true patriot. Your ex-father-in-law would be proud."

CHAPTER TWENTY-ONE

There's an intake of breath, either from Demi or Yvonne—maybe both. These two women, who are barely more than strangers to me, know better than to bring up my complicated history with the chancellor.

Yet Gem doubles down.

"Is this to get Chancellor Bren's approval? Or Gabe's? Or maybe *his*?" She points toward Kalden's distant, retreating form. "Do you even realize how much you center your whole value around these men?"

"That's not true," I bite back, but she's not done.

"After the divorce, you blamed yourself for not being Gabe's perfect little breeding machine. And each year since, you've thrown yourself at any man willing to give you attention. Sun's pits, Orelle! Just a few days ago, you were begging for a proposal from a man almost twice your age whose kisses felt like 'mucus exchanges'—your words, not mine."

A tear breaks free, barreling down my cheek as I stiffen. "You know I was only pursuing him to avoid being eligible for the Hunt."

"Were you, though?" Gem shakes her head and steps in closer, dropping her voice. "I know that's part of it, but I think there's a bigger part of you that believes your existence won't matter until you do enough, be enough, sacrifice enough for a man. I mean, fuck! All of us are literally groomed from day one to think that, so it's not even your fault. And it won't matter how many times I tell you that your existence alone is wanted and useful to me, because I'm just another woman whose opinions matter less than those of our male counterparts."

The tears come more steadily now. I take several long, measured breaths before responding. "Your opinion means everything to me, Gem."

"It shouldn't, though. *Your* opinion of yourself should be the most important. Then, maybe mine at a close second. And T's, of course." She chuckles, trying to ease the tension. "All I'm saying is, you've already given up so much. I'd hate for you to make another sacrifice in the name of patriotism, or worse, chase after a man with an overinflated confidence in his abilities. I want you to choose yourself, to prioritize your survival over anyone else's and be truly selfish for once. But I don't think you will."

I reach for Gem's hand, and she lets me.

"I can't," I whisper. "And it's not about patriotism or chasing after Kalden or Gabe. We finally have a chance to stop this sun-damned cycle of unnecessary deaths. What if this could be the last Hunt? Or at least improve the odds for our successors. Maybe it's naïve of me to hope for that. But if I have to risk my life to potentially save dozens, or hundreds, I will."

Gem doesn't respond right away. I feel her staring at me through her helmet, and I shift my weight between my feet, nervous that she'll keep fighting me on this.

"I won't fault you if you choose differently for yourself." I turn toward Demi and Yvonne, who've graciously given Gem and me the space to work through our shit. "Same for either of you. None of us chose to be put in this mess, but we can make a choice now."

Survival, or sacrifice. Find a semblance of safety further in the forest, or toe the line between sand and grass.

Gem's rigid shoulders relax, but only slightly. "Where you go, I go."

After a whispered exchange, Demi and Yvonne both nod.

"You sure?" I ask.

Yvonne shrugs. "For now."

Demi jabs her elbow into her friend's arm, then adds, "Sticking together as a group feels smarter than going off just us two."

With that, we jog through the patchy shrubbery in the direction that Kalden went. It only takes a few minutes for us to catch up to him, and I suspect he intentionally slowed down for us. Unlike before, he keeps a restrained pace, never straying more than a couple of yards ahead of me. I catch him glancing over his shoulder every so often, but neither of us speaks. Gem catches on, but she too stays quiet.

It isn't until we take a hygiene break to relieve our bladders and retreat from the midday sun that Kalden breaks the tense silence that's festered all morning.

"Do you mind if I talk to Orelle alone for a moment?" He directs the question to Gem, who shrugs.

"That's up to her, but why? Didn't we just agree to stick together?"

Demi and Yvonne swivel their heads towards us to listen.

Kalden clears his throat. "There's something sensitive I'd like to share with her, and I'm not sure it would be appropriate for the group."

I tuck my arms against my chest. "If you make it quick."

"Keep an eye out for any black smoke, but don't follow it until we return." Kalden nods, then leads me deeper into the forest.

I'm about to question how much farther he plans on taking me when he stops and procures two peaches from his knapsack.

"Hungry?" He tugs off his helmet and extends a hand in offering.

Pointedly ignoring the way the twin suns of his irises bear into me, I set my sights on the two fuzzy fruits in his open palm. "When did you get those?"

"This morning, your kiss tasted like peaches." He rolls the corner of his bottom lip beneath his teeth, as if he can still taste me there. Warmth licks across my own lips at the memory of it. "I grabbed a couple on our way back to camp, in case you wanted more later."

The way his tone deepens makes it sound like he's talking about more than fruit.

Or maybe I'm hearing what I want to hear.

My brain chastises the stupid thumping organ in my chest.

"I don't," I snap. "Did you bring me all the way out here just to share a snack and chat about what my kiss tasted like?"

Some of the hardness returns to Kalden's features. "You haven't told the others that our solar sensors are deactivated, so I figured you wouldn't want to talk about this openly. It's time that we have everyone remove their helmets. We could cover a lot more ground, and the others would stand a better chance during the next attack."

I let the words hang in the dense forest air for a moment. "And expose them all to the thing we're taught to hate? I can't ask them to do that."

"Why? The sun isn't our enemy here. You know that as well as I do. All we'd need to do is show them proof that we can harness it while remaining unchanged."

"Are we, though? Unchanged?" I fidget with the tears in my gloves as I admit, "I don't feel the same. There's a constant tingle now in my heart and veins. A warmth. And in my chest, it's like I can sense this—"

"Magnetic pull?" Kalden finishes my thought.

"Yes," I surrender. "How do I know I'm not turning into one of *them*? A Sol? And you too?"

His cheeks attempt to hold back a smile.

"Are you amused by this, Kalden?"

Kalden regains his composure. "No, it's just that they're not . . . I've channeled significantly more power than this, and yet my humanity remains intact. So, I have no doubts that we'll be fine, but I won't ask the others to take their helmets off if you don't think it's a good idea. I trust you. I hope you know you can trust me, too."

The calm steadiness of his voice soothes my fitful pulse. Though I can't be as sure as he is, and I still have so many questions about how Kalden came to know all of this, I *do* trust him. He's proven himself thoughtful, good-intentioned, and assertive—qualities that have kept us alive longer than I thought possible in this sun-drenched expanse. I want to believe he's right, that I'm reading too much into the foreign sensations coursing through me, so I offer a single nod.

He drops his head to eye the peaches still in his hand. "Before we rejoin the others, I really was hoping we could use this privacy to have a quick bite, and to give me the chance to apologize."

"Apologize for what?" I prod, loosening my grip on my folded arms.

"For kissing you," Kalden says, like it's the obvious answer.

"Why? Do you regret it?" My words are stilted by the sudden concern that our heated moment of embrace wasn't all-consuming for him in the same way it was for me.

"No," he says, and my shoulders relax a little at the affirmation. "But you've been quiet all morning."

"So have you."

"Only because I thought I'd pushed you into something you weren't ready for."

"It was just a kiss, Kalden."

"Was it, though?"

My gaze finally lifts to his. Luminous flecks of gold flare around his pupils as he stares into mine, even through my helmet, seeing far more than I'd like him to.

"Yes," I urge.

It's a half-truth. On the surface, it *was* just a kiss. But beneath that, it was like a meeting of souls. As impossible as it sounds, I could swear I'd felt the core of his essence surging up to greet my own. Even now, I sense the pull of it, of him. Beckoning me forward. Urging me to close the distance until I'm once again wrapped in his intoxicating scent of smoky bergamot.

I press my booted heels into the patchy grass, fighting against the impulse. I can't allow myself to give in again—not while Kalden's keeping vital secrets.

"It was a perfectly normal kiss between two consenting adults, so your apology isn't needed."

Kalden lifts a brow, but doesn't counter. "Then what's bothering you?"

"Back there, when that Sol attacked Yvonne—"

"You were amazing," Kalden rushes forward to say. "You did exactly as we practiced."

Blood rushes to my cheeks, but I shake off the satisfaction of his compliment. "You healed her, didn't you?"

He stills, arms falling to his sides. "I did."

"Why?"

Creases stretch across his forehead. "Why did I heal her? She wasn't going to—"

"No, I'm glad you helped her," I cut him off to clarify. "But why didn't you tell me that was possible? You could've said something during our training sessions."

Kalden shakes his head. "There wasn't enough time. The offensive maneuver you did, the flare of solar energy, is a primal release of power. It doesn't require much thought or skill beyond intention. Healing is more complex. You're not just releasing raw energy into someone else. You have to dilute and localize it to the exact right spot. It's not a skill that can be taught in a few hours. And if you attempt it without proper training, it could make things much worse."

He rolls his thumb over the ripe fruit in his hand, then pierces its flesh.

I wince at the juice flowing from the peach's wound. "Oh."

As Kalden takes a bite, I consider his words more carefully. "How do you know so much about this? Did someone train you?"

He nods, wiping the dripping juice from his mouth with the back of his hand.

"My big brother," he says, voice a calculated monotone.

As much as I want to unravel the enigma standing across from me, I don't press it.

Instead, I hold out a palm. "I'll take that other peach now."

CHAPTER TWENTY-TWO

"I'm starting to see why some folks call the aboveground 'the sun's pits,'" Gem huffs as we climb up a steep incline that's more sand than grass, forcing all of us to slow to keep a steady footing.

"It's obscenely hot," Demi pants in agreement.

Yvonne holds up a middle finger at the sky.

Our black leathers absorb the sun like a sponge. And while I could do without the chafing film of sweat between leather and skin, I don't mind how the warm compression of the bodysuit presses firmly into my tense muscles—a minor relief that soothes rather than expunges the budding flare-up. Plus, the blisters stretching along my thighs and down the backs of my ankles give me something else to focus on beyond the increasing pressure beneath my skull that's sharpened from a dull ache to a pulsating stab.

I presume I'm alone in that gratitude as Yvonne pivots her middle finger towards the camera in Demi's helmet. "This is for whoever had the brilliant idea to clothe us in skintight full-body black leathers. Why couldn't you choose a white, breathable cotton or linen?"

"They had to protect us from sun exposure," Demi reminds her friend. "The double-lined leather is less porous than other loosely woven fabrics like cotton or linen."

Yvonne mutters under her breath. Something about stuffing loosely woven fabrics up someone's ass, I think, though it's hard to tell over the ringing in my ears harmonizing with the muted, ebbing roar of what must be the nearing ocean.

Demi pulls out a rudimentary map marked with red circles, similar to the one stuffed into my own knapsack. She eyes it studiously for a moment.

"Maybe we should head that way." She points to her left, where the cluster of trees is slightly denser than the sparser foliage along the forest's edge. "There should be a smaller nest not too far from here to the west. If we stay on the ridgeline, we should still be able to see if we pass by the others, or if any Sols are lurking out on the dunes."

Kalden pauses atop the hill's crest without commenting on Demi's suggestion.

"Hellooo?" Yvonne snaps her fingers as she finishes her ascent and strides up to Kalden. "What do ya say about heading over—Shadows' mercy!"

Hand flying to her chest, she takes a shaky step back.

Demi drops the map. "What? What's wrong? Is it your wounds?"

Yvonne shakes her head, then gestures to something in the distance. Gem and I stumble up the rest of the way to join them.

As soon as I reach Kalden's side, I see it. Several dozen yards to our right, glittering blue water spills into white-capped waves that stretch and retreat across the sand. When I'd glimpsed it earlier this morning, the ocean was little more than a far-off streak on the horizon. Now I'm close enough to hear its rolling melody. And when I breathe, I catch a whiff of the salty moisture Demi's aunt warned her not to drink.

But as impressive and endless as the ocean is, it isn't what sends me to my knees.

A mile or so down the coast, raised domed glass structures supported by stone columns jut out from the sand and continue into the tumultuous waves. A spectrum of colors tints the semi-transparent glass of the outermost domes. Fiery citrine. Sparkling peridot. Pearlescent rose. Winding elevated pathways weave throughout the structures, connecting them to one another and to the central dome that stands proudly at the heart of it all, its glimmering glass as clear as crystal.

My eyes blink rapidly, as if to test whether it's all an illusion induced by the migraine aura clouding the edges of my vision. Surely, there's no way something this resplendent could exist up here, where the only life-forms are animals and mutated former humans.

The world becomes a tumultuous, spinning thing as I spot the tiny specks of luminescent moving figures roaming in and out of the structures and across the pathways. I squint harder. "Are those Sols?"

"They can't be. Sols are selfish creatures. They travel alone or in very small numbers," Gem says, reciting what we've all been taught. "Commander Guffian said the most they've seen together is a group of five."

"And Sols lose their ability to communicate and think critically the moment the sun poisoning corrupts their minds, so they wouldn't be capable of creating all of that." Demi gestures at what seems to be a small village.

"Maybe they're humans, then?" Yvonne suggests.

Gem waves a gloved hand toward the figures in question. "But they're glowing."

Little does she know that I am, too.

Are those people down there like us—humans who have found

a way to harness small amounts of exposure to the sun without sacrificing their humanity? My head swivels towards Kalden, wishing we were alone so I could speak my thoughts aloud.

Demi retrieves her map, dusting off the grains of sand. "Well, whatever they are, if we can see them, they can probably see us. So maybe we should head back towards the trees."

Kalden shakes his head. "Not yet."

"What do you mean, *not yet*?" Gem mocks his intentionally obtuse response. "What are we waiting on?"

Kalden's quiet for several beats, then turns around to face the direction we came from. "Them."

There's not a cloud in the sky as a chillingly familiar thunder rumbles through leaves and sand. The skin along my spine crawls as more reverberations come in quick succession. Too quick. Too many. Like they're coming from more than one source.

My suspicion is confirmed when five black-and-gold forms leap out from the forest across the southern dunes, heading directly towards us. I push myself up to standing, clutching at my plummeting stomach.

Gem whirls on Kalden. "You knew they were coming?"

He unsheathes his knives. "I figured our scent of humanity would lure them in at some point."

Gem grabs onto the hilt of her poniard. "We're supposed to fight them all?"

"Five against five. I suppose the odds could be worse." Yvonne laughs dully.

Two more creatures emerge from the tree line, and we each mutter a curse.

Kalden sighs, straightening his posture. "I was hoping to hold off on this, but I promise I'll explain later."

It's the last warning we get before he twists off his helmet and drops it into the sand, where it begins to roll down the hill.

"What are you doing?!" Gem screams as she lunges to snatch up the helmet. She shoves the headgear into Kalden's chest, but it's too late.

Luminous gold streaks across his face and neck, brightening the dimming marks of his prior exposure. The twin suns of his eyes roll back, and I sense the ecstasy of his surging power as if it's my own. He doesn't leave it at that, though. A pulsing aura ignites around Kalden's body, morphing into flames that engulf the top half of his leather bodysuit. The material incinerates within seconds. Radiant light races from the veins around his throat down his freshly exposed chest and abdomen.

I'd be impressed with how cleanly he's preserved the bottom half of his attire if I weren't in complete slack-jawed shock. How did he do that? The speed and accuracy . . . like he's done it countless times. Just how much sun exposure has Kalden had? How close has he gotten to the edge of his humanity? My arm tightens around my roiling abdomen.

Gem grabs hold of my wrist to lug me away from the gleaming figure beside us. "We need to go. *Now.*"

Demi and Yvonne are already scrambling down the hill.

Kalden opens his eyes, those otherworldly irises finding mine as he latches onto my other arm.

"Don't touch her!" Gem bites out, pulling me closer to her.

His grip doesn't budge.

"There are more coming. At least three. Over there." His gaze slides to the stretch of trees on the opposite side of the hill—the same direction that the others are running towards. "I can't handle both groups at once."

Understanding what he's asking of me, I hang my head. "I might not be much help, especially right now."

The warm hand encircling my arm tightens. "Look at me, Orelle. You have more fight in you than most will ever have. Forget about comparing your abilities to theirs and focus on wielding your own strength. Just like we practiced."

My heavy eyes glance between his, drawing from the steadiness I see in them. Perhaps this is the reason Kalden focused most of our training with me on my back—as if he'd known there'd come a time when agility would fail me.

Stiffly, I dip my chin. "I'll do what I can."

His fingers trail down my forearm as they release their grip, and a wave of energy collides against the tingling, magnetic presence of power in my mind and palms.

It's gone before I can blink, as is Kalden.

"Just like you practiced?" Gem asks sharply, letting go of my wrist.

I shake my head, wishing I had more time to fill her in on everything. But a new set of thundering echoes breaks through the tree line ahead. Demi and Yvonne slide to a halt, heads turning wildly, searching for which way to go next.

Wincing with every footfall, I stumble my way past the frozen duo while releasing my blade cuffs and trusting that Gem will follow.

She does, and I shout, "All I need to do is get my hands on them. It should be enough to incapacitate them, but I'll need help finishing the job. Once they're down, that's when you strike."

"What are y—"

A screech drowns out the rest of Gem's words.

Towering tree trunks snap like twigs as four Sols barrel through the forest, using flares of raw power to boost them forward at an impossibly fast pace. They switch to a regular sprint when they spot me, likely to avoid frying the ripe human before they get their fill.

Three creatures aim straight for me, duking it out for dibs on the first snack, while the fourth splits off towards Demi and Yvonne as they scurry towards the ocean.

The tallest of the bunch, a Sol with long legs to rival Kalden's, takes the lead. As the distance between us dwindles, its blackened tongue lashes out. Instead of dodging, I throw my hands forward, wrapping my fingers around the base of all six pincers as the creature slams its body into mine.

Stars explode across my vision as we crash into the ground, splintering the polarized lens of my helmet. Fresh pain lances through my already throbbing brain, but it isn't alone. The heat coursing through my veins intensifies, demanding to be used. I grit my teeth and release the vibrating energy, sending it into the Sol's writhing, splintered tongue.

Hot saliva drenches my cracked helmet and leathers as it wails in agony, then falls silent.

Before I can catch my breath, the creature is hoisted off me by its greedy kin. Talons rip past my leathers into my throat, heaving me off the ground by my neck. The burnt flesh around its mouth stretches open.

I shove my right hand onto its wrist. The tips of my nightstone blades graze the creature's skin while broiling power pours from my palms.

The Sol flinches away with a shriek, dropping me to the sand and collapsing at my side.

This time, my knees take the brunt of the impact, yet my head is still swimming from the first collision. Legs trembling, I try to stand, but the world tilts off its axis. Or is that me? It's hard to tell up from down as the ground falls out from beneath me, and I buckle onto my stomach. Streaks of crimson drip from my throat, soiling the sand. Blood whooshes in my addled brain, and my body feels so damn heavy. It takes all my focus to roll onto my back and prepare for the next attack.

The third Sol hesitates. Though I'm immobile, it must be catching on that I'm not the easy prey I appear to be. Its burning bloodthirsty eyes shift towards Gem, who's too preoccupied with piercing her blade into the heart of the first Sol to notice the third leaning into its haunches a few feet away.

My breath catches, a scream forming at the base of my marred throat.

I won't be able to send a solar flare without direct contact. I plead with my useless limbs to get up and move, but it's like gravity itself is pinning me down.

"Gem!" I try to call her name, to warn her, but it comes out too slurred and soft.

By some small mercy, she hears me and tugs on the hilt of her poniard, yanking it from the first Sol's chest.

The third creature pounces.

Gem rolls to the side, narrowly escaping the Sol's outstretched arms. While it's course-correcting, she makes a run for it.

With only three steps between them, it strikes again.

Everything stops. My pulse. My breaths. Time itself elongates to a crawl as charred arms wrap around Gem's waist and back. The Sol lifts her off her feet, mouth parting.

Whatever it takes.

I may be broken, but I am not weak—and I will not let her die.

That single thought silences all others as power surges from my body.

An aura of golden flames explodes across sand and grass. The line of fire barrels forward like a wave, engulfing the two limp forms of the fallen Sols before crashing into the third creature's legs. Its bare, charred skin takes to the flames like primed kindling.

Though the golden embers roiling across the ground fizzle out before Gem falls, the blaze surrounding the Sol burns brighter. The creature drops to the glassy sand, rolling to extinguish the flames.

Instead of running for cover, Gem crawls over to the thrashing body and buries her blade in its neck. The Sol shudders one last time, then abruptly stills.

Head slumping in relief, my heavy eyelids fall shut.

Gem is alive, if not safe.

I can finally give into the clawing blackness.

CHAPTER TWENTY-THREE

"Orelle?"

A fuzzy, whooshing sound ebbs in my ears, disturbing the peaceful void. Something jostles my shoulder, but that's not my body anymore. I'm no longer imprisoned.

"Orelle!" A feminine voice breaks through the darkness shrouding me like an endless blanket. "Stay with me."

Why? Why would I want to stay here in this place of pain and monsters when I could surrender to blissful numbness?

Vaguely, I sense a warm hand pressing against my neck, luring me away from the shadows' sedative embrace.

No.

I'm not ready to feel—not when feeling is accompanied by ceaseless pain.

Hot pressure builds beneath the touch, and I fear the flames have returned to claim me, to scorch and devour from the inside out. Yet the inferno takes its time traveling through my veins, like it's searching for something. It gathers leisurely near my knees and throat before winding around my skull. Flashing orbs dance behind my closed lids as the fire pulls back, leaving an incessant tingling in its wake.

My eyes snap open to a vivid blue expanse and three suns, two of which are creased with worry.

The sight of such strong emotion breaking through Kalden's usually controlled mask—and the thought that *I* might be the cause of it—jars me awake. I reach up to brush my fingertips along his downturned lips.

At my touch, his features smooth and settle.

"Thank the shadows you're okay," Gem breathes, pushing aside Kalden to lower her head into the nook between my neck and shoulder.

"It's not the shadows you should be thanking," says an unfamiliar masculine voice, coming from somewhere behind Kalden.

Gem stiffens and backs away from the stranger approaching at Kalden's side.

I move to sit up, pleased to find both the dizziness and numbness are gone. Even my earlier tension and nausea have subsided, though the familiar pressure behind my eyes lingers. I reach a hand across my neck, where the Sol had pierced my skin with its talons, but there's no blood on my leather gloves. No *fresh* blood, anyway.

My gaze lifts to Kalden's.

"You healed me," I say, more of a statement than a question.

He dips his chin.

"The bruises and lacerations were easy enough, but the concussion took a bit more focus." The gentle smile pulling at his lips falls. "I couldn't do anything for the deeper ailments. Wounds like that—ones that have lived within you for nearly your whole life—often intertwine themselves with your core essence. You are who you are because of them. Your resilience. Your resourcefulness. Both were born from a refusal to surrender to your perceived weaknesses. And it would take a healer much more skilled than I to even think about treating them without fracturing your soul."

"It's okay." I offer him a smile, though he can't see it through the deep black tint of my helmet. "I think you're the first person to talk about my condition in a way that makes me feel . . . whole."

"You *are* whole." Kalden grabs my hand, flipping it palm-side-up and rubbing a thumb along the slit in my glove. The motion sends a different kind of warmth flaring through my core.

"You can heal?" Someone chokes back a sob behind me, dousing the new fire within me like a bucket of cold water.

I turn around, surprised to see we're now a mere two dozen feet from the ocean, which explains the whooshing white noise. Demi sits near the edge of the ebbing water, cradling a too-still Yvonne in her arms.

"Your friend is past the point of healing." Kalden bows his head. "I'm sorry."

I stare at Yvonne's unmoving form and notice what I haven't before. Unlike her prior puncture wounds, a gaping hole now runs clear through her chest. The jagged tips of her broken rib cage protrude through her torn leathers. Like the Sol ripped her heart straight out of her body instead of slowly draining her.

Her second chance at life, gone.

Demi hunches over, body heaving. Gem strides to her side in a wordless show of comfort.

My teeth grind together, and I wish I could go back and send out the surge of fire that first moment the Sols broke through the forest.

As if I've conjured one from memory, a guttural wail echoes across the sand, and my body goes rigid.

"Is that—"

"Sounds like Joss needs a hand with the Pyre." A man with bright blond hair and an even brighter smile walks around Kalden to kneel in front of me. "Glad to see you up and moving, little nova."

Like Kalden, his irises are alight with a brilliant gold, as are the veins running along his half-naked body . . . or three-quarters naked, considering the sheerness of his pants.

As if he can sense me staring through my helmet at his semi-transparent bottoms, he shoots me a wink.

Cheeks heating, I ask, "'Little nova'?"

The indecently dressed stranger's smile turns lopsided. "A nova is a strong, rapid outburst of a new star. Or, technically, a star that already existed, but was too dim to really see before."

He pats my legs, then rises.

Was that supposed to be a compliment, or is being likened to a dim star having an outburst some type of ambiguous insult? Whatever the case, this hardly feels like the time for brevity, and I'm not sure how the hell to respond.

Luckily, I don't have to, because Kalden cuts in to tell him, "I'll join you two in a minute."

The blond man nods before jogging towards the other side of the dune.

I push myself to my feet, brushing off the sand from my backside, and nod to the stranger's retreating form. "I take it you know him."

Kalden's features go blank, mask returning. "That's Niles. He's a friend."

"Joss, too?"

He nods once.

My brows pull together. "You have friends who live up here? Aboveground?"

"I do," he answers curtly.

"And they aren't Sols?"

He goes quiet for several seconds. "We aren't the monsters you've been taught to fear."

We. Not *they*.

"I-I don't understand. Are you or are you not a Sol?"

Kalden leans closer. "We can talk about this la—"

"It's a simple question," I say, stepping back.

His shoulders roll forward, but he allows me my space. "I am."

"You're what?" I press, needing him to stop being so vague for once.

"A Sol."

"You can't be," I whisper, though I know it's true. I feel it in my gut, hear the honest steadiness of his tone. "Your skin . . . It's . . . It's not all charred and cracked. You can talk and think and . . . feel. Sols can't do that."

His jaw twitches. "The creatures you know as Sols are actually Pyres."

"Pyres?" I test the foreign word with a grimace.

"There is some truth to what they teach you down there. Sols are humans who've learned to harness the sun's energy. But we aren't bloodthirsty monsters. Our humanity stays intact unless we channel too much power and push ourselves to burnout." Kalden's tone darkens, as do his irises. "When a Sol crosses that line—when they let too much of the sun's power course through them—it incinerates their soul until all that's left is an empty shell of burnt flesh, a mockery of who they once were, with an insatiable hunger for what they lost."

My chest squeezes in on itself.

"You lied to me," I begin, voice shaking as I recall the promise he made during our first training session. "When you vowed that I wouldn't become a monster, you knew I'd assume you meant I wouldn't become a Sol, didn't you?"

His silence is enough of an answer.

"This whole time, you've been telling me a little bit of sun exposure won't take away my humanity."

Gem reappears at my side, voice unsteady as she asks, "How could you expose yourself?"

I squeeze my arms around myself. "Remember what I told you about what happened in the transport tunnel? Well, Kalden saw it. My hand, when it was still glowing. He confronted me during our first training session, then told me there was a way I could harness the sun's power in moderation to fight back without turning into a monster. He even made a pulse promise, but I guess that was a lie."

Black strands spill over Kalden's sweat-streaked temples as he shakes his head. "It wasn't a lie. Not entirely."

"Not *entirely*?" I mock. "Sun's pits, Kalden! Can you stop being so vague and be honest with me? Are Sols fucking allergic to the truth, or is that just you?"

"I meant what I said," he snaps, then takes a breath before adding more calmly, "Sols aren't monsters. You are not a monster."

Gem holds up a palm. "Wait. Are you saying Orelle is a *Sol*?"

More screeching precedes the sound of Kalden's name being called from the opposite side of the nearest dune. The afternoon sun casts a golden silhouette against his dark curls as he turns away from us, peering in the direction that Niles took. And when his glittering eyes return to mine, I kick myself mentally for believing the man in front of me was just a mere human.

"Temporarily, yes. You'll return to your normal human form shortly after sunset, as we all do. The sun bestows its power as a daily gift—one we don't get to keep in its absence." Kalden casts another glance over his shoulder. "I need to go help Joss and Niles with the Pyre, but I promise I'll answer all of your questions later."

Kalden turns and hides his true self no longer, hands extending towards the ground as he launches bolts of energy. His golden-streaked form rapidly retreats through the warm air, taking sand

and dust with him.

Once he leaves us, Gem and I don't speak for what feels like the longest minute of my life.

My eyes drift to the lapping waves while my mind processes through the facts, each one its own brand of grim.

Seafoam spills across the sand.

Yvonne is dead.

The water recedes, taking with it the stream of crimson flowing from her corpse.

Gabe, Aruna, and Twilynn are still missing.

Shimmering waves writhe forward.

Kalden's been lying to me this entire time.

The ocean cowers back.

I've been lying to Gem. Or omitting the truth, which isn't much better.

A roiling wave splashes farther up the beach, catapulting fizzy white droplets into the salty sea air.

The Sols of my nightmares are actually Pyres.

The bubbling foam dissolves, revealing several shells in the sand.

And I'm a Sol.

I peel my attention from the water to find Gem's covered head tilting down at my hands. Radiant beams cut through the slits in my black leather gloves like the first peek of the morning sunrise over the horizon. Its warmth courses beneath my skin, and I crave more of it, like an itch demanding to be satiated.

Whatever it takes—that's what I'd been willing to do to finally feel useful. To prove I'm capable, or maybe even strong. But where's the strength in risking my humanity? What good am I to Gem, or to anyone else, if I become the thing we're fighting against?

Perhaps my death would be preferable.

Backing away, I squeeze my fingers into fists, focusing on the mechanical release of the blades instead of the craving. Because if what Kalden said is true, that Pyres are born when a Sol harnesses too much power, then the last thing I need to do is indulge.

Or I *will* become a monster.

If I'm not already becoming one.

CHAPTER TWENTY-FOUR

"Where are you going?" Gem asks, trailing behind as I trudge along the dampened shore in no particular direction other than *away*. When I don't answer, she presses, "Orelle, please don't run from me."

"I'm not running," I finally say, not bothering to turn around as I glare at the too-slow progress of my feet.

Fingers grab onto my shoulder, halting my steps. "Yes, you are. But you can't run away from this."

"Don't." I swat away her hand. "Don't touch me. I don't want to hurt you."

She steps closer. "You'd never do that."

I flinch back, tossing up my arms. "How do you know? I don't even know who I am anymore, let alone what I'm capable of."

"I do."

"Look at me!" I snap, raising my glowing palms. "I'm a Sol, Gem. A sun-damned *Sol*. The enemy we were sent out here to kill."

She folds her arms tightly against herself. "Kalden said it isn't permanent."

A bitter huff escapes me. "I'm not so sure I'd believe anything he says right now."

"Fair enough," Gem relents. "But you still seem like you. Well, minus the golden veins."

"I don't feel like me. Not anymore."

Gem tilts her head. "What feels different?"

"Everything," I say. "It's like the sun itself has been infused into my veins."

She's quiet for a beat before softly asking, "Does it hurt?"

I consider the buzz beneath my skin, how I'd thought it pleasant before I fully grasped what was happening. "No."

"Is it bothering you in any way?"

"No," I repeat. "Well, it wasn't, until Kalden admitted that it makes me a Sol. It's like a warm, tingling pressure, but it didn't feel uncomfortable before. Now it's all I can focus on."

She softly murmurs, "Hm."

"What?" I ask, releasing and sheathing the blade cuffs as she assesses me.

"I think Kalden's telling the truth. If you were turning into one of those . . . those creatures, you'd probably be feeling a lot more than a warm tingle. Not to mention, you're able to have a lucid conversation without thirsting to rip into my chest and your skin hasn't blackened to a crisp. So, maybe he's right. Maybe Sols aren't monsters." Gem steps in again. "You might feel, and look, a little different, but you're still my best friend."

Palms prickling beneath her gaze, I tuck my hands behind my back.

"No," she says firmly, pulling my arms forward and intertwining her fingers with my own. "No more hiding."

Tears spill across my eyes, muddying my already murky vision. "How can you not hate me?"

"I'm pissed you didn't tell me sooner, but I don't hate you, Orelle. Don't think I ever could. I just want to understand why. Why did you do this?"

"Why do you think?" I try to pull away, but Gem tightens her grip. "I'm the reason we didn't make it to Deor. If it weren't for me slowing us down, you wouldn't have gotten hurt or evicted from your home. And then you took it easy on me during training, and I still couldn't keep up. I was going to get myself killed and drag you down with me, like I always do."

"That's not tr—"

"It is, though. We both know I'm not built for surviving, Gem. Why else would you leave Taur? Why would Gabe abandon his family, his city, if he was confident that I'd make it? I was tired of feeling too weak. Like my death was inevitable for all of us. So, when Kalden told me there was a way I could finally do something about it, I took it. For the first time in ten years, I felt like my life was truly in *my* hands. *I* got to decide my fate. Not Gabe or his father. Not some random guard looking for a quick release. Not even the people that I love, like you, Taur, or my parents. And I guess . . . I wanted to prove I was more than a broken throwaway."

Gem leans her helmet into mine, voice breaking as she says, "If you saw yourself the way I do, you'd know there's nothing to prove. Your existence is a gift, not a burden. You keep saying you're broken, but what I see is a whole entire woman who rebuilt herself from nothing when she could've easily given up; a woman who's persistent and selfless. I mean, sun's pits, Orelle! Even on your worst days, you go out of your way to make me laugh, even if it's at T's expense. You taught me life doesn't have to be painless to be full. And my life is abundantly more full with you in it."

We sniffle at the same time, making a breathy snicker bubble up from my throat as Gem finally breaks our contact.

I shake the last of the tears from my eyes. "A simple 'I love you' or 'I forgive you' would've sufficed."

"I don't think it would've. I needed to get the truth through that thick skull of yours." Gem raps her knuckles against the crown of my helmet. "But in case it wasn't clear, I do forgive you. And you know I'll always love you."

My puffy eyes crinkle at the sides. "Maybe I've been going after the wrong marks. First, you compliment my big head, and now the love confession. When can I expect the official proposal?"

She shakes her head, and I swear I can sense her nose scrunching. "You're disgusting, you know that? You're practically my sister."

"But if I wasn't?" I ask, waggling my brows, though she can't see them.

"Orelle," she groans.

I hold up my palms. "Sorry. You make it too easy."

The sight of my ripped gloves sends my smile falling.

Even with my face covered, Gem catches the shift.

"What are you going to do now that your secret is out?" She gestures to the hidden camera.

The hole in my chest that Gem had patched over cracks back open as I stare at the reflective surface above her browbone, straining to see whether the telltale pinprick of red light glows beneath the sun's glare. When I don't spot it, my lungs grab onto a rebellious breath, hoping that perhaps Kalden deactivated the recording devices prior to our battle—yet the air is once again stolen from me when my gaze travels to Demi.

Amidst the chaos, there's been no time to consider that my actions would be captured by witnesses or cameras. Now that they have, the only way I can return to Caligo is in chains, regardless of whether this change is temporary. Any other action would undermine what we're groomed to believe.

"As soon as they allow the sun to mark their veins, they lose their humanity. Forever."

Though I'd first heard the warning from my mother, she hadn't been alone in that belief. She'd simply echoed the sentiment drilled into her from her parents, neighbors, and friends. A lie repeated and carried through generations to disguise itself as truth. For what? What do the leaders of Caligo stand to gain from keeping its residents in the dark? What benefit is there in ensuring we stay uninformed and under-resourced?

The answer buzzes in my palms: power.

If more people knew the truth—that Sols are separate from Pyres and that they're able to retain their humanity—how many would choose to leave behind the cramped, musty city for a chance at freedom? Freedom to live wherever they want to live. To love whoever they want to love. To procreate, or not procreate, on whatever timeline they decide on with their partner. Would there even be a city left for those in power to lead once people recognized Caligo for what it is: a cage parading as a haven?

I'd like to think people would take their own fate into their own hands, but will the truth be enough to break through the generational grooming? Or are they so far gone that they perceive lies as truth and truth as lies?

I truly don't know. But what I do know is that I won't be able to return to find out. Because there's no way the full footage from Kalden's revelations will make it to the edited episode to be presented to the masses. Whatever the cameras caught will be warped to fit the usual narrative.

I can practically envision it now. Flashes of Kalden's golden veins and my own glowing palms underscored by dramatic instrumentation. Maybe even a voice-over lamenting our betrayal and demanding our execution. A line drawn with Caligo on one side and me on the other.

"I can never go back," I say, finally answering Gem's question.

She nods, as if she suspected as much, but offers nothing further than her steady presence as I roam aimlessly up the rolling sand, maneuvering around the patches of marram grass.

I'll never see Taurance again. I won't be there to witness her transformation into a mother, to see if her baby gets those glittering jade irises or her infectious laugh. And if Gem returns, I won't see her again, either. Just like that, the women who've become my sisters—the family that picked me up and patched my heart back together when I needed them most—will be forever out of my reach.

A strong gust of wind douses me in the ocean's salty air, but my cheeks are already stained by the bitterness of grief.

CHAPTER TWENTY-FIVE

It isn't until I nearly walk straight into Kalden that I realize I must've subconsciously followed the ever-present pull of his energy. He steadies me with a hand on my shoulder, pupils flicking to Gem, who halts a few paces behind, before returning to mine.

"Are you okay?"

My raw, red-rimmed eyes lift to his through the shadowed lens of my helmet, and I again wonder how he's able to see past the deep, polarized tint. I shake my head, the only answer I can give right now.

Not pushing for clarification, he keeps his steadying palm on my shoulder. I lean into it, into him, knowing I probably shouldn't let my guard down around the man who intentionally misled me. But Kalden's not alone in his deception. At least he chose to lie to a stranger, not his best friend.

I'm so lost in the spiraling thoughts that it takes me another minute for the scene to register. Standing next to Niles is quite possibly the most striking woman I've ever seen. Like her companion, the woman's attire is borderline indecent, with a thin iridescent band of fabric stretching across her breasts and a second, slightly larger band wrapping across her waist. The sun bathes practically every inch of her well-endowed figure in mesmerizing patterns of gold, tracing from her bare feet up to her short black curls that hang over the side of her angular face, framing large upturned eyes straining to focus on the Pyre kneeling before her. Its feral black-and-gold gaze glowers at the ground, but it makes no attempt to free itself from the hands that clench either side of its head.

My mouth falls open at seeing the charred creature's submissive posture.

Predicting my questions, Kalden explains, "Joss is skilled at controlling certain electrical signals. She can temporarily disrupt the pathways between the brain and the body to immobilize an opponent while sifting through the electrophysiological activity corresponding to specific memories."

"In simpler terms, she can read minds," Niles clarifies with an eye roll from Joss's side, holding one of his hands atop hers while the other rests on a pair of cuffs dangling from his back pocket.

Kalden's jaw twitches. "There's more to it than that. Joss sees the frequencies almost like a static montage. Not every memory is as clear and whole as others. It takes immense effort to weave through all the signals and form a coherent image of what the bearer of the memory truly experienced. That type of mental energy can quickly burn through her borrowed power, which is why Niles is lending Joss some of his own."

I blink slowly, trying to wrap my mind around the revelation that Sols can read memories. "Is it safe for her to be that close to the Pyre?"

"As long as she maintains control, it'll believe it's restrained. But I got these, in case things get a little feisty," Niles says, tapping on the cuffs.

"What memory is she looking for?"

Niles lifts a blond brow, letting Kalden take the lead.

"There's been a significant increase in both Sol disappearances and Pyre sightings. It's not uncommon to lose a Sol or two a year to burnout. Though most of us learn from a young age to recognize the signs that we're nearing that edge and how to deescalate, there are some who take on more than they should and ignore the warning until it's too late. But in the past fifteen or so years, the annual number of Sols succumbing into Pyres has shot up to a couple dozen. This anomaly seems to be localized to the villages surrounding Caligo. That's why I went there in the first place. To investigate—"

The high-pitched whistle of an object cutting through the air silences Kalden. He barrels into my side, sending us both toppling into the sand and narrowly avoiding the missile arcing towards Joss, Niles, and the Pyre.

Niles's eyes go wide. He tugs on Joss's hand seconds before impact, and a translucent aura of gold pulsates out from them. But the two Sols aren't fast enough to escape the thick bloom of smoke that explodes from the missile as it strikes the Pyre's skull.

The black particles ascend into the sky, rapidly expanding into a cloud of false night, pluming over Kalden and me. The dense nightstone air is like prickling ice. It crawls down my throat and settles on my bits of exposed skin, intent on extinguishing any trace of the sun's warmth. Pushing up on all fours, I heave out a violent cough, struggling to breathe past the claustrophobia of the nightstone merging forcefully into my lungs.

Kalden does the same at my side, spitting out wads of black-tinted mucus while limping into the heart of the smoke, where his friends last stood.

A minute passes, and the fog begins to lift, revealing three motionless bodies in the sand.

The first is the Pyre, or what remains of it, which isn't much beyond a mutilated lower half.

Several feet away lie Niles and Joss. Their once-beaming veins flicker as the nightstone eats away at the sunlight's energy. But it's Joss's arms that make my stomach churn. Her forearms end abruptly in severed stumps of sinew and bone where her hands were mere minutes ago, now cleaved by the blast.

Kalden reaches his palms over both of their hearts and closes his eyes in concentration. The remnants of his magic flood to his hands before pouring into the Sols. Through their tarnished skin, thick golden cords wrap around the faintly beating organs, bolstering them with the borrowed power.

"Get back, Elle!" Gabe screams from somewhere behind me.

The relentless ice needling through my veins overtakes any relief I might've felt at the sound of his voice. With no small amount of effort, I lift my head to see my ex-husband sprinting down the hill, a second missile in hand. As he stokes the igniter, I'm hit with the sobering realization that he intends to strike again—except this time, there will be no chance that Kalden and his friends will escape the blast.

I can't let that happen.

I crawl closer to the three Sols, banking on the hope that Gabe hasn't yet realized that I'm one of them. And if he has, maybe his lingering feelings for me will be enough to give him pause.

Mercifully, Gabe pulls the igniter away from the missile's wire, pocketing it before closing the remaining distance between us.

"Elle!" He doesn't wait for me to respond as he grabs underneath my arms, hoisting me away from Kalden, Niles, and Joss.

"Let me go." My words are a raspy mutter, but Gabe must hear them, because he stills.

"They're Sols, Elle! Didn't you see? They're marked by the

sun's mutation!"

Jerking away from his slackened grip, I angle my body between Gabe and the Sols, slowly backstepping. "Don't pretend like you don't know the truth. Sols aren't the monsters that your father and all the chancellors before him have portrayed them to be."

"What are you talking about?" Gabe's pitch heightens. "Did you not see how they killed those women back in the meadow? How can you defend that?"

"Pyres did that, not Sols."

"Pyres?"

"Shadows' mercy, Gabe! You can drop the act. I know about the lies. How everything we've been taught about Sols is really a twisted truth about Pyres. That exposure to the sun alone doesn't take away a person's humanity unless they channel too much of its energy. That it's all a ploy to keep us trapped below and your family seated in power."

"Did *he* tell you that?" Gabe asks, nudging his chin towards Kalden.

"He told me about the Pyres, but I pieced the rest together myself."

Gabe huffs an exasperated breath. "And you believe him?"

"I do," I say firmly, gaze narrowing on Gabe's hand as it returns to the igniter in his pocket.

"He's the one who lied to you, Elle. How can you not see that? I don't know what kind of magic he's been using to disguise himself as human, but just because he doesn't look like the other abominations doesn't mean he isn't one."

A spark comes to life at the end of the igniter, and I brace my hands on either side of my helmet. If any evidence of my earlier exposure lingers on my face, it could either stoke the man into firing the second missile or force him to think twice about his demonization of Sols. Hoping for the latter, I tug off the headgear, throwing it into the sand between us.

"If he's an abomination, then so am I."

Gabe falters a step, lowering both hands. "W-What did you do?"

"Found a way to survive."

"No." He drops both the missile and igniter before rushing forward to pick up my discarded helmet, dusting it off. "No, we can fix this. We have to! Before it's too late."

Without meeting my gaze, Gabe tries to hand me the headgear, as if I took it off by accident. I stare at the lump of anodized aluminum without accepting it and note my reflection in its cracked lens. Even beneath the false night, my usual amber irises are alight with a fading gold.

"Elle, please," Gabe begs as I make no move to grab the helmet from him. "You can't let them see you!"

"If you're worried about the cameras, you're too late. They've already captured my confession. And I have no intention of putting that back on."

A tremor shakes through his clenched grip, though his eyes remain downcast. "You have to. I won't let you destroy yourself like this. I can't stand here and watch you become a monster."

His fear is palpable, and I don't think he's faking it.

Which means Chancellor Bren has also kept the truth from his son.

"I'm not destroying myself. The reaction is temporary. Look at me, Gabe," I plead softly. And when his head finally lifts, I give him a reassuring smile. "See? It's already fading."

"I don't understand," he admits on a shaky exhale.

Kalden appears at my side, holding an unconscious Joss in his arms. "Orelle isn't losing her humanity, if that's what you're worried about. The last of the solar energy will drain from her body soon enough. And it won't come back until she's re-exposed to direct sunlight. But what's more concerning is whether my friend survives your murder attempt."

"Her veins . . . they were glowing," Gabe stammers. "I thought she was going to hurt Elle."

"Both Sols and Pyres bear the mark of the sun, but we aren't the same. We Sols maintain our humanity. We feel, eat, love, and shit just like any other humans would, but with an added boost of borrowed power during daylight hours."

Niles sluggishly rises to his feet, all traces of his prior brightness gone from his narrowed cerulean eyes as he continues where Kalden left off, stalking closer to Gabe. "And unlike you, we have no interest in unnecessary bloodshed. We prefer to keep our distance from you Shades, since you're the ones who tend to escalate into violence."

"We need to get Joss to Lucis," Kalden says, reminding Niles there's no time to pick a fight. "She's stable for now, but I'm not sure how much longer she'll stay that way. We need to staunch the bleeding."

"Can I help?" I ask, already releasing the blade cuffs to slice off the leather sleeves of my bodysuit.

Thanks to how skintight the material is, I nick my shoulder with the sharpened nightstone tip several times, sending fresh daggers of ice to devour the little warmth that remains in my veins. I hiss through my teeth. There's irony in my pain tolerance drawing the line at tiny slices when it hardly bats an eye at my usual migraine attacks, or the puncture wounds I'd gotten around my throat from the Pyre's talons.

Once I finish ripping off the second sleeve, I hand both pieces to Niles. "You could use these as makeshift bandages until we get her proper medical attention."

Niles nods his gratitude, wrapping the leather around Joss's amputation sites.

Gabe grabs hold of my left arm. "You're going with them?"

"Where else is there for me to go? I can't go back. Your father will either have me executed or sent to the Abyss."

"Maybe not, if I talk to him . . ."

"No, Gabe." I take a measured breath. "He already hated me before, for my inability to comply with breeding expectations. Even if the footage of my confession doesn't make it past the production team, anyone who sees it will know I'm proof that our beliefs, our whole system, are built on lies. I was already disposable to him, but now I'm a threat."

Gabe doesn't respond, so I tug free from his grip.

Once my back is to him, he rasps, "Then I'm coming, too."

I whirl back around. "What?"

"I'm not letting you walk into a den of Sols alone." Gabe's gloved fists clench at his sides, voice lowering. "We can't trust them, Elle. Just because they look more normal than the other creatures doesn't mean they aren't dangerous."

Niles scoffs a few feet beside us. "You nearly kill me and Joss, and yet you have the nerve to accuse *us* of being dangerous?"

He pulls out the cuffs from his back pocket.

Gabe steps away, head shaking.

"The only way you're coming with us is if I know you won't be shooting a missile at my back."

"I won't," Gabe insists.

Niles leans in closer, nose scrunching. "I don't believe you. You still fear us. Fear and hatred are two sides of the same coin, especially for *your* kind. Your bigotry makes you distrustful of anything or anyone that doesn't align with what you deem as right and good. It's why you didn't hesitate to throw that explosive. Your eyes told you we didn't look like the charred creature beside us. Our skin wasn't seared. Our posture wasn't threatening. Yet you dehumanized us anyway, simply because our veins differed from yours."

Seconds pass. When Gabe finally responds, he does so by unhooking the belted pouch containing the remaining missiles and shoving it into Niles's open palm.

Niles waits expectantly, eying the igniter protruding from Gabe's pocket. "That, too."

He hands it over, and Niles secures the cuffs around Gabe's wrists.

A familiar rhythmic whir stirs in the salty breeze behind us, tugging at a memory I can't quite grasp as we make our way closer to the beach. My shoulders roll back a bit when I see Aruna and Twilynn looking relatively intact, though both flinch as the Sols approach.

"What in the burning pits of the sun are you doing?!" Aruna curses at Niles, who ushers a restrained Gabe forward. "That's Chancellor Bren's son!"

Jaw clenching, Niles points to the woman lying limp in Kalden's arms. "He did that to her. If Joss doesn't make it, I won't give a fuck who he is. Murdering an innocent life has consequences."

"Innocent?" Aruna spits. "You're mutated abominations!"

Kalden's voice is calm, yet firm. "You've all been lied to. It takes more than sun exposure to mutate into the creatures you've been told are Sols. Despite the temporary powers gifted to us, we're as human as you are."

Twilynn angles her head towards me, then Gem, who stands at my side. "You believe that?"

"I do," Gem says. "Think about it. We're told Sols are too engrossed in their hunger to communicate, that their intelligence gives way to animalistic instinct. If that were true, we wouldn't be having this conversation."

Kalden adjusts his grip on Joss. "We really don't have time to explain more right now. The bandages help, but she still needs a mender. Follow us, or don't."

"I can't leave her," Demi roughly whispers from where she hovers over Yvonne's body.

"I'll carry your friend back to Lucis for a proper burial, if you'd like," Niles offers.

She gives a stiff dip of her chin.

"If you try to run, I will catch you," Niles warns before releasing Gabe to lift Yvonne.

My spine prickles as I fall into step behind Kalden while the others trail behind, continuing our trek into the den of Sols.

CHAPTER TWENTY-SIX

These people aren't monsters. Though we've only been inside the village for a matter of minutes, I've seen enough to erase any lingering doubts.

On the surface, Sols have features that are distinctly inhuman—like incandescent eyes and gold-streaked veins shimmering beneath their skin—but anyone who bothers to study their interactions for more than a few minutes would realize how undeniably normal they are. Men and women amble around while chatting animatedly with their neighbors about the cloud of false night bleeding into the southern outskirts of the village, drawing a harsh line between shade and sun across the outermost domed structures.

Conversations soften into whispers as Kalden passes with Joss in his arms, and Yvonne in Niles's, but crescendo closer to a regular volume by the time I meander past at the tail end of our group. The onlookers exchange theories about what happened to Joss.

"Does it have something to do with the black cloud?"

"Where did it come from?"

"How long do you think it'll last?"

"I wonder what the High Sol will do about it."

"Should we be worried?"

The children don't seem to share these concerns as they chase one another through the shallow waters below the raised pathways, daring each other to test who's brave enough to get the closest to the darkened edge.

A little girl with dark blonde curls and full cheeks catches my eye as she leaps across the top of the domes. I jolt forward, heart racing as I envision her falling through the ten-foot gap between the round structures. But my fear is proven misplaced as she sticks the landing with a giggle.

My throat tightens as she jumps to the next dome, and the next. Moving so freely.

No one tells her to get down. Nobody warns her that she could hurt herself or cause a scene. In fact, the few people who glance her way give the child a little cheer of encouragement. It's a stark contrast to the expectations of modesty, humility, and restraint placed on the young daughters of Caligo.

As if she senses my attention, the child turns her head in my direction with a grin that stretches almost the entire width of her face. I smile back and offer a quick clap before catching back up to Gem at the tail end of our group.

We follow the winding path towards the heart of the village, passing by a myriad of vibrant glass structures, even more dazzling up close than they were from afar. We come to a halt outside one of the more generously sized domes, its white glass walls more opaque than some of the others. Hovering within the open doorway is a vertical layer of suspended lucent liquid.

Kalden adjusts his grip on Joss, then disappears beneath the doorway.

Answering my unspoken question, Niles sticks his leg through. "It cleanses and sterilizes those who enter. Fairly standard protocol in most mending facilities."

When he pulls back his leg, the gore that was caked around the hem of his pants is gone.

My lips form an O as I stare, dumbfounded by the "standard protocol." How is there anything *standard* about a gravity-defying vertical bath?

Niles waves for us to file in, carefully maneuvering Yvonne so her feet don't hit the doorframe.

No one seems particularly eager to follow, so I step up to the threshold, closing my eyes and holding my breath before passing beneath the layer of liquid. Warmth seeps over my skin and leathers, yet I find neither my hair nor attire is the slightest bit damp as I cross inside. The only evidence it affected me at all is the absence of grime where blood once coated the neckline of my bodysuit.

A petite older woman with bright white hair ushers both Kalden and Niles behind a partition of curtains, permitting Demi to follow as she reaches for Yvonne's lifeless hand.

A younger male rushes around a glass tabletop to greet the rest of us, blocking the path forward. His eyes widen when he takes in the head-to-toe gear of the others, yet his smile doesn't falter. "How can I assist you?"

Nobody offers an immediate answer, so I step forward to say, "Uh, we're here with them."

"Are you friends of the High—?"

"Kalden," Niles says as he circles back to the entryway. "They're friends of Kalden. Except for this one. He's responsible for Joss's injuries, so I'll be taking him to the holds once we're done here."

Gabe flinches as Niles grips his shoulder. "The holds?"

"Temporary confinement."

Aruna pushes me aside to stand in front of Gabe. "Like a prison cell? You can't take him away from us! The chancellor's going to see this and—"

"There's no signal," the mender interrupts to say.

Aruna angles herself towards the younger man. "What?"

His cheeks turn rosy. "You're from the Shade cities, yes?"

My brows arch at the new term—Shades. Is that what they call those of us who reside within Caligo and its two brother cities?

"This is the latest batch of sacrifices the Shades sent out on the Hunt," Niles explains, confirming my suspicion.

"I see," the young mender says, his vivid green-and-gold irises flicking to Aruna's helmet. "Like those who've come before you, I presume you've all been equipped with a recording device. These devices typically emit a specific frequency, yet I sense no signal, so it's doubtful the recordings are being delivered back to your leader."

Aruna's gloved hand flies to the tinted lens above her brow bone before she whirls back to Niles. "One of you did this, didn't you?"

The Sol holds up his palms. "Don't look at me."

"If you hurt his son, Chancellor Bren will find out," Aruna warns.

"Even if that's true, which I doubt, thanks to these things not working . . ." Niles flicks her helmet. ". . . the chancellor has no jurisdiction here, thank the sun. I also have no intention of hurting his son. All I'd like to do is ask him a few questions about why he attempted to kill us while unprovoked, and what his intentions are with this new weapon."

Aruna crosses her arms, doubling down. "I won't let you take him."

Niles steps in closer, and even though the nightstone's effects have depleted the enhanced glow from his veins, there's an intensity in his cerulean gaze that tells me he doesn't need the boost of magic to best an opponent. "I don't remember asking for your permission."

"It's okay, Aruna," Gabe assures her. "I can handle his questions."

Aruna continues holding her ground in front of Niles for several stretched seconds before cowering away from the Sol.

The mender's polite smile returns. "Are any of you injured?"

No one answers.

Accepting that Sols aren't the evil creatures we feared them to be is one thing, but I can understand why the others would be hesitant to interact with them, regardless of how kind they seem. Especially since, unlike me, they haven't spent the past few days warming up to the idea that there's a positive side to the sun's power.

"What about you?" the mender asks, gesturing to the tears in my bodysuit.

"Oh, um, Kalden took care of those already."

His attention shifts to the tiny cuts on my upper arm. "But not these?"

Niles answers for me. "She cut herself with a nightstone blade."

Blood rushing to my cheeks, I squirm as the mender's brows furrow. "Not on purpose. I was trying to remove my sleeves so we could use them to staunch Joss's bleeding. I'll be fine."

He nods. "You will be, but I'd recommend at least two hours of sun exposure to counteract the lasting effects of the nightstone. Otherwise, the lacerations may take longer to heal and could become prone to infection."

"Niles almost got hit with a nightstone missile," I say, eager to get the attention off me.

"Almost," Niles emphasizes, scooting aside a stack of papers to lean against the glass tabletop.

I cross my arms. "You lost consciousness."

The mender inspects the dilation of his pupils. "Could be a

concussion, or vasovagal syncope. Do you have any aches in your head or neck?"

"None of concern."

"Any nausea? Dizziness?"

"No." Niles meets my gaze, then rolls his eyes, as if I'm to blame for the mender's fussing.

"Can you recall the events prior to the impact?"

"I was standing next to Joss, lending her some of my power as she searched through the Pyre's memories, when I saw a dark object hurtling towards us. I tried to pull her away, but wasn't fast enough." His brow furrows. "Next thing I remember is waking up to a pitch-black sky and Kalden channeling the last of his waning energy into me."

"You said it was a nightstone missile," the mender says, glancing back at me. "Can you explain to me what that is?"

The mender's calm smile finally falters as I give a brief summary of Gabe's invention of airborne carbon nightoxide.

"And each of you breathed this in?"

"Yes."

"I see," he says with a frown. "There's no way of knowing how long the effects of inhaled nightstone particles will last. It might take a few hours or days of consistent sun exposure to cleanse the toxins from your body."

Niles rises from the table. "We won't be able to channel until it's fully gone?"

The mender tilts his head. "Not necessarily. As it fades, your harnessing abilities should gradually be restored, but you may find your bandwidth significantly more limited. I recommend avoiding prolonged channeling until your system is completely free from the nightstone. Anything more than quick bursts of power may increase your chances of burnout."

Jaw clenching, Niles dips his chin. "Let's hope that won't be necessary."

"We'll arrange her burial a half hour after first light tomorrow," the female mender says to Demi while Kalden ushers us back outside. "Until then, I want you to get some food and rest, okay, dear?"

Demi's covered head barely moves as it hangs downcast.

Niles breaks off from our group to take Gabe to the holds, while Kalden leads the rest of us on a brief tour of Lucis.

My fingers twitch with the urge to pull Demi into an embrace, but Twilynn beats me to it, which is likely for the better. If I were her, the last thing I'd want is to be in close contact with a Sol, or someone who *was* a Sol. Though the light left my veins more than an hour ago and I am not the creature that took her friend's life, it isn't an easy thing, undoing that groomed hatred. It's a truth made evident each time Aruna's hand flinches on the hilt of her dagger when a passerby gets too close.

"What do you think's in there?" Gem asks, and I blink, shifting my gaze to the large center dome she points towards—the one I'd spotted when the village first came into view.

I shrug. "Maybe it's the living quarters for whoever's in charge around here?"

Gem leans in, voice dropping. "Do you think they have a chancellor, too?"

"We don't, and it isn't," Kalden says over his shoulder as he steers us through a particularly crowded pathway lined with men and women holding pliable poles over the bridge's ledge. "That building there is our communal greenhouse. We have several larger crops a few miles northwest, but most of our produce is grown right there in the main dome, where residents can pick vegetables, herbs, and fruits at their discretion."

"How do the rations work?" I ask, glancing at the back of my left hand out of habit, though my glove conceals the marred brand from view.

A middle-aged woman to my left sets her curved pole down against the railing before turning towards me. "Rations? Honey, we don't do that tiered nonsense here. There's more than enough to go around, as long as folks don't get greedy."

Brows pulling together, I stop walking. "You know about the tiers?"

She scoffs. "All too well. I was in your shoes once, you know. Got selected about twenty-three years ago to be a Huntress. Would've ended up dead like the rest of 'em if it weren't for Irene's birds."

My pulse picks up as I recall Demi's tale of the golden birds guiding her aunt to safety. "Who's Irene?"

The woman's pole begins to bend, and she turns back around to tug it towards her, twisting the gear near its base until a writhing speckled fish emerges from the water's rippling surface. Her brown-and-gold eyes crinkle at the sides, and I presume she's forgotten all thoughts of our conversation until she calls over to me once more. "Ask him."

CHAPTER TWENTY-SEVEN

An hour later, I'm scooping up the last of the rice from my bowl as Gem admits to Kalden, "I see why you thought the food they gave us before the Hunt was barely edible."

After several days of us snacking, Kalden organized an entire feast for us beneath an open pavilion nestled along the village's western edge. The late afternoon sunlight beams across the horizon, casting an amber glow across the array of now-empty porcelain dishes and two empty chairs—Aruna and Demi opted to stay behind in the shared bungalow that Kalden escorted us to prior to the meal. Thanks to the nightstone in our lungs offering us temporary immunity from the sun's effects, Gem and Twilynn agreed to let Kalden disarm the sensors in their helmets so they wouldn't have to wait until sunset to eat.

"That's because the food they feed you down there is grown with an artificial photosynthesis," Niles comments while leaning back in his chair, "making it deficient in both natural vitamins and flavor."

I wipe away the tangy sauce from the corners of my lips. "How do you two know so much about Caligo?"

Kalden and Niles share a look.

"Our mothers were born there," Kalden answers after taking a long swig of wine.

When he doesn't expand, Niles chuckles. "Damn, Kalden. You can't just drop that on them without expanding on the details."

"Actually, that's exactly what I expect from him," I say, sipping the deep berry liquid from my own crystal glass and ignoring the heated sensation of Kalden's eyes on my face.

"You two are that familiar already, huh?" Niles glances between us with a lopsided smirk. "What else have you come to expect from him?"

I sense there's more to Niles's question beyond the flirty little game he's presenting it to be, but I play along anyway. "He's calculated, yet selectively considerate. Quick to make decisions. Led more by his own moral compass than by duty. Obsessed with control, to the point where he pretends to be unaffected by trivial things like emotions, but he has his tells."

"I do?" This time, the question comes directly from Kalden.

I finally lift my gaze to his, struck by the intensity of his molten irises, even without the sun's luster.

"Your eyes," I breathe. "They're the only place you can't hide what you're feeling. Like right now, your pupils are dilating. Maybe in surprise, but your hooded lids tell me it's mostly satisfaction."

Kalden rewards me with a rare lift of his full lips. "Good to know you've been studying me so closely."

"Maybe I wouldn't have to if you weren't so insistent on acting like a personified puzzle."

"I think you like the challenge." One corner of his mouth lifts higher than the other, and it's truly ridiculous how much that simple movement awakens every nerve in my body.

Gem clanks her fork onto her plate, and I shoot her an apologetic glance, but she takes a sudden interest in ridding the tablecloth of invisible dirt.

"So, your mothers were from Caligo?" I ask, attempting to bring us back to Kalden's blunt confession.

Niles answers first. "They were both selected for the Hunt about forty years ago. Their group left them for dead after a Pyre ambush about seven miles south of here. Kalden's father was returning from a trip to our southern capital when he found them, pulses faint, but still beating."

"He healed them?" I ask.

Kalden nods.

"I guess your hero complex is hereditary, then."

Niles huffs in amusement, but Kalden's smirk falls. "I'm no hero."

"Not this again," Niles groans. "That wasn't your fault."

"What happened?"

Niles shakes his head. "It isn't my story to tell."

A muscle twitches in Kalden's jaw as he stares at his empty glass. "About nine months ago, my older brother, Aurick, came to me in a panic after his partner didn't come home the night before from his hunting trip with his sister. Aurick wanted my help in casting out an electromagnetic wave to detect where he went. You've probably already noticed that Sols can sense each other's energy. And the more often we're around someone, the more we pick up on their unique essence. It's almost as easy as breathing, especially when we're in close proximity. But the farther we are from the person we're trying to detect, the more it drains our power."

Kalden's eyes gloss over as he continues recalling, "I'd already spent a good amount of energy that day, so I tried to assure Aurick that maybe his partner had extended his trip. I honestly thought he was overreacting. So, Aurick decided to do it alone."

The wine sloshes uneasily in my stomach, my gut sensing what likely happened from there.

Niles rests a hand on his friend's shoulder, and Kalden exhales slowly.

"It happened so quickly. One minute, I was grabbing produce from the greenhouse. The next, I felt his essence burning away. Smelled the bitter ashes of it. By the time I got to Aurick's home, it was too late. He'd burned through it all—his clothes, his skin, and his humanity." Kalden blinks, releasing twin beads of tears down his cheeks while making no attempt to wipe them away. "I kept him restrained for a week while I tried everything to bring him back. Even let him feed from me, hoping my essence would replace what he lost. Probably would've died if it weren't for Niles barging in to get him off me. I knew then that it was time to put an end to it. My brother had already died, and I couldn't keep pretending I'd find him in the mockery of his corpse."

An icy pressure weighs on my lungs as I imagine the devastation of losing a sibling in that way, and no one speaks for a long minute. What's the right way to respond to that level of horror? Perhaps there isn't a "right" response, no right words beyond a simple acknowledgement of his grief.

"I'm so sorry," I say.

"Me too," Gem echoes.

Even Twilynn nods her agreement.

Kalden fidgets with his empty glass before pushing it away. "I didn't tell you that to gain your sympathy. I just thought you should know that I'm not the hero you think I am. If I weren't so selfish, Aurick would still be here."

"Aurick knew the consequences of channeling that amount of power by himself," Niles says gently. "He could've asked someone else for help."

"Two things can be true," Kalden admits.

I sense Gem's eyes on me, and I turn to find her jade irises glittering.

Two things can be true.

Like Kalden, I made a selfish decision that pushed Gem away. But I'm not the only one making choices.

Gem could stay with me. Now that she's had some time to get to know Kalden and come to her own conclusion about the Sols, I suspect part of her wants to. But I also know a larger part of Gem could never choose to turn her back on her twin, even if it means going back to the stifling darkness of Caligo. And as much as I'll miss her—miss them both—I can't blame Gem for choosing Taur over me.

I nudge my boot into hers beneath the table. She nudges mine back.

Heavy silence compresses against the glass columns of the domed pavilion.

"Your mothers," I begin to ask, hopeful my prodding doesn't build onto the thick quiet. "Are either of them here?"

Niles's smirk returns. "Eager to meet the parents already, little nova?"

I share a soft smile. "I'd like to meet the two women who survived the Hunt and made a new life for themselves."

Eyes filling with pride, Niles shares, "I could take you to meet my mother in a couple days, if you'd like. Once you've had time to settle in. And Irene is away on travels, though she should be coming back soon, right Kalden?"

Kalden nods, but I barely notice as Niles's words scratch at something I heard earlier.

"Irene's birds," I say, repeating what the stranger had said after we left the menders.

Both men share a look before turning their full attention towards me.

Brows arching, Kalden asks, "Who told you about that?"

I fiddle with the cloth napkin, folding it into squares. "There was a woman on one of the bridges earlier—the one with the people and their wired poles."

Niles cuts in. "You mean the fishing deck?"

My forehead pinches, recalling how she'd reeled in a speckled fish. "Maybe? Anyway, she told me she'd been in a past Hunt and that she survived because of Irene's birds."

Twilynn perks up, quietly chiming in to ask, "Like the ones Jacqueline saw?"

"Demi's aunt had a similar experience," Gem explains to the Sols. "Saw some glowing birds that guided her back to Caligo."

Kalden leans back in his chair. "On the first anniversary after my mother's near death, after she had time to acquaint herself with her abilities, she wanted to help the new recruits somehow without having to explain that she wasn't the same as the monsters they were meant to hunt. So, she sent out winged solar constructs to act as her second set of eyes."

"The birds weren't real?" I ask, trying to wrap my head around how that's even possible.

"No, they're real," Kalden corrects. "As real as the blast of power you cast to level the Pyres earlier. But instead of a warm-blooded animal, her constructs are an amalgamation of energy manipulated into the shape of her choosing."

Gem lets out a breath. "Shadows' mercy, that sounds . . ."

"Difficult," Kalden supplies.

Niles snatches the last bunch of grapes from the center of the table while clarifying, "Especially when the constructs are as detailed as Irene's. And the distance she's able to push them is no easy feat. Would push a lesser Sol to burnout. It's a marvel she keeps it up year after year."

Kalden shrugs. "It's worth it for her. She's not always able to locate the Huntresses in time, but when she does, that's one less life stolen by Caligo's lies."

"Did she send any this year?"

Kalden's gaze turns downcast, and Niles clears his throat, answering on his friend's behalf, "No. Ever since Aurick, she's been . . . more cautious with her channeling."

"Right," I say, kicking myself mentally for steering us back into sensitive territory. "Well, thank you for putting this meal together—though I'm not convinced you didn't 'construct' all this food into existence."

Niles shakes his head. "Eating a construct would be highly inadvisable, unless you enjoy the flavor profile of acrid radiation and having your taste buds melted."

Tongue souring, I scrunch my nose.

Kalden graces us with an almost-smile. "I can assure you that no solar constructs were used in the preparation of this meal, but I'll pass along the compliments to the culinary staff."

Niles lifts his glass in a toast before downing the rest of its deep berry liquid.

"They outdid themselves. Pulled out all the stops for the return of the High—you." He winces. "Sorry."

Kalden waves off the apology. "It's time I tell them the rest."

My eyes skate over the lavish dishware and intricate floral arrangements. Even the food itself tasted like luxury. The whole private dining setup is brimming with an extravagance that I should've questioned sooner.

"You're the High Sol, aren't you?" I say, remembering the term I'd heard floating around during our arrival.

Both Kalden and Niles turn their widened eyes to me.

"Where did you hear that?" Kalden asks, his gaze flicking to his friend with suspicion.

Niles holds up his palms. "Wasn't me."

"It really wasn't," I confirm, then explain, "When you were leading us through the village earlier, I heard people gossiping about the High Sol and what he planned to do about the black cloud."

"And you presumed that was me?"

"Not initially. But between you having this grand feast organized for us on very short notice, and Niles almost slipping up, it's not a far reach."

Gem nods. "It makes sense. You're a natural leader, albeit a reluctant one."

Kalden arches a brow, and I point out, "You swooped in with our training sessions when that guard made it clear he wasn't concerned about preparing us for the Hunt."

Gem chimes back in to add, "And once we were released, you took charge and kept calm, even when those Pyre things attacked us."

Kalden lifts his chin, irises gleaming as he glances between us. "I guess I haven't been as covert as I thought."

"So, what does it mean to be the High Sol?" Gem asks. "Are you the elected leader of this village, or were you born into it?"

"The High Sol isn't a genetically inherited or formally elected position. It's something you are or aren't."

Niles gives Kalden a teasing look before clarifying on his behalf, "Every Sol has their own bandwidth for how much of the sun's power they can channel before reaching burnout. Some can only use a few short bursts of raw energy each day. Others can draw from it long enough to achieve a highly specialized task, like Joss. A few of us can sustain more prolonged periods of channeling, but even we have to cap it after a few hours. Sometimes shorter, depending on how much focus and power the task requires. Then there are the High Sols, blessed by the sun with an unfathomable bandwidth."

Kalden groans. "'Unfathomable' is a stretch."

Niles slaps a hand on his shoulder. "I once saw you sustain a magnetic field barrier for ten hours."

Brows lifting, I ask, "I take it that's impressive?"

Niles nods. "I'd reach burnout after maybe two hours. Three, tops."

"Damn." Gem tips her cup at Kalden. "Do you even have a limit?"

Shadows flicker in those golden irises. "I do."

Just when I think he's about to return to his intentionally vague ways, Kalden surprises me by sharing, "I nearly reached it once. After Aurick . . ." He clears his throat. "Channeling often has a pleasurable heat. A consuming warmth that magnifies each of our senses. But when a Sol is nearing burnout, it becomes scorching. It overtakes all feelings. All emotions."

A shudder claws down my spine. "How close did you get?"

Kalden's haunted gaze flicks to mine. "As close as a Sol can get before becoming a Pyre."

CHAPTER TWENTY-EIGHT

We return to the shared bungalow while Niles circles back to the mending facility to check on Joss. The generous abode is one of the larger structures along the village's waterside edge. The exterior glass walls are inlaid with tiny orange, yellow, and blue shards to create a mosaic of the sunrise over the ocean. A spiral staircase circles up to a raised deck encircling the bungalow's roof.

Catching Gem's eye, I nod towards the steps, and we ascend them together.

Neither of us speaks for a while, preferring to relish the view.

Eventually, Gem breaks the silence to confess, "I think you're going to like it here."

"Maybe," I admit, fingers gripping the aged wood railing. "There's still so much I don't know."

"Yeah, but look at this." She waves a hand at the green-and-gold landscape to our left, then the ocean to our right. "Kalden doesn't seem so bad, either."

Warmth blossoms across my face. "He isn't why I'm staying."

"No, I know. What I said about you chasing the approval of men was—"

"Right," I finish for her. "You were right to call it out. I don't do it consciously. I think it's more of a groomed instinct than a deliberate choice, and I'm not sure if I'll ever shake it fully. But I think I stand a better chance at shedding those habits here than if I were to return—if going back was an option."

My vision blurs as I replay the events that make that impossible.

"I am proud of you, you know," Gem says quietly. "For being selfish. Adapting. Surviving. Maybe not in the way I would've chosen for you, and definitely not one I'd choose for myself. Then again, it led you here, so maybe it was the exact right path. Plus, seeing you fight those Pyres was badass."

"Badass?" I cringe. "I was concussed and literally fighting *on* my ass."

"So? Taking three creatures down by just flailing your arms around is impressive."

"Okay, hold on. There was a bit more to it than flailing my arms." I nudge my elbow into Gem's arm, and she jumps back, eyes wide. "I wasn't—I'm fully drained of power right now."

Her parted lips morph into a grin. "I know, but you should see your face right now."

I groan. "You're evil."

"I've got to get my revenge while I still can."

My shoulders sag forward as I fidget with the fraying stitches along the side of my leathers from where I cut myself right before our departure. "Does that mean you've decided to head back?"

Gem's voice falls to a broken whisper. "I have to. T's gonna need me. I know we'll be separated once I'm back, but it'll only be a few levels between us. At least I'll still be able to see her, even if we aren't sharing the same cabin."

"I understand." I tuck my curls behind my ears while I ask, "Would you . . . Do you think you could see yourself staying here if you didn't have to go back for Taur?"

She releases a slow breath, leaning her back on the railing. "I'm not sure I'd be as eager to go back, especially knowing all the trauma and death that's come from the chancellor's lies. But is it horrible to admit there's a familiarity in the darkness? I know you've always said it's like a cage, but it's been my home my entire life. Most of the halls I can navigate with my eyes closed. It's predictable, if not safe, and I don't think I'm ready to give that up."

I get where she's coming from. The unknown has left me feeling disoriented more than once since we left Caligo behind. Yet unlike Gem, I welcome the jittery rush that fills my chest when I consider how much there is to see and learn.

"I'll miss you," I whisper, voice cracking as I rest my head on Gem's shoulder.

The very fact that she allows me to do so tells me all I need to know, but she says it anyway. "I'll miss you, too."

Neither of us is ready to part, so we linger, discussing the hastily made plan that the other Huntresses put together prior to dinner. This time tomorrow, they'll request that Gabe is released, so the five of them can begin their return during the cover of night, though they'll also request to be given back the nightstone missiles, just in case they encounter more Pyres.

"Aruna thinks we'll be welcomed home as heroes, since we've taken out fifteen 'Sols,'" Gem huffs, using her fingers to put air quotes around the word. "And with our cameras disabled, we should be able to make a case to suggest the conditions of the Hunt have been met."

"Heroes, huh?

She chews on her lip. "You think it's a naive plan, don't you?"

"I think it has a lot of contingencies," I admit. "Have you considered what might happen if the Sols aren't ready to release Gabe? I mean, he nearly murdered someone today, Gem. And if they do allow him to leave, there's no way they'd let him take those missiles."

"Maybe they'd entrust them to us? Heading back without Gabe wouldn't be ideal, but if we're adequately armed, we should make it," Gem says, though her strained pitch gives away her doubt.

I sigh, picking at a splinter in the wooden railing while counting each potential fallacy. "If they give you the missiles, who's to say you'll have enough if you run into another horde of Pyres? And if you have enough or manage to avoid them, do you truly believe the chancellor would be quick to accept the word of four Tier Threes as evidence that you've fulfilled the terms of return, without Gabe there to vouch for you?"

Gem hangs her head, a response in and of itself.

"I figured you'd be gone by now," I say while spotting Kalden waiting at the bottom of the stairs.

Dark circles streak beneath his closed lids as he leans against the bungalow's mosaic wall. "Gone where?" he asks, eyes remaining shut.

"To check in with the mender," I say, like it's the obvious answer.

"Niles circled back a few minutes ago. Joss is stable. The transfusions were successful at removing the nightstone from her veins. The menders intend to finish regenerating her hands tomorrow."

"They can do that?" Gem asks, following behind me on the stairs.

Kalden dips his chin. "She woke up long enough to tell Niles that she saw an older man wearing a navy suit with a silver moon emblem in the Pyre's memories."

Gem's brows pull taut. "The chancellor?"

I shake my head. "When would he have interacted with a Pyre? I've never heard of him going aboveground, even at night."

"Also could've been Commander Guffian or one of the gate guards." Kalden shrugs. "I plan on swinging by to ask Joss for more details tomorrow, if she's feeling up to it."

I nod, treading closer as I descend the final step. "Will you be feeling up to it?"

"Why do you ask?"

"You look like sh—"

"Exhausted," I say, cutting Gem off.

Kalden's lips twitch in a half-smile, but it falls quickly. "The sun's gifts aren't without cost. The more we harness, the closer we're tied to our circadian rhythm. As night falls, we'll be in a near comatose state. Very little can wake us until the sun itself decides it's time to rise."

"Why does that feel like a challenge?"

His hooded eyes finally peek open at that. "We can make it one."

"*Uck.*" Gem groans. "I'm out."

I grin. "See you in the morning."

"Mm-hm." She waves a hand over her shoulder before disappearing into the bungalow.

A gleam of renewed energy dances in Kalden's irises as he holds out an arm. "I'd like to show you something."

I feign a grimace. "Please tell me that isn't an innuendo. I swear, if you pull your pants down right now, I'll follow Gem inside."

Kalden chuckles. The sound is just like everything else about him—edged in a warmth that leaves me craving more.

He leads me around the winding pathway past a few more sizable bungalows, then stops at a more modest structure, the slightest bit bigger than our cabin back in Caligo. Unlike most of the neighboring homes, its exterior glass walls are fully opaque. As if the owner prioritizes privacy over vibrant transparency.

"Awfully bold of you to take me to your home on the brink of sunset."

He lifts a dark brow. "What gave it away?"

I point to the solid glass. "You and your walls. Always hesitant to let people in."

He blows out a breath. "I've always been like this. Ignorant of most social cues and decorum. Content with being alone. But after losing Aurick and nearly burning through my own humanity, it got worse. I think a part of my soul never fully recovered from that. Emotions that used to come easily just . . . don't. I'm not sure I realized how numb I've felt until I saw you in that tunnel."

The memory of our meeting flashes to mind. "You looked angry."

"Not at you." He shakes his head, forehead creasing. "I caused that earthquake. I needed a way into Caligo to see if the Shades had any more info on the missing Sols, without barging in through the front door. And I remembered what my mother had told me about the transport tunnels, so I waited until the city was asleep before sending a blast of power into the ground. I hadn't expected anyone to be there. When I saw you, I was terrified that I'd hurt an innocent. And maybe a bit frustrated. I'd wanted to get in and out without drawing notice. But there you were, noticing me."

I hold up a finger. "*You're* the one who came up to me with that boulder. I wouldn't have noticed you at all if you'd stayed hidden."

"Probably, but I couldn't do that."

"Why?"

"When I first heard someone shuffling around, I wanted to make sure they weren't gravely hurt. Then I saw you reach into that beam of sunlight, and I was curious to see how you'd react. After months of apathy, there you were, making me feel too many things. Curiosity. Frustration." Kalden's chest rises and falls as he leans in. "Anticipation."

A heady shiver skirts down my spine.

"Hold on." I press a palm into his chest, ignoring how the heated contact pulses through me. "How did you make yourself look so normal?"

When we'd met, there'd been no trace of the sun's golden light in his veins or eyes.

"This," Kalden says, reaching up to take off the nightstone pendant resting below his collarbone, then he snaps it open like a locket. "The outer shell is painted with a matte onyx that's meant to imitate nightstone, but the inside is sunstone."

He places the open pendant in my palm. The orange-and-yellow stone glimmers as I lift it for a closer look.

"It allows us to stow away our power when needed," Kalden explains.

"Like nightstone?"

"Nightstone depletes. Sunstone stores. It acts as a vessel, either temporarily or indefinitely. A Sol can reabsorb whatever they channeled into the vessel at any given time without the presence of the sun."

My eyes flick back up to his. "Even at night?"

He nods. "Only until the Sol uses up the amount of power that was put into the stone."

"Wow," I breathe, marveling at the unassuming stone for several more seconds before handing it back to Kalden.

"Keep it."

My brows pull together. "I can't."

"Why not?"

I shrug. "You might need it."

Kalden's mouth quirks up a bit. "I have more of those inside."

"So, you're not gifting me some rare, special necklace?" I tease while pulling the golden chain around my head and settling the sunstone pendant atop my ragged bodysuit.

"I like seeing you wear my things." His irises glint for a moment before he shifts on his feet, kicking a loose pebble free from the wooden planks of the suspended bridge. "Technically, I could've drawn from it to heal Gem's head injury from the falling debris, but I wasn't sure how you'd react, and I didn't want to chance it. I'm sorry."

I dip my head to acknowledge his apology. "I probably would've freaked."

"Maybe, maybe not. You're handling all of this better than most who are forced to confront the fact that their entire belief system is built on a lie."

"Give it a few days. Once the shock wears off, I might just go ballistic," I tease with a breathy chuckle.

Kalden's head tilts to the side. "That would be a valid response, you know."

"To be honest, I think part of me isn't all that surprised. After Gabe and I divorced, I had to face a lot of ugly truths about Caligo—truths that I'm ashamed to say I didn't really grasp until they had a direct negative impact on me. The Hunt's eligibility system is an obvious issue, but it's just another symptom of the discriminatory tiers. They bleed into everything. If you aren't an able-bodied male, you get little say in what jobs you're allowed to work, where you're allowed to live, who you're allowed to love. Little boys are sent to organized learning programs, while the girls stay home with their mothers to learn how to cook, clean, sew, speak, not speak, and any other domestic duty deemed necessary for fulfilling our primary purpose in life: supporting our future husband. It's a system that does more than foster our codependency. It rewards it, which doesn't make for a functional relationship for any of us."

I press my palm onto my forehead and lean against the cool glass of Kalden's home before continuing, "All that to say, I already knew how much Chancellor Bren and his purists loved to twist a narrative for their gain. It's shitty, recognizing how deep the brainwashing goes, but is it weird if I also feel relief? The truth equips me to choose possibilities I didn't know existed. And for the first time in a while, I feel . . . empowered. Like the future is truly mine to choose."

"It is." Kalden smiles, and holy shadows, I forgot how breathtaking happiness looks on him. "So, what would you like to do next?"

I turn, taking a few steps away as I pretend to mull it over. Finally, I spin on my heel, stopping right in front of the arched glass door set within a gilded frame.

"I'd like you to let me in." I rush to tack on, "If you'd like."

Kalden's grin brightens, sending a wave of heat through my veins more potent than the sun itself. He steps towards me, close enough for me to see each individual fleck of gold in his irises and the gleaming umber strands that fall against his temples.

"I'd like nothing more."

CHAPTER TWENTY-NINE

Silken sheets caress my skin as I wake in the predawn hour the next morning, basking in the scent of smoky bergamot. I try to roll closer to the edge of the bed, but the warm, sturdy arm wrapped tightly around my waist prevents me from doing so.

A fervor pools low in my stomach from last night's memories.

After inviting me in, Kalden had given me a tour of his modest one-bedroom home, indulging my every little inquiry about his various books and knickknacks. He'd even offered me a change of clothes and privacy as I'd ripped the disgusting leathers from my body. By the time we made it to his bed, the sun had finished its descent beneath the horizon, and we'd both succumbed to our exhaustion.

Despite the lack of physical entanglement, it was quite possibly the most intimate evening I've ever spent with a man. Never have I felt so in control—or so valued for my mere presence alone, not what I can offer—than when I'm with Kalden. As many questions as I had for him, he had for me. And not once did his eyes wander or glaze over, even when I rambled on about rebuilding my life post-divorce with Gem and Taurance, and the anxieties of starting over yet again.

Gem believes I'm going to like it here in Lucis, and I already do. I'm sure, in time, its flaws will be revealed, along with Kalden's. That's the thing, though. No one is without flaws, but finding somewhere or someone that allows us to reveal those imperfections and accepts them exactly as we are . . . Well, that's enough to make a girl feel like she's home.

A beam of amber light shines through the circular window at the top of the ceiling's dome, and Kalden finally stirs. He tightens his grip on my waist, rolling me over until I'm pinned between his arms.

"Good morning," he says, curls falling along his face as he presses a kiss on my forehead.

I lift my fingers to brush them through his disheveled hair. "Did you sleep well?"

He dips his chin. "Too well. How long have you been up?"

"Long enough to discover you're more animated while unconscious than when you're awake."

His angular brows raise, but only slightly. "I doubt that."

"It's true. You made some interesting noises," I say, releasing a close-mouthed grumble before crescendoing to a whimper, though it comes out more like a moan.

Kalden's hooded gaze fixates on my mouth. "That *is* an interesting noise. I think I'd like to hear it again."

Blood blooms beneath my cheeks. "Only if you earn it."

"Is that a challenge, or a promise?" He leans in close, the rough bass of his voice sending tingles across my lips, and I'm struck by the memory of being in a similar position a handful of days ago. Like then, my back arches, yet this time he doesn't flee as I guide his face to mine.

"Both," I whisper, then claim his mouth with my own.

Hands travel down the length of my sides, inching closer to the hem of my borrowed tunic. His fiery touch awakens every inch of my body. I welcome it. If death by Kalden's fire is to be my fate, then I will gladly burn in this insatiable inferno, but I'll be taking him down with me.

He submits to my lead, allowing me to shove him onto his back.

"You're radiant," he says, dilated pupils beaming up at me as they devour my mussed curls and swollen lips.

My smile grows wider as I realize I believe him. I feel radiant. Alive. In control. I get to choose what I want. *Who* I want.

And I want him.

My fingers grab onto the translucent tunic, itching to pull it off.

"*Orelle,*" a familiar voice calls from outside, halting my hands. "Orelle! Where are you?"

Kalden stiffens beneath me. "Sounds like I'm not the only one who needs you."

I mutter a curse before climbing off both Kalden and the bed, tripping gracelessly as my foot gets caught in the twisted sheets. "Coming!"

Once I regain my balance, I jog towards the arched front door, swinging it open to find Gem walking past with her helmet firmly back in place.

"Over here!"

"There you—sun's pits, Orelle!" She throws her hands across the polarized lens, blindly shoving us both inside and kicking the door shut. "Where are your clothes? Demi and the others are waiting on us."

"Yvonne's burial," I say, eyes widening as I remember what the mender said about starting a half hour past first light. I spin around and rush back to the bedroom to tug on my boots.

Kalden, who's already pulled on a fresh pair of pants, offers a new, off-white tunic. "As much as I appreciate your current attire, I thought you might prefer something less revealing for your friend's burial."

"Thanks." I pull it on without removing the iridescent fabric beneath. "I'm decent now."

Gem heaves a sigh. "Good. Let's go."

Kalden steers us to the northwestern edge of Lucis, where the dunes give way to rolling green hills. We don't stop until we reach the first in a scattered line of cypress trees so Yvonne can be laid to rest eternally beneath their shadows, as per Demi's request.

Niles and the young man who assisted us at the mending facility yesterday carry Yvonne's body on a bed of black silk, and a bouquet of black roses covers the fatal wound in her chest.

When I first saw the flowers, Kalden explained, "It's customary to bury our fallen with white roses, but the menders agreed black would be more fitting, given her upbringing."

The considerate gesture makes my eyes well up as the two men lower Yvonne beside the roots of the cypress, taking care to set her down gently.

The female mender kneels a few feet away before motioning for us to do the same. "In Lucis, we view dawn as a rebirth. But for Caligans, it is an end, which is why we've gathered together at this hour to honor the life of Yvonne Starow, beloved daughter and friend. This earth was blessed by her existence, so it shall cherish her forevermore within its embrace."

She places a kiss in her sunlit palm before pressing it to the dirt. Niles and the young mender do the same, along with Kalden, who kneels at my side.

Demi hunches forward to grab Yvonne's hand, holding it to her heart one final time.

"I love you," she whispers hoarsely. "I'm sorry for not telling you sooner."

As the mender digs her nails further into the dirt, the ground rumbles beneath my knees, a fissure splitting in a precise line around the bed of roses. Tears burn my eyes as Demi releases Yvonne before she's lowered into the earth's open womb.

Twilynn scoots forward, wrapping an arm around Demi's shaking shoulders. Gem follows, standing steady beside the two women while waving me over. Even Aruna inches the slightest bit closer, though notably keeping her distance from me on Demi's opposite side.

And there the five of us stay, offering our presence over words until the ground fully closes over our fellow comrade and friend.

CHAPTER THIRTY

"Hold up, little nova." Back on the bustling raised walkways of Lucis, Niles pulls me behind the rest of the group to ask, "I've got to swing by the holds to ask Gabe some questions, and I was wondering if you'd be willing to tag along?"

My brows shoot up. "Me?"

"No, the other little nova." His cerulean irises glisten. "Yes, you. I was hoping if you're there with me, he might be more forthcoming, or more willing to hear what we have to say."

I bite on the inside of my lower lip, but nod. "Sure. I can't guarantee he'll listen, but we can try."

"Perfect." He grins, wrapping an arm around my shoulders. "Kalden, I'm stealing your girl."

"Have fun. I'll meet you there in a bit," Kalden calls back from his position at the front of our group, waving without looking.

Aruna glances over her shoulder, and I feel the prickle of her glare cutting through her helmet as Niles steers me down a set of stairs that spill out onto a lower pathway, but sensation dissipates after we round the first bend.

"You know, little nova, when Kalden told me he was going to Caligo to investigate the Pyres, I never would've predicted he'd come back with a woman. A Shade, nonetheless."

"Is that a bad thing?" I ask quietly, recalling what he'd said to Gabe about "our kind" being those more prone to violence.

Niles tilts his head. "Depends on the Shade, I guess. Not all the women that Irene has saved are grateful for her intervention. She began by guiding them here, towards Lucis. Most accepted the help and shelter, but a few . . . Well, they took it upon themselves to fulfill their duty as Huntresses by attacking our people. After the last incident ended in the death of both a Sol and the Shade who killed her, Irene switched to leading the women back towards Caligo."

Though the deaths didn't occur by my hand, the weight of them sits on my chest. Throat swelling, I rasp, "I'm sorry."

Niles squeezes his arm around my shoulders. "Don't be. Kalden trusts you, and I do, too. You've proven that you see us as fellow humans, not the monsters you're practically bred to fear. Plus, you already make one hell of a Sol. If you were able to send out that solar wave with minimal training, imagine what you'll be able to do a few months from now."

The pressure in my chest eases, and my lungs expand more easily as I consider finding my own way to help future Huntresses avoid the fate of Yvonne, Meridna, Faron, and Blair.

Minutes later, Niles leads me into a nondescript dome with gray opaque walls and no windows.

"Back again?" asks a striking woman whose golden veins trace mesmerizing patterns across her hairless head.

Niles nods. "Brought some company with me this time."

"Help yourself," she says, not bothering to glance up as she flips to the next page in her book.

"Will do." Niles strides around the woman's desk, kneeling beneath the bottom drawer to procure a ring of keys.

Lifting a single brow, I ask, "That's it?"

"What's it?" Niles pushes a brass key into the aged knob and shoves open the thick, wooden door.

I shrug, lowering my voice as we pass into a dimly lit hall with numbered doors. "I figured your prison cells would be secured by some type of magical barrier, only accessible by Sols with a specific type of energy field or something."

Niles chuckles while bolting the door into place behind me. "The holds aren't a prison. They're more like a temporary holding facility for those who pose a moderate risk to themselves or others, so they aren't meant to be a long-term residence for high-threat individuals."

"Where do they get sent? The high-threat individuals?"

Hand stiffening on the keys, he replies, "A conversation for another time."

Niles pauses in front of the door marked by the number three, giving me the space to take a measured breath before nodding and unlocking the brass-plated door.

"Elle?" Gabe rises from the padded cot that's notably wider and plusher than the one I've slept in for the past decade. He moves the draping chains latched to his wrists, stepping over them towards me before retreating back as Niles shuffles in at my side. "What are you doing here?"

"I'm here to help," I say, keeping my voice steady, calm.

The artificial amber light highlights the wrinkle between his auburn brows as they pull together. "Help who? Him, or me?"

"Both, I hope."

Gabe's rosy lips pull down. "Where's your uniform?"

Warmth floods my cheeks as I glance at the layered tunics I borrowed from Kalden.

"Couldn't stand the stench anymore," I say instead, figuring the truth won't help us win my ex-husband over.

With his mouth thinning, those midnight-blue eyes rove around my body, lingering on my exposed legs, arms, and face. "You aren't . . . glowing."

I fold my arms against my chest. "The nightstone I inhaled—from the missile you nearly hit me with—is still in my system."

"I didn't . . ." Gabe lifts his hands, as if to indulge his habit of running his fingers through his hair, but the weighty chain tugs on his wrists. "I was trying to protect you."

"I didn't need your protection. Not from them."

"These missiles," Niles begins, using our conversation as a segue. "How many did you bring with you?"

Gabe swallows. "A dozen."

"And you've only shot off two?" He nods, and Niles presses, "By that count, there should be ten missiles left in the bag you handed to me. There are only eight."

It isn't phrased like a question, so Gabe just blinks.

I roll my eyes. "Where are the other two missiles, Gabe?"

His shoulders rise, then fall. "Must've dropped them at some point. Maybe back in the meadow, or when we slept together beneath the trees. I'm curious, Elle. Were you already lying to me then, or did the deception come later?"

Niles's wide gaze flicks to mine, and I shake my head. "First off, I fell asleep *beside* you, after making it very clear I had no interest in pursuing anything further than friendship. And second, to be honest, yes. I'd begun my training with Kalden prior to that night, though I didn't intentionally wield the sun's power until Yvonne nearly died the next morning."

Gabe's features twist into a snarl. "How could you?"

"How could *I*?" I laugh darkly. "We were sent out here to die, Gabe! Me. Gem. The others, too. Did you really expect me to play the good little martyr?"

"Of course not! I snuck out for you, Elle. To save you."

"I'm not your wife anymore, Gabe. You made sure of that ten years ago, when you cast me aside out of fear that my infertility would affect your duties to Caligo. But did you ever consider how it affected *me*? Having the dream I spent my *entire* life planning for ripped away by my own body? I hated myself. Every time my cycle restarted, it broke me. And instead of helping me put together those pieces, you stomped on them and threw me out. But it's been a decade, and I'm no longer some broken thing that can only be made whole by a man. I found a way to hone my jagged edges into a weapon, to protect myself and the people who were there for me when you weren't."

His mouth falls open, but no words come out, so I continue, "So, forgive me if I refuse to stand here and beg for your understanding. The only thing I'm sorry for is not entrusting Gem with my intentions sooner, but I'm not sorry for finding a way to survive without your help."

My labored breaths fill the stretching silence until Niles finally asks, "You two were married?"

I turn towards the Sol. "Yes."

"Shit, little nova. You should've told me sooner. I wouldn't have made you—"

"It's fine," I say, brushing off his apology. "You didn't make me do anything. I came here to help."

Gabe's wan face pales further. "You sound different, Elle."

My chest heaves with a sigh. "That's because I am, but not because of the sun or the Sols."

His jaw clenches as he turns his head away.

"Do you have any more questions I can help with?"

Niles rubs a palm along the back of his neck. "Uh, I think I'll swing by again later by myself."

I nod, slipping past him and pausing at the door. "You've got a good heart, Gabe. Consider making room in it for more than just your constituents."

CHAPTER THIRTY-ONE

Rich hues of blue and gold spill through the mosaic walls across the aged wooden floorboards as I tread towards the kitchen the next morning, led by the faint scent of blueberry muffins and buttery toast. I rub the lingering sleep from my eyes while passing through the doorway, expecting to see a few of the Huntresses enjoying their breakfast. But the large circular table to the right of the walnut cupboards is vacant, minus the four plates of half-eaten food.

Maybe they weren't that hungry?

Brows furrowing, I head back into the hall, until I reach the other rooms at the back right of the rounded bungalow. The creases in my forehead deepen as I take in the empty beds notably void of their gear and weapons.

Did the plans change?

No.

Gem promised me last night that they'd give it another day before asking Niles about releasing Gabe. She wouldn't have left without saying goodbye.

I step outside, bare feet thumping against the wooden pathway as I search for signs of movement, in case they got restless and went for a walk before the still-sleeping village wakes. I break into a jog, aimlessly following the winding paths between the domes.

Just when I think I'm well and truly lost, I spot the gray opaque walls of the temporary confinement facility Niles had taken me to yesterday. Though I never got her name, perhaps the female stationed there would be willing to point me in the right direction, if she's even awake yet.

I reach for the door, surprised to find it's already cracked open.

"Hello? Sorry to bother you, but—" My words abruptly end when I slip inside and find no one manning the desk. I rush towards the door to the back hall. It, too, has been left ajar.

Needles dance along my skin as I push into it . . .

The third holding cell is empty.

Gabe isn't here.

Gem and the others are missing.

"Shadows' mercy," I curse, then run back outside, aiming towards the village's edge.

My chest tightens when I spot them a few minutes later: five figures clad in head-to-toe black treading south through the dunes below, backs turned on the village. But it's the way the shortest of them walks stiffly, as if being tugged forward, that sends me back into motion.

Gem.

The cool ocean breeze whips through my curls as I lean forward and leap off the platform, sending Kalden's sunstone pendant thumping against my chest. Sand greedily absorbs the footfalls of my dissenting legs. I cast a few glances at the brightening horizon to the east, pleading with the glowing orb to make its ascent.

As if it hears the unspoken plea, the sun mounts the horizon moments later, gracing the left side of my body with its light. A welcome tingle settles into my veins. With luminous hands streaking in my peripheral vision, I press onward with labored breaths.

If only I could give myself a boost, like the way the Pyres used thrusts of energy to leap across the dunes . . .

Maybe I can?

I direct the influx of power to my palms, letting it build to a potent warmth. Though the vibrations grow, I wait a few seconds longer, then release the flare toward the ground.

Grains explode from the dunes below as my body catapults dozens of feet off the earth.

I *really* didn't think this through.

Arms flailing, I spiral downward and scramble to reclaim a grip on the pulsing force throbbing within my hands, directing a more measured burst at the rapidly approaching sand—just enough to slow the momentum of my fall.

I land ass-first into the warm powder. The collision is relatively gentle, as if the fall spanned a couple of feet instead of several dozen. Rising, I reset my sights on the familiar figures that disappear over the nearest crest, then repeat the steps. I mount the top of the dune and nearly stick the second landing before swaying to the side.

"Elle? What are you doing here?" Gabe stretches out an arm, ushering the Huntresses to take cover behind him while clenching a rope in the opposite hand—a rope that ends in a knot around Gem's wrists.

My nostrils flare. "What am *I* doing? What in the fiery furnace are *you* doing?!"

Fists shaking, I lean forward.

Gabe drops the rope, letting it fall to the sand beside his feet. "I wasn't going to hurt her. I only needed to make sure she wasn't going to warn you of my escape."

"So what if she had? They weren't going to keep you as a permanent prisoner, Gabe. You would've been free to go in a couple days, if not hours."

He shakes his helmeted head. "You don't know that."

"I do," I say. "The only reason they restrained you was to protect against unnecessary violence."

"Do you hear yourself, Elle? You're defending them! Sun's pits, you've *become* them!"

I throw my hands up. "Is that truly so bad?"

"Yes." The word is low, rough. A surrender and a condemnation. "Just because they've evolved doesn't mean they aren't monsters."

I descend farther down the dune, stomping straight up to Gabe. "Monsters? I'm not sure what you thought you were seeing back there, but I saw giddy children and generous neighbors. People who not only welcomed a bunch of strangers into their community but cared enough to host a memorial in honor of our fallen. Strangers that recognized our lives are something worth celebrating, not sacrificing. So, if you're looking for monsters, maybe you should look closer to home."

He tenses, and I take advantage of the moment to pull Gem's poniard from where it hangs around his belt. A hand grabs my wrist, and I don't think twice before releasing a flare into it.

Gabe crumples to his knees with a yelp.

Once, I might've knelt beside him and begged for forgiveness. Inflicting pain on any man, let alone my ex-husband, wasn't a thought I'd allowed myself to entertain, even for the men who shared no such qualms. Perhaps it was the ever-looming threat of being a Tier Three throwaway one misstep away from getting locked in the Abyss, or my deep-seated desperation to prove myself worthy, fighting back was a concept reserved only for our mandated training sessions.

Now, though, I don't bat an eye as I sidestep around Gabe's contorted form and cut off the knot from around Gem's wrists. If resorting to violence to defend my friend makes me the villain he believes all of us Sols to be, then so be it.

Gem's shoulders sag. "Thank y—Look out!"

Something blunt slams into the backs of my knees, swiping my legs out from under me.

"Get away from us!" snarls Aruna as she unsheathes her short sword.

Gem pushes herself between us. "Aruna, quit it! Orelle isn't here to hurt us, and you know that."

"Do I? What do you call that?" She points a finger towards Gabe, who pants as he slowly returns to standing.

"Justice," Gem says with a shrug. "And a long time coming, too."

Before Aruna can spit another retort, a metallic hum slices through the air, growing louder by the second.

I return the poniard to Gem.

"More Pyres?" she asks.

"I don't think so. It almost sounds like . . ."

Black-adorned figures emerge from the top of the opposite ridgeline, dozens of heads bobbing as they march in formation in uniforms nearly identical to Gabe's, with added armor plating. They halt at the peak as one breaks from the line to descend the hill first. The rising sun glints off rows of pins and badges secured to navy armor, and I know who it is before he speaks a word.

"Step away from my son!" Chancellor Bren bellows, his voice spreading across the valley.

It takes several seconds before it registers: he's talking to me. I clench my flickering fists. "I won't hurt him, and I think you know that."

The chancellor stiffens. "Of course you will. You're a Sol."

"I am," I say, since there's no use denying that. "But you and I both know that Sols are not your true enemy. The Pyres are."

He tilts his head, and for a moment, I think he might continue the ruse. "You're still wrong about one thing, dear. I have no true enemies—none that are capable of defeating me."

The chancellor pulls a remote from beneath his armored vest, pressing a thumb into a singular red button. My muscles clench as I wait for a barrage of missiles or other projectiles to rain down on those of us in the sandy valley. None come. Instead, familiar thundering booms reverberate beneath my bare feet, striking in rapid succession. Someone behind me gasps as the first Pyre mounts the ridge, its charred legs burrowing into the sand a few yards in front of Chancellor Bren and his men.

It isn't alone. Three more of its kin leap forward. Then ten. A dozen. Too many for me to fight alone. The Pyres nearest us lean forward, readying to close the gap.

Power surges to my hands as I do the same, preparing to do what I must to protect the Huntresses at my back.

"Stop," Chancellor Bren says plainly while pushing the button a second time.

As one, the Pyres halt in place, their taloned hands writhing towards the collars at their throats.

Gabe steps forward, cradling his still-sore hand to his chest. "Father, what have you done?!"

"What I must to preserve our great city—the same thing you will have to do, when your time comes." The chancellor lifts the remote. "Control first, above all."

Gabe shakes his head. "It's Caligo first."

"They're one and the same, son. Caligo would not exist without control. It's the pulse of the city, and we're the ones who must keep it alive. Otherwise, our people would disperse into chaos."

Gem strides up to my side. "You're controlling the Pyres?"

Chancellor Bren nods. "I am."

"Then why continue the Hunt?" I ask. "Why keep sending us out here to eliminate the threat if there is no threat? What's stopping you from liberating our people?"

"I believe I've already answered that, dear," the chancellor says before heaving a sigh. "I was really hoping it wouldn't come to this."

"Come to what?" Gabe asks.

Chancellor Bren lifts two fingers in a signal, and Commander Guffian breaks forward from the pack. "Commander, there's been a change of plans. We cannot have the remaining Huntresses return to Caligo. They've witnessed too much and now pose a threat. Kill them."

"Father, no! They're innocent!" Gabe shouts, and the chancellor holds up a hand.

"Innocent? Son, do you not see the treason flowing through her body?"

Aruna runs forward, distancing herself from me. "What about us? I swear, I won't say anything!"

Chancellor Bren hesitates a moment before shaking his head. "What if you change your mind? If I allow you to return only for you to slip up? Or worse, find yourself missing the sunlight? Longing to feel its warmth? No. Your bodies may not be contaminated yet, but your minds are, and I cannot allow that to fester."

Aruna pivots her appeals to Gabe directly. "Gabe, please!"

Gabe tenses, turning his head between Aruna, his father, then finally to me. "Are you still you, Elle?"

"Now isn't the time, Gabe." I shake my head while pointing to the navy-clad figure who's always stood between us. "You have to tell your father to stop."

The icy rigidity of the chancellor carves through Gabe's voice. "This is the *only* question that matters, Orelle! I followed you up to this sun-damned graveyard to save you. And now you're standing here—you, but not. Make me believe that you're the same woman who clung to me in the reservoir when we were sixteen, or the same woman who jumped into my arms before we crossed the threshold into our home on the eve of our wedding. I know your body's infected, but tell me your mind is yours. That it hasn't been twisted by those abominations. If you do that, maybe I can find a way to save you." His voice softens to a plea: "Please, Elle."

The memories of ignorant bliss haunt my next breaths . . . but I'm not the same. Could I really ever go back? Though I know the answer, the heaviness in my throat grows as I consider what Gabe might do if I say no to him now.

"I can't deny I've changed, but I *am* still me, still human."

He shifts his weight uneasily, as if sensing the difference in my tone—the firm confidence of a woman who no longer measures her identity based on the perceptions of others. Or is he actually considering his father's delusions?

The oscillating glow of the light pulsing along my veins quickens with my heartbeat.

Gabe takes a single step backwards, angling towards his father. "I don't recognize *what* you are anymore, but it isn't human."

Chancellor Bren's voice rings out. "Step away from the Huntresses, son. I'll manage this difficult decision for you. Commander Guffian, eliminate the remaining loose ends. Ladies, I'd advise you not to resist. It will be over quickly."

The chancellor's host descends in formation from the opposing dune while the chancellor, commander, and Pyres remain along the ridge.

Aruna is the first to run, booted feet sliding as she spins back towards the village. Twilynn and Demi follow. As the first row of guards charge the remaining distance between us, Gem and I turn to flee as well. She leans to grab my arm, relieving some of the weight that hinders my feet.

"Go!" I yell at Gem. "I can flare-jump away. I'll buy you time."

She continues to yank on my arm. "No! I won't let you burn out."

I relent and allow Gem to ease my escape. We continue to climb the opposing dune towards Lucis. As we crest the hill, I turn away from the village that faintly shimmers with the morning dew and twist to see the guards gaining ground, losing sight of Gabe in the columns of black helmets and padding.

But he was already lost to me, wasn't he?

I never should've forgotten that he'll always be his father's son.

The mechanical whir that has stalked us throughout the Hunt crescendos, grating against my aching skull. A large cart, identical to those that transported us from the entrance of Caligo, careens through the valley at our flank, outpacing our ascent.

"Gem, you've got to let go. I—We don't have a choice. We have to fight." I wrench my arm from Gem's firm grip. Nimble fingers quickly reattach themselves to my shoulder before relinquishing.

"Make this the last choice they get to take from us." Gem only retreats a few steps.

The Caligans came to see a monster. Maybe they've made one instead.

My teeth grind together as I turn and unsheathe my own weapon, calling forth the tingle beneath my skin.

I'll stop before I burn.

Fire flows down my veins, and I extend a hand toward the cart. A magnetic pulse erupts from my outstretched fingers, humming with brightened strokes of light. Crackles resound across the dunes as the stunning blast reaches the steel-framed transport, tipping it onto its side. Dust detonates in a cloud around the fallen vehicle as it tumbles into the valley and impacts the corner of the guard formation.

A motorized echo continues to stir the air as I spin to find the others arming themselves against the outpouring soldiers from a second cart blocking our path towards Lucis. I reach out my hand again, aiming to stun the man leading the blockade. My jaw slackens as the subsequent burst dissipates instead of disarms, as if the black chestplate I'd been aiming at swallowed the full weight of the flare.

"Shit!" I backtrack closer to Gem. "Their armor is made of nightstone."

The guards at the base of the hill reform their disjointed line, and begin to advance, tightening the invisible noose around our necks with each step. Gem and I clamor towards the group of three women who have their weapons pointed at the five guards frantically spreading to surround us.

Twilynn's wail pierces through the whine of the transport's engine. "Please, stop!"

Still, the advance continues from all sides as the Huntresses become the hunted.

"I'll make sure the rest can't follow, but the others are too close. You need to fight! Each of you. All that armor's gotta be weighing them down. Dodge like Kalden taught you." I stare at my illuminated reflection in the visor of Gem's helmet before she dips her head.

The Huntresses split into pairs. Gem and Demi attack the leftmost guard while Aruna and Twilynn attack the right. Averting my eyes before the pairs clash, I turn to fight my own battle.

The sun's radiative reflection simmers within me. I summon the heat again, kneeling to plant my hands deep within the grains of warm powder, just as the mender had at Yvonne's burial.

Pinpricks race along my neck.

How far can I go?

The sand pulses with my heartbeat. Grains jump in time with the escalating rhythm while my feet sink deeply into the rumbling ground. A chasm forms, splitting across the dune and entrenching those who've yet to reach the peak. Thrashing limbs pry against the flow of rock and sand without avail. The guards that don't find support are sucked into the earth's depths—an abyss of my own making.

I staunch the outpouring energy and attempt to unbury my limbs from the compacted terrain. My arms pull free easily enough, but the dwindling strength in my aching muscles is no match for the earth's greedy hold on my legs.

"Gem, help!" I shout, watching a few remaining guards scale the rift. The commander tugs Chancellor Bren and his prodigy further from the crumbling edge.

"Holy shadows, Orelle!" A dark poniard dripping with blood falls at my side, and trembling arms wrap around me before pulling to release my legs from their cell.

I scan the blood streaking across Gem's leathers. "You're okay?"

Without a response, Gem picks up her dagger and rushes back towards the fight.

Glancing down at the sand coating my knees and shins, I busy myself with wiping off the chafing grains, protecting my heart for one more ignorant breath before looking to see whether I sent the other Huntresses to their deaths.

The last guard falls on his knees, succumbing to Aruna's blade as it plunges into the gap between the helmet and breastplate. Each Huntress nurses a wound, but all are standing, except for Demi. Her frame caves in on itself as she kneels, clutching at the steady crimson spouting around the dagger jutting from her ribs. Twilynn darts toward her while the rest of us take up a defensive circle around the two.

"Stop! Pull back and reform!" Commander Guffian's voice carries over the wind, though I can barely make out what he's saying over Demi's choked wail.

The chancellor turns a knob on the remote, and the Pyres settle into their haunches. Their foreign power pushes at my senses before they release it to propel themselves over the valley. Familiar thunderous cracks ring out as the wave of Pyres ascends, nothing but ravenous hunger in their black-and-gold eyes—eyes that will match mine, if I push myself much further.

The echoes of their assault reverberate around us as a dozen glowing figures land mere yards away. Scorching energy rains from above. The heat of the strike glasses the sand around several Pyre's feet.

My lungs lift with renewed vigor as I realize the newcomers aren't Pyres at all.

CHAPTER THIRTY-TWO

Kalden, Niles, Joss and another Sol make landfall in front of us, dust exploding from beneath their feet. Niles tugs at the air, and the Sols leap ferociously into a barrier he's erected out of sand and willpower.

Kalden glances at Gem and Twilynn, who hover over Demi. "Don't remove the blade. We need to deal with this first."

I tread to his side, voice unsteady as I ask, "Can you stop them?"

Kalden's lips thin. "It doesn't matter if we can or not. We fight anyway. And if one of us burns, we do what we must. Whatever it takes."

Whatever it takes.

Whether Kalden knows it or not, his words are an echo of my parents' plea. Though theirs was a call for survival, his is a call for sacrifice. Kalden will kill every Pyre, drive the Caligans back underground, and seal the nightstone door shut himself if he has to. I have no doubt that he'd scourge his humanity completely if that's what it took to protect the people he cares for.

But I won't let him do that alone.

"Kalden!" Niles struggles against the talons and tongues lashing through cracks in the sandy blockade. "Could use your help when you're done batting lashes at your girl. I can't hold the barrier much longer on my own."

"I've got him," I say to Kalden.

Niles lifts a brow as I race to his side. "You got anything left?"

Almost no part of me isn't consumed by the sun's warmth. If it weren't for the cool, lingering thread of nightstone sliding its way back and forth from my heart to my fingertips, I'd say it was almost pleasant.

"It doesn't matter. We do what we must," I urge, repeating Kalden's command.

Niles smirks. "I've heard that before. But not many people can keep up with him. It's okay to hold back. All I need you to do is place your palm here and don't let go."

He nudges his chin towards his shoulder, and I do as instructed. Before we close the breaks in Niles' fortification, Kalden and the two other Sols dive into the pack of Pyres, forming constructs of energy into thin curving blades and piercing staffs. Between each lash, the constructs vanish, only to renew for the next blow. We hold the barrier a little longer until the grunts taper. Niles drops his hands and allows the sand to fall back into place.

The dusty battlescape comes into view. A Pyre appears through the choked air, tongue splintering as it readies to feed off of whatever humanity I have left. I shove my hands forward and push an uncontrolled blast of solar energy out in panic.

Niles reacts faster than me, and a sharp-headed spear of light hurls through the air and embeds itself through the chest of the Pyre, passing completely through it before evaporating. The creature's lower half is paralyzed, but it continues to grab at the sand, pulling itself closer to me. Bending to retrieve a discarded nightstone blade from the ground, I wait for the Pyre to thrust its pincered tongue towards me. I swipe the blade across the thick tendrils, severing them from the Pyre's throat. Blood pours from the blackened creature's gaping mouth. Only seconds pass before the squirming motion stops.

A multitude of Pyres sprawl motionless from the edge of the shield's remnants to the chasm, yet a dozen more must've been released while the barrier was formed. A new horde catapults themselves across the opposite dune to where Kalden, Joss, and the other Sol now hold a defensive position.

Niles points towards the Sols. "They need help. Can you stay here?"

Before I can offer an answer, Niles compresses the sand with a flare and propels himself over the valley to attack the Pyre pack from behind.

I glance down at the nearest threat: the cluster of black-armored guards, no longer in disarray. Ranks reassembled, the chancellor's men reascend the hill around the rift's border.

Sweat pours down my temples. If I push myself too much further, I might not be able to come back. I can't turn into a Pyre here. Gem, Demi, Aruna, Twilynn . . . They can't handle fighting the guards and an ally turned foe. But maybe I can stop all of this another way.

I glare at Chancellor Bren, sitting untouched and unfazed across the dune while Gabe, Commander Guffian, and several shadows stand around him. With a surge of energy, I hurtle myself over the valley. A hiss escapes through clenched teeth as my leading ankle rolls on impact.

His shadows rush forward forming a wall between me and their leader.

I stagger forward. Just a few more bursts, that's all. I beg the heat gathering in my blood.

"Stop this!" Gabe pleads.

"Why?! He wants us dead. All of us. Our entire lives have been at your father's mercy. I won't let our deaths be the same." My weight shifts forward as I lift my palms towards the wall of men.

He chokes out my name. "Orelle!"

Chancellor Bren places a gloved hand on his son's shoulder. "Now do you see? The Orelle you knew is gone."

The commander pulls the chancellor further behind the line of guards, but not before my attention flicks to the box in Bren's hand. If I can take the controller, maybe I can take back control.

Shifting all of my weight into my good ankle, I launch myself over the guards. I clear the front line, but the commander grabs my injured ankle during the descent. Neither of us are able to guide the landing, and I crash into the chancellor's sturdy frame.

His visor lens shatters as it smashes into the ground. Chancellor Bren's shadows rush forward to retrieve their leader, but I grab the Pyre control box from his belt and tuck myself alongside the chancellor's dazed body.

My skin broils.

Just one more. That's all I need.

Grains scatter beneath me as I expel one more burst while clinging to the chancellor. Our bodies spin through the air, until I can't hold him anymore. We both land in the fray of Sols and Pyres.

I scramble for the remote and twist the knob.

Nothing happens.

The handful of remaining Pyres notice my intrusion and the scent of pure humanity laying on the ground motionless a few yards from me. I frantically twist the knob further and press the only button on the controller. The Pyres that were closing in on the chancellor suddenly seize, bodies stiffening and dropping in unison. The entire field of battle quiets for a moment. I stand on one trembling leg and lurch toward the chancellor, pulling him to his feet.

Kalden and Niles finish off the incapacitated Pyres before appearing next to me.

"Thank the sun you did that," Kalden huffs, his glowing veins obfuscated by reddened skin.

I peer at my own hand and see a similar hue. The blood in my veins grinds through my body. The pressure threatens to spill from my eyes and ears.

I grip Chancellor Bren's arm tighter. "Give the order to return to Caligo. Before any more of your men die."

Gabe inches closer to us before Kalden shouts, "We don't want to kill him, but if you take one more step, you'll be the next chancellor!"

Gabe's purposeful steps stiffen from the threat, and he comes to a halt.

Commander Guffian follows his lead.

"You don't have the right to command my men." The chancellor's bent knees straighten. Turning his gaze to avoid the sun's rays through his broken visor, he lifts his head and shouts across the dunes. "Who are you, men of Caligo, to listen to this woman—a feeder turned traitor? You have orders from the highest office above or below ground!"

All my hopes of a peaceful retreat crumble. I prepare to summon whatever power I have left.

Chancellor Bren continues, "Let's be done with this. Kill them all!"

The guard formation marches up the hill, where the vulnerable Huntresses are attempting to slide a heavily bloodied Demi towards the village.

Kalden's fist connects with Chancellor Bren's head, lifting him from the ground and disconnecting the snug helmet from its wearer. Golden rays trace across the chancellor's exposed face.

"*No!*" Gabe's voice rings into the clear sky.

"Order them to stop!" I scream at Chancellor Bren.

The crumpled man on the ground clutches at his cheeks. "What have you done? You've infected me!"

Niles hurriedly kneels beside the chancellor. "We need to restrain hi—"

A blast of energy erupts from Chancellor Bren's hand, and Niles falls back.

His body lands motionless.

Sensing my racing pulse, Kalden assures me, "He's okay. Unconscious, but alive."

The chancellor pulls himself up from the sandy impression left by his impact. "I'll help you meet the fiery destruction you so desperately crave!"

I glance over my shoulder and watch the guards closing in on the Huntresses . . . and Gem.

Twilynn and Aruna have crested the next dune so far in front of the other two that they might make it to the village. But they left Gem dragging Demi through the sand, leaving a thinning trail of blood and a swarm of guards fresh on their heels.

I kneel to my side, where a fallen Pyre lies. The clasp of the collar around its singed neck unhooks after several awkward twists and pinches of the mechanism. I wrap my fingers around it, pulling it free.

The chancellor lifts his head, twisting towards me. But before he can react, Kalden directs a kick into his stomach, causing him to collapse once more.

I wrap the collar around Chancellor Bren's neck, and it clicks easily into place. "Call off your men! Now!"

"No, no, no!" Through gasping coughs, he claws at his throat. "You can't!"

"I'm done asking." I stand over him, casting a shadow across his hunched frame, and jam my thumb into the button on the black box still in my left hand.

The chancellor's body convulses, and he lets out an eerie garbled cry. Red skin blooms across his nose and quickly spreads along his face before emanating a glow. I step away while flickers of heat from his eyes threaten to burn me.

No. I need him to give the order to stop the guards.

I reach in to remove the collar, but the increasingly white-hot heat of his skin makes me recoil. Kalden grabs my arm and pulls me away. He picks up Niles and follows quickly after me. While I turn to shuffle back, Gabe stops and falls to his knees not far from the scorching shell of his father.

The sand surrounding the chancellor begins to flow into a glassy bubbling pit. The glowing form of what was once a man lifts to its feet. The deep navy armor falls away, engulfed in flames on the ground. Its form stretches and wretches. A fiery orb expands from its skin and lifts into the clouds followed swiftly by a blinding light.

A quick glance reveals that the guards, the shadows, Gabe, even Gem have slowed or stopped to learn the fate of the chancellor.

An explosion of fiery magnetic force washes past me and Kalden, forcing us prone.

When we look back, Chancellor Bren is no more. In his place stands a monstrous black charred form with talons where its hands used to be. The creature gags, six long wiry tongues spilling out of its throat. A bitter smoke wafts through the air, stirring the acid in my stomach.

"I-I didn't mean to . . ." My legs shake while Kalden pulls me to my feet.

"That's not how it normally happens," he says raggedly.

A roar resonates from the freshly turned Pyre, and it staggers towards us, gaining its bearings before taking small bounds.

I fumble for the box that fell into the sand. The creature takes a final leap, and I press the button. Convulsions tear through what remains of the chancellor, and the figure lands roughly. It stills for a few seconds before shifting forward.

Again, I press the button, and it finally stops its attempts to lunge. I stare into the black-and-gold irises that were once an icy blue. Circling the button with my thumb, I wait for the chancellor's charred shell to make its next move. It finally turns and lifts its tongues into the air, as if sensing the plentiful humanity on the other dune, then jumps towards the group of outlying guards who've been watching the spectacle.

Hundreds of guardsmen scatter across the golden landscape, and the chancellor's husk tears apart his own forces as they haphazardly retreat towards Caligo.

Commander Guffian grabs Gabe's shoulder and pulls him up. "Shadows, secure your new chancellor."

Gabe peers over his shoulder as he's prodded and pushed within a circle of bodyguards, and I sense his condemning glare prickling down my spine.

I don't think he'll ever forgive me for what I just did to his father. And yet, something in me feels like I only revealed his true nature. To so many of the women in Caligo, Chancellor Bren has always been a Pyre, feeding on our humanity. His twisted words tore through us and made us believe we deserved a life of sacrifice.

I watch the sole Pyre chase the group of fleeing guards into the forest, leaving a trail of bodies and blood in its wake.

CHAPTER THIRTY-THREE

Scarlet clouds streak across the sky like blood as the sun approaches its descent. Although there's been no sign of the chancellor's men since they bolted into the forest, I keep a watchful eye on the horizon, waiting for any hints of movement or unnatural black smoke from the unaccounted-for nightstone missiles.

"They won't strike again so soon," Kalden says, placing a steady palm along the base of my spine. "Not until Caligo's had time to adjust to their new chancellor."

I dip my chin. "I know."

Warm lips press against the crown of my head, and I lean further into him, inhaling his smoky bergamot scent.

"If you change your mind, you're welcome to sleep at my place tonight."

"I know," I say again, turning my head to look up into those molten irises. "But I think it's best if—"

"If you stick with the girls?"

I nod.

"I understand. They're lucky to have you as a friend. I know you blame yourself for what happened to Demi, but don't forget the three other hearts still beating tonight. Gem, Twilynn, Aruna . . . They're alive because of you."

I lift a hand to brush the black curls away from his face. "And I'm alive because of them."

"Thank the sun for that," he says, leaning in, yet waiting for me to bridge the final gap.

And I do, but not before casting a final glance at the horizon and the glimpse of the moon bleeding through the reddened sky.

TO BE CONTINUED...

You've reached the end of *This Safe Darkness*, Book One in the Sols & Shades duology. For announcements about Book Two, follow Alexis on Instagram @alexismaragold or keep an eye on her website alexismaragold.com.

If Orelle's story resonated with you, please consider leaving an honest review on Amazon, Goodreads, StoryGraph, or your platform of choice.

ACKNOWLEDGEMENTS

In the spring of 2022, I set out with a concussion and a dream to write my first novel. In the 3+ years since, I've somehow written three more completed manuscripts, signed with a literary agent, connected with bookish friends across the globe, and now I'm publishing my debut.

Though *This Safe Darkness* is the first book I'm getting to share with readers, it isn't the first book I've written. Technically, it's my second and fourth—I wrote the original version in 2022 after shelving my first novel, revised it thoroughly with beta readers and my agent, then scrapped it all in 2025 after completing my third novel to rewrite an entirely new version of this story with only the core pulse intact.

Throughout this journey, there were multiple times I considered walking away. In fact, there was a time when I didn't pick up a book for four months. My self-worth had gotten so tied up with my lack of querying success that I had to step aside to remember my value isn't dependent upon what I produce or accomplish. Days after deciding I was ready to come back, I received an offer of representation. *[Insert a clever quote about growing pains often preceding achievements].*

I wouldn't have made it here if it weren't for a multitude of people who've come alongside me, but at the top of my list of people to thank is my dearest friend, husband, and muse: Michael. It is the privilege of my life to be wholly known and loved by you. Thank you for indulging that random car chat in the fall of 2022 when I asked, "What if day and night were switched? Like, what if humans were nocturnal? *Why* would they be nocturnal? Do they fear the sun?" Thank you for bringing me countless bedside meals while I holed up in my mental writing cave. Thank you for being my first ever beta reader, editor, and co-contributor for the battle scenes. If it were up to my own conflict-avoidant devices, fight sequences would consist of a few sentences and punches, so let's all say, *"Thank you, Michael!"* I love you endlessly.

Second on the list is my favorite (and only) child. My brightest sunshine. Thank you for grounding me back into reality when my mind tries to drift too far. Thank you for being patient when Mama misses out on playing because of the usual flare-ups and/or writing deadlines. Thank you for cheering me on. Being your mother is a joy and an honor. Also, please don't read this book until you're much older, okay? Great.

To my parents, Charles and Eileen: thank you for celebrating my ambitions. Between American Idol auditions in my teens, songwriting, performing in school musicals, trying out for television pilots, and pivoting into a fourteen-year graphic design career, you always believed in my voice and passion for storytelling. Turns out I have a lot to say—a whole novel's length, to be exact.

Thank you to my siblings, Hope and Bronte, who have often been my backbone before I developed my own.

I'm immensely grateful for my in-laws, Lorri and Bill, who consistently show up for our family, even when it means driving across multiple state lines in one day. Both of you are the pinnacles of love in action.

Writing can sometimes be a very solitary experience, so it's a beautiful thing when fellow writers and book lovers rally together to provide community. Alyssa McKnight, Brittney Arena, Harper Hawthorne, Kendall Annette, Lindsey B., Maggie Rapier, Mariel Pomeroy, Meredith, Monica DeLoy, Paris Soto, S.K. Harper, Susannah B., and Thea Brickman. You are all incredibly brilliant, generous, and supportive. Thank you for answering my many questions, body doubling in writing sprints, commiserating in the low points of publishing, meeting up for a good yap, and sharing your work(s) with me. I value our friendships deeply.

To my critique partners and overall wonderful humans—Alicia, Angela, Kate, Kelley, Kelly, Melanie, Lia, RJ, and Rachel—huge thanks to each of you for being willing to provide priceless feedback and encouragement. Your keen eyes truly enhanced my craft, and your existence enriches the world. I appreciate each you of very much.

To both of my therapists (the one I had while living in Missouri and the one I've been fortunate enough to connect with in the past year): words don't suffice for how much both of you have impacted my life. Thank you for not only listening but also hearing me. Thank you for sharing in my excitement as I've navigated this writing journey and for sitting through hours' worth of bookish rambles.

Of course, I can't forget to shout a huge word of gratitude to my editors: George and Robin. Not only was your feedback spot-on and actionable, but it also was immensely affirming. Thank you for elevating this story into something I'm proud to share with readers.

Lastly, I'd like to thank the young man who rear-ended my vehicle in April 2022. If it weren't for that accident causing me to have a concussion—and the subsequent impaired judgement—I truly don't know if I would've worked up the nerve to write my first book. Because of you (plus some time off combined with doom scrolling on bookstagram), I was able to ignore that voice of doubt and finally write a whole entire novel after literal decades of filling up notebooks, word docs, napkins, and emails with book ideas. Thanks, dude.

ONE LAST FUN FACT

Did you know that the setting of *This Safe Darkness* was inspired by Jockey's Ridge along the coast of North Carolina? Although there are some differences between the dunes of Caligo and the real-life state park, the dunes and their proximity to the ocean, the species of vegetation and foliage, as well as the disorienting desert-like feeling were all drawn from my own experience visiting Jockey's Ridge. It's one of those places where you almost feel like you're in another world. If you ever find yourself in or near the Outer Banks, I highly recommend adding it to your list of must-see places.

www.ingramcontent.com/pod-product-compliance
Lightning Source LLC
Chambersburg PA
CBHW020914310726
48980CB00011B/884/J

* 9 7 9 8 9 9 3 3 6 2 3 4 2 *